PROJECT RAPHAEL
A DR. STUART MYSTERY

STEVE SKINNER

Other Dr. Stuart books by Steve Skinner

Five South

Copyright © 2021
Steve Skinner

All rights reserved. This book or any portion thereof may not be reproduced or used in any manner whatsoever without the express written permission of the publisher except for the use of brief quotations in a book review.

ISBN (Print): 978-1-09839-703-6
ISBN (eBook): 978-1-09839-704-3

To Jim Gaynor

Poet, teacher, editor, philosopher.

After all these years, still my best man.

1

"Oh, this is heavenly," sighed the girl.

The young tech executive's dreams were coming true. A beautiful girl reclined on the soft bench, letting her fingers run over the polished teak woodwork of the sailboat's cockpit. The boat glided smoothly across San Francisco Bay. The only sounds were the gentle slapping of the water against the bow and a slight hum from the wind in the wires. It was late morning and sunny. Last night's fog had burned off and the air was relatively warm. For San Francisco, that is. There was a gentle breeze, enough to propel the nine-meter single-masted sloop at a steady clip, but not so windy as to create any chop in the water.

The young executive looked admiringly at his date, noting the contours of her breasts as she lounged in the cockpit. Her cream-colored Irish wool sweater and designer jeans conformed perfectly to her body. This was their third date, a romantic sail on the bay. His plan was a morning sail to anchor off Angel Island for lunch, maybe a short hike ashore in the afternoon. Then back to the St. Francis Yacht Club for dinner with a view and, if things went as he hoped, back to his apartment for the night. A bottle of Dom

Perignon chilled in the galley refrigerator along with half a wheel of brie. A fresh loaf of sourdough bread was stored in a cabinet. The sailboat was polished and prepped in the most seductive possible way. He felt himself getting aroused in anticipation of the entire day and night with this positively gorgeous creature.

He was sailing with just the mainsail because that was easiest for him to do alone. The objective was smooth and romantic, not fast and exciting. Three or four container ships rode high, anchored in the middle of the bay, awaiting loading at the docks in Oakland. A slow-moving Hyundai auto carrier was underway, heading west through the Golden Gate. An experienced sailor, he was certain that the waves from the auto carrier would be barely perceptible on the sailboat. He kept one hand on the wheel, but his eyes were fixed on the girl.

They didn't see the object in the water in front of the sailboat, so both he and the girl were startled out of their reverie when the bow bumped into something.

"What was that?" asked the girl, looking into the water, "Did we hit something?"

He leaned over and looked along the portside. He caught sight of the body as the sailboat glided by.

"Holy shit," he said.

She screamed.

♦ ♦ ♦

Dr. Matt Harrison of the San Francisco Medical Examiner's office groaned when Franklin Howard, the morgue attendant, called him. Harrison was tall and gangly with rimless glasses and light blue eyes that fascinated women. Fortunately for Matt, other men also found his eyes attractive.

"You're up, Dr. Matt," said the young black man, "Sorry, but you just caught a floater out of the bay."

"Our side of the bay or the Oakland side?" asked Matt, hoping to avoid an unpleasant experience.

"Our side," replied Franklin, "I'm setting up the autopsy table now."

"How bad is the decomp?" asked Matt.

"Bring your clove sticks or a cigar," advised Franklin.

Matt groaned again and reached into the top drawer of his desk. He removed two sticks of clove, which he would insert into his nostrils while he performed the autopsy. Bodies found floating in the bay were notorious for their stench in the autopsy room. All the medical examiners and morgue staff used either the clove sticks or smoked cigars during the autopsies of floaters. Without them, not even the most experienced morgue staff could stand the smell.

"Did we get x-rays?" asked Matt.

"Yes, sir. Up on the view boxes in the autopsy room," said Franklin, "I had the techs shoot full body films before I put her on the table. Figured you might want a picture before you start taking things out."

Matt stuck the clove sticks in his nose, then entered the autopsy room. A bloated and discolored body lay on the steel table, the head propped up on a plastic support. He averted his gaze to look at the x-rays displayed on the wall-mounted lighted view boxes.

"Well," said Matt, "There appears to be plenty of air in the lungs, so the odds are we're not looking at a drowning."

Franklin nodded in agreement.

"Oh, hell," said Matt, still looking at the images.

"What, Dr. Matt?" asked Franklin.

"It's a kid," said Matt.

♦ ♦ ♦

Dr. Raymond Stuart was never totally comfortable in a tuxedo.

Stuart was fifty, with salt and pepper hair cut short, almost military style. Medium height, very physically fit. One might have thought him handsome in a rugged sort of way, if one was not bothered by the glass eye. Stuart's right eye was a prosthetic, very well made and nearly a perfect match for the normal left one. The only obvious difference was that the right eye didn't move. Stuart found the glass eye to be annoying. When he was alone or with close friends, he removed it and wore a black eye patch. For formal occasions or while working with patients, he inserted the glass orb and put up with the discomfort.

"Well, if it isn't Ray Stuart," said the Dean of the medical school, extending a hand, "Nice to see you this evening."

Stuart smiled and shook the hand. It was the Dean, after all. Normally, the man wouldn't remember that Stuart existed. But formal dinners were for formal phoniness. This was why, whenever possible, Stuart avoided large social gatherings.

"It's all about the residents and their families," Stuart said, "It's their graduation dinner. I really love seeing these young doctors heading out into the world. Makes me feel good about the future of medicine."

"You look pretty good in a tuxedo," teased the Dean, "Tonight you look like a man who is Professor of both Orthopedics and Pediatrics."

"I can't say that it's comfortable," Stuart replied, "but this seems to be the required uniform for the country club. Not the sort of place I usually hang out. I'm here because of these young men and women as well as the wives, husbands, and partners who survived the ordeal of being married to doctors who work eighty hours a week. It's often harder on them than the residents themselves."

"Please enjoy yourself, Ray," said the Dean, "Good to see you here. I'm sure it means a lot to the residents."

"Thank you," Stuart replied. He would enjoy honoring the graduating residents. The faculty, on the other hand, too often used this evening for excessive drinking and pompous self-promotion. He had little appetite for phoniness and vacuous chitchat.

"Ray Stuart, God it's been a long time. You look pretty good, considering all that you've been through."

Stuart took the outstretched hand of Dr. Wallace Godfrey. Godfrey had once been chairman of the division of plastic surgery at

Sutro State, but had left the academic life a decade earlier to pursue a very lucrative private practice career. Godfrey was tall and strikingly handsome, black hair with just a touch of grey around the ears. His baby blue eyes were as clear as the sky on a summer day, radiating friendliness and inspiring confidence, important considerations to his wealthy patient clientele.

"Good evening, Wallace," said Stuart, "You're looking prosperous. Private practice agrees with you."

While he and Godfrey worked very closely together for years, Stuart never really considered Godfrey to be a personal friend. There was a vanity about the plastic surgeon that prevented Stuart from being totally comfortable.

"Oh, yes, Ray, the nips and tucks and boob jobs more than pay the bills," said Godfrey quietly, so that none of the other guests could overhear, "But my practice also allows me to pursue the one true love of my life."

"Project Raphael," said Stuart, "How's that going?"

"Bigger and better than ever," said Godfrey, "You wouldn't recognize it. We run five medical missions each year into El Salvador and have recently started to schedule missions in Ecuador."

"Still doing a lot of cleft palate surgery?" Stuart asked.

"Oh, much, much more," Godfrey replied, "We actually have a full-time mission hospital and clinic in El Salvador."

"Seriously? Did the government give it to Project Raphael? Do you share it with the health ministry?"

"No, we built it," said Godfrey, "We don't have to borrow space from the health ministry any more. We actually have our own staff there year-round, some American and some Salvadoran. We now have follow-up of surgical cases and great communication with the doctors in the US."

"That should allow your teams to perform more complex procedures," said Stuart, "if you have your own people there to take care of the patients post-operatively."

"Not only can we take on bigger cases in El Salvador," Godfrey continued, "but I've developed a network of sympathetic contacts in hospitals and universities all over the United States, which allows us to be able to bring some particularly difficult patients here for operations we could never attempt in Central America."

"Wow. That's much more elaborate than when I went on missions with you," said Stuart with true admiration, "We used to go down for two weeks. I'd operate on a bunch of babies with clubfeet. You'd fix a few dozen cleft palates and we'd be on our way back to San Francisco before the natives could ask 'who are those guys?'"

"Oh, yes," continued Godfrey, "Things have grown since those days. You know, another benefit of my private practice is that I've gotten to know some very wealthy and generous people in the Bay area. Many have been helpful with financial contributions to the Project. Lately I've even found a few benefactors for the project from outside northern California."

"Grateful patients or business contacts?"

"Patients," said Godfrey, "You know, when a doctor takes care of a celebrity, word gets out. You have the same thing in orthopedics. The doctor who successfully operates on some big sports star finds himself sought after by other athletes and wannabe athletes. The same is true in plastic surgery. When people see one of my patients on the big screen and admire the face or other alluring parts of the body, they want the same surgeon to take care of them. It's uncanny. This didn't happen when I was just another member of the faculty. But people come from literally all over the world to see me now."

"They must be pretty demanding," Stuart said, "Personally, I've never been wild about taking care of rich people. They think they're the only ones that matter."

"And they're right, Ray," Godfrey replied, "There are different classes of people for a reason. The rich and famous got that way by being smarter, more creative, harder working."

"Not to mention greedier and less scrupulous."

Godfrey laughed. He and Stuart had been having this same argument for decades.

"Truce, Ray," said Godfrey, "We're on neutral territory. No arguing when we're both wearing tuxedos."

"Fair enough," said Stuart, "I'll change the subject. Are you still teaching residents? Why did you come to this dinner tonight?"

"I lecture at the medical school and take an occasional resident as an observer in the office," replied Godfrey, "But mostly I'm here to honor the residents who've gone on missions with Project Raphael. Residents in plastic surgery, ENT, general surgery, and orthopedics come to El Salvador. They see a lot of conditions that we never see in the US and get to do a lot of interesting operations. The residents love the experience. And, hopefully, when they're out in practice, they'll want to volunteer in the developing world themselves."

"Good for you, Wallace," said Stuart, "I mean that."

"Thank you," said Godfrey, "Ray, why don't you join us on a mission? We could certainly use your expertise."

"I haven't done any surgery since the auto accident four years ago," said Stuart.

"I'm sorry to hear that," said Godfrey, "You used to be one hell of a surgeon. Even if you don't operate, we could still use you. I need someone knowledgeable in our clinic and someone to teach the residents. You'd be perfect."

"I hadn't given it much thought," said Stuart, "But yeah, maybe I would be interested in another mission. It would be a contribution to my own recovery, a chance to get away from the routine and do a little good."

"Praise the Lord," smiled Godfrey, "I won't forget this, Ray. I'll be in touch."

💧 💧 💧

Gabriella Cortez laughed and talked at a hundred words a second as she and her two friends walked the unpaved streets of Cedros. There were only four or five streets in the village. Buildings were mostly painted concrete and stucco, roofs of corrugated sheet metal. Some houses had forlorn little flower boxes, but generally there was little color except for the drab beige of dust. By contrast the foothills to the east were lush with trees and vegetation. Overall, Cedros was an uninspiring place to grow up, but the energy of teenage girls was irrepressible.

"I liked the green skirt that Sofia Reyes was wearing in the magazine," said Martina, Gabriella's best friend, "I want one like that."

"Me, too," said Gabriella. She was fourteen, but looked older. Her body had blossomed early into womanhood. She was very pretty with nice curves. Her breasts were already developed. Yet she retained the perfect light brown skin and perky smile of a child.

"No way your mother would let you wear it," said Elana, always the serious one, "It's way too short."

"I could wear it," Gabriella replied with teenage bravado, "My mother doesn't tell me what to do."

"Dream on, girl," said Elana, "Until you get a job and move out, you'll do what your mother says."

A red Nissan cruised slowly by the three girls. Two young men were inside.

"Hey, baby, what's happening?" a handsome man in his early twenties leaned out of the passenger window.

"Nothing for you," snapped Elana. To the other girls she said, "Keep walking."

"Why so unfriendly?" asked the man.

"Don't pay them any attention," Elana said, "they're *Los Cóndores*."

Gabriella wasn't very good at taking advice. The young man was very, very good looking.

2

DETECTIVE DUANE WILSON was a tall, muscular black man, a product of the streets in the Hunter's Point district of San Francisco. He was as good a cop as the department had, smart and proud. Duane had worked his way through San Francisco State and got his detective badge in short order after joining the force. Now he was assigned to homicide.

Other cops often thought that Duane was aloof, a loaner. Duane was rarely seen at the cop bars after his shift. He did his job extremely well and was respected for his professionalism, but had no close friends in the department. In truth, Duane was a warm and friendly man. He was also still in the closet as far as the department was concerned. Even in a city as tolerant as San Francisco, Duane dared not take risk of full exposure. He couldn't hide the fact that he was black. He could still try to hide the fact that he was gay.

"Okay, tell me about this," said Wilson, leaning forward to put pen to notebook. He was seated at Matt Harrison's desk in the San Francisco Medical Examiner's office.

"Female, teenager I'm guessing, found floating not far from Angel Island by a guy in a sailboat whose plans to get laid went down the toilet," said Harrison, "He called the Coast Guard, who fished out the body and called us and SFPD when they got her ashore. My guess is that she'd been in the water five or six days. Maybe longer."

"Lots of guesses, Matt," said Wilson, "Is this a homicide or an accidental drowning? Why'd you call me?"

Duane Wilson and Matt Harrison had been partners for three years. Matt was quite open about his sexuality and proud of his relationship with Duane. Duane and Matt found that their jobs often required them to collaborate professionally, an arrangement they both found enjoyable.

"For a start," said Matt, "she didn't drown. She didn't have water in her lungs. That, I'm sure, had something to do with why the body came up to the surface. She was dead when she went into the water."

"How'd she die, then?" asked Duane.

"That's the part I'm not totally sure of," said Matt, "She's been in the water a while, so some tissues are decomposed or have become fish food. There was no fracture of the hyoid bone in her neck, which is commonly seen with manual strangulation. I couldn't find any evidence of gunshot wounds or knife wounds. It could have been a knife wound, possibly, if she bled out from a severed artery or something. But there was no damage to the heart, lungs, liver, or other organs that would be consistent with a knife wound. Do you want to see the body?"

"Absolutely not. And I don't want to smell it either. I've had the experience of seeing one of your floaters and let's just say that it didn't help me to solve the case. It didn't do much for my appetite for supper that night either. I'll take your word and respect your expertise in some things, like floaters. I think you're telling me that you have a teenage girl who was dead when she went into the water, but no explanation of what killed her? Could it be suicide? A drug overdose and somebody dumped her body? Why homicide?"

"It has to do with her feet," said Matt, "Or rather her lack of feet."

"Huh?"

"The body has no feet," said Matt, "Before you ask, no, nobody cut her feet off. I think that a weight or something was tied around her legs to weigh down the body when she was tossed in the bay. Between the crabs and fish and whatever else was eating the flesh and the standard decomp, the ankle bones separated from the shin bones, to put this in terms you would understand, and the body floated free. The feet and the weight are still at the bottom of the bay."

"Is this a theory of yours or do you have evidence?" asked Duane.

"There are scratches, scoring on the tibias, or shin bones, that seem to have come from a metal chain," said Matt.

"Your professional opinion is that somebody killed her, wrapped a chain around her ankles, attached a couple of concrete blocks, like in the old mobster movies, and tossed her in the bay?"

"Sort of, yes."

"Did she have drugs in her system?" asked Duane.

"We've sent some tissue and urine for toxicology, but results won't be back for a few days. Those tests might not be helpful. If she'd taken drugs for a long time, like an addict, we may see some drug in the tissues. If she took something only once and it killed her, we're not likely to find anything."

"Was she sexually assaulted?"

"Can't tell. Too long in the water."

"Who was she? Any idea?"

"Not a clue," said Matt, "Nothing on her body to identify her. No fingerprints we can use. We've sent some DNA to see if she's in the system."

"Can you describe her so we can look at missing persons?" asked Duane.

"I am going to say she was about four foot ten or eleven, maybe eighty pounds, brown eyes, black hair."

"Asian?"

"I can't tell," said Matt, "I can tell you that there was one other thing. She has a deformed spine."

"Like a hunchback?" asked Duane.

"Well, the classic hunchback, as you call it, is a deformity we call scoliosis. She had what we call kyphosis."

"What's that?"

"Kyphosis does occur in kids, but this deformity is the kind that little old ladies get when they get old and their spine bones collapse."

"Old ladies? I thought you said this was a kid."

"It is a kid," said Matt, "and the spine thing is something I've never seen before."

"Really?" asked Duane, "With your fancy Boston education and all the years of training, you've never seen this before?"

"No," said Matt, "I'm a pathologist. I'm not an expert in kids' bones."

"Well," said Duane, "we both know somebody who is an expert on kids' bones. He's a hell of a smart doctor and a pretty good detective."

"Dr. Raymond Stuart," they said together.

Dr. Yousef Al-Saffar spun his desk chair around and enjoyed the view of the Red Sea. He propped his feet up on a short file cabinet to give them rest. It had been a long day in the operating room and it felt good to sit down. His office was richly appointed in a modern style, with a huge glass-popped table for a desk, a throne-like chair made of gleaming stainless steel and supple leather. An entire wall was devoted to mementos of the doctor's accomplishments. Photos of Al-Saffar with celebrities and world leaders hung next to diplomas from the finest universities in the world. Al-Saffar was from a wealthy family, remotely part of the genealogical web related to the royal family. He had been educated in England, but received his medical training in Chicago.

The doctor was tired, but felt the kind of satisfying fatigue that comes after a job has been done very well. Looking at the beautiful scenery relaxed his mind. The double lung transplant that he performed that day would secure many, many healthy years for his patient. That felt good.

Dr. Saffar was the chief medical officer and head of the transplant program for the Al Saud Medical Center in Jazan, Saudi Arabia. Located across the street from a park right on the waterfront, his third-floor office included a spectacular view of the Red Sea. The rustling branches of the palms in the park were framed by the dark blue of the water, highlighted by white transient lines of waves. In the distance the water changed instantly into the azure blue of the clear sky.

Jazan is, for the most part, a modern city. Like much of Saudi Arabia, oil is the lifeblood. Large refineries and storage containers squat on the land. Docks for tanker ships bustle with trade. The mountains to the east are decorated with elegant tourist hotels, rustic walls, and mansions for the richest citizens. For the most part, the old stucco buildings, the thatched huts of historic Arabia have been relegated to historic tourist attractions, though some of the old stone architecture is still beautifully preserved at the university. Palm trees still line the streets, which are full of people, women in full *hijabs* waited upon by imported Filipino servant girls.

The hospital, on the north side of the city, was a marvel of modern medicine. Everything was state of the art, with every imaginable medical device. No expense had been spared when the hospital was built and every amenity was available to the exclusive patients who came for care. The Al Saud Medical Center was a strictly private facility, caring only for the wealthy, the famous, and the powerful.

The hospital had no emergency room. Patients came by appointment only. There was no outpatient facility, but elegant medical offices were located in a separate building in the complex. Patients were seen privately in the doctors' offices. Some patients were actually admitted to the hospital for diagnostic work-ups and tests, if that was more convenient for the patients or the doctors. For most of the patients, doctor and hospital bills were minor financial nuisances. Obstacles and annoyances created to save money for insurance companies were ignored.

This, Dr. Saffar mused, was medicine as it was supposed to be. Patients were treated as though they were the most precious creatures on earth. At the Al Saud Medical Center, the patients were indeed the most important people on earth.

The hospital provided expert medical care and many types of operations were done there. Cardiac bypass and valve replacement surgeries, joint replacements, and plastic surgery were some of the more common procedures.

But the crowning jewel of the hospital was the transplant surgery program. This was Dr. Al-Saffar's specialty. Transplantation of kidneys, livers, hearts, lungs, and occasionally the pancreas. The success rate was exceptionally good.

Today Dr. Al-Saffar gave a movie star a new set of lungs and a new lease on life.

The doctor's reverie was interrupted when the hospital administrator, Ali Darwish knocked on the open doorway and entered.

Ali and Yousef grew up together as boys. While Yousef pursued medicine, Ali chose the business world. They were like brothers, united in purpose and principle.

"How did the operation go?" asked Darwish.

"Perfect," smiled Al-Saffar.

"Healthy donor lungs?"

"Excellent."

"Do you have a few minutes?" asked Darwish, "There are a few things we need to discuss."

Dr. Al-Saffar took his feet down and turned to his desk. Ali Darwish was an essential full partner in the operation of the hospital. Not a doctor, he still understood the mission of the hospital and did everything possible to facilitate its success.

"Are we in financial trouble again, Ali?" Dr. Al-Saffar asked.

Darwish laughed.

"Not trouble, exactly. You can go on putting new lungs into famous actors who still smoke a pack and a half a day. I'm pretty sure I can keep you in business."

"I knew you could. We provide excellent surgery for excellent patients. To do that, we need excellent management."

"It might help me if we could bill the insurance companies for at least part of the care," Ali said, "Our patients are mostly wealthy, but they expect rather lavish accommodations, which cost money. The cost of care is very high. Some of them, like your movie star, don't quite cover the costs."

"You know how I feel about insurance companies, Ali," Al-Saffar said, "Once you start accepting their money, you must also accept their rules. They tell you which tests you can do, which treatments are permitted, how long a patient may stay in the hospital, how much you can charge. Those are decisions that should be made by doctors, men who are educated in the diagnosis and treatment of disease, not by accountants looking to save money on the bottom line."

"I do understand, Yousef. We rely only on what our patients pay for our services. For the most part, they're happy to compensate us for the amazing things you do for them. But even some of them find the bills a hardship. Your dedication and generosity toward the patients make my life challenging. It would be easier if I could negotiate with the insurance companies and at least capture partial payments."

"The insurance companies care only about money," the doctor argued, "Take the man I operated on today. He's a world-famous actor. His gifts and talents have delighted people all over the world. After surgery today, he can continue to do that. He enriches all of humanity by the work that he does. Now, he has a bad habit, an addiction really, something he has trouble controlling. No insurance company would approve a lung transplant in a man who is still smoking. Months could be wasted filling out forms and filing appeals, but the insurance denial is inevitable. Because of this hospital, a brilliant man can have life, more time to deal with his addiction and hopefully quit smoking. Meanwhile, his life's work goes on. Nobody can put a price on a life like that."

"No, you're right. Your work makes a difference in the world. I'm grateful to be able to help. We do tend to come up a little short financially when we rely only on payments from the patients. I do my best to secure as many revenue streams as I can to facilitate your work."

💧 💧 💧

Gabriella was walking alone, on her way home from school, when she saw the red Nissan again. The handsome young man was alone, driving the car. He really was good-looking.

Gabriella waved to the man.

The Nissan pulled over to the side of the dirt road ahead of Gabriella and the man got out. He was tall and slender, clean-shaven with perfectly barbered hair cut just above the collar of his silk shirt that was open enough to reveal the hair on his chest. He had a small tattoo of a condor on his neck.

"Hi," the man said, revealing a perfect set of gleaming white teeth, "I'm Hector Velasquez."

"I'm Gabriella Cortez," she replied.

"You live here in Cedros?"

"Yes."

Hector pointed to the books she was carrying.

"You go to school?"

"My last year."

"You plan to continue after the mandatory years?" he asked.

"I don't know," she said, "I haven't decided."

"I was just going to get a beer at the *tienda* up ahead," Hector said, "Would you like to join me?"

Red flags waved and alarms sounded in Gabriella's head. As long as she could remember, her mother and her teachers warned her about older men who were strangers making seemingly innocent offers. This Hector was the personification of the kind of temptation she had been taught to avoid. And the tattoo on his neck branded him as a gang member.

On the other hand, the *tienda* was a public place with outdoor tables. It was a sunny afternoon and lots of people were on the street. There weren't many things to do in Cedros or many interesting people to meet. Whatever else he might be, Hector was as handsome and sexy as a movie star.

Most importantly, Gabriella was fourteen and could make her own decisions.

"I don't drink beer," she said, "but you could buy me a Fanta."

3

THE FOG WAS in and the air outside was cold. Raymond Stuart lived in a house situated on a bluff overlooking the Pacific Ocean, south of San Francisco and just north of Half Moon Bay. Stuart loved the rugged isolation of the coastside. He loved the rhythmic sound of the waves and the smell of the salt air. He loved the coolness and the gentle blanketing of the fog every evening. With a fire in the fireplace, he got out a well-worn Gibson acoustic six-string and checked the tuning. Stuart was comfortable in jeans and a plaid flannel shirt, his eyepatch covering the empty socket.

He began with "Blackbird" by the Beatles. He enjoyed the left-hand fingering as he moved up and down the fretboard. He made no attempt to sing, just enjoyed the intricate guitar work, which reflected a classical style. Stuart regretted that he had never studied classical guitar. He was just about to segue into "Hotel California" when the phone rang.

Stuart picked up the old land line phone. Almost nobody ever called him on this line.

"Hello?"

"Ray?" It was a woman's voice, not quite familiar.

"Yes."

"This is Kathleen Atwood. Do you remember me?"

Stuart felt a slight twinge in his chest.

Oh, yes, he thought, I remember you.

Kathleen was a stunning brunette with long wavy hair and soft light brown eyes. She was also the best operating room nurse he had ever known. Together they had been through surgical triumphs and near disasters. In the operating room, he and Kathleen had functioned as one being, swift and sure and efficient. More than just professional colleagues, there was always something more between them, something always left unspoken. Perhaps to avoid ever facing their real feelings, he and Kathleen exchanged witty and deprecating banter. On the surface, they seemed to insult each other. Beneath the surface there was enormous professional respect. And, perhaps, something that neither of them ever talked about.

Stuart had not talked to Kathleen since his auto wreck four years ago. The wreck broke both his legs and cost him his right eye. Stuart had not done a single operation since that wreck.

"Kathleen, you know I could never forget," he said, "How are you? This is a surprise."

"I'm fine, Ray," she said, "I miss you, you know. Are you ever coming back to surgery?"

Stuart looked at his hands that moments ago were flying over the guitar strings effortlessly and accurately. It wasn't his hands that kept him out of surgery. Nor was his eye holding him back.

"I don't think so," he said, "The car wreck and all. I'm spending most of my time teaching residents and students, covering clinics and working in my lab. I'm content to leave the glory of the operating room to the younger surgeons."

"That's too bad, Ray. I hate to say it, but you were the best. We were a terrific team."

"Yeah, we were good. You still working?"

"Yeah," she said, "Gotta pay the bills, you know. I don't do quite as much orthopedics as I used to. I'm doing a lot of plastics now."

"Really? You're tormenting a whole new group of surgeons? Plastics? I wouldn't have expected you to like that. Tummy tucks and face lifts, what could be more boring? On the other hand, plastic surgeons are so full of themselves that they provide fat targets for your insults."

She laughed.

"I'm nice to them," she protested, "I always show great respect for the surgeons."

"Yeah, right."

"You're special," she said, "I needed to let a little air out of your balloon from time to time. To keep you on the ground. Anyway, I got interested in plastic surgery because of working the teams in El Salvador. You know, with Project Raphael."

"Are you still doing those trips then?" he asked.

"At least twice a year," she replied, "To be honest, that's why I called. We have a mission planned for next month. I'm the charge nurse for the operating rooms on the mission trips. Anyway, I was talking with Dr. Godfrey. He told me that you might be interested in working another mission. I'm calling to tell you that I hope you will."

"I'm not planning to operate in El Salvador if I don't operate in San Francisco," he said.

"That's what Dr. Godfrey said. But you might teach the residents and students and work in the clinic."

"I told Wallace that I'd consider joining as a clinic doctor," he said, "You're going?"

"I just told you that I am," she replied, "It would be good to see you, to work with you again."

"You just made up my mind," he said, "El Salvador, here I come."

💧 💧 💧

She was too old to be raising a four year-old. Pepé was her fifth child and she was tired. Her oldest, a seventeen year-old daughter should be helping with the little one, but she was lazy and ungrateful.

Muriel Salas rubbed her aching knees. The gesture seemed to help a little, but the pain and weariness never seemed to go away.

Pepé was, she thought, a problem child. Too much energy. He was slow in his speech. He didn't walk until he was more than a year old, but now made up for his slow start by running everywhere. And the yelling. The only time the boy was not yelling was during the few hours he was asleep.

After only a few morning hours, she had reached her limit with the boy. It was more than she could take. The running, the yelling, the continuous damage to the modest house in the impoverished village were too much. She handed him a battered soccer ball and chased him out into the street to play with all the other undisciplined urchins. It seemed like madness, all the noise and the running feet of little children. Still, Pepé and his little friends seemed to have fun, kicking up dust in the village of Nahuizalco.

So, every day, she dressed Rafael, fed him, played with him for an hour or two, and let him out. He came back for lunch, filthy, then went out again. That was the daily routine.

♦ ♦ ♦

"Hi, Matt," said Stuart, arriving at the coroner's office, "How've you been?"

"Great, Dr. Stuart," replied Dr. Harrison, "I'm sorry to have been out of touch, but, on the other hand, it's nice that you don't have to get involved in the kind of unpleasantness we deal with around here."

"Yes," said Stuart, "We should see each other socially, not professionally. If we're working together, something bad has happened to some poor person. What have you got?"

"Teenage girl found floating in the bay," Matt began, "Not a drowning. She was dead before she went into the water. No obvious cause of death. No sign of violence. No drugs in her system that we could detect. But somebody tied some chains around her feet before she was tossed into the bay. The fish and the decay caused the ankles to cut loose as the bones separated. Without the chains, she floated to the surface. Duane and I consider that suspicious. And she had a spine deformity, a kyphosis, that I don't understand."

"Kyphosis?" asked Stuart, "Not scoliosis?"

"Kyphosis," repeated Matt.

"Do you have some x-rays?"

Matt called up the x-rays of the dead girl on his computer and displayed them on a large monitor. Stuart studied them. He began with the films that showed the bones of the skull, hands and arms, legs. Finally, he looked at the neck and spine.

"Do you have a lateral?" he asked.

Matt changed the x-ray view. Stuart looked closer at the black and white image.

"How about a chest x-ray?" Stuart asked.

"Well, sort of," said Matt, bringing up another image, "There's air in the lungs. I'm not sure what else you can see after her time in the water."

Stuart studied the x-ray.

"Do you still have the body here?" he asked.

"Sure," said Matt, "It's still an open case. She's a Jane Doe. Nobody's come forward to claim the body."

"Can I look at it?"

"Do you really want to?"

"Yes, I do," said Stuart.

Matt picked up the phone on his desk and called Franklin Howard.

"Franklin, can you get the teenage female floater out on the table for me?" Matt asked, "Yes, ten minutes should be fine. I'm bringing Dr. Stuart down with me to look at the body, so please get another set of gloves, a mask, and a gown for him."

Matt opened the drawer of his desk, took out four clove sticks, and offered two to Stuart.

"You might want these, Dr. Stuart," he said, "Floaters smell pretty awful."

"Yes, I know, Matt. But no thanks on the clove."

"Cigar?" Matt asked, "Lots of the pathologists smoke cigars in autopsy. Works just as well as the clove. Personally, I don't like the smoke or the aftertaste of cigars."

"I'll pass on the cigar, too," Stuart replied, "Who knows, I might just smell something to help solve the mystery."

"I sure hope not, Dr. Stuart."

They rode the elevator to the lower level of the medical examiner's building, changed clothes and entered the autopsy room. Franklin had the body ready and stood next to the table, ready to assist.

"Franklin Howard," said Matt, "this is Dr. Raymond Stuart, an expert in children's orthopedics from Sutro State."

"Pleased to meet you, Dr. Stuart," said Franklin, "Dr. Harrison tells stories about you. Are you here to help solve the mystery of what happened to this girl?"

"Well, Mr. Howard," Stuart said, "I'm here to look at things and see if I can help. Can we open the chest and have a look inside?"

"Yes, sir," said Franklin. He reached for a pair of scissors and cut the heavy sutures that held the edges of the Y-shaped autopsy incision together.

"The internal organs were removed, Dr. Stuart," said Matt, "They're in separate jars, if that's what you want to see."

"I know, Matt," said Stuart, "And I may want to look at the lungs later, but right now I'm interested in the spine. Mr. Howard, do you have a chest spreader?"

"Right here."

"Good," said Stuart, taking the instrument. He placed long flat paddles on either side of the chest, then attached them to a ratchet-like frame and cranked open the chest. "Yes, that's what I need to see."

Stuart thrust his hands inside the body and felt the bones of the spine.

"Do you have a bone curette?" he asked.

"In the drawer," said Franklin, "I'll get you one."

Stuart took an instrument that looked a little like a spoon on a long handle and scraped the bones of the spine from the inside of the body.

"Here," he said, handing some tissue to Franklin, "Get some microscopic slides on that. And make sure to have the lab do an acid fast stain on some of it."

"Acid fast?" asked Matt, "Are you saying that this girl had tuberculosis?"

"I'm certain of it," said Stuart, "This is a classic case of a Pott's abscess."

"I've never seen one," said Matt, "I have vague memories of books and slides in medical school."

"Um hum," mumbled Stuart. He took his hands out of the chest cavity and moved toward the head. Tilting the neck back, Stuart opened the mouth and stared inside.

"Well, your girl had active tuberculosis, pretty advanced," Stuart began, "You haven't seen a Pott's abscess because they're so rare in the United States. We do a reasonably good job of treating TB in our country. Not so in other, less developed nations. We think we have poverty in our inner-city ghettos, but it's nothing compared to some so-called Third World countries. Those countries usually have what they call universal health care, with free care for all citizens. The truth is that that there is no health care except for the very rich, so every citizen has equal access to nothing at all."

"Tuberculosis is a very common and serious health problem in the developing world," Stuart went on, "And, untreated, this is the sort of clinical picture you get. Your girl is about thirteen or fourteen, judging by the growth centers I saw on the bones. Foreign, I think. She has several teeth filled with dental amalgam. That hasn't been used in this country to fill cavities since before this girl was born. My guess is that she's from Central or South America. You might test the filling amalgam for rexillium and for mercury. Both are toxic and can cause side effects. That's why you won't find them used in the United States, but knowing what's in the amalgam may help you narrow down her country of origin. You can also send off some DNA for analysis and get a pretty good idea of her racial and ethnic characteristics. That should give you a pretty good idea of where she came from."

"Did she die of tuberculosis?" asked Matt.

"That would be my guess," said Stuart.

"A teenage girl with TB whose body was dumped into San Francisco Bay?" asked Franklin, "Why?"

"Here's my explanation. You've got a girl, maybe from Central America, certainly poor. Even in developing countries, only the poorest get tuberculosis this bad. She dies from TB, maybe here in the Bay area or on the way from her home country. Somebody didn't want her body to be found. So, somebody ties a weight around her ankles and dumps her body in the bay. Why? I think you're looking at a victim of human trafficking," said Stuart.

On a day when he had no surgery scheduled, Dr. Al-Saffar was still busy. He had lots of paperwork to do. Even though he and his hospital did not get involved with insurance companies or governmental health care systems, Dr. Al-Saffar believed in the value of documentation. It was just good medical practice. Every detail of every patient was contained in the computer files at the Al Saud Medical Center. Available at the fingertips of any doctor on staff, every lab test, x-ray and bit of social and financial data was digitally immortalized.

Besides reviewing computer data, Dr. Al-Saffar had some important phone calls to make. His secretary announced that he had Dr. Alexander Balderis on the phone from Moscow. He also told Dr. Al-Saffar that Dr. Balderis was fluent in English, so they would not need a translator.

Alexander Balderis was the premier expert in liver disease in Russia.

"Hello, Dr. Balderis, I'm Dr. Yousef Al-Saffar of the Al Saud Medical Center in Saudi Arabia," he began, "One of your patients, a Mr. Gregor Blinov, contacted me. He learned of our hospital's liver transplant program from one of my other patients."

"I know Mr. Blinov very well," said Dr. Balderis, "but I had no idea that he had contacted you. He's been a patient of mine for years, though I haven't had any impact on his life at all. He has scrupulously ignored my recommendations, prescriptions, and advice. I'm a little surprised that he voluntarily contacted any doctor."

Al-Saffar smiled. He was accustomed to listening to frustrated doctors.

"Mr. Blinov said that you told him that only a liver transplant could save his life," Al-Saffar said.

"Gregor Blinov is the CEO of one of the largest oil companies in all of Russia," Dr. Balderis said, "He's one of the closest friends and trusted advisors to the President of the Russian Federation, which makes him one of the most powerful and influential people in my country. Many say that Blinov's progressive ideas will shape the future of Russia. Unfortunately, he is also a hopeless alcoholic. His liver has been failing for years. I've tried every trick I know to get him to stop drinking. Frankly, Dr. Al-Saffar, I think he's a lost cause. I don't think that he'll ever stop. Gregor Blinov is going to literally drink himself to death."

"Would he survive a liver transplant?"

"I don't know," replied Dr. Balderis, "I may have told him that a transplant was his only hope. Mostly, I was trying to scare him. I'm not sure he's healthy enough for surgery. It doesn't matter, in my opinion. An alcoholic who's still drinking and determined to continue is not an appropriate transplant candidate anyway."

"He asked me to schedule an appointment to have a look at him," said Dr. Al-Saffar, "I feel like I owe him at least an independent evaluation. Could you send me a copy of his medical records?"

"Of course," said Dr. Balderis, "You're welcome to them. I hope you have more success than I've had."

"Thank you, Dr. Balderis," said Al-Saffar, "Mr. Blinov seems like an extraordinary man. He deserves an extraordinary effort."

4

Giancarlo Valdez maintained a mansion with a spectacular ocean view for his private residence. The estate was protected with electronic surveillance cameras, electrified fences, and ten loyal men of *Los Cóndores*, each armed with a pistol and an automatic rifle.

Giancarlo was thirty-eight, short and stocky with hair that was beginning to thin out. His face was as rough as the surface of the moon, pocked with holes from severe acne as a youth and scarred from a lifetime of fighting. He was not an attractive man. But what caught the attention of everyone he met were his eyes. They were as black and cold as coal. Giancarlo's eyes betrayed no emotion, no humanity. They were reptilian.

Valdez was the leader of *Los Cóndores*, one of the largest and most vicious of the Salvadoran gangs. *Los Cóndores* was present in every corner of El Salvador. Hundreds of government officials and law enforcement officers were on the payroll. Giancarlo was not content to be a big fish in the small pond of El Salvador. He had greater plans.

In recent years, the gang established a beachhead in the United States. They were relatively small players, based in Oakland, across the bay from San Francisco. They made money selling drugs, primarily cocaine, on the wholesale market. For now, anyway, *Los Cóndores* had too few men and inadequate firepower to challenge the established black, Latino, and Asian gangs for territory. So, those gangs became customers of *Los Cóndores*. Giancarlo had good connections in South and Central America, so it was not difficult for him to get the drugs into the US.

Valdez was always looking for ways to make more money. He found business partners wherever he could. Today he would host an individual known to most of gang members only as the Client.

The black limousine pulled up in front of the mansion on the circular driveway. A liveried chauffeur opened the door for the Client, whose eyes were hidden by dark glasses. Giancarlo watched as the Client was escorted inside. They had been in business together for several years. It had been profitable, if somewhat distasteful.

The Client was shown into the gang leader's private library. The Client did not remove the sunglasses. Giancarlo always felt that the Client lacked respect for him. It was a source of some annoyance. Still, this was business. He didn't have to like the Client as long as the money was good.

"How can I help you today?" asked the gang leader.

"We are going to need subject DFR265," said the Client, "The name and the last address we had for him are on the papers. He should be four years old."

Giancarlo took the papers from the Client. Glancing at them, he grunted his approval.

"When do you want him?"

"End of this month," said the Client, "I'll transfer a quarter of your fee into your bank account immediately. Another quarter when DFR265 is on the boat, and the final half on arrival at the destination."

"Very well," said Valdez.

"There is another matter," said the Client, "Are you interested in another route for getting large shipments of cocaine into the United States?"

"I'm listening."

"You and I are already making regular shipments of human cargo from El Salvador to Oakland," said the Client, "There's more room in the containers."

"And you propose to use some of the shipping space for drugs?"

"Yes. The containers are going anyway. Why not use the space to maximum advantage?"

"Are you developing a drug distribution system in the United States?" Giancarlo asked, his brows raised.

"Absolutely not."

"You have a distribution system for the girls," Giancarlo countered, "Why not expand to drugs?"

"Selling drugs is your business, not ours."

Giancarlo looked at his guest suspiciously.

"Then why are you offering to ship drugs for us?"

"We've had a profitable business partnership," said the Client, "Why not build on it?"

"What's in it for you?"

"We want twenty-five percent of your take on what we ship in our containers."

Giancarlo chuckled.

"Yet you consider me to be a thief and a thug," he said, "Five percent."

"Twenty percent."

"Seven percent."

"Fifteen percent."

"Ten percent and I let you leave my house alive," said Giancarlo.

"Very well," said the Client, "We have an agreement."

They shook hands and the visitor left.

Giancarlo picked up the papers that the Client left, then picked up his phone and called the *Los Cóndores* lieutenant in San Miguel.

"Jorge, I need you to pick up a package," said Valdez.

"Of course, *Jefe*," said the man.

"His name is Pepé Salas and he should be about four years old," said Valdez, "Our latest information is that he lives in the village of Nahuizalco. I want him healthy and unharmed. Bring him to me in Acajutla in ten days."

"As you wish, *Jefe*," said the man.

♦ ♦ ♦

"You don't know anything!" screamed Gabriella Cortez.

She threw a terra cotta pot, flower and all. It smashed into the wall.

"You're only fourteen!" replied Anna Cortez, "You're too young to have a boyfriend. You don't know what you're doing."

"You're the one who doesn't know what she's doing!" replied Gabriella, "Hector understands me! Hector loves me!"

"Hector is old enough to be your father and he's nothing but a cheap thug."

"He's not! Hector is twenty. He has a good job. He works in security. And, he has a future, which is more than I can say for you in this pathetic village!"

"Hector is a gunman for *Los Cóndores* and he protects drug dealers with a shotgun," said Anna, "There's nothing wrong with Cedros. It's good enough for me."

"It wasn't good enough for my father," said Gabriella with a sneer, "He ran away to San Salvador. That seems like a good idea. Hector promised to take me to San Salvador."

"No! I forbid it!" shouted Anna.

"Hector and I have been dating for a month. Nothing bad has happened. I don't need you to boss me around. I'm fourteen and I can decide for myself!" yelled Gabriella, slamming the door as she ran out.

Gabriella actually hated fighting with her mother. She loved her mother very much. She just wished that they could have an adult conversation, that her mother would at least try to see things from her point of view.

She was in her last year of school, at least the last one she was required to attend. The future seemed uncertain. She wasn't sure that she wanted to get any more education, but an education might be a ticket out of Cedros. Getting out of Cedros was her one certain goal. The little rural village was oppressive, hopeless. Most of the kids her age wound up working on local farms. Or in some menial, dead-end job like her mother had, doing other people's laundry.

Gabriella had dreams. In her mind, she could be a princess, live in a palace with a handsome prince. She often fantasized that her prince would come find her on the dirty streets of Cedros, and sweep her away to his palace.

Just in case her prince couldn't quite find Cedros on a map, Gabriella thought about finishing high school and maybe going to college. Education could get her a good job, far away from Cedros.

Perhaps more importantly, Gabriella was in love. Her first love. Hector Velasquez was the first man that she had ever felt this way about. Hector was a real man, handsome and worldly, not like the awkward boys her own age with pimples and a bad smell.

Was Hector the prince she dreamed about?

Raymond Stuart always felt self-conscious when people praised his work. On one hand, he knew he was good. He held himself to a very high standard and had trouble when others didn't live up to it.

Stuart also knew that, deep inside, he was seriously flawed. He had what the psychologists called a lack of self-esteem. The persona that he presented to others was that of a serious, thoughtful professor, genuinely modest and quiet. On the inside he was very insecure indeed.

One of Stuart's flaws was that he could not interpret the feelings of women. He was thinking of Kathleen Atwood a lot since she phoned him. The two of them used to be close, professionally, before his auto accident. An intuitive team in the operating room, Kathleen knew exactly which instrument he needed at any time during the procedure. During his surgical career, he worked with hundreds of nurses in surgery, but only with Kathleen did he find this synchronicity.

She was an attractive woman. That was obvious. He was never sure about her feelings for him. What if all the phony insults and deprecating banter contained an element of truth? For whatever reasons, he never could bring himself to talk with her about personal, emotional, romantic topics. After the accident, he put her out of his mind, somehow convinced that his injuries had made him hopelessly unattractive to any woman. A solitary life was, he believed, part of his penance for what he had done.

The sound of Kathleen's voice when she called him on the phone stirred old memories, old yearnings. Stuart couldn't get Kathleen out of his mind. Irritated with himself, he picked up the phone and called her number.

"Hello," she said.

"Kathleen?" he asked.

"Ray," she said, "I'm happy you called."

"Well, good," he replied, "I thought we might discuss the mission to El Salvador over dinner."

"I'd like that," she said, "When?"

"How about tomorrow?"

"Perfect. What time?"

"I'll pick you up at six thirty," he said, "Are you still on Moraga?"

"Same place," she said, "Where did you have in mind?"

"I was thinking of La Cave, the little quiet French place in the Richmond district."

"I love it."

"Yes, I remember."

Kathleen Atwood's pulse raced in anticipation of the date. She tried not to look too eager when she watched Stuart park his Jeep in front of her house. She resisted the temptation to open the door even before he rang the bell.

Kathleen was dressed to look her best. When she opened the door, she looked carefully for Stuart's reaction. It seemed to her that Stuart forgot to breathe for just a few seconds. She wore a sleek green dress complimented by an emerald necklace. The high heels accentuated the shape of her legs. Her long wavy brown hair cascaded over bare shoulders.

"Wow!" Stuart whispered.

"We're not in surgery now, Doctor," Kathleen said. Every woman was pleased to get a response like that from her date.

"So far, so good," she thought.

The drive to the restaurant was short.

"I'm embarrassed to bring you to a nice restaurant in a Jeep Wrangler," Stuart said, "I should have rented a better car, or maybe a limo. At least a taxi."

"Ray," she said, "I'm going to dinner with you. I know you. And the Ray Stuart that I know drives a Jeep. It fits you. There's nothing phony about you. A rental car or a limo would be phony."

Once inside the restaurant, Kathleen ordered a glass of Chablis. Stuart opted for ginger ale.

"Ginger ale?" she asked, "What happened to the Johnny Walker black label?"

"Not since the accident," said Stuart, "The accident changed a lot of things in my life. Giving up alcohol is one of the lesser things."

That was a surprise to Kathleen. The Ray Stuart she knew was a hard drinker and a prized date for any surgical nurse. Now a teetotaler? What else was different with him? She felt awkward.

"Will it bother you if I...?" she said. She was self-conscious about ordering wine.

"No, go ahead. It won't bother me at all."

Once they ordered their dinners, Kathleen began the conversation. She kept it safe, focusing on professional issues. That was what they always did. Kept it safe. Kathleen desperately wanted that to change, but she didn't know how to make that happen.

"You'll really be impressed with what Dr. Godfrey has done with Project Raphael," she said, "It's all much bigger, better organized than it was in the days when you went on mission trips. There's a full clinic, two full-time operating rooms, plus labor and delivery. There are twenty inpatient beds. They even have a full-service clinical lab and, you won't believe this, a blood bank. The place is staffed all year round."

"A blood bank?" asked Stuart, "That would solve so many problems. It would allow so many more operations. When I went on missions, we had to be careful not to do any operations in which we might lose enough blood to require a transfusion. We were more likely to lose a patient from a fatal transfusion reaction than from any surgical misadventure. That always limited the surgical options."

"We're doing much bigger cases. Since we're staffed year-round, patients can stay longer. The nursing staff and many of the doctors are Salvadoran, ones that we've trained. Dr. Godfrey is in frequent contact all year long, using a special telemedicine connection."

"He told me that a team from San Francisco goes down about five times a year," said Stuart.

"Yes," she said, "The Salvadoran staff at the clinic select patients for the visiting physicians from the U.S. to see, depending on the kind of specialists we're bringing down. We have clinics and then set up a surgical schedule. It's really efficient."

"It doesn't sound like you need me taking up space down there," said Stuart.

"Oh, no," she smiled, "You won't wriggle out of this one. There's a lot for you to do. First, they're really excited about having you work in the clinic. They're already calling in patients who are so complicated that nobody can figure out what to do with them. All lining up for the famous Dr. Stuart."

"A whole clinic of insoluble cases?"

"Yep. For two solid weeks."

"I better pack some aspirin," he said, "It sounds like I'm going to have a lot of headaches."

"Plus, they want you to teach residents," Kathleen added, "The U.S. residents from Sutro State, of course, but Salvadoran residents as well. When we have a team going down, the Salvadorans always send their orthopedic residents and some in pediatrics as well. How's your Spanish?"

"Well," Stuart smiled, "Maybe a wee bit rusty. Haven't used it much in the last four years. But it should come back quickly."

Kathleen stopped talking and just looked at Stuart for a moment. She just had to express herself.

"Ray, it is going to be terrific to work with you again," she said.

Stuart blushed.

"I can't quite tell you how much I'm looking forward to it," he said, "Frankly, you're one of the main reasons I agreed to be on the team."

She looked down at her food for a moment, thinking. His words weren't what she expected; they were what she hoped for.

Then her gaze went right back to his eye. She had to ask some hard questions.

"Ray, why didn't you call me?" she asked.

"You mean after the accident?"

"Yes."

"There was a lot going on," he tried to explain, "Not just with the physical recovery. There were other things. Mental things. Emotional things. Maybe some spiritual things."

"You could have talked to me," she said.

"It was complicated."

"Four years, Ray," she said.

"I'm sorry," he replied, "It's still complicated."

She knew that she wasn't going to get any better explanation. Not now, anyway.

"So, what have you been doing since the accident?" she asked, "I know you don't operate anymore."

"I do a lot of consulting around the medical center. I see a lot of patients. Mostly kids, of course, but some adults," Stuart said, "I teach the residents and students. I still run the gait analysis lab. And I've got a couple of research grants that I'm working on in the lab."

"Sounds like you're keeping busy," she said.

"I also have a new gig," he said, "I don't quite understand how I fell into it, but I've become a kind of consultant to the San Francisco Police Department and the medical examiner's office."

"I heard around the hospital how you helped the police catch the hospital administrator and the director of nursing last year."

"Yeah," he said, "That might be how the amateur medical detective business got started."

She decided to try again at a personal question.

"Do you still play the guitar?" she asked, "I used to love hearing you play and sing. Do you remember on our missions to Central America? After a long day in surgery and at the hospital, the team used to go have dinner together. Then, we'd get drinks, sit outside. Somebody always seemed to produce a guitar and we'd sing songs until everyone was so tired and we had to get up and do it all again the next day. You were pretty good on the guitar. I mean, are your hands recovered enough to play?"

"You ask a lot of questions," he said.

"That's what you get for going four years and not calling me," she replied.

"Yes, I still play guitar," he said, "and my hands are fine for playing. I haven't lost anything on the guitar. I may be a little better than I used to be because I have more time to practice."

"And do you still sing?"

"No," he said, "And that's enough questions in the 'music' category."

Kathleen decided that this evening was a start.

5

DETECTIVE DUANE WILSON anticipated his friend's reaction.

"Jesus, Duane, this place gives me the creeps," said FBI Special Agent Walter Reynolds.

Reynolds was a tall, thin African-American in his mid-thirties. Conservatively dressed in a brown three-piece suit, he was not the sort of individual who would attract attention in a crowd. He was assigned to the FBI Human Trafficking Task Force out of the San Francisco office.

Duane Wilson smiled at Reynolds. They were in the lobby of the office of the San Francisco Medical Examiner.

"You crack me up, Walt," said Wilson, "With all the horrible shit you deal with, you get uncomfortable just being in the lobby."

"Just knowing that in the basement there are drawers full of dead bodies makes me cringe," said Reynolds, "Why do we need to have the meeting here? What's wrong with my office?"

"Dr. Harrison thought you might like to examine the body yourself," said Duane.

"And does Dr. Harrison think that there are pigs flying over Union Square?"

They arrived at the office of Dr. Matt Harrison. Duane introduced Walt. Neither Duane nor Matt let on that their relationship was anything other than professional.

"Pleased to meet you, Agent Reynolds," said Matt.

"Call me Walt," replied Reynolds, "What have you got?"

"A teenage girl, probably thirteen or fourteen that was fished out of San Francisco Bay a few days ago," said Matt, "She was tossed into the water after she died. Whoever threw her in tied a chain around her ankles to weigh her down, but the chain and her feet fell off, allowing the body to float to the surface."

"Not a pretty thought," said Reynolds, "But what makes you think she is a human trafficking victim?"

"There was no sign of violence to her body and no drugs that we could detect," Matt continued, "I called in Dr. Raymond Stuart from the medical school at Sutro State as a consultant. He figured out that the girl suffered from severe tuberculosis of a degree not often found in the U.S. By looking at her teeth, he believes that she came from a foreign country, a poor one, perhaps from Central or South America. He thinks that she died from tuberculosis and I agree."

"This Dr. Stuart suspects that she is a trafficking victim?" asked Reynolds.

"Yes," said Matt, "We've sent off a DNA sample, which should tell us pretty specifically where in the world she came from."

"It makes sense, Walt," added Duane, "Neither we nor the Oakland PD have any missing persons reports that fit the description, especially with the TB. I think maybe she arrived here dead on some sort of transport or maybe she died soon after arrival. There is no evidence that she was murdered in a violent way."

"If she was a sick kid brought into this country against her will and she died in transit, you may be damn sure she was murdered. If she died while they were trafficking her, that in itself is murder," said Reynolds, "The bastards who bring these girls in have absolutely no respect for human life. They are the most despicable criminals on the planet."

"That's why I called you," said Duane.

Reynolds frowned.

"If we can link this to a criminal group, it's capital murder, potentially a death penalty case. The threat of a needle in the arm may shake up some low-level creep enough to give us some names of the leaders of a trafficking group. Most of the trafficking in the San Francisco area is coming out of Asia, but there's plenty coming from Central and South America as well. This is a huge worldwide problem. It's estimated that there are twenty-one million victims of human trafficking worldwide. About fourteen million are in forced labor and another five million are sex slaves."

"But governments all over the globe have condemned human trafficking," said Matt, "There are a bunch of international treaties. You would think that the combined power of law enforcement worldwide would be able to shut this down."

"You ought to know that money talks," Walt said, "Human trafficking is big money. About $150 billion dollars in profit per year. That kind of money can buy a lot of blind eyes and even cooperation from law enforcement."

"Assuming that our Jane Doe is a victim of trafficking," asked Duane, "Where will you start?"

"I'll start a file," said Walt, "It'll help if you let me know the results of the DNA test when you get them. That should help us direct our investigation to Asia or Central America. We'll coordinate with SFPD."

"Might be a good idea to loop the Oakland Police Department in as well," said Duane.

"Agreed," said Walt.

"Do you think she came in by sea, given that we found her in the water?" asked Matt.

"Unlikely," said Walt, "Most of the human trafficking victims come in overland, in trucks and busses. Some by air. Very, very few by sea. Most likely she died and they just dumped her body in the bay. We have sources of information. I'll put the word out about this dead girl and see if anything develops. You haven't given me a lot of evidence right now."

"Would it help if Dr. Stuart talked to you?" asked Matt.

"Let's see what the DNA test shows," said Walt.

♦ ♦ ♦

"Ray, may I introduce Bill Conklin," said Wallace Godfrey, "Bill's the business manager for Project Raphael. He's the man who makes it all work."

Stuart offered his hand to the balding, overweight man in the ill-fitting suit. The three men were sitting down to an elegant lunch at the Top of the Mark.

"Ray has signed on for our next trip to El Salvador," Godfrey continued, "He and I go back many years, to when our medical missions were just week-long adventures in the rural hospitals of Central and South America. Ray was the head of pediatric orthopedics at Sutro State University back then. He's forgotten more about sick kids than most surgeons learn in a lifetime."

"Yes, I've heard of Dr. Stuart," said Conklin, "You're something of a legend both in San Francisco and in the mission world. I'm delighted that you're joining us this trip. I think you'll be impressed with the changes that Wallace has made in the organization. You know that Project Raphael has its own hospital?"

Godfrey beamed like a proud father.

"Our hospital is in Acajutla. You've been there, Ray, so you know the place. Right on the Pacific coast, in the northern part of the country."

"Why'd you pick Acajutla?" Stuart asked.

"It's a lovely spot, really," Conklin answered, "There's a port so we can get our shipping containers in easily with our medical supplies and equipment."

"Kathleen Atwood told me that you maintain a year-round clinic and keep the place staffed all year by a combination of Americans and local professionals," said Stuart, "That's a huge improvement. One of the worst parts about our old missions was that we would come into town, operate, and leave. The poor locals were stuck with our complications. It limited the treatments we could provide. Kathleen also said that you had telemedicine connections to San Francisco."

"Yes, that's true," smiled Godfrey, "We can look at the patients by telemetry and consult with the doctors in El Salvador."

"Now, you're talking, Wallace," said Stuart, "Now you're bringing first class medical care to a third class country."

"Not quite first class by American standards," said Conklin, "But certainly by the standards of the developing world. Whenever you have time, Dr. Stuart, please contact me with your passport data and other information so I can get you cleared by the Salvadoran Ministry of Health. I can also get your plane tickets. Do you want to fly first class?"

Stuart looked at Godfrey. "Do you fly first class?"

"Oh, I don't fly with the team at all," smiled Godfrey, "I go on my yacht. It serves as a kind of mobile office and headquarters during the mission. Also, from time to time we have a patient that we need to transport back to the United States for more sophisticated surgery. Do you remember when I told you that we've been able to make contact with certain US specialists to treat some patients in the United States? People who require operations or treatments we can't do in El Salvador? Well, I have a stateroom on the yacht specially equipped with all sorts of hospital equipment. I often use the yacht to transport these special patients to San Francisco. I also have a nurse who's part of my regular crew. She takes care of those patients on the voyage from Acajutla to San Francisco."

"We ship our supplies and equipment by sea," added Conklin, "We own two shipping containers. We ship them out a few weeks before the mission team flies down to El Salvador. Local contractors deliver the containers right to the hospital. It's all very convenient."

"I'll say," said Stuart, "I remember hauling hundred-pound cardboard boxes through foreign airports and waiting hours for somebody to either inspect them or not, then haul them again to another place for shipment to the hospital."

"Oh, yeah," laughed Godfrey, "Those were the good old days, all right. One massive screw up after another. Seems like the representatives of the health ministry never quite got the word to the officials at the airport, who had no idea what to do with a mob of gringo doctors and sixty heavy boxes full of everything from aspirins to anesthesia machines. We had some funny experiences with those boxes."

"I remember once, in Peru, I think, when some guy in a police uniform saw us coming in at Customs with all these giant boxes," Stuart recalled, "He demanded that we open each box for his personal inspection. He wanted to see our packing manifests. Somehow he thought that we'd counted each surgical sponge and hemostat."

"I remember that guy," Godfrey added, "I was in charge of that mission. Do you remember what he was threatening?"

"When it came to discussions or difficulties with the authorities, I tried to keep a low profile," Stuart said.

"As I recall very well," Godfrey said, "Suddenly, the good Dr. Stuart was *non habla Español*. Well, this idiot, I think he was a police lieutenant or something like that, threatened to put the whole group under arrest. It took forever, but I finally found somebody in the Ministry of Health to sort the thing out."

"I remember sitting there on the boxes for about two hours," Stuart said, "I had to pee so bad I thought I would explode."

"No more of that bullshit, Ray," Godfrey assured him, "Bill has arrangements with US Customs here in San Francisco and Oakland as well as the customs office in Acajutla. Everything goes like clockwork. No wasted time, no stress."

"That in itself should justify your salary, Bill," said Stuart.

"The containers have been a godsend," said Godfrey, "All Bill's idea, of course. And, with so much space, we can ship more equipment than in the old days, when we had to cram things into boxes that we could manipulate by hand."

"This trip, for example," said Bill, "We're transporting two dozen wheelchairs and a load of canes, walkers, crutches, and other durable medical equipment. We have an arrangement with a local company to maintain the wheelchairs for the patients who need them."

"That would be a very valuable service," said Stuart, "Disabled people in the developing world need wheelchairs. While kind donors in the U.S. may donate used, or even new chairs, there's generally no way to maintain them. They fall apart and become just another part of the trash that litters Central America. How well I remember seeing broken medical and surgical equipment scattered in the fields, just junk that can't be fixed in those countries."

"Exactly the issue we're addressing," said Godfrey, "Bill has this local company that we've started working with. We supply new chairs and other equipment as well as parts and tools for repairs and maintenance. They do the work, send us the bill, and the chairs keep on rolling."

"I hesitate to ask, but are you also doing electric wheelchairs?" asked Stuart.

Godfrey beamed with pride.

"Indeed, Ray, that's what's in one of the containers for this trip," he said, "Our first load of electric wheelchairs and the parts and tools needed to maintain them."

"Fantastic," said Stuart.

"You didn't answer my earlier question, Ray," interrupted Conklin, "Do you want to fly first class to El Salvador? Most of the surgeons prefer first class."

"No, thank you," said Stuart, "I'll fly coach."

"Try to get him seated next to Ms. Atwood," said Godfrey with a wink.

People and chickens scattered as the blue van sped down the single street of the village of Nahuizalco. The van swerved to a stop in front of a shabby house. Half a dozen dirty little children played in front of the house. They all looked up when the van arrived.

Four men with their faces covered in black balaclavas exited the van.

"Pepé!" shouted one of the men.

One scruffy little boy looked right at the man in the ski mask. The other children looked at Pepé.

"This one," said the man in the mask, pointing at the little boy.

One of the men scooped up Pepé and turned toward the van. Pepé let out a screech. The other children scattered. A peasant woman came running out of a nearby house, screaming for her son.

A masked man shot the woman right through the heart.

The dust settled and the chickens returned to the street after the van sped away. Such things happened often in El Salvador.

6

Ray Stuart had the middle seat on the flight to San Salvador. The window seat was occupied by Kathleen Atwood. She slept for most of the trip, frequently leaning her head against Stuart's shoulder. He made no effort to move or reposition her. Stuart enjoyed the feel and smell of Kathleen's hair. The sense of closeness with Kathleen was pleasant.

The aisle seat was occupied by Dr. John Talbot, one of the anesthesiologists on the trip. Talbot was part of the Sutro State University Hospital staff, a long-time colleague of Stuart's. Talbot had been on many mission trips to Central America over the years. He was a veteran of the "old days" when Stuart participated frequently.

Talbot was a chatty fellow who loved to talk about the current mission and reminisce about previous trips.

"Ray, you won't believe the new facilities," said Talbot, "The anesthesia machines are state of the art, the same model we use at Sutro State. Did I mention that Wallace asked for my advice when we made the purchase? Of course, I selected the best. We have two, one for each operating room at the hospital in Acajutla. A third machine is being sent down in one of the containers. It should be there already. While you folks are in the clinic, I'll check it out and get it ready to go. That way we will have a high-quality backup machine all the time."

"Sounds like a vast improvement over some of the equipment you used to use on our mission trips," said Stuart.

"O God, yes," said Talbot, "Do you remember that place in Guatemala? My first trip, I think. They had this anesthesia machine from World War II, it was so old. I had never used one, just seen pictures in history books. I don't think the tubing had been changed since the Eisenhower administration."

"Oh, I remember," said Stuart with a grin, "The first thing you did was rip out all the old tubing and start rebuilding the machine from the floor up. Literally. You had bits and pieces of the old gadget strewn all over the floor. We were trying to unpack surgical gear, but there was no space because of your anesthesia repair shop."

"There were a couple of gaskets that had simply rotted away," continued Talbot.

"As I recall, when you hooked up the new tubing and started to run anesthetic gasses through them, there was a huge leak," said Stuart, "You had nitrofluorane filling the operating room and damned near put all the nurses and surgeons to sleep."

"Oh, yeah," said Talbot, "I sort of forgot that part of the story. Well, that sort of thing will never happen again. This new facility is great, I tell you. We even have a full-service clinical lab. Every single patient that gets an anesthetic has a full blood count, urinalysis, and chemistry profile. All of us in anesthesia are thrilled. It's so much safer this way."

"Does that mean you don't have to cancel as many cases?" asked Stuart.

"Come on, man," said Talbot, "We only cancel cases when we're worried about the safety of the patient. We're not going down to these countries to kill off the poor people. You surgeons get all the glory, straightening out crooked feet and fixing cleft palates with a stroke of the knife. But these people are malnourished, uncared for. You guys have no idea what sorts of diseases they have. Giving anesthesia to some of these people is like dancing in a minefield."

"I know, I know John," said Stuart, "I was just joking with you. What may be a simple procedure for us surgeons can be a hair-raising nightmare for you at the head of the table. I'm really glad that you have reliable equipment and a clinical lab. I'm not going to be operating this trip, but I'll certainly have a look at this anesthesia Wonderland of yours."

Stuart had his own private room at the modest, but clean hotel near the waterfront in the town of Acajutla. Most of the senior surgeons and anesthesiologists had their own room, while residents, students, nurses, and other personnel were generally paired up with roommates. The hotel was a ten-minute bus ride from the hospital and clinic. Even though it was Saturday, Stuart was eager to see the new facility.

From the outside, the Project Raphael Clinic was an unimpressive two-story structure. Squarish functional architecture, simple and unassuming. There was a single sign above the main entrance identifying it as a hospital. Inside, things were different. Cheerful bright colors, polished tiled floors, and lots of lights. There were plenty of readable signs posted directing people to the clinics, clinical laboratory, obstetrics unit, and surgical suite. Stuart was impressed.

"Ray!" boomed the voice of Wallace Godfrey, "Welcome to Project Raphael. What do you think? Can I give you a personal tour?"

"Hi, Wallace," said Stuart, shaking his head. Godfrey was wearing a beige tropical suit, expensive Italian loafers, and a Rolex. The ego never stopped shining. "When did you arrive?"

"A couple days ago," smiled the plastic surgeon, "We had fair seas and following winds, as the sailors say. The Arariel had a great voyage."

"Arariel?"

"That's what I named my yacht," said Godfrey, "I have a kind of angel fixation, you know. The angel Raphael is the one who performs the healings on behalf of God. In Jewish mythology, Arariel is the angel who is more or less in charge of the seas. I thought it would be a good name for the yacht."

"You're not Jewish."

"A technicality. I can appropriate things from any religion or culture that I want. And I like the name Arariel. She's a beauty. Seventy meters with eight staterooms. I had one made into a kind of hospital room and another remodeled into an office. I run the whole Project Raphael from the yacht when we're down here. We have a crew of nineteen, which includes the nurse who cares for any patient that we might be transporting to the States for special surgeries."

Godfrey proudly led Stuart on a hospital tour. There was a spacious, clean surgical suite with modern operating tables and lights. Gleaming anesthesia machines and sophisticated patient monitors were in each room. There was a four-bed recovery room with monitors for each bed. There were two six-bed medical wards, one for men and one for women, plus a four-bed pediatric inpatient unit. A separate wing housed a four-bed obstetrical unit with its own labor and delivery rooms. Stuart noticed that there were plenty of clean sheets and blankets, a relative luxury for a hospital that cared for the poor of Central America. There were only two men, one woman, and two children in the hospital at the time. Godfrey explained that the hospital had deliberately reduced the census to make room for the rush of patients that would result from the work of the newly arrived team from the U.S.

The facility had its own x-ray suite, where plain x-rays and ultrasound examinations could be obtained rapidly and efficiently. The clinical laboratory reminded Stuart of one at Sutro State University Hospital. He wandered over to inspect some of the machines, curious about the kinds of tests that could be run.

"Come on, Ray," Godfrey urged, "They're just lab machines. What could be duller?"

"I was curious about the sorts of tests that I might order," explained Stuart.

"Each new patient has basic labs done at initial registration at the clinic. When you see someone in the clinic, the basic lab results are already there. That makes clinic visits much faster and more efficient. And each person coming in for surgery has pre-operative labs. If you want more tests, you can get them. You'll see when we get to the clinic," said Godfrey.

Finally, they came to the clinic. It was a bright and cheerful large outpatient unit with sixteen examining rooms arranged in two sections of eight rooms each. Godfrey explained that they could run two types of clinics simultaneously.

"Tomorrow afternoon, you'll have the A section for orthopedics while plastic surgery has its clinic in the B section," Godfrey explained, "There's a large common waiting room. The clinic staff will call the patients and place them in rooms for you. Each exam room has basic diagnostic tools, an x-ray view box, and a rack with paper forms. It's still El Salvador, Ray, and we're a long way from an electronic medical record. We still write on forms here. An old school doctor like you will be very comfortable with this. There's the lab requisition form and the x-ray form. We also have surgical and medical admission forms and doctor's order sheets."

"Like the old days in the United States," said Stuart, "But far better than the old days in El Salvador."

"You orthopedic guys order lots and lots of x-rays," said Godfrey, "And our techs can handle most of them. They have a few years of experience with the most common views. We don't have a CT scanner or an MRI machine here. Theoretically, you could get those kinds of tests in San Salvador, but do me and Bill Conklin a favor and don't order any. Our budget just won't handle that sort of thing."

"You've done wonders here, Wallace," said Stuart, "All with private funding?"

"Yes," said Godfrey proudly, "All of this was built using private donations. We have an adequate operating budget as well. My goal is to set up a foundation to support the clinic. I want the earnings from the foundation to cover operating expenses completely. If I can pull that off, Project Raphael can be financially independent of me. I won't live forever and I want to go to my final rest secure in the knowledge that the work of the clinic will continue."

"Are you thinking of stepping aside?" Stuart asked, "You're too young to retire."

"Not yet," Godfrey replied, "I've still got quite a few years to be useful. I have established a board of trustees, though. They're already involved in running the hospital and clinic. They help with fundraising. It means that I'm not irreplaceable. Project Raphael can continue, no matter what happens to me."

"Admirable," said Stuart.

"Enjoy yourself on this mission, Ray," said Godfrey, "I'll see you around the next couple of weeks. Maybe you would join us for dinner on the yacht one evening?"

"Us?"

"Oh, yes, my wife came along," said Godfrey, "She enjoys the cruise and the beaches of Acajutla."

"I'd be honored," said Stuart.

After Godfrey left, Stuart wandered around the facility looking for Kathleen. He found her at the loading dock behind the hospital, directing a group of young muscular Salvadoran men in the unloading of two shipping containers, which were attached to tractor-trailer trucks. Bill Conklin was with her.

"Hi, Dr. Ray," said Conklin, "Did Wallace give you his personal tour?"

"He did," said Stuart, "He's very proud of this place."

"Good," said Conklin, "These are the shipping containers I was telling you about. The smaller one there, the twenty-footer, is full of the surgical supplies and medications, as well as some instruments that your team will need for the next two weeks. That's Kathleen's responsibility. The larger container is a forty-footer and that's the one we're using to transport our wheelchairs and other durable medical equipment. It also has Dr. Talbot's new anesthesia machine."

Conklin stopped to yell at two of the young men who were wrestling a large crate out of the container.

"Careful with that," yelled Conklin.

Stuart saw by the label on the crate that it contained the precious anesthesia machine. He had nothing useful to contribute to the work at hand, so he tried to stay out of the way. Stuart only had one eye, but he was a highly trained observer and he missed very little. He noticed that the trucks were labeled "LC Freight" and featured a small image of a condor. The young men who were working hard to unload the containers had a tough look about them. He could see a tattoo of a bird, a condor, he thought, on the necks of several of the workers.

Stuart noticed that some of the young men were carrying pistols stuffed into their pants. It took him a moment to remember that El Salvador was a violent country, with a murder rate ten times as high as Chicago. The streets of El Salvador were battlefields for rival gangs. The police and government were corrupt and many companies had to arm their employees for safety reasons.

Stuart watched the men unload boxes and wheelchairs for a while. The two containers were parked side by side at the loading dock. Ever curious and always observant, Stuart thought that when looking at the inside, the larger container didn't seem twice the length of the twenty-foot container, but just slightly longer. Tucking that observation away in his memory, he went off to see other features of the hospital.

♦ ♦ ♦

"You paying for the coffee?" asked Will Chen.

Duane Wilson grinned. What a typical greeting from Will. Not a "hello" or a "good morning," but an inquiry of who would be picking up the tab today.

Will was a short, wiry Oakland police detective who seemed to always be in motion. His eyes darted all around the room and his feet always seemed to be tapping some beat that only existed in Will's mind. Duane Wilson wondered if the man ever stopped moving. But Will was a good cop and a good friend. Duane and Will had collaborated on dozens of cases over the years.

They were in a coffee shop at Jack London Square.

"Sure, I'll buy the coffee," said Duane, "It's a lot cheaper on your side of the Bay."

"In that case, I'll have a slice of apple pie with mine," said Will.

Duane grinned and ordered the coffee and pie.

"We have a case in San Francisco that I'd like to run by you," said Duane, "A girl, thirteen or fourteen years old. She died of tuberculosis. Somebody tied a chain around her ankles and dropped her body in the Bay. Between the fish and the chain, the feet fell off and she floated to the surface."

"This is not good for my appetite, Duane," said Will with a frown.

"We have this doctor that consults with the ME's office sometimes," Duane continued, "He thinks this girl was from Central America. El Salvador or Guatemala or someplace like that. He thinks this girl is a victim of human trafficking. The FBI is in on the case and they think the doctor might be right."

"You didn't invite me for coffee because you missed my smiling face. You want to know what's happening in Oakland with human trafficking," said Will.

"Yep," said Duane, "Anything on the street in your neighborhood?"

"Well, Oakland is a major port and there's plenty of human trafficking coming through here," said Will, "Not on the water, of course, but on the freeways. Most of the victims come across the Mexican border in trucks or vans. A few fly into private airports."

"We have the same thing in San Francisco," said Duane, "In addition to the Central and South American victims, we get quite a few from Asia."

"We do too," said Will, "Our department works with the FBI on the human trafficking problem, but it's damned hard. The victims are kept underground, out of sight. They don't speak English and are, for the most part, just transiting through Oakland on their way to somewhere else."

"Sounds just like San Francisco," said Duane, "We don't get many leads either. If the good citizens of our city are keeping sex slaves in their mansions, nobody talks about it. And nobody can keep track of all the prostitutes in the Tenderloin. Who knows how many of them were brought in here against their will from Asia or Central America?"

"Don't forget eastern Europe," said Will, "A lot of these victims come from the old Soviet republics like Uzbekistan or Kazakhstan or some other godawful country that ends in 'stan.' Some of them come voluntarily, lured by promises of a better life, a good job, maybe a rich American husband. They find themselves in hopeless debt to some asshole who smuggled them in. Then they get addicted to heroin and they become slaves for life."

"It's not a long life for most of these people," said Duane, "Do you know who's smuggling the victims in?"

"Lots of players in that game," said Will, "There's lots of money in it. Mexican cartels, Chinese tongs, Russian and Albanian mobs mostly."

"Any local gangs involved?" Duane asked.

"Not really," said Will, "Local gangs are, well, local. They don't have the kind of capital to invest in transportation of human beings. They're very territorial and have almost no power or influence outside their own turf. To play the human trafficking game, you need international connections and lots and lots of money. Our street gangs in the East Bay are small time punks, peddling drugs and extortion mostly."

"What about some of the newer gangs that have come over from Asia or out of countries like Guatemala and El Salvador? Don't they have connections to the gangs in their home countries?"

"I suppose that's possible," said Will, "But most of our Asian and Latino gangs are home grown. There are some rumors of Salvadoran gangs working in Oakland, but they're very small and, so far, they can't make much inroad into the territories of the black, Latino, and Asian gangs that have been here much longer. The local boys are bigger and stronger."

"Do me a favor and keep an ear open for me, Will," said Duane, "For some reason, the case of this poor girl is eating at me. I really want to catch the bastards who brought her over here to die."

7

GABRIELLA GIGGLED WHEN Hector slipped his hand inside her dress and caressed her breast.

"Perfect," Hector thought. "Young and sexy. Just the girl I'm looking for."

"Come away with me," Hector whispered in her ear, loving the soft feel of her breast and the clean smell of her hair.

"Where would you take me?" Gabriella asked.

"To San Salvador," he said, "The big city with lights that never go out. I'll buy you clothes of the finest fabrics and the latest styles. We'll eat at world class restaurants, drink wine, go to nightclubs and concerts. We could make love on silk sheets in the best hotels. No more of this filthy village with dirt streets. Not for you, my princess."

"Ooh, Hector," she said, "You make it sound like Heaven."

"It is Heaven. Come with me."

"My friend Elana says that I should stay away from you. She says you're a hoodlum."

"You need better friends."

"Well, my best friend, Martina, thinks that you're cute."

Hector nibbled gently at Gabriella's ear. She laughed and wiggled.

"I think I like Martina," he said, "You need to introduce me. Is she anything like you? Because you are the sexiest thing I've ever seen."

"Hey, I thought I was your girl!" she said, giving him a playful punch.

"You are, Gabriella. Believe me."

"Do you love me, Hector?" she asked.

"More than anything," he said.

Hector was aroused. This was going to work out very well indeed.

♦ ♦ ♦

Sunday morning in Central America brought pleasant memories for Ray Stuart.

Clinic wouldn't begin until the afternoon. He met Kathleen for an early breakfast. They had decided to reprise one of their old traditions from previous medical missions. They walked to the nearest church, about half a mile from the hotel, and attended Mass.

Like many churches in Central America, this one was plain. A few poor-quality, faded paintings hung on the walls. The dreary images were of saints and Jesus, usually teaching or healing somebody. Everybody in the pictures looked like they were Mayan. There were no stained-glass windows. A painted statue of the Virgin Mary stood on one side of the altar. A plaster Jesus hung on a wooden cross above a stone altar. The pews were rough wood, unpainted and hard. The people were poor, dressed in cheap clothes and smelling like they were in need of a bath.

Some things about Central America, Stuart thought, never changed. He reached for Kathleen's hand and gave it a gentle squeeze.

Kathleen smiled at Stuart as they knelt. Local Salvadorans stared at them curiously. Kathleen and Stuart didn't need words. The situation was too familiar. They were back at work, caring for people in a foreign land. Worshiping with the locals was an important part of a mission trip for them. It reminded them who they were and why they were there.

The team assembled for clinic after lunch. Kathleen and her team of nurses went off to the surgical suite to unpack boxes, sterilize instruments, and prepare for two weeks of very busy surgical schedules. Stuart joined three other orthopedic surgeons, a resident, and a medical student. They had met in the airport and on the plane to El Salvador. Most were from the San Francisco area.

Dr. Penny Levin flew in from Los Angeles and met the northern California group when they changed planes in Houston. She was a pediatric orthopedist on her first mission with Project Raphael. She impressed Stuart from the beginning with her firm, confident handshake and friendly approach. He was looking forward to working with her for the next two weeks.

Dr. James Brauer was a tall man with a large belly. He was in private practice in Danville, California, an expensive community in the East Bay. Brauer had been quick to point out that he was a personal friend of Wallace Godfrey. He was a veteran of many missions. Brauer was a large financial contributor to Project Raphael and had solicited even more money from his rich friends at his country club in Blackhawk. He wore expensive clothes and jewelry. Since they were in an impoverished Central American country, Stuart wondered who Brauer was trying to impress.

Dr. Peter Cain made Stuart smile just meeting him. Cain radiated an infectious warmth and energy. Cain was very fit and dressed well in casual, but expensive clothes. Cain was on his first foreign mission. His specialty was actually sports medicine, which he practiced in a private office in Marin county. When they met at the airport in San Francisco, Stuart was surprised that a surgeon interested in sports medicine would even consider a mission like this. Cain explained that, in his view, sports medicine had raised the standards of orthopedics. No longer was it sufficient to get a patient back to work. Rather, a real success of treatment had to get the patient back to the recreational activities the patient enjoyed as well. He was eager to share his knowledge and skill with ordinary working people in the developing world.

"Hi, Elizabeth," Stuart waved to a young woman who was standing off to the side.

Dr. Elizabeth Potter was a third-year resident at Sutro State. Stuart knew her from his work at the university. She had a lot to learn, but was bright and competent. Participation on Project Raphael missions was a tradition for orthopedic residents.

At the airport, Stuart had briefly talked with Dennis Nichols, a fourth-year medical student at Sutro State. Nichols was a bookish young man with thick glasses. Stuart was eager to get to know him better.

"Are you interested in orthopedics, Dennis?" Stuart asked.

"I don't know," Nichols replied, "Maybe. Probably not."

The conversation was interrupted by the San Francisco nurse in charge of the clinic. In her mid-forties with an efficient, no-nonsense attitude, Ann Conforti knew how to get doctors to focus on the work at hand.

"Let's go, boys and girls, there's work to be done," announced Ann.

She guided the group to the A section of clinic. With eight examination rooms in the section and four senior surgeons, she gave two rooms to each. The resident and medical student could follow any senior surgeon or be called to look at interesting patients. There was a surgical scheduler, three Spanish interpreters, and several nursing assistants available to help the team.

Stuart spoke serviceable Spanish. He was not assigned one of the professional interpreters. Rather he was assisted in his clinic rooms by a Salvadoran nurse whose English language skill supplemented his Spanish.

One of the first of Stuart's patients was a seven year-old boy named Eduardo who was having trouble walking. He was there with his mother and little brother. His mother explained that he walked normally as a toddler, but had increasing difficulty as he grew older. He had big muscles, she noted, pointing to his overdeveloped calves, but seemed to be weaker and weaker as each month went by. The local doctors could not figure out what was wrong.

Stuart knew the diagnosis before he examined the child. Still, he made a point of watching the boy walk in the examination room. Then he hoisted the boy up on to the table and carefully checked the motion of every joint and the strength of each muscle group.

"He has excellent motion," Stuart said to the mother as he stretched the little boy's ankle, "Do you do this at home?"

"Yes, Doctor, every day," the mother replied.

"You do a good job," said Stuart, "Would you mind if I showed Eduardo to our student doctors?"

"Not at all, Doctor," she said.

Stuart turned and addressed the little boy.

"Can I bring in some other doctors to see how well your mother takes care of you?" Stuart asked. He nodded eagerly in assent.

Stuart asked the nurse to invite the resident and medical student in to the room.

When the students entered, he asked them to watch Eduardo walk. Then he asked Eduardo to lay down on the floor. The boy complied.

"Now, stand up, Eduardo," said Stuart.

The resident and the medical student watched as the little boy struggled to get his feet under him, bracing his knees straight with his arms. Then he marched his hands up his legs, pushing himself upright.

"Very good, Eduardo," said Stuart.

Stuart repeated the rest of his physical examination for the benefit of the resident and student, then asked them to step outside into the corridor and wait for him. Stuart remained with the family. After a few minutes, the mother, Eduardo, and his little brother emerged from the room and headed for the waiting area. Stuart followed into the hallway.

When the family was out of hearing range, Stuart turned to the medical student.

"What did you see, Dennis?" Stuart asked.

"He walks funny,"

"Can you be more specific?"

"I don't know," said the student.

"Well," asked Stuart, "Did you ever see him bear weight on his leg with his knee bent?"

"I don't think so. I really didn't notice."

"He never did," Stuart continued, "Why would that be?"

"Because it hurt him to bend his knee?" asked Nichols.

"Maybe," said Stuart, "But he never appeared to be in pain during any part of the exam. Is there another explanation?"

"Is he weak?" asked Nichols.

"Yes, he is," said Stuart, "Which muscle is weak if you can't stand on a bent knee, Dr. Potter?"

"Er, well, the quadriceps, I think, sir," said the resident.

"Do you know Eduardo's diagnosis, Dr. Potter?" Stuart asked.

"No."

"Have you ever heard of the Gower's sign?"

"Yes, I read about it somewhere," she replied.

"Have you ever seen a positive Gower's sign?" asked Stuart.

"I think maybe I just did," said Elizabeth Potter.

"How about you, Dennis," asked Stuart, "Have you ever heard of the Gower's sign?"

"No, sir."

"Can you explain it to him, Dr. Potter?"

"Well, the Gower's sign is what Dr. Stuart had the little boy do when he asked him to get up off the floor," Elizabeth began, "His quads are weak, so he keeps his knees stable by using his hands and arms. Until he gets upright, then he can lock his knees in extension and free up his hands. It's a sign that is virtually diagnostic of muscle disease, most likely muscular dystrophy."

"What else did you notice about Eduardo's musculoskeletal system?" Stuart asked.

"Well, it looks like his calf muscles are really developed," said Nichols.

"It's called pseudohypertrophy, Dennis, and mostly it's a result of atrophy of the other muscles, which makes the calf look big and strong," said Stuart, "Plus, the calf muscles are about the only ones he has to propel himself and keep him upright. They're doing double duty. Yes, Dr. Potter, this is muscular dystrophy, Duchenne's type."

"Excuse me, Dr. Stuart," asked Elizabeth, "But how can you tell it's Duchenne's and not some other kind of muscle disease."

"Because his mother is normal appearing and his little brother has it, too," said Stuart.

"Huh? His brother?" asked Nichols.

"Yes," said Stuart, "He also has what looks like calf hypertrophy and, while he walks fairly well, never bends his knee in single leg stance."

"How did you notice the brother?" Nichols asked, "Did you get him up on the table before we came in?"

"No, Dennis," said Stuart, "You need to train your eye to look at everyone in the family, especially in pediatric specialties. The exam room is full of clues to the diagnosis. You must learn to look everywhere and at everyone, not just the patient."

"Can the little boy be helped, Dr. Stuart?" asked Nichols.

"I'm afraid not," said Stuart, "Duchenne's muscular dystrophy is a hereditary disease found almost exclusively in boys. It's relentlessly progressive and will kill him, probably before he's twenty."

"Oh, my God," said Nichols.

"Did you tell the mother, Dr. Stuart?" asked Elizabeth, "I mean, did you tell her that her son was going to get weaker and die? And that her younger son would share that same fate?"

"No, Elizabeth, I didn't," said Stuart, "What good would that have done anyone?"

"Aren't we supposed to tell our patients the truth, to the best of our knowledge?" asked Potter.

"No, Elizabeth, we're supposed to act with compassion," said Stuart, "If we can help the patient, we tell them what we can do, even if it means painful surgery or risky procedures. But when sharing our knowledge will only break their hearts and cause pain, I think the compassionate thing to do is keep our mouths shut."

"So, what did you tell the mother, Dr. Stuart?" asked Nichols.

"I told her that we have many such cases in the United States," said Stuart, "And that I was quite confident that I understood Eduardo's problem. I assured her that it is a case of weakness of the muscles and that Eduardo isn't lazy, as she sometimes thinks. I told her that there are no operations or medications that will help, not even in the United States. I explained that in the U.S. we treat the children with physical therapy, encouraging them to maintain strength and keeping the joints moving. I told her that she was doing as good a job as any physical therapist I know in the U.S. and I commended her devotion and love for her children."

"And she was okay with that?" asked Potter.

"Of course she was," said Stuart, "She came a long distance and brought her son to see the fancy doctor from San Francisco and he told her that she was doing everything possible for her boy. She doesn't have to feel guilty or cursed because she was born into poverty in El Salvador. What more could I have done for her? Often in medicine, the most important thing is not how much you know, but how and when you use your knowledge."

"Outstanding," Dr. Yousef Al-Saffar whispered to himself, looking at his computer screen.

He found a perfect six-point match for his patient who needed a kidney transplant. The Al Saud Medical Center, as a private institution, was not limited to donor lists within Saudi Arabia. Rather, the hospital belonged to a worldwide confederation of hospitals and clinics, all linked by computer through the servers which resided at his hospital. While the confederation shared all sorts of information, Al-Saffar was particularly interested in possible organ donors.

His success rate with organ transplantation was far better than most programs worldwide. The doctor attributed some of the success to his own skills as a surgeon and physician. Partly, though, was his ability to secure excellent tissue matches using his global connections. This particular donor was currently in Shanghai.

Using an intercom, he called his personal secretary.

"Please get the doctor for Prince Tariq on the phone."

In minutes the light flashed on Al-Saffar's desk.

"Yes, Doctor, we have found a donor for the Prince," Al-Saffar said, "A perfect match. Let's schedule admission to our hospital for Tuesday the twenty-fifth of next month. We'll plan the kidney transplant for Thursday the twenty-seventh. I anticipate that the prince will be hospitalized for a week to ten days."

"I'm impressed that you found a donor so quickly," the doctor said, "A perfect match is a blessing from Allah."

"Allah smiles upon the prince and the royal family," said Al-Saffar, "It is a pleasure to be entrusted with the care of such blessed people. I am humbled to be of service."

The world of medicine would never know how far superior Dr. Al-Saffar's results were to other centers. He wrote no scientific papers for publication in medical journals. His practice was exclusive, dependent on discretion.

There was a knock on the door. Ali Darwish entered. Dr. Al-Saffar could not restrain sharing his joy at having found a kidney for the prince.

"Congratulations," said Ali, "I understand that you saw Dorothy Watson, the British author, in your office earlier this week."

"Yes," said Al-Saffar, "a remarkable woman. Did you know that she has published sixteen best-selling books? She has a most amazing and insightful mind. She's brilliant."

"And she's sick," added Ali.

"Tragic," said Al-Saffar, "Simply tragic. How unfair is fate. She's actually not that old and, other than the viral cardiomyopathy that has affected her heart, she's quite healthy. With a new heart, she could live to be ninety. The woman is a genius. We could assure that the world has the benefit of her contributions for decades to come."

"I hate to bring this up, Yousef," said Ali, "but she's a British citizen. She's made a lot of money selling her books, but I'm afraid that she can't afford a heart transplant. The British National Health Service is unlikely to help pay for the operation in Saudi Arabia when the same procedure is available in the United Kingdom."

"It's not the same procedure!" said Al-Saffar, "Do you have any idea how many people die in the UK while waiting for a heart transplant? They don't care how brilliant she is, what an exceptional human being she is. We've got to help her. For the good of all humanity, we've just got to save her."

8

Giancarlo Valdez arrived at the warehouse near the docks at Acajutla in an armored limousine with four bodyguards. There was nothing subtle about the arrival. The car pulled up in front of a steel overhead door. Two guards exited and took positions behind the vehicle, eyes scanning the neighborhood, assault rifles at the ready. Two others stood on either side of the overhead door. When they were satisfied that things were safe, the door to Valdez's Suburban opened and he quickly stepped inside.

Pablo Ortega was waiting inside to greet the leader of *Los Cóndores*, accompanied by another eight armed gang members, some men and some women.

"*Jefe*," said Ortega respectfully.

"Are we ready for the next shipment?" asked Valdez.

"Yes, *Jefe*," said Ortega, "Six girls ready to go."

Valdez grunted approvingly.

"Let me see them."

Ortega led Valdez deeper into the warehouse. There was a large cage with iron bars in the center. Only one door permitted access to the cage. Six cots with blankets lay on the floor. Six terrified girls stared at the visitors. A female guard unlocked the door. Both Valdez and Ortega entered.

"In a line, girls," said the guard.

The girls formed a makeshift line facing the gang leaders. All looked at the floor. One little girl started to tremble and a tear ran down her face. Valdez looked the girls over one by one.

"This one is very fat, Pablo," said Valdez, pointing to a girl, "Where do you find a fat girl in El Salvador?"

"Sometimes fat girls visit our country from Argentina, *Jefe*," said Ortega, "And we all know that teenage girls often run away from their parents."

"But who would want a girl this fat?" asked Valdez with scorn.

"I am told that there are many men who prefer their girls with a few extra curves," smiled Ortega.

"Perhaps," said Valdez, "Well, it's not our problem. Once we get these girls to North America, the Client will take care of them."

Moving on to the next girl, Valdez stared at the little one, who was now crying silently and shaking.

"How old is this one, Pablo?" Valdez asked.

"Eleven, *Jefe*."

"Lovely. Excellent work. The Client will be very happy with this one."

The little girl almost collapsed. An older girl standing next to her wrapped arms around her to support the youngster. Valdez and Ortega ignored them.

"Oh my," said Valdez with a smile, "Where did you find a redhead?"

"In San Salvador, *Jefe*," replied Ortega, "They are rare, but can be found."

"Many people consider redheads to be exotic," said Valdez, "The Client should pay us a little more for finding this one. I must remember to mention this when I next talk with the Client."

Finishing the inspection, Valdez and Ortega discussed the provisions needed for the girls. The trip to the United States would take about two weeks. Food and water, toilet facilities needed to be provided. It was not good for business if their "products" arrived in port sick, malnourished, or dead.

"And now," said Valdez, "How about the smaller, more valuable cargo?"

Ortega led him to a different corner of the warehouse. A guard opened a locked door and they entered a comfortable, well-appointed apartment. The contrast between these rooms and the squalid prison where the girls were kept was striking. The apartment had a spacious living room, a well-equipped kitchen, a comfortable bedroom with twin beds, and a play room stocked with toys and stuffed animals.

"Greetings, *Jefe*," said the matronly woman inside.

"Ah, Daniella, you look lovely," said Valdez. His cold reptilian eyes showed his insincerity. "How is our little guest?"

"He's healthy and thriving, *Jefe*," she answered, "Ready for his voyage to America. He's gained a kilo and a half since he's been with me."

"Excellent, excellent," said Valdez, "I will see him now."

Daniella Santiago, a fully trained nurse, retrieved a cute four year-old boy from the playroom. One look at Valdez and his armed henchmen sent the boy into hiding behind Daniella's skirts, clutching to her leg.

"Come on, Pepé, say hello to the nice *Señor* Valdez," she coaxed.

The little boy stayed behind her, terrified of the pock-marked face and cold eyes.

"Pepé," said Valdez, "A lovely name. He looks good, Daniella. Good job."

♦ ♦ ♦

"What do you, see?" asked Stuart, holding his arm across the door into the examination room, blocking the entrance.

"A mother and a little girl," replied Dr. Pedro Sandoval, a mid-level resident in orthopedics from San Salvador.

"Look at the little girl," said Stuart, still blocking the door, "What can you learn from here?"

"Nothing," replied Sandoval, "I must go into the room, talk to the mother, and examine the child."

"Oh, Doctor Sandoval," said Stuart, "You can learn a lot from right here. Things that may not be revealed once you go into the room and possibly scare the child. Now, is the little girl healthy or sick?"

"Excuse me, Dr. Stuart?"

"Is she healthy or sick?" Stuart repeated.

Sandoval looked into the room where the little girl was climbing on the examination table, attired in her prettiest dress, which was getting seriously wrinkled during her exploration of the room. She was jabbering to her mother and giggling.

"She looks healthy," said Sandoval.

"Yes, she is," replied Stuart, "And that tells you a lot right away. You're not looking at a serious infection or a tumor or a major neuromuscular disease. This is a very functional little girl. Now, why is she here?"

"I need to examine her and talk to her mother," Sandoval protested, "How can I tell why she's here just from the doorway?"

"Just watch carefully."

The little girl climbed down off the table and scampered into her mother's arms.

"How does she walk?" asked Stuart.

"Quickly," said Sandoval.

Stuart laughed.

"Yes, indeed. And on the lateral border of her right foot."

Still in the doorway, Sandoval looked at the girl some more.

"You're right," he said, "And the outside of her right shoe is more worn than the inside."

"Well done. So, Dr. Sandoval, why do you think the little girl is here?"

"Ah, Dr. Stuart," Sandoval replied, his eyes lighting up, "My guess is that she has residual deformity from an old clubfoot."

"Excellent," said Stuart, lowering his arm and allowing Sandoval to enter the room.

The little girl indeed had been born with a congenital clubfoot. She had surgery in San Salvador as a baby. After surgery, she had worn casts for six months, but the family was too poor to afford a brace for a longer time, as would have been recommended. As the child grew, some of the old deformity recurred, causing her heel to turn in slightly and the forefoot to turn in. Sandoval was gentle, but skillful in his examination of the child. She smiled at him as he manipulated her feet.

"What will happen if we do nothing?" Stuart asked.

"Well, sir," began Sandoval, "She's only four years old. As she continues to grow, I expect that her clubfoot deformity will continue to recur and her deformity will get worse."

"What would you expect by the time she's skeletally mature?"

"She should have a serious deformity, which will impede her walking, cause her pain, and make her rejected by others."

"Well said," said Stuart, "Is there something you can do now to improve her fate?"

"I think so," said Sandoval, still manipulating the feet, "She could have a repeat soft tissue release operation with proper casting and bracing, since that's available at no cost here at Project Raphael. But, from what you've already taught me in the last several days, at age four soft tissue surgery won't be adequate. She'll need some surgery on the bones of the foot in order to restore proper alignment and complete correction."

"Very good, indeed, Dr. Sandoval," said Stuart, "Have her stick around today until Dr. Levin gets out of surgery. Show the case to Dr. Levin and see if she agrees. If so, you need to scrub in when the little girl has her operation."

Sandoval was a quick study, a sharp mind and Stuart's time in clinic flew by when Sandoval was there. There was a bounce in Stuart's step when the clinic staff broke for lunch.

Stuart found a paper plate and loaded it with rice, beans, and chicken. It was a lovely day and he went outside the clinic and found a table at which Dr. Peter Cain and the medical student, Dennis Nichols, were dining. They, too, had been in the clinic all morning. Cain's specialty in California was really sports medicine, but he was seeing all types of adult patients in El Salvador.

"Hi, Ray," said Cain, "Please join us. I was just explaining to young Dr. Nichols how a reconstruction of the anterior cruciate ligament can restore stability and improve performance in an athlete."

"Are you doing ACL reconstructions here?" Stuart asked, "How do you rehab the patients?"

"Yes, I've done a few this week," Cain replied, "The physical therapy department here is remarkably good."

Stuart excused himself when he finished eating. He had a little time before the afternoon clinic. He wanted a closer look at the physical therapy department.

As Cain had said, the facility was good. Stuart admired the quality equipment. He made a mental note to start sending some of the children for physical therapy. He also decided to have lunch with the therapists to discuss techniques.

On the way back to the clinic, Stuart passed the clinical laboratory. He remembered that he had wanted to look inside when Godfrey took him on the tour, but Godfrey was in a hurry. Stuart decided to check out the equipment.

The clinical laboratory staff was also at lunch, but the door was unlocked and Stuart went in. He was impressed with the size and cleanliness of the lab. He saw neat racks of blood and urine samples, each with computer generated labels. He noted that the whole laboratory seemed to be connected in a small computer network, a remarkable thing for a small facility in El Salvador.

Stuart looked at the machines themselves. Each appeared to be modern, if not state of the art, devices. He didn't notice any machines that seemed to be out of service, which he found surprising, given the difficulties in maintaining sophisticated technology in the developing world. One machine in particular caught his eye. It was a Maxwell FSC, a sophisticated device used for DNA analyses and in both blood banking and tissue typing. Stuart marveled at the inclusion of this particular piece of equipment in the lab.

Gabriella was thinking about sex.

Nowadays, she seemed to always be thinking about sex. Hector had a lot to do with that. Sooner or later, she knew that she would have sex with him. Deep inside, she was curious. Deeper inside, she was scared.

School was over for the day. She wasn't going to stop at home before she met up with Hector. They arranged to see each other at a local *tienda*. He would drink a beer and buy her a Fanta. There were some tables and benches where they could sit and talk.

She sighed. Not so long ago, she didn't even want to be a teenager. Her life seemed pretty good as a little girl. It was uncomplicated. She had seen teenagers in the village. Nothing about them made her want to be one. Too much drama.

Her body had betrayed her. Something inside her started making some sort of hormones and, without actually consulting her, the body turned into a teenager. And everything changed.

Her heart beat faster when she saw Hector's handsome face.

"Hi," she shouted, picking up her walking pace.

Hector rose from his chair and embraced her.

"You're more beautiful than ever," Hector smiled, "How about a kiss?"

She kissed him quickly, blushing. They were, after all, out in public.

"Did you learn anything useful in school today?" Hector asked, mocking her.

"I learned that boys get dumber and dumber every day," she retorted.

"Until they become men," Hector said, "Then they acquire wisdom."

"Maybe some men acquire wisdom," Gabriella, "Others just have fewer pimples and bigger egos."

"Not me," Hector said.

"Are you hiding some pimples?" she teased, "Because you sure have a big ego."

"I have a realistic sense of my own attractiveness," Hector said, "And my own importance."

He was attractive, she thought. Slender, yet well-muscled. A handsome, chiseled face. Dark, sexy bedroom eyes. A dazzling smile of pure white teeth. She wasn't impressed with the tattoo of the condor on his neck. Nor was she happy about the pistol he kept stuck in his pants. But he looked enticingly good to Gabriella. Such a difference from the boys her own age.

"Where are you taking me this weekend, Mr. Big Shot?" she teased.

"Well, there is a party in a town near here," he said, "Lots of my friends are going."

"*Los Cóndores* friends?"

"Sure," he said, "They're the best friends I've got. They're like family."

Gabriella's own friends were giving her mixed advice. Martina, her best friend, was jealous. Martina was adventurous. She said that if Gabriella got tired of Hector, she volunteered to take Gabriella's place.

Elana had a different opinion. She had a strong distrust of gang members, perhaps because her brother had been severely beaten by members of *Los Cóndores*. Elana urged Gabriella to get rid of Hector. In that regard, Elana sounded like Gabriella's mother.

"My mother thinks you're a bunch of thugs."

"Yeah, well your mother needs to wake up and realize that you're no longer in diapers," Hector said, "You're old enough to pick your own friends."

Gabriella just wanted a little respect. Gabriella still loved her mother very much. If her mother really loved her, she would respect Gabriella's choices.

"I'm looking forward to the party," Gabriella said.

Ann Conforti, the head nurse of the clinic opened the door of Stuart's examining room and stuck her head in.

"Excuse me," she said, "When you finish with this child, can you confer with Dr. Brauer?"

"Of course," said Stuart.

Stuart asked the medical student, Dennis Nichols, to have a look at the next child, assuring him that he would return after he consulted with Dr. Brauer.

"How can I help you, Jim?" Stuart asked.

Brauer pointed to an x-ray of a child's pelvis and hips hanging on the view box.

"About a year old," said Stuart, "The left hip is totally dislocated. This kid is not going to do well in life if that hip isn't put back."

"My thoughts exactly, Ray," said Brauer, "Is there any hope at all of getting this back in the socket without surgery?"

"Not really," said Stuart, "You might be able to put the kid to sleep, examine her with total muscle relaxation and be able to put the hip back into the socket, but it won't stay. Even if you could get the hip in and hold it long enough to put a cast on, this is the sort of hip that will re-dislocate even in a good cast."

"In your opinion, it will require an open reduction," said Brauer.

"That's right," said Stuart, "It needs surgery."

"That's exactly what I thought. I'll put it on my schedule then," said Brauer.

Stuart looked at Brauer quizzically. This man did general orthopedics, not pediatrics. Most of his patients were wealthy adults. Brauer read the doubt in Stuart's expression.

"Don't worry, Ray," he said, "I've been doing these cases for years. I know how to do these."

"No offense intended, Jim," said Stuart, "But when was the last time you were in a baby's hip?"

"Just last year," said Brauer, "Right here in El Salvador. Turned out great. That's one of the best things about coming down here, you know. It keeps my skills in pediatrics up. It's hard to get cases like this at home with so many pediatric orthopedists around. The pediatricians send all the cases to the universities or the Children's Hospital. They forget that there are competent surgeons right in the community who can easily handle straightforward cases like this."

"Do you do a lot of pediatric cases here with Project Raphael?" said Stuart.

"Yes, quite a few," said Brauer, "They're a change of pace and a lot of fun."

9

GABRIELLA FELT LIKE a princess riding in Hector's Nissan to the party. She dressed in a stylish skirt and top. The skirt was very short. Her mother didn't know that she had it. Gabriella knew that her mother would disapprove. Hector said it was sexy.

They drove about an hour to a town about five times bigger that Cedros. The party was at a large house. The music was loud and the people were amazing. Gabriella quickly figured out that she was the youngest person at the party. All the men sported condor tattoos on their necks. Most had pistols in their belts. The girls were mostly in their late teens or early twenties, lots of makeup and a few tattoos of their own. The clothes that the girls wore looked like they came right out of the fashion magazines she liked to look at. Most of the people were smoking cigarettes.

"Hector, I'm not sure I fit in here," she said, "Everyone's much older. These girls look like fashion models."

"Baby, the way you look tonight, you'd fit in at any party," Hector replied, "You might want to have a beer. That'll help you relax."

"I've never tried a beer," Gabriella admitted.

"It's part of growing up," he said, "I'll get you one. You'll like it."

Hector moved off in the direction of the bar. Gabriella looked around at the partygoers. Nobody was paying any attention to her. She felt self-conscious. She hurried after Hector.

"Here you go, baby," Hector offered her a bottle of beer, "Or do you want a glass for that?"

Gabriella glanced around. The other girls at the party were all drinking their beer directly from the bottle.

"This is fine," she said.

Hector took a long pull at his beer. Gabriella brought the bottle to her lips and took a tentative sip.

The beer was bitter. She wanted to gag.

"You like it?" Hector asked.

"Oh, yes," she lied, forcing a smile.

Hector and Gabriella mingled with the crowd at the party. There were so many people. She couldn't remember all the names. Hector was very gallant, introducing her proudly as his girlfriend.

Music came from a large stereo system and people began to dance.

"Come on, baby," Hector motioned, "Let's party."

Gabriella took the opportunity to set the bottle of beer down and join Hector on the dance floor. She watched the other girls undulate to the music and tried to copy their motions. The expression on Hector's face told her that she was doing something right. Gabriella danced more provocatively and Hector responded with a proud, yet predatory grin.

A slender girl in a black dress, smoking a cigarette, approached Gabriella when the music stopped.

"Hi, I'm Briana," the girl said, "Nice dance moves."

"Gabriella. Thanks."

"Are you Hector's girl?"

"I sure hope so," Gabriella replied.

"By the way he looks at you, I think you're the love of his life," Briana said, "Hector's a handsome guy."

"He's fantastic," Gabriella said.

"I haven't seen you around," Briana continued, "Is this your first *Los Cóndores* party?"

"Yes," Gabriella said, "Have you been to these before?"

"Many times," Briana.

"I hope I get invited back," Gabriella said, "This is really fun."

"I'm very certain that we'll be seeing each other again," Briana said, moving away, "I need another drink."

Briana gave a wave and a smile at Hector, then glided through the crowd toward the bar.

Gabriella and Hector danced and laughed. Everyone at the party was happy and friendly. Gabriella felt welcome and accepted. Eventually, Hector went off in search of more beer. A tall, heavy-set man approached Gabriella. He had a glass of what Gabriella assumed must be whiskey in his hand.

"Hey, beautiful," the man said, "I like your moves. Wanna dance with me?"

"No," she replied.

"What the hell do you mean, 'no'?" he asked.

"I mean I don't want to dance with you," she said.

"It's a party," he replied, "Everybody dances with everybody else."

"Not me," she said.

The man grabbed her around the waist with his free hand.

"C'mon, let's just party, baby," he said.

Gabriella slapped him hard in the face. Shocked at her reaction, the man let go.

Spotting Hector across the room, she turned on her heel and headed in his direction. The man stood there, rejected and confused.

"Hector," she asked, "Who's that fat guy over there?"

Hector looked in the direction she pointed. The man was still staring incredulously at Gabriella.

"That's Esteban," he said, "He's an important man in *Los Cóndores*. Why is he staring at you?"

"He's rude," she said.

"What did he do? What did you say to him?"

"He wanted to dance with me," she said, "I think he wanted more than that. I told him no."

"Well," said Hector, "That explains the expression on his face. Esteban isn't used to being refused anything."

"He needs to get over it," she said.

As the evening progressed, the party guests supplemented their beer with marijuana and a little cocaine. Hector offered both to her.

"Hector, I don't think so," Gabriella said, "I've had my first beer tonight. Let me take one step of growing up at a time."

"Okay, baby," Hector said, "No pressure."

She loved the dancing. Proving to be a quick study, she made up some new moves and added a few flourishes of her own to what the other girls were doing. Hector proved to be an excellent dancer. People gathered and cheered as she and Hector whirled around the dance floor.

"Hector, this is great," Gabriella said, puffing a little when they took a rest. She had traded her beer for a Fanta, which was much more pleasing to her taste.

"Oh, baby, stick with me and there's a whole lot more coming. You and I are just getting started."

"You could have any one of these girls," Gabriella said, "They're closer to your age. They're much more mature. Why don't you date them?"

"Because I'm in love with a sweet, gorgeous girl from Cedros," he answered, "She's special. A little bit innocent, a little bit adventurous. A little bit curious and a little sassy. Compared to her, these girls are just ordinary."

Gabriella smiled at him. Hector's words made her feel good inside.

The party went past midnight. When they finally walked to Hector's car, she was exhausted but ecstatic.

"This has been the most wonderful day of my life," she murmured, resting her head on Hector's shoulder.

Gabriella fell asleep in the car riding back to Cedros.

It was the second Monday afternoon of the mission. The plastic surgeons finished their schedule early and Kathleen opened a second orthopedic room. Dr. Levin was doing multilevel tendon releases on a girl with cerebral palsy. It was a long and tedious procedure, with multiple incisions and wounds to close, but not a difficult operation. Kathleen sent the best assistant surgeon, the resident Dr. Potter into the other room to help Dr. Brauer do an open reduction of a hip on a one-year-old. Kathleen thought little of this, as she knew that Dr. Brauer had operated on children many times at Project Raphael. Kathleen got busy with planning the surgical schedule for the next day, assigning nurses and figuring out which packs of instruments would be needed for each case.

About an hour after Dr. Brauer began his operation, Kathleen was interrupted by the anesthesiologist, Dr. Talbot. He was worried about the way that the operation was going.

Dr. Talbot explained that the child was stable under anesthesia and the blood loss had not been excessive. But Talbot had heard the conversation on the other side of the drape. He related parts of it to Kathleen.

"Are you sure that's the rectus femoris tendon, Dr. Brauer?" Dr. Potter had asked.

"Sure, it's always right here," Brauer replied.

"The professor at Sutro State says it looks like a silver fish," said Potter, "That doesn't look like a silver fish to me."

"Have you ever assisted on an open reduction of a baby's hip before?" asked Brauer testily.

"No, sir," she replied.

"Then shut up and hold that retractor," said Brauer, "Jesus H. Christ, I can't see shit in here."

Talbot had seen enough operations to suspect that things were not developing as they should. He got one of the other anesthesiologists to relieve him for a few minutes. After briefing the relief anesthesiologist on the case, assuring her that the child was stable, Talbot went to find Kathleen.

"Brauer is totally lost in that baby's hip," Talbot blurted out to Kathleen, "He has no idea where he is or what he's doing."

"Damn," said Kathleen, "Can't Dr. Potter help?"

"Shit, she's just a junior resident," said Talbot, "She's never seen an open reduction before. She sure as hell hasn't seen one now."

"What do you think I can do about this, John?"

"You could scrub in and relieve the surgical nurse," he said, "Hell, you've done hundreds of babies' hips with Ray Stuart. You could probably get Brauer back on track."

"Damn," said Kathleen again, "Dr. Levin is just getting into a long case in the other room. I'm not a doctor, John. I can't go in there and take over. Let me go back there and have a look. Maybe I can think of something."

When Kathleen reached the operating room, things had gotten worse. Unable to actually find the hip joint, Dr. Brauer had made a second incision along the baby's thigh and, with a power saw, had removed a section of the upper femur. The bleeding was worse and the anesthesiologist was increasing the fluids. Kathleen watched for a while, taking in the situation. Wordlessly, she left the operating room and returned to the front desk of the surgical suite. Picking up the phone, she dialed the clinic.

"Clinic, Ms. Conforti," said the voice on the phone.

"Ann, this is Kathleen Atwood in the OR. Which doctors are in orthopedic clinic?"

"Dr. Cain and Dr. Stuart and the medical student."

"Can I speak with Dr. Stuart?" asked Kathleen.

"Just a minute."

Kathleen bit her lip, knowing what she was about to ask could be painful.

"Hello," came Stuart's voice.

"Ray, this is Kathleen in the OR," she said, silently praying for strength, "Jim Brauer is trying to do an open reduction on a baby's hip. He's totally lost. He hasn't found the hip joint after nearly an hour and a half. He cut the femur; I don't know why. It's a mess."

There was a long silence on the other end of the phone.

"Is Dr. Levin available to help him?"

"No. She's just starting a long case of her own and she only has one of the Salvadoran residents as an assistant."

Another long silence.

"Ray," said Kathleen softly, "I don't want to ask this of you. I know you haven't operated since the accident. I don't quite know why, but, well, this may be really hard for you. I'm just thinking of this poor baby."

"I'll be up in a few minutes," said Stuart, "See if you can get Brauer to just stop for a while, maybe cauterize a few bleeders. I'll ask Peter Cain to finish up the clinic."

Kathleen returned to the operating room, scrubbed herself into the case, and relieved the instrument nurse, who was more than happy to get out of there.

"We're having one hell of a time," said Brauer when he saw Kathleen.

"I know, Dr. Brauer," she said, "I hope you don't mind, but I've asked Dr. Stuart to come take a look. Maybe he can help."

"Stuart?" asked Brauer, "I'd love his input. I hope that he won't just look, but actually scrub in and give me a hand."

"I thought that Dr. Stuart didn't do surgery anymore," said Dr. Potter.

"He's making an exception in this case," said Kathleen.

She saw Stuart dressed in scrubs at the scrub sink. He had removed his glass eye and wore the patch. Just seeing him go through the routine of scrubbing his arms and hands brought back memories. She feared that she may have offended or hurt him. With the baby's health on the line, Kathleen knew that the time for personal feelings would come later.

Kathleen looked hard into Stuart's eye as she helped him with his surgical gown and gloves. She saw the steady gaze of the great surgeon she knew.

"Want two more hands and one more eye?" Stuart took a position opposite Brauer at the table.

"Well, we could use a little help," said Brauer, "We're having a little trouble finding the femoral head. I shortened the femur in hopes that things will become more clear, but we haven't had much luck."

Stuart looked into the main incision and poked his finger at some structures.

"May I?" he asked.

"Of course," said Brauer, "Do you want to stand over here? I think you're going to become the surgeon at this point. You've got more experience with the tough cases than I do."

"Not necessary," said Stuart.

"Dr. Stuart is left-handed," said Kathleen, "He's already on the side of the table that he likes."

"Kathleen, may I have a peanut?" Stuart asked.

Kathleen had already prepared a small piece of gauze held in the tip of a curved clamp. She slipped it into Stuart's open hand. Stuart kept his gaze inside the incision, not looking at his hand. He knew the instrument would be exactly what he needed placed in exactly the right spot.

Stuart gently moved a tendon, then cleared some tissue. Soon they were all looking at the pale white capsule of the child's hip. Kathleen handed him a long-handled scalpel with a tiny blade. Stuart incised the capsule in the shape of the letter "T." Amber joint fluid flowed into the wound. Dr. Potter removed the fluid with a suction catheter. When she did so, they were all looking at the shiny white cartilage of the ball of the child's hip joint.

Stuart, gently positioned the hip back into the normal socket, then sutured the capsule back tight so the hip was held in the proper place. Using a small metal plate, he put the femur back together where Brauer had cut it. Stuart then moved the leg through a full range of motion. The hip remained stable in the socket.

"That was impressive, Ray," said Brauer, "After years of absence from the OR and with only one eye, you've still got it."

"Thank you, Jim," said Stuart softly.

"Dr. Potter and I can close this up if you like," said Brauer, "And we'll get this baby into a cast. Do you want to see the x-ray when we get the cast on?"

"I would appreciate that. I'll go back to the clinic."

"I'll bring the x-ray down there for you," said Dr. Potter.

Kathleen noticed that Stuart said nothing to her and did not make eye contact.

That evening, the team was having dinner together in the hotel. Word had gotten around that Stuart had returned to surgery and salvaged a near disaster. Many of the nurses and doctors stared at Stuart, glancing away when he looked back at them. Kathleen found the whole scene to be uncomfortable. She was sure that she'd hurt Stuart. She wanted desperately for him to talk to her.

Wallace Godfrey made an unusual appearance in the dining room. There was nothing humble about his entrance. Godfrey loved attention. Dressed in his tropical suit, he stood out among the tired staff, who wore mostly jeans and tee shirts. Godfrey went straight to where Stuart and Kathleen sat, sitting down in an empty chair.

"I heard about today, Ray," said Godfrey, "Does this mean that you're back as a surgeon?"

"No sense wasting time with diplomatic chit-chat, is there, Wallace?" said Stuart, "I don't know. Today was a special circumstance. A colleague needed help and I knew how to help him. What else could I have done?"

"If this means you've decided to come back to surgery, should we set you up with a schedule in the operating room?" asked Godfrey.

"No, not this trip," said Stuart, "I have some thinking to do."

10

FELIPE PEÑA ASSEMBLED all twelve members of the Oakland branch of *Los Cóndores* at their headquarters, a well-appointed office in an industrial park not far from the shipping docks. *Los Cóndores* rented the adjacent warehouse as well as the office. Oakland was the destination for the abducted girls taken in El Salvador and transported by shipping container to the San Francisco Bay. Once the containers were off-loaded at the port, they were taken by truck to the warehouse. The warehouse itself had been customized similarly to its counterpart in El Salvador, with showers and toilets, cots and accommodations for the girls when they arrived. The girls were locked up at all times, of course, under the guard of gang members. In the office, Peña had the paperwork which showed the destination of each girl, how much had been paid, and whether or not any more money was owed to the gang. Each girl was cleaned up, dressed up, fed, and dispatched by car or van to her new "home."

Los Cóndores was just a transport service in the human trafficking business. The Client found the buyers. The Client placed an order for how many girls were wanted. The order was placed in El Salvador and the gang members there obtained the girls. *Los*

Cóndores in Oakland made most of its money from selling wholesale cocaine to local gangs, but the girls were a very profitable side hustle.

Felipe Peña was the leader of the Oakland branch. Right now, he had a problem. The neighboring black gang, 8 Gangsta Blood, was putting the squeeze on the longshoremen at the Oakland docks where the girls and drugs arrived. *Los Cóndores* needed unencumbered access to those docks. In addition, Felipe was interested in expanding into the lucrative retail cocaine business on the streets. The nearest gang turf was that of the 8 Gangsta Blood.

Felipe needed to make a move.

"Contact Nine Mil, boss of the 8 Gangsta Blood," said Peña to one of his men, "It should be easy to find him. Just pass the word to one of his homeys. They can always be found at the corner of 8th Avenue and 12th Street, selling shit. Get the word to Nine Mil that I want to set up a meeting. I want to negotiate a business deal. I suggest a neutral turf, a location in San Francisco that I'll select. It's OK if he wants to bring his whole posse."

The gang member departed. Felipe addressed the remaining men.

"Listen, *mes amigos*," Peña said, "We're gonna make a move on 8 Gangsta Blood. We rent a warehouse in San Francisco. On Revere Street in Bayview. It's supposed to be a backup if something compromises our place here in Oakland. I need a couple of you to go there now. I want you to scout for good places to watch who goes in and comes out of the warehouse. The places need to be well hidden. Nearby rooftops are ideal. I also need about a hundred fifty gallons of cheap gasoline."

"Felipe," said one of the gang, "There are over forty members of 8 Gangsta Blood. We only have twelve of us in the Bay area."

"Who said anything about a fight?" asked Peña, "I'm talking about a business meeting."

The meeting was scheduled for six o'clock two days later. At five-fifteen, Nine Mil Brooks, the leader of the 8 Gangsta Blood, arrived at the warehouse in San Francisco accompanied by twenty heavily armed members of his gang. All were young black men, wearing red headbands. Most of them had tattoos of a dog's paw on their neck or their hand. A few had teardrops tattooed below an eye. Each carried an automatic pistol. Two had shotguns and three more wielded automatic rifles.

Nine Mil looked around the street. Most of the windows were so covered in dirt that they were opaque. He saw nothing on the rooftops, no people, no reflections, no guns. He was wary, nervous. He didn't like meeting with the Salvadoran punks of *Los Cóndores*. A business meeting, they said. Bullshit.

He didn't like meeting in San Francisco. It would have better if they met on his turf. But the Salvadorans weren't that stupid. It wouldn't matter, he thought. The outcome would be the same. These punks were going to yield to the power of 8 Gangsta Blood or they would die right here, this evening.

Nine Mil posted two men with assault rifles outside the door to the warehouse. He sent another to the roof. These men had walkie-talkies and could warn him at the first sign of treachery. Once inside the warehouse, Nine Mil took stock. There were wooden crates and a few fifty-five gallon drums haphazardly scattered on the floor. The big doors were all locked. He stationed his men around the open area, some concealed behind crates and drums. He and his top lieutenants stood in the middle, facing the doors.

A quick search revealed no evidence of the Salvadorans. His men could find no signs of a trap. The lookouts at the door and on the roof reported all clear. Satisfied that 8 Gangsta Blood had arrived first, Nine Mil lit a cigarette and tried to relax.

"Got two guys with rifles on the door and one on the roof," whispered one of *Los Cóndores* from a fourth-floor window across the street into a hand-held radio, "All others inside."

"Juaquin, you on the roof?" asked Peña in Spanish.

"Yes, behind a ventilator. He didn't see me."

"Carlos and Esteban, you ready?" Peña radioed.

"Ready."

"Go." Peña ordered.

The two 8 Gangsta Bloods at the door fell silently as the silenced rounds from across the street cut them down. Juaquin, the *Los Cóndores* man on the roof, crept stealthily behind the black man. With his left hand, he covered the lookout's mouth while the right hand cut the man's throat. Great gushes of blood drenched both of them. The black man struggled a little, then collapsed into a pool of his own blood.

Juaquin wiped the blood off his hands on the dead man's clothes, then fingered the radio.

"All clear."

The back gate of a parked truck opened and six members of *Los Cóndores* rushed the warehouse. Some fastened chains to the exit doors and padlocked them all. The rest poured cans of gasoline all around the warehouse. The man on the roof dumped six five-gallon cans of gasoline on the roof and down the ventilation shaft. Then all but Peña scampered away. Peña lit a flare and tossed it into the gasoline.

Nine Mil heard the "whoosh" of fire outside. Almost simultaneously, there was a trickling sound as liquid dripped out of the ventilation duct. Suddenly, everything was on fire.

Nine Mil and three of his men ran toward the doors hitting the opening bars hard. The doors didn't budge, held tight by heavy chains on the outside. One of his men fired his pistol at the doors in frustration. Bullets ricocheted around. They all ducked instinctively.

The last thing that Nine Mil saw was the explosion of a fifty-five gallon drum of gasoline, highlighting the silhouettes of this men running all directions in panic.

Peña took a few moments to admire his work. The whole thing was a rather spectacular bit of pyrotechnics. There were muffled explosions as gasoline containers inside ignited. Little staccato pops as the trapped gang bangers fired their weapons in futility against locked doors. Every so often, he thought he heard a scream. Flames licked around and under the chained-up doors. Very satisfying work, he thought.

It was five forty-five in San Francisco and traffic was gridlocked as usual. By the time the fire trucks arrived, the entire warehouse was engulfed. There were no witnesses. As the firefighters unloaded their gear and their hoses, Peña and his men of *Los Cóndores* were on the 101 freeway, creeping along in traffic at a snail's pace toward the San Mateo Bridge.

💧 💧 💧

"The gentlemen from Bahrain are here, sir," said the secretary.

"Thank you. Send them in."

Dr. Al-Saffar was curious and anxious to meet these men. Messrs. Rashad and Jarra according to their papers and introductions. Dr. Al-Saffar had never heard of Rashad and Jarra. Even though the men came well recommended, he checked their backgrounds. He could find no evidence that Rashad or Jarra existed.

Because the references were from within the royal family, the men were given an appointment. However, Dr. Al-Saffar doubted that their names were Rashad and Jarra and he doubted that they were from Bahrain.

Both were dressed in western business suits, understated but clearly of high quality. Seville Row, Al-Saffar guessed. Rashad was clearly the more important. He was in his mid-forties, perfectly barbered all the way to his close-cut beard, which was flecked with grey. His hands were too rough for a life of pampered leisure and his face had spent much time in the sun. Jarra was younger, taller, lithe and athletic. Jarra walked half a step behind Rashad and carried a leather briefcase. He waited until the older man was seated before taking a chair himself.

"How good of you to see us, Dr. Al-Saffar," said Rashad.

"How can I help you?" asked the doctor.

"We represent a very important individual, who unfortunately has a very serious health problem," said Rashad, "Our employer suffers from end stage renal failure. He has recently begun dialysis, but a transplant seems to be the only alternative."

"Why can't he remain on dialysis?" asked Al-Saffar, "That's a perfectly good alternative."

"Our employer is a very important man," said Rashad, "In our business it's essential that he be able to travel. For him, travel often involves long distances and often on short notice. He cannot be tied to a dialysis machine."

"There are home dialysis machines that are quite portable," Al-Saffar said, "Regular dialysis units can be found all around the world. If your employer has the financial wherewithal, he can get dialysis anywhere."

"Doctor, we are quite aware of the availability of dialysis units and the portable devices," Rashad said, in a voice that betrayed some irritation, "These are not practical options for our employer."

"And just who is your employer?" asked Al-Saffar.

"He prefers to remain anonymous at this time," said Rashad, "We must insist that your respect his privacy. You will learn his identity when he arrives for the transplant."

"That's not acceptable," said Al Saffar, "No one, not even the king himself, can just arrive at my hospital and receive a transplant without a thorough and complete medical examination by me."

"We can arrange for such an examination," said Rashad, "We will take you to our employer."

"Where is he?"

"You don't need to know."

"I must have access to my equipment," said the doctor, "This facility has every modern medical testing device. I take pride in assuring that each of my patients has the best care that medical science can provide. The people who come to me for transplant care are some of the most important people in the world. Their health and their lives are invaluable. I won't do substandard work. I cannot do a pre-operative evaluation anywhere but here."

Rashad looked at Jarra in thoughtful silence. After a few moments, he spoke.

"It may be possible for us to bring our employer to you," he said, "but we will have to insist on some very special conditions. You see, doctor, security is an issue for our employer. An issue of the greatest importance."

"I understand," said Al-Saffar, "Security is a major issue for many of our patients. I assure you gentlemen that our security force here is of the highest quality."

"We'll provide our own security, Doctor," said Rashad, "And we're going to require an entire wing of your hospital."

"An entire wing?" Al-Saffar was shocked, "Have you any idea of how much that will cost?"

"Doctor Al-Saffar," said Rashad with a smile, "We would not be here if cost was an issue."

"Well, you must arrange for your employer to come to the hospital," said the doctor, "I'll do a complete physical and laboratory evaluation. It will take about three days. Then, if your employer is a suitable candidate for a transplant, we can begin to search for a donor. Do you have a donor already? A relative perhaps who might be a match?"

"We do not have what you call a volunteer donor, sadly," said Rashad, "One of the reasons we selected your facility is its reputation for obtaining excellent donors."

"Well, then, when would you like to schedule the admission for the evaluation?"

"We'll contact you, Doctor Al-Saffar," said Rashad, "In a gesture of good faith, Mr. Jarra will leave his briefcase with you. It contains two million dollars in United States currency. Will that be adequate?"

"Yes," said Al-Saffar without a change in his facial expression, "That should be an adequate initial payment."

11

STUART CAME TO the last patient of the last day of the mission. He was going to be the first doctor to finish. Kathleen and her surgical crew had finished cleaning up and had packed the instruments that needed to go back to San Francisco in boxes. The team of American health professionals was happy, but exhausted.

Ann Conforti put the last little boy in an exam room.

"Dr. Stuart, this is Manuel Cuellar," said Ann, "He's three and a half. He was born right here in our labor and delivery department. His mother is worried that he is pigeon-toed."

"Don't you get tired of seeing kids with in-toeing and bowlegs, Dr. Stuart?" asked Dennis Nichols, the medical student.

To be sure, there had been lots of children in the orthopedic clinic over the last two weeks with problems that would get better on their own. If Stuart minded seeing these patients, he never let on.

On the other hand, Dennis Nichols had failed to impress Stuart. Nichols was sloppy and expected to have everything handed to him. If he had any problem-solving skills, he was reluctant to employ them.

"No, Dennis, I don't get tired of seeing these kids," said Stuart, "I know, and by now perhaps you know, that almost all in-toeing resolves by itself. There are, of course, pigeon-toed adults, but there is no functional problem with being pigeon-toed. Some of the greatest athletes of all time have been pigeon-toed. However, just because I know this is nothing to worry about, and you know that this is nothing to worry about, does not mean that Mrs. Cuellar knows that this is nothing to worry about. Human decency requires that we thoroughly examine this little boy, give his mother our professional opinion, and let her know that we take her seriously."

Manuel was a happy and friendly little fellow. He was fascinated by the little stuffed parrot that Stuart had in his pocket. Stuart squeezed the parrot and it made a little squawk that delighted the toddler.

Stuart decided that he had time to make one last effort to teach Nichols something. Since Manuel was so cooperative, he took the medical student through the entire physical examination of a child. Not just the musculo-skeletal system and the leg alignment assessment, but also the eyes, ears, nose and throat, neck and chest, heart, abdomen, and even the neurologic examination. At the end, Stuart explained to Mrs. Cuellar that she had a wonderful, beautiful, and healthy little boy, that he would outgrow the pigeon-toe. She left the clinic impressed and happy. The little boy was delighted when Stuart gave him the stuffed parrot as a gift.

"Well, that's it," said Ann Conforti as Stuart and Nichols exited the exam room, "Let me say that it was a great pleasure to have you on this mission, Dr. Stuart. I hope you'll come back again soon."

"Thank you for all your help, Ann," said Stuart, "You run a very efficient and welcoming clinic here. I'm pretty sure that I'll come back."

"And you, young doctor Nichols," Ann asked, "Have you decided on a specialty yet?"

"I am leaning toward dermatology," said Dennis.

"Excellent choice, for you," said Stuart.

Stuart thought it was a perfect choice for this student. Lots of money, little pressure, normal business hours. Empathy and compassion were not necessary.

"Hey, Professor," said Kathleen, striding into the clinic. She wore blue jeans and a short-sleeved blouse instead of her usual scrubs. "You done yet?"

"All done," smiled Stuart, "Looks like you're ready to escape this place."

"Yep," she said, "And, as a reward for your hard work the last two weeks, I want you to know that you and I've been invited to dinner on the yacht tonight."

"Godfrey's yacht?" asked Stuart.

"How many yachts do you know in the harbor?"

"How did you rate that invitation?" Stuart asked.

"Well, if you want to know the truth, I think that he wants to thank me for running such a productive surgical suite these last weeks," said Kathleen, "He's allowing me to bring a guest."

"Is that an invitation?" Stuart asked.

"It is. Are you available?"

"As it turns out, my schedule is clear," said Stuart, "Dinner on a yacht? I forgot to pack my tuxedo."

"What I have on is the best outfit I brought," said Kathleen, "While not in any way up to his elegant personal standards, I'm pretty sure that Wallace understands."

The yacht was far more impressive that either Stuart or Kathleen had imagined. It was gleaming white and illuminated by countless party lights. Sleek and modern and huge, well over two hundred feet long, with a wide gangway sloping gently to the dock, the vessel nearly took their breath away. While Stuart knew little about yachts, he could only guess that this one cost tens of millions. Even for Wallace Godfrey it seemed extravagant.

A uniformed crew member greeted them at the gangway, checked a clipboard to confirm their invitations, and guided them to the dining room. Along the way, Stuart looked at the staterooms. Most of the doors were closed, but he could estimate the size and they corresponded to the most luxurious rooms available on commercial cruise ships. One had a door ajar and he peeked inside at the sumptuous furnishings.

The dining room was comparable to a five-star hotel. Two tables for four to six, covered by white linen cloths and set with fine china and crystal stemware. Godfrey rose from his chair to greet Stuart and Kathleen.

"Ray, so glad you could come," said Godfrey, "And Kathleen, you look gorgeous."

"Dr. Godfrey, you're very flattering," said Kathleen, "But dressed in clothes more suited to gardening than fine dining, with no makeup, and exhausted from two weeks of hard work, there's no way that I'm gorgeous. However, you're very charming."

Godfrey laughed.

"Let me introduce you," he said, "My wife, Lois."

A tall, blonde woman in a formal evening gown, festooned with jewelry rose and offered her hand to Stuart.

"How do you do?" Lois asked, clearly indifferent to any answer.

Stuart studied the new Mrs. Godfrey with the educated interest of a surgeon who knew what was possible in the operating room. She was at least twenty years younger than Wallace. Her breasts and buttocks were, well, ample, traits that many men found stimulating. The skin around her eyes, neck, and cheeks was so tight that it looked like wax.

When Dr. Godfrey was on the faculty at Sutro State University, he had a different wife. Now that he was in private practice, a more ornamental spouse must have been required. The new Mrs. Godfrey was a living testimony to the power of cosmetic surgery. Stuart thought ruefully that when Wallace Godfrey got tired of his first wife, he simply divorced her and made himself a new one.

"I'm Dr. Raymond Stuart," he said, shaking her hand, "Wallace and I used to work together on medical missions to the developing world. That was quite a few years ago, probably before you two were married. I'm happy to meet you now. May I introduce Miss Kathleen Atwood, the head nurse in our surgical suite for this mission."

Dr. Godfrey continued the introductions.

"Ray and Kathleen, you both know Bill Conklin, our business manager."

Hands were shaken and smiles were smiled.

When the steward came around with the wine, Stuart politely covered his glass.

"Not drinking, Ray?" asked Godfrey.

"No, thank you, Wallace," replied Stuart, "Not since the accident."

"Perhaps an ice tea?" asked the steward.

"Yes, thank you," said Stuart.

Just before dessert was served, Kathleen excused herself to visit the bathroom. As she walked down the hall, the door to one of the staterooms opened and a little boy rushed out, almost running into her.

"A-a-a-h-h-h!" squealed the boy.

Kathleen stopped and stared at the child. He looked to be about four or five years old. In a heartbeat, the door to the stateroom opened again and a woman rushed into the corridor. She was in her late forties, somewhat plump, with rosy cheeks and a radiant smile.

"You get back in here, you little scamp," said the woman, grasping the boy by the upper arm.

"A-a-a-h-h-h!" wailed the boy.

"Sorry for the intrusion, madam," said the woman as she dragged the child back inside the stateroom.

When she returned to the dining room the crème Boulet had been served. Stuart was talking for the first time all evening.

"Wallace, there are so many children here with untreated clubfoot deformity," Stuart said, "Our American team is treating them with surgery. In fact, the most frequent operation we are doing in orthopedics with Project Raphael is a clubfoot correction. For the older children, that's really the best option, but at home we have almost completely stopped treating clubfoot operatively in babies."

"Why?" asked Godfrey.

"We have a technique of serial casting of baby clubfeet that has proven extremely successful with superior results at long term follow-up to surgical correction," said Stuart, "It requires excellent cooperation on the part of the family and good quality bracing after the foot is corrected. But I've seen the quality of the braces you're getting from the company that does the wheelchairs. The braces are very good and I'm sure that they could make the clubfoot braces for the babies."

"How often are the casts changed?" Godfrey asked.

"Weekly."

"Who would do the casting?" asked Godfrey, "We only bring American orthopedic teams down five times a year."

"I can train your cast technicians to do the work," said Stuart, "It's been done in Africa with excellent success. Technicians without formal degrees are doing the majority of the clubfoot casting in several African countries and the results have been very good."

"Well, if you'll promise to come down on our next mission, you're on," said Godfrey.

"It's a deal," said Stuart.

"Let's work out the details when we get home, "Godfrey said, "Perhaps we could have lunch, you, Bill, and I. Maybe we could get this started on our next mission."

"Dr. Godfrey, may I interrupt?" asked Kathleen.

"Of course," said Godfrey.

"I saw a little boy on board. Is he the child of one of the crew?"

"Oh, no," said Godfrey with a grin, "He's a special patient. He has a brain tumor, a meningioma. We are taking him to the United States for surgery."

"Really?" asked Stuart, "How old is he?"

"Four or five, I think," said Godfrey.

"With a meningioma?" said Stuart, "Are you sure?"

"Quite sure," said Godfrey, "We sent him to San Salvador and got an MRI."

"At considerable cost," interjected Conklin.

"Well, a few dollars," said Godfrey, "But I was able to persuade Dr. David Goldman at Stonybrook in New York to do the surgery for free. Dr. Goldman feels confident that the tumor, which is benign, can be removed safely and in its entirety. The child can be expected to recover completely and lead a long and normal life."

"It's so kind of you to do things like this, Wally" said Lois, "No wonder I fell in love with this man."

◆ ◆ ◆

Gabriella Cortez gazed into the mirror and smiled.

She liked what she saw. Perfect teeth. Perfect skin. Long eyelashes accenting soft brown eyes. These, she knew, along with a body that was in full adolescent blossom, were her tickets out of the hellhole in which she lived.

She wondered if her mother had been sexy or beautiful when she was fourteen. Had her father and mother kissed and cuddled like she did with Hector? Was her mother once as dizzy with love as she was now? It seemed inconceivable. Gabriella tried to remember how her parents interacted when she was a little girl. Try as she might, she couldn't recall them ever being affectionate to one another. Perhaps that was why her father left. Gabriella was terrified that she would end up just like her mother.

Gabriella couldn't get the party she attended out of her mind. It was like a fairy tale, an event that was fading away, one she couldn't totally remember yet she would never forget. Of course, she didn't tell her mother that she was going. She was careful that her mother never saw the short, revealing skirt she wore. When she came home late at night, somehow her mother knew. While Gabriella invented lies and excuses, evading questions with consummate skill, her mother knew.

The deteriorating relationship with her mother was breaking Gabriella's heart. They couldn't seem to just have a calm, intelligent discussion any more. Gabriella knew that soon she would go off with Hector with or without her mother's permission. After a time, she would return to Cedros and show her mother that she was mature enough to be away from the village. Her mother would see that she was happy and healthy, that there was nothing to fear. She would prove to Elana that she had been right about Hector and she would have stories to make both Elana and Martina jealous.

12

Detective Duane Wilson parked the police car near the scene of the fire. He saw the battalion chief detach himself from the other firefighters and walk toward him. The street was soaking wet and the ruins of the warehouse were still smoldering. Duane shuddered at the scene, not so much because of the cold San Francisco air, but because he was back in the "hood" where he grew up.

"I gather that this is more than just a warehouse fire," Duane said to the battalion chief.

The firefighter nodded grimly.

"This is a massacre," said the firefighter, "We've got multiple casualties. We're still finding bodies, but this was a mass murder."

The firefighter led Duane through the smoking rubble on the street. Black tarps covered two bodies on the sidewalk.

"These two may have helped set the fire," said the chief, "They're not badly burned at all. We found them right where you see them, on the sidewalk, outside the building. Look at this."

There was a heavy chain across the ruins of the double steel door right next to the bodies. The doors had been chained and locked shut, preventing anyone inside from escaping. Some of the wall had collapsed, leaving the inside of the warehouse wide open. The roof had collapsed. Firefighters moved cautiously inside, sifting through the debris and marking the location of bodies.

"Arson investigators are here, but I can tell you what I know at this point," the chief continued, "All the doors to the warehouse, as far as we can tell, are chained and locked. It looks like the accelerant used was gasoline. Some may have been dumped on the building from the outside, but it looks like a fair amount of gasoline was stored inside. So far, we have fifteen bodies inside, all burned beyond recognition. I'm sure there will be more. And we've found quite a few guns inside."

"Guns?" asked Duane.

"Yes, lots of them. Handguns and long guns, some assault rifles, I think."

"This is a gang operation," said Duane.

The fire chief nodded.

They spent a few minutes walking around inside the ruins of the warehouse. Duane had no idea how anyone could find anything in such a mess. He stopped by a little red cone on the floor. It marked the location of a charred skeleton. Duane knelt down to look at the blackened skull. He noticed that the teeth were all capped with gold. He grunted. That gang-banger was probably very proud of his shiny "grill." Duane thought that maybe the victims were members of a black gang. In this neighborhood, the skeleton could have belonged to one of his childhood friends. A few feet away were the remains of a semi-automatic handgun. He grunted and headed back toward the street. A firefighter from the arson squad was standing near the two bodies on the sidewalk. A medical examiner's van had arrived and two attendants were preparing to load the bodies inside.

"Not so fast, fellows," said Duane, showing his badge, "Let me have a look before you take these bodies."

The arson squad member approached and offered his hand.

"Paul Edwards, arson investigator," he said.

"Duane Wilson, homicide."

Duane looked into the face of the dead young black man. He turned the man's head to reveal the number "8" tattooed on the neck. Taken aback, Duane pulled the tarp back more to expose the man's hands. On the right wrist was a tattoo of a dog's paw.

"I'll be damned," said Duane.

"Do you recognize the tattoos?" asked Edwards.

"This guy is 8 Gangsta Blood," said Duane.

"Neighborhood gang?"

"No, and that's what's puzzling," said Duane, "8 Gangsta Blood is an Oakland gang."

Kathleen had the window seat on the plane out of San Salvador. Stuart made the sacrifice and took the middle seat so that he could be next to her. One of her young surgical nurses happily took the aisle. Exhausted from the hard work over the last two weeks and the farewell party the night before, the young nurse was asleep before the wheels came up.

Kathleen nudged Stuart with her elbow. She checked again to make sure that the nurse in the aisle seat was sound asleep. Then she whispered, hoping that nobody else would hear what she and Stuart said.

"Last night Wife Number Two really put me to shame," she said, "Did you see that dress and all those jewels? I felt like the queen of the grubs."

"She didn't spend two weeks working fourteen-hour days in the surgical suite," said Stuart, "Getting dressed for dinner may have been the most stressful thing she had to do."

"Why did she come on this trip?"

"Wallace said she enjoys the cruising and loves the beaches at Acajutla."

"She sure didn't talk much at dinner," Kathleen said.

Stuart looked at Kathleen quizzically.

"Women like that are meant to be seen, not heard."

Kathleen scowled at him, thought about making a comment, then changed the subject.

"Professor, your thoughts on the last two weeks, excluding last night's dinner?" she asked.

Stuart looked at her gently in that way she loved. She knew that he was selecting his words carefully.

"Mixed feelings," he said, "And I'm not sure I want to share all of them on the plane. The mission brought back memories that I enjoy. It was good to come down here and help some of these kids. We can only help a few. We haven't done anything really to improve the health of the majority of Salvadorans. On the other hand, we've been able to make a difference for a few kids. The most impressive thing is what Wallace has been able to do with the new hospital and clinic."

"Isn't it amazing?" said Kathleen.

"Not just the facility," said Stuart, "but what Wallace is doing with it. He's not just treating patients, but he's helping to educate young Salvadoran doctors and nurses. That'll have the biggest impact over the long haul. The Salvadorans are smart people. What they lack is good education, quality equipment, and modern technology. It's these young professionals who'll really make a difference."

"That sounds pretty enthusiastic. Why the mixed feelings?" asked Kathleen, "Was there something that you didn't like?"

Stuart raised an eyebrow and frowned a little.

"That's the part I'd prefer not to discuss on the plane," he said.

She knew that if Ray Stuart didn't want to talk, pressing him would be futile. She hoped that he would open up to her when he was ready.

Stuart had left his Jeep at the Park 'N' Fly at San Francisco International. He offered Kathleen a ride home and she happily accepted. As soon as they were on the freeway, she resumed her questions.

"Now that there's nobody to eavesdrop, Ray," she said, "What parts of the trip didn't you like?"

"It's not that I didn't like things," he began, "Rather, there were parts that were troubling. I was pretty disappointed in the medical student."

"And that showed, Professor," she teased, "The student was a dunce and you knew it. He probably thought he did a great job and that you liked him. But for somebody who really knows you, well, your distaste was pretty obvious."

"Was it that apparent? I take it that you don't think he's going to nominate me for Teacher of The Year?" he said.

"Actually, he might," she replied, "You're good at being polite. He might actually ask you for a recommendation for residency."

"That wouldn't be a good idea," said Stuart, "I'm a poor liar and if I told the truth he wouldn't get a residency at all. What was that kid doing in El Salvador, anyway? He didn't give a damn about the poor people in the country and he had almost no interest in learning. Tell me he was better with the plastic surgeons."

"Not much," said Kathleen, "They were underwhelmed as well. My guess is that he's padding his résumé in hopes of getting a better residency when he graduates."

She was hoping for something more important than his opinion of the medical student.

"Was there anything else?" asked Kathleen, "Maybe when I pressured you into operating?"

"Yes," said Stuart, "That was troubling in a couple of ways."

"You saved that baby's hip, Ray," she said, "There's nothing wrong with your surgical skills. You operate as well as you did before the accident. That should make you happy."

For a moment, Stuart took his eyes off the road and looked right into Kathleen's.

"I'm not happy," he said.

"I'm sorry that I put you in that position, Ray," she said, "But I had to do something. Dr. Brauer was lost in there. For the sake of that child, I had to ask you."

"I know," he said, "I understand. I guess I wish it hadn't happened."

"Dr. Brauer said that he could do the case," she said, "So we let him book it. Besides, he said that you'd consulted with him on the procedure and agreed with the plan."

"I did agree with the plan," said Stuart, "I didn't realize that he wasn't competent to perform the operation. And that's one of the things that bothers me about medical missions like this."

"What do you mean?"

"I mean that Brauer is like so many American doctors with fancy private practices at home. A poor person couldn't get an appointment in their offices. The first question that the office staff asks about a patient is what the insurance coverage is. They treat the wealthy and well-insured, then drive home in a fancy car and take the wife to dinner at the country club. They come on these missions and do a bunch of operations that they would never attempt at home, just to look like heroes. Then they go home, patting themselves on the back because they're such great philanthropists and brag about their great generosity to all their friends. The hypocrisy is nauseating."

"But they and their rich friends make big donations to keep charities like Project Raphael going," Kathleen said, "We do a lot of good in these countries."

"Yeah," he admitted, "That's what bothers me."

When they got to Kathleen's apartment, Stuart helped her carry her bag inside. They stood awkwardly close. She had to say something.

"Ray," she said, "I don't want to wait until the next mission to see you."

"Neither do I," he admitted.

Stuart drew her closer and they kissed, softly and tentatively.

💧 💧 💧

"Come on, girls, get in the container," said Pablo Ortega "Move it, move it."

Six frightened girls stared into the big metal box. The interior walls were lined with soundproof foam panels. Six sleeping bags were rolled up atop air mattresses. In the back was a toilet. Stacks of boxes and cases of bottled water filled the back third of the container. Timidly, they climbed up the ramp and inside. Ortega followed and addressed the girls.

"Now, pay attention," he said, "This is your home for the next two weeks. You're on your own. Nobody will be able to hear you if you cry out or bang on the walls. We want you to arrive at your destination in good health. Everything you need is here. The toilet works with chemicals. It's for peeing and shitting only. Don't put your tampons or garbage into it or you'll have a very smelly journey. There are cases of bottled water. Drink it sparingly. The water is not for washing. There are cases of food. You have twenty-four different meals to choose from. Eat two of these each day and you'll have enough for the journey. Eat more and you'll be hungry at the end. There are cans of fruit. Eat the fruit in the morning for breakfast and the boxed meals for lunch and dinner. There are two lights that run on batteries and spare batteries. Do you understand?"

Most of the girls nodded their heads. The littlest one started to cry silently.

"Bon voyage," said Ortega with a smirk.

Ortega descended out of the container. Two of his men closed the big steel doors and Ortega attached the seal as the shipping agent. One of the men took the papers certifying that the container was being shipped empty, along with the official signature of the Acajutla harbormaster. The man climbed into the cab of the truck on which the container rested, closed the door with the name "LC Freight," and started the engine.

13

San Francisco police detective Duane Wilson called Stuart two days after his return from El Salvador.

"Dr. Stuart," said Duane, "Can we meet? I want to talk to you about the girl we found in the bay, the one that Matt Harrison consulted you about. And I want you to talk to the FBI agent who's now in charge of the investigation."

"Sure, Duane," Stuart replied, "Set it up."

They met two days later in the FBI office. Wilson introduced Stuart to Special Agent Walter Reynolds. Since everything was pointing to the death of the girl being related to human trafficking, the FBI was taking the lead on the case. Reynolds took charge of the meeting.

"Dr. Stuart, your suggestions proved quite useful," he began, "First, the dental amalgam did contain mercury and rexillium. Our laboratory at Quantico says that the composition of the dental filling is most consistent with amalgam used in Central America. Second, the DNA analysis of the chromosomes suggested that the girl was mostly native American."

"Did they look at mitochondrial DNA?" asked Stuart.

Reynolds raised an eyebrow in admiration. Duane had no idea what they were talking about.

"Yes, in fact they did," said Reynolds, "And that analysis showed that the girl was of Mayan ancestry, of a tribe found mostly in modern El Salvador."

"Dr. Stuart just got back from El Salvador," said Duane.

"I doubt that he brought a handful of girls to sell into sex slavery," said Reynolds.

"Hardly," said Stuart, "But I don't think it would be difficult. The poverty in El Salvador is horrendous. I can see that some girls might fall for a line that promises them riches and good jobs in the US. Or, it would be relatively easy for human traffickers to kidnap girls. There are lots of gangs on the streets, and lots of violence. Even the men who transported our medical equipment and supplies were armed."

"El Salvador is a mess," agreed Reynolds, "The level of gang violence is out of control. The government agencies, including law enforcement, are corrupt. I'm afraid it would be easy for a ring of traffickers to work there."

"If the girl we found in the bay was a victim of human trafficking and she came from El Salvador," asked Duane, "Are we looking for Salvadoran gang activity?"

"It's possible," said Reynolds, "The gangs in El Salvador are involved in drug dealing, extortion, murder for hire, and prostitution. We suspect that they'd love to get into the human trafficking business since the profits are so high. But so far we have nothing to indicate that they're actually active in trafficking."

"Are there Salvadoran gangs active in the San Francisco Bay area?" asked Stuart.

"We think so," said Duane, "As of now, there's been little activity that we can connect specifically with gangs from El Salvador. There are rumors that some Salvadoran gangs are trying to establish themselves somewhere in the Bay area. Without much success, at least that SFPD knows about. Our own Latino, Asian, and African-American gangs have most of the market in drugs and extorsion cornered. It's pretty hard to break into that sort of business."

"The FBI has a hint that there's a Central American gang trying to break into the Oakland and East Bay communities," said Reynolds, "We just have sketchy information at this point."

"Does the gang have a name?" asked Duane.

"Rumor has it they're called *Los Cóndores*," said Reynolds.

Duane resolved to talk to his friend Will Chen in Oakland about *Los Cóndores*.

♦ ♦ ♦

Joint captivity forged a firm friendship among the six girls. Corina, the sixteen year-old redheaded girl, emerged as the leader.

The prevailing mood inside the container gradually morphed from terror to resigned depression. The lighting was adequate. The meals were nourishing, if not tasty. The toilet worked.

Linda was also sixteen. She was the overweight girl whose family had been visiting San Salvador from their home in Argentina. Linda was from a wealthy family and had the best education. Corina relied on Linda for advice. Corina decided that all of the girls needed to support Paula, who was only eleven. Paula was from a small village in El Salvador. It was understandable that Paula would often suffer panic attacks and tearful breakdowns.

Corina set up a rotation so that someone was always pounding on the wall and yelling. She didn't want to take even a little chance that a potential rescuer would walk past a silent container.

In reality, no one cared. The container was nestled in the hull of the SS Hermione, a veteran coastal freighter that worked its way from Acajutla, El Salvador, to Oakland, California and back again. The Hermione carried a variety of cargo, some in shipping containers, some loose or in crates. Once stowed in the hold, the container holding the girls was ignored by the crew.

Inside the container the sounds of the ship were muffled, but continuous. There was a low rumbling from the ship's engines that never changed. Periodic banging sounds from the ship's equipment or cargo superimposed themselves on the ever-present low frequency noise.

The girls quickly lost a sense of time. Their bodies fell into a kind of synchrony and they found themselves awake or asleep together. With nothing to do inside the container, they slept a lot. When they were awake, each told her story. Friendships grew out of their common adversity.

At first the voyage was smooth. The container was situated near the center of the ship and was only minimally affected by the rolling of the waves. Though the girls didn't know it, they had been out of Acajutla for three days when the first storm hit.

At first, the change was subtle. The sound of the engine rumble slowed slightly. The ship and the container began to roll from side to side, more and more as they sailed into the storm. A few items, food containers and water bottles, fell off packing boxes and rolled on the floor. Then the container began to tilt forward and backward as the ship pitched in the waves. Girls began to hold onto the sides of the container or each other for stability. Finally, the container bobbed up and down as the ship moved from wave crest to bottom. Even in their protected position in the hold, the pitching and rolling of the vessel were severe.

Several girls groaned and lay down on their air mattresses. Some closed their eyes. Some clutched at their abdomens. The container pitched and rolled and yawed with the ship in the storm.

"I'm sick," said Linda.

"Don't throw up here, get to the toilet," said Corina.

"Someone else is at the toilet," whimpered Linda just before she vomited onto the floor of the container.

Other girls got sick. The floor was too unstable for walking. A couple of girls crawled toward the toilet to puke.

Corina fashioned sickness containers out of plastic bags, empty food containers and water bottles. They were not ideal, but helped control the mess, since only one girl could kneel at the toilet at a time.

Only Corina and young Paula escaped the seasickness. It was up to them to clean up as best they could. Paula was totally terrified. She just wanted Corina to hold her.

The stuffy air of the container now was polluted by the rancid smell of vomit. Urging Paula to let go and help, Corina mopped and scrubbed, using bottle after bottle of water. She jammed as much of the mess into plastic trash bags as she could, tying them tight in a futile effort to contain the stench. Paula was at her side, mopping, bagging and crying.

Corina remembered the priest in church talking about Hell when she was a little girl. Now she was experiencing it.

Stuart and Kathleen headed south along the Great Highway as the sun began to set over the Pacific Ocean. On the rare days when the fog stayed offshore and he could actually watch the sunset, Stuart loved the scene. The beauty of the orange and blue sky over the deep blue of the ocean made it hard to keep his eyes on the road.

Dinner reservations were at the Moss Beach Distillery. It was one of Stuart's favorite restaurants. They had a table by the window so that they could appreciate the sunset.

"I know why you like to come here," teased Kathleen, "You like the ghost."

"I'm a scientist," replied Stuart, "I don't believe in ghosts."

"But the Blue Lady is different," she said, "She's a romantic ghost and you relate to her. She was a married woman having an affair with a mysterious lover. Her husband found out and attacked them on the beach. She was murdered on the beach right down there. But her lover survived the assault. I've heard that there have been quite a few sightings of her walking the beach, searching for her lover."

"It's baloney, but it sells a lot of abalone," Stuart said.

"You made a rhyme," she giggled, "Baloney and a-balone."

"You're impossible," Stuart retorted, "Behave yourself or I'm going to stop taking you out in public."

"I think you like the ghost story," Kathleen insisted, "The Blue Lady reminds you of yourself, lonely, walking the beach at night in a sad search for the love of your life."

"Have I ever mentioned how annoying you are?" he said with a grin.

"Many times," she replied, "But nobody, including me, pays any attention to your opinion. I remember the time when the dean of the medical school came down to surgery to watch one of your operations. Like all surgeons, you were pretty puffed up, so proud of yourself."

"I always behaved professionally in the operating room."

"Yeah, right," she said, "And when the dean came in, you introduced the surgical team to him. Do you remember what you said about me?"

"Something appropriate and professional, I'm sure."

"You said that I was the worst surgical nurse in the state of California," Kathleen pronounced, "It was the most embarrassing moment of my career. In front of the dean, for God's sake."

"I was probably trying to get an increase in the surgical staff budget," Stuart said, laughing, "If I told him how bad the nurses were, maybe he'd let us hire some more."

"You're lucky that you didn't get a scalpel stuck straight through your hand," she replied.

"Don't give me that," he said, "You've stuck me and kicked me and hit me in the OR so many times that I could file assault charges."

"I only provide little clues when you're doing the wrong thing in the operation," she insisted, "Somebody has to keep the procedure moving in the right direction."

"Maybe it wasn't the accident that made me stop operating," Stuart said, "Maybe it was that I couldn't take the abuse anymore."

"You love it and you know it."

Stuart knew that she was right. The teasing and joking and insults were fun.

All through supper the banter continued. Stuart felt happier than he had been in a long time. When they worked together on the baby's hip in Acajutla, good feelings from the past clicked back into place. But something was different. Stuart didn't just see Kathleen as his best surgical nurse. Something had grown. He couldn't keep his eyes off Kathleen while they laughed and joked.

"If you're so interested in ghosts walking on the beach," he said, "What do you say to going back to my house? I have some stairs that lead right down onto the beach. We could go down for a moonlight stroll and look for ghosts together."

"Sounds mysterious and romantic," she said, "I'm in."

Stuart's house was on the cliff right above the ocean. The cold air off the water made Kathleen shiver. They went inside to get her a warm jacket. Stuart's home was furnished mostly in natural woods. There were no flowers or knickknacks. There were some very nice paintings on the walls, almost all of them seascapes. Lots of bookcases. No television. It was compulsively neat. When he had bundled Kathleen in to a jacket that was far too big for her, they went out the back door and onto a path which led down to the water. Stuart had a combination of old railroad ties and stepping stones along the path to make it stable and secure. He held her hand to assist her on the descent. A three-quarter moon provided gentle light over a tranquil sea. Stuart put his arm around her and they stood silently on the sand. The only sound was the rhythmic breaking of the waves.

Kathleen snuggled closer to Stuart. He responded by tightening his hold. They just stood there for perhaps ten minutes before Kathleen spoke.

"I get it," she said, "I understand why you live here."

"Do you?" he asked.

"This is peace," she said, "Whether it's shrouded in fog or clear like tonight, it's peace. No racket, no cell phones, no pages. It's your cocoon, the place you come to think."

After a while, they climbed back up the path. Stuart put a couple of logs into the fireplace while Kathleen brewed tea. Snuggled on the floor in front of the fire, they kissed.

"I think I could get used to this," she said.

14

Duane reluctantly entered the autopsy room. Matt Harrison was gowned and gloved, up to his elbows in a body, assisted by Franklin Howard.

"Hey, Detective," said Franklin, "How you doin', bro'?"

"I'd be doin' better somewhere else, bro'," said Duane, "This place gives me the creeps."

"Shit, man, you get used to it," said Franklin, "Dead people are safe. It's the ones that's still alive gonna hurt ya."

"Sorry, to call you down here, Duane," said Matt, "I just thought you'd want to know what I found right away. I finished the autopsy on the first guy from the street. This is the second guy. Your two gang bangers on the sidewalk didn't die from the fire. They were shot. There was no evidence of smoke inhalation in the lungs of either of them. They were dead before the fire started. Each was killed by a gunshot wound. Rifle wound, to be precise. I sent the bullets to your ballistics lab, but my guess is that they were 308 NATO rounds."

"308 NATO rounds?" asked Duane, "Those are military."

"Well, I think you have a war on your hands," said Matt, "A gang war. If I had to make a bet, I'd say that these bullets were fired from an AR-15 assault rifle."

"None of the neighbors heard any gunshots before the warehouse caught fire," Duane said.

"Come on, man," Matt interjected, "You grew up in Hunter's Point. Bayview is pretty much the same sort of neighborhood. In the first place, there's so much racket down there, it would be hard to hear a cannon fire. In the second place, who in that neighborhood would tell the cops if they did hear gunshots? And, in the third place, gunshots in that neighborhood are heard all the time. The folks down there are used to it."

"If they heard gunshots, they'd tell me," Duane said, "I'm one of their homies."

"Pardon me, Mr. Detective," interrupted Franklin, "But you ain't no homie any more when you become the police. That's my 'hood', too, bro'. No matter where you were born or the color of your skin, ain't nobody in that 'hood' gonna talk to the police. When you put on the uniform, you become blue, not black."

Duane didn't want to face the fact that Franklin was telling the truth.

"They could have used a sound suppressor," Duane said.

"Can you put one of those on an AR-15?" Matt asked.

"Yes, it's possible," Duane said. "How about the victims inside the warehouse? Have you looked at any of them?"

"Not much to look at," said Matt, "But at first glance they all look like young males. African-American. There were seventeen of them inside the warehouse. All burned beyond recognition. We'll try to identify them through dental records and DNA."

"If these two guys were shot dead before the fire started, they probably weren't the arsonists," said Duane, "More likely they were the lookouts on the street. And, if so, then maybe the victims inside the warehouse were also 8 Gangsta Blood. What the hell were they doing in a warehouse in San Francisco?"

Corina sat up straight, all senses focused. The strong movements of the ship had changed to a very gentle rocking. The constant noise of a ship at sea also was reduced. The batteries on the lights that Esteban Ortega had supplied them had died. None of the girls knew how long they had been in the dark. None knew how long they had been at sea or whether it was night time or daylight outside.

The stench in the container was almost unbearable. Six girls confined in a small space for nearly two weeks without a shower or a bath made for some serious body odor. The vomit didn't help. She hadn't been able to find any place to put the vomit. The stench made some of the girls nauseated. The ventilation in the container was adequate to keep them from suffocating, but not nearly good enough to freshen the air.

A loud metallic crash hit the container, muffled by the extensive sound insulation inside the box. The girls were all sitting on the air mattresses when the container was lifted. The sudden movement toppled the eleven year-old over. She whimpered and one of the older girls put a reassuring arm around her.

Felipe Peña watched the crane operator pick up the forty-foot container. Peña chewed on his lip as the container swayed slightly in the breeze. As usual, it was cold on the dock in Oakland at eleven o'clock at night. There were a few poor lights, nothing like the blazing illumination at the main docks of the port, where the big container ships were loaded and unloaded. This dock was ideal for Peña's business. It was small, with little traffic. The large docks had a perpetual traffic jam of trucks, containers, people, and officials. Nothing could be less interesting than the SS Hermione, a weathered coastal freighter that had seen better years.

The swaying container stabilized and the crane operator lowered it skillfully onto the trailer of the truck bearing the sign LC Freight. A second, smaller container was loaded onto a second truck. No officials challenged the trucks as they pulled away from the dock and onto the freeway.

"The patient from Bahrain has arrived, Doctor," said the secretary, gently opening the door to the office.

Dr. Al-Saffar knew that the patient was not from Bahrain, but he still had no idea who the patient really was.

It was nearly midnight at the hospital. The entire south wing of the third floor of the hospital had been cleared. Only the essential staff was present. Dr. Al-Saffar didn't know the exact time that his special new patient would arrive, so he opted to work late in his office. Dr. Al-Saffar hated wasting time.

Hospital security cleared the small convoy of SUVs onto the hospital grounds. Armed guards alighted from the vehicles and scanned the entranceway to the hospital. Three of them entered the building and, when they were confident that there was no danger, motioned to others to escort the patient inside.

Al-Saffar donned a crisply pressed white lab coat, adjusted his tie in a mirror, and proceeded to the reserved wing. Armed men lined the corridor.

"You will pardon the intrusion, doctor," said the man called Rashad, "But we cannot be too cautious. Security for our employer is of paramount importance. Now, if you will kindly empty your pockets into the container."

Jarra held out a plastic bin. Dr. Al-Saffar deposited his stethoscope, a penlight, his wallet and watch, several pens, and a small notebook inside. The man called Jarra waved a metal-detecting wand over the doctor, then patted him down. Then he took the penlight and the pens apart, inspected them, and returned them to Al-Saffar.

"Very well, doctor," said Rashad. He opened the door and followed Al-Saffar inside.

The patient was seated on the bed. Al-Saffar could tell that the man was tall, with a long beard and a mostly bald head. He was thin and looked chronically sick. His skin had a pale, greyish color which Al-Saffar noticed in the bright hospital light.

Dr. Yousef Al-Saffar looked into the cold brown eyes of Khalid Al-Quatani, the leader of Quabdat Allah, the Fist of God. Dr. Al-Saffar's new patient was the most wanted terrorist on the planet.

💧 💧 💧

Felipe Peña supervised the process when the trucks hauling the two containers arrived at the warehouse that served as the Oakland headquarters of *Los Cóndores*. Both trucks were backed up to the loading dock, but only the container with the girls was opened. Armed gang members stood on the loading dock, while others opened the doors into the lighted warehouse.

"God, this smells like shit," complained Felipe, "Get the girls out now. And Pablo, get a hose in here. Marco, get the girls into the warehouse and into showers. I can't stand the stench."

Gang members pushed and shoved the girls out of the container. After days of darkness, the stark lights inside the warehouse were blinding. Paula cried out and covered her eyes. A slap from a gangster quieted her.

Inside the warehouse was a large cage made of chain link. There were cots with blankets in the cage as well as piles of women's clothes. But the girls couldn't go directly into the cage. They were led to a large bathroom facility with multiple shower heads, not unlike a barracks or dormitory. Soap and towels were stacked at the entrance. The facility had sinks and toilets and mirrors. Despite the terror and humiliation, the girls luxuriated in the hot water, soaking and washing for the first time in two weeks. Their spirits were raised a little just by feeling clean.

Their captors left them in the bathroom for three quarters of an hour. Then Peña ordered them out of the bathroom and his men herded them toward the big cage.

"Ooh, look at the fat one," said Marco, a short, skinny man whose face was scarred from severe acne, "I want to fuck the fat one."

"You can't fuck any of them," said the man named Juaquin, "Felipe will kill you if you try. They're for the Client who paid good money for them. We don't own them."

"I'd pay to fuck the fat one," replied Marco.

"For me, I'd want the red-haired one," sneered Carlos, a tall, handsome young man, "I've never fucked a red-haired girl."

"And if you try, Felipe will have a special death for you," said Juaquin, "I heard that the red-haired girl is bringing in nearly double the money."

"Hmmm, I bet she's worth it," said Carlos.

The girls were shoved into the cage. They were left to themselves to select cots and find clothes in the piles. The cage was padlocked and the leering gang members stood outside and watched them dress.

Pulling a bandana over his nose to reduce the stench, Peña went into the container. Using a screwdriver, he removed several plywood panels from the back wall, behind the shelves where the food had been stored. With the panels removed, he and Juaquin removed a dozen packages of uncut cocaine. They took the cocaine to the office in the warehouse. They secured the cocaine in the safe.

There was work to do, arrangements to make. Peña studied some papers. He was a stickler for documentation. Every dollar paid, every name and address to which he needed to ship a girl, every phone call, email, or text message was kept in his impeccable files. If the big boss from El Salvador ever came to inspect Felipe's work, he wanted everything in order, down to the penny.

Peña called his men together around the cage where the girls were held.

"Stop staring and listen to me," Felipe ordered, "None of these girls stay in the Bay area. We need to get them all moving tomorrow. About mid-morning. I don't want them in the morning commute traffic. All are to be moved in cars or vans."

"These two are going to Oklahoma City," said Peña, handing two sheets of paper to Juaquin, "They go to a whorehouse."

"We'll send them with Esteban in the Chevy van," said Juaquin. He pointed out the girls to Esteban, who nodded in assent.

"Fine," said Felipe, "The fat girl goes to Seattle. Send her in the Toyota with Marco."

"Not Marco," said Juaquin. He had heard Marco's lustful desires expressed earlier.

"Why?"

"Just trust me," said Juaquin, "I'll take the fat girl to Seattle."

Marco looked disappointed.

"All right," said Felipe, "This one just goes to Fresno. A short drive. Send her in the Civic with Pablo. And the little one is special.

Carlos will take her in the Lexus all the way to Boise, Idaho. They'll pretend to be father and daughter."

"Whoever bought her is sick," said Juaquin, "It even disgusts me."

"Nobody asked you. We get paid to transport the merchandise."

"What about the girl with the red hair?"

"Ah, yes," said Peña, "I'm taking her to Chicago myself in the RV."

15

ST. FRANCIS WOODS is one of the most prestigious neighborhoods in San Francisco. Stuart wasn't surprised that Dr. Wallace Godfrey lived in an elegant mansion in the fanciest part.

The housekeeper let Stuart in. The hallway itself was bigger than Stuart's house. There was a spiral staircase on either side leading up to a balcony. An enormous crystal chandelier hung from the second-floor ceiling. The floor was polished marble. Two marble statues in the classical Greek style stood near the staircases.

Lois Godfrey greeted Stuart in the hallway.

"Hello, Dr. Stuart," she said, "Did you have a good flight home?"

"Yes, thank you," he said, shaking her hand, "Did you enjoy your time in El Salvador? There can't be much to do for two weeks."

"Oh, I find ways to entertain myself," Lois said, "The shopping isn't much, but the beaches are lovely. I've been in Acajutla several times now, and I've made a few friends. We enjoy playing tennis."

"Do you have a medical background?" he asked, "Have you considered working with us in the clinic?"

Stuart could not imagine Lois working in the clinic in any capacity, but it seemed to be a polite and respectful line of conversation.

"Oh, heavens no," she replied, "Before Wally and I married, I was in the business world. Sick people make me nervous. I'll happily leave them to you and Wally and the nurses."

Stuart chuckled.

"You two have business to discuss. About the clinic," Lois said, "He told me that you were coming. He's arranged for the two of you to have lunch in the dining room. I'll show you where it is."

"Will you be joining us?" Stuart asked.

"Oh, no," she said, "All that medical stuff is so boring."

Lunch was elegant and delicious. It was served by the woman he thought was the housekeeper, who also seemed to be the cook. Somehow Stuart doubted that the new Mrs. Godfrey did much cooking. The conversation stayed focused on Stuart's proposed new clubfoot program.

"We'll need at least ten dozen cases of two-inch plaster and cast padding. We need to have a supply at the clinic after we return home."

"No problem," Godfrey replied, "I'll make sure that Bill orders it and gets it into one of the containers. We should have plenty of room for the next mission."

"I'd like to take Ron Delgado, one of the cast technicians from Sutro State along on the trip," said Stuart, "He knows the casting technique well. Ron is also fluent in Spanish. He does a lot of the real, hands-on teaching of the residents. He'll be invaluable for teaching the Salvadoran residents and techs. He's also very good with babies and anxious moms."

"Done, done, and done. Give Bill Conklin your list of needs. I can't tell you how excited I am about this, Ray," said Godfrey, "You're going to have a big impact on the kids we serve at Project Rafael."

Stuart couldn't help but grin. The prospect of starting a clubfoot casting program in El Salvador was deeply satisfying. It had been a long time since he felt this excited about anything in medicine.

"Now that you have good bracing right there at the clinic, we can correct clubfoot deformities without surgery. Which reminds me, we should take one of our orthotists along, to show the locals how we make the good clubfoot braces." Stuart grinned at Godfrey, "I know, tell Bill Conklin."

"Just make sure that all these people will fit on the plane," joked Godfrey, "I'm very happy that you're back on the team."

"It feels good, Wallace. I'm happy, too."

"It's a whole new dimension in providing health care to the developing world," Godfrey said, "Things are on a far grander scale now. I can't exactly tell you when the transition happened, but it was a few years ago, after you stopped going on missions. We used to beg and scrape for a couple of bucks here and there. We begged medical and surgical supply companies to donate boxes of sutures and old equipment. We pressured pharmaceutical representatives to give us free samples of drugs. Somehow everything changed. Now I entertain CEOs and foreign dignitaries. The checks flow in.

And the more money we get, the bigger the program becomes. The bigger the program, the more checks come in. I tell you, Ray, it's a damn good feeling."

"I can only imagine," Stuart said.

"Have you thought about getting back into surgery? The job you did on that baby's hip on our last mission was pretty masterful. All the team members were talking about it. Even Jim Brauer thought it was impressive. He's going to think twice about doing more operations down there on little ones."

"If Jim's going to stop operating on kids in El Salvador, maybe that alone was worth my effort," said Stuart, "I'm not sure that US surgeons should be traveling to developing countries to perform operations they would not be allowed to do in their own American hospitals. Just because other countries don't have medical malpractice lawyers doesn't give us license to work outside our competence when we're on missions."

"I always thought that a well-trained American surgeon was an improvement over no surgeon at all, or one of the local bunglers," Godfrey replied.

"I don't agree," said Stuart, "First of all, when our surgeons go to other countries and operate outside their expertise, we can create medical messes that the local doctors have to clean up when we come back to the US. The patients may very well be better off with no surgery at all than an operation that's poorly performed. Or one with serious complications. Second, I think that the doctors in the developing world are just a smart as the ones in the US. The Salvadoran residents I met on the last trip were bright and quick.

The problem is that they don't get very good training and they have to work with shabby equipment. Honestly, in the long haul, we could do more good by helping to train doctors in the developing world and helping them get good equipment than just coming down there like Butch Cassidy and the Sundance Kid, dazzling everyone with our magical operations and our incandescent egos, then getting on the plane to fly back to our opulent lives in San Francisco."

"Wow!" said Godfrey, "I guess I pressed your button, Ray. A fine sermon, Reverend. But you evaded my question. You showed me and everybody else on the team that you haven't lost your touch in the operating room. Are you going to start doing surgery again? In El Salvador or in San Francisco?"

"I'm thinking about it. For now, don't book me any cases for the next mission. Let me concentrate on the clubfoot casting program."

"Fair enough, Ray. It's your decision. I'll schedule you in the clinic, for teaching the residents, and the clubfoot program."

"Thanks, Wallace."

"You know that you made quite an impression down there," said Godfrey, "The Salvadoran residents raved about your teaching."

"I'm glad they learned something," said Stuart, "I'm not sure that I can say the same for our young medical student."

Godfrey laughed.

"Our young Mr. Nichols, our doctor-to-be, is a bit of a dud, isn't he?"

"I really don't know why he came," said Stuart.

"The experience looks good on his residency application."

"For dermatology?"

"Dermatology is really competitive. Being part of a Project Raphael mission may give him just the edge he needs to secure a good dermatology residency."

"Jeez, Wallace, why did you let him on the team? He was a drain on our energy. The Salvadorans must have noticed that he really didn't give a damn about them."

"God, Ray, it really has been a while since we worked together," said Godfrey, "I've forgotten how naïve you can be. If you really care about the poor people in places like El Salvador, and I know you do, you have to learn how to butter up some people who are not naturally inclined to be so dedicated. Nichols' father is a billionaire. He made his money in real estate. He donated half a million dollars to Project Raphael. For that I think we can put up with his idiot son for a couple of weeks."

"So, you let Nichols' father buy his son a place on the team so he could have a sweeter resume when he applies for a dermatology residency?"

"His father and I didn't actually have that discussion," said Godfrey, "But for a half million-dollar donation, I'd put Jack the Ripper on the team. Every time."

"Doesn't that bother you at least a little?"

"Not one bit, Ray. I sleep very well at night and never, ever get indigestion. By the way, the same concept applies to your friend and colleague Dr. James Brauer."

"What?"

"Oh, yes. Actually, I have you to thank for that, too. Jim was so impressed with the surgical rescue you performed, and the grace that you showed by not embarrassing him, that he upped his donation by an additional six figures as soon as we got home."

"Brauer had no business operating on that baby."

"That's reality, Ray. Jim Brauer is happy that you're coming on the next trip. He knows that if he screws up on another kid, you can bail him out."

Stuart just groaned.

♦ ♦ ♦

Dr. Yousef Al-Saffar couldn't stop the shaking in his hands. For a surgeon, this was particularly troubling. He knew what was causing the trembling. He also knew exactly when it had begun. The shaking was from fear. It started with his examination of his new patient, Khalid Al-Quatani, the leader of the terrorist group called the Fist of God.

Al-Quatani was a physical mess. A diabetic since childhood, the terrorist leader had consistently ignored all medical advice. Now in his early 50s, his blood sugar was totally out of control. Dr. Al-Saffar generously characterized his patient's use of insulin as "occasional." When the terrorist did take his insulin, the dose was erratic, determined as much by how Al-Quatani felt as by what his doctors prescribed. He was a textbook illustration of the ravages of untreated diabetes. His vision was impaired from diabetic retinopathy. The circulation in his feet was tenuous. He had already lost some of the feeling in his fingers and toes, demonstrating that the peripheral nerves were degenerating.

The terrorist leader was at his hospital because his kidneys had completely failed. Al-Quatani was prescribed dialysis, but he rarely complied. The doctor understood that his patient was a fugitive, moving around the globe with security guards and multiple hideouts. Still, the Fist of God had ample financial resources. Dr. Al-Saffar thought that Al-Quatani and his followers could have done a much better job of taking care of his kidneys. The doctor surmised that dialysis was inconvenient and not a priority for terrorists.

Without a transplant, Dr. Al-Saffar knew that Al-Quatani would die. Even with a transplant, the prognosis was poor. The patient had a long history of non-compliance with medical advice. Any patient who received an organ transplant needed to be on drugs to suppress the rejection process. A healthy immune system would attack a transplanted organ, even one with good tissue compatibility. The drugs to suppress the immune response needed to be taken faithfully for the rest of the life of an organ recipient. It was unrealistic to think that Al-Quatani would take the medicines needed to prevent rejection. For dozens of reasons, no government-sanctioned transplant center would have ever considered Khalid Al-Quatani to be a transplant candidate.

Dr. Al-Saffar saw himself as a major contributor to world stability. He held in his highly skilled hands the lives of some of the most powerful and important individuals in the world. His hands had preserved the lives of titans of industry, some of the most important artists and entertainers, and many of the most important political leaders on the earth. He was proud that he could make a contribution to the betterment of mankind in this way.

"Excellent surgery for excellent patients," was Al-Saffar's personal motto.

Khalid Al-Quatani did not qualify as an excellent patient. The terrorist was a loathsome, evil man. The world would be better off without him in it.

If he didn't come up with a transplant and perform the surgery perfectly, it was likely that the terrorists of Quabdat Allah would kill him. He resolved to do the surgery and get Al-Quatani out of his hospital and out of his life. What the terrorist did about his own health after the surgery was not the doctor's problem.

It was essential that Dr. Al-Saffar find a donor for Al-Quatani. He couldn't put this patient on a legitimate transplant list. He couldn't reveal this patient's name or health status.

The men who called themselves Rashad and Jarra, members of Quabdat Allah themselves, produced a list of volunteer kidney donors for their chief. Over three hundred members of the terrorist organization volunteered. These were men and women who were willing to give their lives for their cause. Donating a kidney to save the life of their leader was, to them, a small sacrifice.

Unfortunately, Dr. Al-Saffar's problems were not limited by his patient's poor health and non-compliance. Al-Quatani was O negative and had relatively uncommon HLA antigens, the most important tissue types in transplant surgery besides the normal blood typing. The rarity of the Al-Quatani's tissue type made finding a donor particularly difficult. None of the volunteer donors was a match. Maybe he could get away with a partial match, but there were risks of an immediate rejection or failure of the transplant in the first months after surgery. The possibility of immediate rejection was most frightening. He had seen one when he was still in training, but never since he had been in practice. The rejection process begins right on the operating table. Doctors might be able to slow the process and keep the patient alive for a few days, but the transplant was doomed to failure in such cases. With the patient he was treating, Al-Saffar knew that, if the patient didn't leave the hospital alive, neither would he. Out of both a sense of professional pride and fear for his personal safety, he desperately needed a donor who was perfectly compatible with his patient.

Dr. Al-Saffar sat at his computer alone in his office, trembling fingers working the keyboard, opening some of his special files. His hospital had access to organ donors throughout the world, donors whose names did not appear on other lists. Some were desperately poor individuals who would sell a kidney for cash. It was quite astonishing how many poor people there were, especially in large undeveloped countries. These potential donors didn't care who the recipient was as long as they and their families were adequately compensated. There were other potential donors with data in the computer as well, most of whom would not be compensated for their sacrifice. He entered Al-Quatani's information and ran the program looking for the best match.

Dr. Al-Saffar caught his breath as the results appeared on his screen. For a full two minutes he just stared. There was an

O-negative person with a full six-point match. Fifteen years old and presumably healthy. Easily located in Mumbai.

Dr. Al-Saffar was only dimly aware that his heart rate slowed when he found the perfect donor for the terrorist. He didn't notice that the trembling in his hands stopped.

16

Stuart and Kathleen arrived together at the departure gate at San Francisco International Airport, ready for Stuart's second mission of the year. Many of the Project Raphael team members were already there, chatting and laughing, catching up on stories. Stuart shook hands politely with Dr. James Brauer. They would see each other in El Salvador, since Dr. Brauer would be sitting in the First Class section.

A young brunette with a long pony tail and glasses approached.

"Dr. Stuart?" she asked.

"Yes."

"I'm Margaret Goodman, fourth-year student at Sutro State." She extended her hand.

"Pleased to meet you," he replied, shaking her hand. Remembering his experience with the previous student, Stuart bluntly asked, "Why are you on this mission?"

"I'm going into pediatrics," she said, "But my real interest is in global health care. I have a Master's in Public Health."

"You're going to have fun being chained to this old codger for the next two weeks," interjected Kathleen, extending her own hand. "I'm Kathleen Atwood, head nurse in the surgical suite."

"I'm looking forward to it," said Margaret, "In fact, the prospect of two weeks in a developing country with Dr. Stuart as my professor is one of the main reasons I signed up."

"You must be a glutton for punishment," said Kathleen.

"Do you already have a residency lined up?" Stuart asked.

"Yes, sir. I'll be at UC San Diego next year," she answered

Stuart was relieved that the medical student on this mission was not just trying to pad her resume.

A handsome young man dressed in jeans and a hoodie joined them. He also extended his hand.

"Hi, Dr. Stuart, Ms. Atwood," he said, "I'm Mike Pirelli."

"Mike is one of our better orthopedic residents," said Stuart as hands were shaken all around.

"I'll do you a favor and not tell anyone you said that," Kathleen said, "It would spoil your well-deserved reputation as a curmudgeon."

"Thanks," Stuart replied, "It was just a momentary lapse into civility. Mike, have you decided what to do after residency?"

"I'm probably going to take a fellowship in trauma," Pirelli said, "I expect that there are a lot of cases in El Salvador that are the result of trauma. All the residents say that these Project Raphael trips are very educational."

"Well, a medical student interested in pediatrics and global health and a resident who's go to specialize in trauma," said Stuart, "The dinner conversations on this trip should be very interesting."

"Do either of you speak Spanish?" Kathleen asked.

"I had three years of Spanish in high school and one more in college," Margaret said, "But I've never actually tested my skills in a Spanish-speaking country."

"All I know is *taco, burrito,* and *cerveza,*" said Pirelli.

"It'll take a while to get your Spanish up to speed, Margaret," Kathleen said, "But it should come. Don't be afraid to speak Spanish to the people. They'll be delighted to help you. They consider it a great courtesy when you try to speak their language. Dr. Pirelli, you'll be happy to know that the team has several professional translators with us. But you might want to expand your Spanish vocabulary in the next couple weeks. May I suggest that you start with *por favor, con permiso,* and *gratias.*"

"What are those?" asked the resident.

"Look them up," said Stuart.

The two young men blended in well with the other unemployed and bored males on the dirty street of the Salvadoran village of Cedros. Smoking cigarettes, striking poses, going nowhere.

Hector Velasquez was dressed in dirty jeans and a shirt open to his navel. He leaned closer to speak softly to his companion. The other youth was shorter and muscular. A tattoo of a condor was prominent on his neck. He looked tough and hard.

"Did you pick up my signal when we passed the house?" Hector asked.

"The yellow house two streets over with the red door. The woman was wearing jeans and a red blouse," said the thug.

"Right," said Hector, "Every day the woman is alone in the house at four o'clock. You can take her then. Get there before she starts to cook. I want the kitchen to look clean."

"Where do you want me to take her?"

"I don't care," said Hector, "I don't want her body found for a very long time."

"Consider it done."

Later, after he had changed into fancier clothes, Hector met up with Gabriella at their usual cantina. She preferred that he not come around to her house because of her mother's disapproval of the whole relationship. This was fine with Hector. He disliked the old bitch anyway.

"I know that today was your last day of school," said Hector with a smile, "That calls for a celebration. In San Salvador."

"Really?" Gabriella smiled.

"Oh yes, my love. Today's the day," he said with a smile.

"When do we go?"

"Right now."

Hector kissed her and led giggling Gabriella to his car.

"Hector," she protested, "I need to stop at home. I need to get some things."

"My darling, where you're going there are new clothes beyond your imagination," he said, "I'll buy you what you need and a suitcase to put them in."

"Really?"

"My love, you are about to experience a whole new life style." Hector had been looking forward to this day for a long time.

"Now, get in the car."

Detective Duane Wilson stepped into the coffee shop at Jack London Square, accompanied by his friend, FBI Special Agent Walter Reynolds.

"That's Will Chen in the booth over in the corner," said Duane, gesturing toward the table occupied by the wiry Oakland police detective.

"Who's your friend?" asked Chen, his eyes darting between Duane and Reynolds.

Reynolds extended his hand.

"Walter Reynolds, FBI."

"Good," said Chen, "What we're going to talk about may interest you. Duane, you're buying."

"As usual," said Duane. The server came to the table, "Three coffees, please."

"And a slice of apple pie," added Chen.

"So, what you got, Will?" asked Duane.

"The fire or ambush or massacre or whatever it was you had across the bay has pretty much destroyed the 8 Gangsta Blood," said Chen, "Most of the top guys were killed. No great loss to Oakland or society, if you ask me."

"Do you have some idea about who might have done it?" asked Duane, "Or why? Or why they did it in San Francisco?

"Yes, and maybe and no," said Chen, "8 Gangsta Blood made most of its money in drugs and extortion. They're a nasty violent bunch of bastards, but no worse than our other gangs. The warehouse massacre killed off a lot of them. The survivors are too weak to hold the turf, so the neighboring gangs have moved in to take their corners and their customers. Some of the survivors joined the neighboring gangs and a couple decided to move out of town. It's been surprisingly peaceful, to tell the truth. Anyway, one of the former members of 8 Gangsta Blood came to us. He traded what he knew for some financial assistance relocating to L.A."

"So, you got a confidential informer from the 8 Gangsta Blood?" said Duane.

"In a manner of speaking," said Chen, "It's really only a one-off tip. This dude told us what he knew and is getting the hell out of town. Our informer heard about the new gang in Oakland that we talked about, *Los Cóndores*. As I told you, they're pretty small. Now they're operating on 8 Gangsta Blood turf. There was supposed to be a meeting with the leaders of *Los Cóndores* in San Francisco at the warehouse. Our informant doesn't know who chose the San Francisco location or why. Anyway, the Blood was going to put the newbies in their place."

"And instead, the Blood got annihilated."

"That's the theory," said Chen, "It's possible that this little gang from Central America is making a move. Now, *Los Cóndores* is on our radar."

"Holy shit," said Reynolds, "*Los Cóndores* making a move in the Bay Area."

"And maybe starting a war," said Duane.

"Well, the war with 8 Gangsta Blood is already over. *Los Cóndores* won that war with a decisive first strike," Chen said, "I suppose that the massacre at the warehouse might be the opening salvo of a bigger war against Bay area gangs."

"Yeah, I've learned a little more about them since we last talked" said Reynolds, "Some of the meanest, cruelest most violent bastards in the world. We really don't want them in the US. In El Salvador they're involved with extortion, prostitution, murder for hire. Very nasty boys."

"Are they capable of pulling off a massacre like the one in San Francisco?" asked Duane.

"More than capable," said Reynolds, "Cold blooded murder is their stock in trade. They're smart and totally ruthless. Will, do you have any idea what *Los Cóndores* is up to in Oakland?"

"Cocaine," said Chen, "At least that's what we think. Not on the streets, like the other punk gang bangers. Farther up the food chain. We think that *Los Cóndores* is acting as a wholesaler. They may be the source from which the local gangs buy product for sale on the street."

"And 8 Gangsta Blood was one of their customers?" asked Duane, "So why kill off a customer?"

"We think that *Los Cóndores* may be getting into the retail cocaine market," said Chen, "In the last week or so, we're seeing Latino salesmen on some corners of what used to be 8 Gangsta Blood turf."

"Does *Los Cóndores* have the manpower to cover the old 8 Gangsta Blood turf?" asked Duane.

"Or the firepower?" said Reynolds.

"No," said Chen, "We think that there are only a few *Los Cóndores* foot soldiers in Oakland. It looks like they're still mostly in the wholesale sales business to other gangs. They're just getting started on the streets. There may be another angle, one that may be of interest to Walter and the FBI."

"What's that?" asked Reynolds.

"Part of the old 8 Gangsta Blood business was extorsion on a portion of the Oakland docks," said Chen, "I think it's possible that the Blood were interfering with the importation of cocaine from Central and South America to *Los Cóndores*. The Blood may have been trying to take a cut of the importation profits, or even take it over themselves."

Reynolds let out a whistle.

"Will, do you have any evidence that *Los Cóndores* may be involved with human trafficking?"

"No."

"And the FBI can't connect them with human trafficking in El Salvador or anywhere else," Reynolds added.

"But it's possible that *Los Cóndores* is getting into the extorsion business at the Oakland docks," Will said.

"Jesus," said Duane. He couldn't stop thinking that maybe cocaine wasn't the only thing that *Los Cóndores* was bringing in to the Oakland docks.

17

GABRIELLA KNEW THAT, sooner or later, the moment of decision would arrive. She knew that one day Hector would ask her to get in the car, tell her it was time to leave Cedros for a new life. Over and over, Gabriella had played this scene in her mind. She was going to have to choose between her mother and a hopeless future in Cedros or Hector and a mysterious adventure in the larger world. Well before this day, Gabriella knew what she was going to do.

She got in the car.

As they drove, Gabriella thought about what her decision was going to mean. One of the most important things was that she was going to have sex with Hector. Probably tonight. She felt little butterflies fluttering in her heart, making it beat faster. She was nervous, but she knew that this day would come. It happened to every woman, she told herself. Tonight, it would be her turn. Part of her knew that she would get through the experience and be happy about it. Part of her was afraid that she wouldn't.

Gabriella drank in the scenery with her eyes as they drove. In her fourteen years, she had never really been far from Cedros. Everything she saw was new. Rural El Salvador wasn't much to look at, but it was fresh and interesting to her. Hector concentrated on his driving and Gabriella on the scenery.

Gabriella had, at best, a rudimentary education. She did, however, know that San Salvador was an inland city. So, when she saw the ocean, she was puzzled.

"Hector," she said, "I thought we were going to San Salvador. That's the ocean!"

"I have little surprise for you, my love," he replied, "I've planned a short beach excursion first."

"Really?" she asked, "I don't have a swimsuit!"

Hector grinned.

"Part of me wants to say that I'd prefer you go in the water without one," he said, "But everything will be provided. I love you, Gabriella. You need to learn to trust me."

She reached her hand to his and gave a squeeze, then resumed her gazing out the window. Hector was right, of course. He was her handsome prince. He knew about the world outside Cedros. She did need to trust him. That was part of being in love.

"I love you, too, Hector," she said, "I'm so excited!"

After several miles of glorious beaches, they arrived in Acajutla. Gabriella was dazzled by the luxurious resort hotels and spectacular grand houses.

"Hector, did you see these places?" she said, "This doesn't seem real."

"Oh, it's real," he replied, "And we're staying in one of the nicest resort hotels tonight."

"Which one?"

"I'm going to let it be a surprise," he said.

Gabriella stared at each hotel in succession, picturing herself checking in to a luxury suite, making love to Hector in a king-sized bed with satin sheets. The fantasies were thrilling.

The drive took them past the resort hotels and into the city. Large commercial ships rested in the harbor. The sights and sounds of El Salvador's busy port filled her senses. Cranes loaded and unloaded containers. Pallets of goods crowded the docks. The smells of salt air and fish were new to her, strange and fascinating. Gabriella was overwhelmed.

Hector pulled the car up to a large warehouse. The large overhead door was closed and locked. A smaller door was on the left.

"Come on," said Hector, "I need to pick up a few things from my friends before we check into our hotel. Come on in."

Gabriella hopped out. Hector held the door for her as she entered the warehouse. He closed it behind them. The warehouse was large and clean. Several tough-looking young men and a couple of girls loitered about, some with pistols in their belts, one or two with rifles slung over their shoulders. In the middle of the warehouse was a large steel cage, ten feet high and forty feet on each side. Inside the cage were air mattresses and sleeping bags. And three young girls.

At the sight of Gabriella, the three girls rushed to the side of the cage, shouting and yelling.

"Run!"

"Get help!"

"Get us out of here!"

"Run now, girl!"

Hector grabbed both her arms and held her very tightly.

"Hey," Gabriella protested, "Let go. You're hurting me."

"Can't let you go, baby," Hector said, "You know how much I like to hold you."

One of the thugs with an assault rifle slipped it off his shoulder and pointed it at the girls in the cage.

"Get back! Shut up and move away from the door!" ordered the man with the rifle. The girls cringed and stepped back.

Another thug took a key and opened the door to the cage.

"In you go," said Hector.

"Wh-wh-what's happening?" she protested, "I don't understand."

"Stupid girl," said Hector, "You're going to the big city alright. Lots of glamor and shopping. You're going to San Francisco. And you're not coming back."

Hector shoved Gabriella into the cage. She almost lost her balance, but recovered and grabbed the steel bars as the thug locked her in.

"But my mother will miss me," she cried.

"Your mother is dead," said Hector without emotion, "Nobody is going to miss you. You're just another missing kid in another filthy village in a country that nobody cares about."

A tall heavyset man walked over to the cage and leered at Gabriella. It was Esteban, the gang member who Gabriella had smacked at the party.

"Well, well, well," he said with a grin, "Hector's little hellcat has come back. Maybe now you and I will dance."

Gabriella's fairytale dream turned into an unimaginable nightmare.

♦ ♦ ♦

Mike Pirelli, the orthopedic resident approached Stuart in the middle of his somewhat chaotic clinic. Pirelli was scratching his head.

"Dr. Stuart, you gotta see this kid," said Mike, "I've never seen anything like this."

"Well, Mike," said Stuart, "You sure know how to get my attention."

Stuart followed Pirelli to an examination room.

"What's the mystery case, Mike?" Stuart asked.

"At first I thought it was some kind of practical joke," said Pirelli, "Like maybe the nurses were playing a trick on the new resident. I thought that they'd bought some really gross rubber feet at a novelty shop or a Halloween store and put them on this kid just to freak me out."

"Novelty shop feet?"

"And then I looked really close and touched them. The feet were real! Well, then I was really freaked out. You just have to see this, Dr. Stuart!"

Stuart gestured to the resident to stay outside in the corridor. Alone, he opened the door to the examination room. The lone occupant was a boy in his early teens. His face reflected a mixture of embarrassment, fear, and hope. Stuart offered the boy his hand.

"I'm Dr. Stuart. What's your name?"

"Juan Torres."

"Are you here alone?" Stuart asked. "Where are your parents?"

"I came alone," said the youth, "My parents said that no one could help me, that I was wasting my time."

"How did you get here? Where do you live?"

"I'm from a village about twenty kilometers from here. I walked."

All the time that Stuart was talking to the boy, he kept his eye on the lad's face, not the feet. Stuart had seen the feet as soon as he opened the door. He knew the diagnosis already.

"What do you hope that we can do for you, Juan?" Stuart asked.

Juan pointed to his feet. Stuart knelt, looked at the feet closely and began to touch them and move them.

Juan's feet were grotesque. They appeared to be nearly twice the normal size. The skin was thick and hard as plastic. They were filthy and almost black with soil. Deep fissures, like tire treads, but deeper and without a pattern crisscrossed the bottom of both feet. The skin was very thick and rigid. Stuart noticed lots of dirt and a few small pebbles lodged in the fissures. Gently, Stuart probed the skin and joints all over the feet. He noticed that the inner two toes looked normal, but the outer three were hugely overgrown. He also noticed that the skin over the top of the foot and the inside part was softer, more supple, and normal in thickness.

"What is the worst problem with your feet, Juan," Stuart asked the boy, "What bothers you the most?"

"Pain."

"Where is the pain?"

"On the bottom. When stones get stuck in my feet, it hurts to walk."

"You're not bothered by how your feet look?" Stuart asked.

"I know they're ugly. I don't like the way they look. I can't find shoes that will cover them up," said Juan, "And I don't like it when people make fun of me. But I could accept that if I didn't have the pain. And I could find work if I didn't have the pain."

Stuart nodded in understanding.

"Juan, we're going to get some x-rays. They're pictures of the bones in your feet. It won't hurt. The nurse will take you to another room where they'll take the x-ray pictures. I'll look at the pictures of the bones and talk with the other doctors. Then the nurses will bring you back to a room like this one. I and the other doctors will come and talk to you. We'll let you know if we can help you. Don't be discouraged."

Stuart went into the corridor, grabbed a requisition form and ordered the x-rays. Giving the form to the nurse, he engaged Dr. Pirelli, who was waiting eagerly for Stuart to speak.

"Have you ever heard of Proteus syndrome?" Stuart asked.

Pirelli shook his head no.

"Go find Margaret Goodman," said Stuart, "Bring her here. This is a very interesting case. From many points of view. She should see it, too."

Pirelli scurried off and by the time he returned with Margaret the x-rays were back. The resident and the student stood on the flanks while Stuart studied the films.

"Proteus was a character in Greek mythology," Stuart began, "Proteus was able to alter his physical characteristics. So, the disease that bears his name is characterized by human tissues that can greatly alter their appearance. Bone and skin are typical tissues to be affected. In bone, we generally see grotesque overgrowth. It can affect single bones, or several. It's not unusual to see a normal bone right next to one that has grown to gigantic proportions. When skin is involved, it tends to be overgrown as well, becoming thick, coarse, and corrugated. The deformities of Proteus syndrome are quite grotesque."

Pointing to the x-ray, Stuart continued.

"Mike, look carefully at the appearance of each bone in the forefoot. There's gigantism of the bones of the lateral three rays of both feet. The feet are fairly symmetrical with little difference between the right and the left. We tend to focus on these huge giant bones. We need, however, to notice that the inner two toes and their metatarsals are actually quite normal."

Stuart took his hand and covered the image of the abnormally large bones.

"You're right, Dr. Stuart," said Pirelli, "If you just look at the medial rays, they appear normal."

"This looks gross," Margaret said, "Do the feet look as bad as the x-rays?"

"Worse," said Pirelli.

"Be careful," said Stuart, "What's important isn't what you and I think about the patient's problem. The only person who defines the goal of treatment is the patient himself. In Juan's case, we're so appalled by the appearance of the feet that we want to get rid of the ugliness. Juan, however, is not so interested in how his feet look as the fact that stones get lodged in the fissures and it hurts to walk. Sure, he knows his feet are ugly. He'll accept ugly if he can walk without pain."

"Is there anything that can be done for the boy?" asked Margaret.

"Let's go see Juan and see if we can come up with a plan," said Stuart, opening the door to the exam room.

Stuart led the doctors into the room and introduced them to the youth. Margaret and Pirelli each took a turn examining Juan's feet. Finally, Stuart knelt and held Juan's left foot.

"To give this boy pain relief," Stuart began, "we have to get rid of the fissured skin on the bottom of his foot. Most of the skin that he walks on is abnormal, but not the part on the most medial side."

Stuart drew imaginary incisions on the foot with his finger.

"We need to make the foot smaller to get good skin on the weight-bearing surface. Suppose we remove the outer bones at an angle from the second toe to the base of the lateral forefoot. We take out the bad skin on the bottom. Using the good soft skin on the top of the foot, we swing it around to the bottom and suture it to the good skin on the medial bottom of the foot."

"That's a big flap of skin, Dr. Stuart," said Pirelli.

"Yes, it is," Stuart replied, "I've never heard of this being done before, so it's not fair to ask one of the other surgeons to perform the procedure. Mike, will you put this on the surgical schedule? I'll do it myself."

18

OVER THE NEXT several days, more girls were added to the cage. As her rage cooled to a steady simmer, Gabriella became very observant of events in the warehouse. Gabriella was disgusted to see that Briana, the tall girl she met at the party, was one of the guards over the captives in the cage. Briana and another girl supervised them when they were allowed out to use the bathroom and shower. Briana smiled at Gabriella in a nasty, condescending way. Gabriella ignored her.

Gabriella was startled when a loud electric motor began to raise the overhead door. She stared intently as a couple of *Los Cóndores* gang members wheeled a stretcher like the ones used in ambulances into the warehouse, past the cage, and toward the back of the open area. Two women accompanied the stretcher, one older and rather plump, the other tall, dressed in elegant black, with dark glasses and a big hat. The form under the sheets on the stretcher was small, probably a child.

Gabriella saw the group with the stretcher disappear through a door. After a few minutes, the gangsters with the stretcher and the tall woman in black re-emerged and left.

Gabriella had no idea what was going on behind the door, but she knew that it was bad.

◆ ◆ ◆

When he had seen the last patient in the clinic, a clerk intercepted Stuart to tell him that Dr. Godfrey wanted him to call. There was a phone at the front desk.

Stuart stopped by the surgical suite after he had spoken to Godfrey. Kathleen was just leaving for the day.

"You look tired," Stuart said.

"You don't look so hot yourself, Doctor," she replied with a grin.

"Want to go to dinner on a yacht tonight?" he asked.

"Yeah, I'm pretty much done," Kathleen replied, "I need to take a shower and put some makeup on."

"Wear your best dress," he added, "The blue one with the spaghetti straps."

"Too bad," she said, "I left that dress in San Francisco. I did bring the plaid skirt and a nice blouse to go with it. I was hoping that we'd get invited to the yacht again. No way was I going to be embarrassed by being under-dressed."

Dinner on the Arariel was splendid, as it had been before. Lois Godfrey was radiant in a short white dress that flaunted her shapely legs. Wallace Godfrey complimented Kathleen on her appearance. Lois was more than polite. She was the perfect hostess. William

Conklin, the business manager of Project Raphael, was the fifth person at the dinner table.

Godfrey was ebullient.

"Ray, Kathleen, so glad you could join us," Godfrey gushed.

Pleasantries were exchanged.

"I'm hearing great reports about your clubfoot program, Ray," Godfrey said, "This could make a big and lasting difference in El Salvador."

"I have good help and willing students," said Stuart.

"The other doctors are talking about your latest surgical triumph," Godfrey said, "Quite an inventive procedure."

"When you're confronted with a problem you've never seen before and the status quo is unacceptable, it's imperative that you invent a solution that hasn't been done before," Stuart replied.

"Your solution was brilliant," said Godfrey, "The boy now has a foot of normal size with good, normal skin. He'll be healed and back to have the other side done by the time of our next mission. Are you going to do that operation?"

"Now that I've started a professional relationship with Juan, I can't abandon my patient," said Stuart with a smile, "so I guess I'm committed to the next trip."

"It's good to have you back as a regular member of the team," said Godfrey, "You'll do a lot of good here."

Kathleen smiled and gave Stuart's hand a squeeze.

"Lois and I were talking," said Godfrey with a conspiratorial wink to his wife, "We wonder if you and Kathleen would be interested in sailing home with us on the Arariel. Think of it as a kind of special 'thank you' for all that you've contributed to Project Raphael on these last two missions. As a bonus, perhaps, it might give you and Kathleen a little time to relax together."

Lois grinned. Stuart looked at Kathleen.

"That would be very nice," Kathleen said.

Stuart kept his eyes on Kathleen, but said nothing. He just nodded his head.

"Then consider it done," said Godfrey, "Pardon me for being intrusive, but will you be needing one or two staterooms?"

"Two," said Stuart and Kathleen together.

Eight girls now shared the cage. They slept side by side on air mattresses and sleeping bags. Each day they were allowed out, one at a time and watched by one of the female guards, for a shower and a change of clothes. There were real toilets near the showers, they were far better than the portable potty inside the cage.

Each girl in the cage had a story to tell. For four of them, the story was almost identical to Gabriella's. A charming young man with a nice car and lots of money found the girl in some small, hopeless village. As each girl described the details, it seemed as though the men were following a script. There were promises of a life of excitement, adventure, and luxury, just like Hector had promised. Simple girls with dismal futures seized on the fantasies the men were peddling. Like Gabriella, most had willingly gotten into cars with the gang members, ready to see their romantic dreams come true.

Two girls had been forcibly kidnapped. These were the youngest, aged eleven and twelve. One had gone to the store for groceries and never returned home. A girl from Guatemala was taken as she walked home from school. The oldest girl, nineteen, had a pistol shoved in her face one evening as she closed up the *tienda* where she worked.

Each individual girl reacted to their situation in her own way. The two youngest ones were paralyzed with fear. They spent most of the time crying. Two were depressed, resigned to whatever horrible fate awaited them. They each sat alone, mostly silent. One girl was delusional. She thought it was all a joke, a sick joke that would end with her boyfriend's return and a riotous party with the gang members. Two remained hopeful. Surely, they thought, the police would learn of their abduction and rescue them. They spent each day trying to catch glimpses of the world outside the warehouse, searching for their saviors.

Gabriella was angry. She was angry at Hector. She was angry at herself. Her mother and Elana were right about Hector. She owed them a big apology. If she could get out of this cage, Gabriella was going to go home.

Before he left, Hector said that her mother was dead. Was that another one of Hector's lies? Was he just trying to make the whole experience more painful? She had to ignore Hector's lies for now. She had to get out of there.

Gabriella struggled, but kept a tight grip on her emotions. She studied the guards, young men and women in their late teens or twenties. She learned the habits of each guard. She eavesdropped when they talked, trying to discover some little bit of useful information. She marveled that the guards just talked normally, as though the girls in the cage didn't exist. Even the female guards behaved as though the captive girls weren't even there, unless the guard was escorting a girl to the showers. Soon, she realized that the guards didn't consider the girls to be real people, with real minds, and real ears. The girls were just objects to the guards. Gabriella thought that maybe she could use their indifference. She looked carefully for an opportunity to act.

"Listen," Gabriella whispered to the other girls, "I'm going to get out of here. If you can, follow me. If you can't I'll send help for you."

"How are you going to get out of here?" asked one girl, "It's impossible."

"I don't know yet," Gabriella replied, "I haven't figured out the details. But I want you all to be ready to move when I give the signal."

"What signal?"

"You'll know it when you see it," Gabriella said with more confidence than she felt.

"You'll get us all killed," said another girl.

"Gabriella, don't talk about escaping," said another, "It's too dangerous."

"What's dangerous is doing nothing," said Gabriella, "Staying with these bastards is worse than getting killed."

"They can kill us and go out and get eight more girls easily," said one girl, "Just like they got us."

"I don't think so," said Gabriella, "I don't think they have time. I heard some of the guards talking. We're to be shipped out of here soon."

"When?"

"I don't know exactly," said Gabriella, "But soon. They're going to sell us for money. I don't think they'll kill us. We're only worth money if we're alive."

"They'll hurt us," whimpered a crying girl.

"No," said Gabriella, "We're worth more money if we look good and we're healthy. We can use this to our advantage."

"You're crazy, Gabriella," the oldest girl said decisively.

The mission was coming to a close. Only small operations, ones that didn't require the patients to stay long in the hospital remained. Project Raphael had a regular staff of Salvadoran doctors and nurses. Still, the North American team didn't feel right about leaving a patient with potentially serious post-operative complications behind in El Salvador. There were follow-up clinics to schedule. Many patients would come back for physical therapy, braces, medications.

Stuart spent the last morning in the clinic, watching his newly trained cast technicians and Salvadoran doctors apply the clubfoot casts to babies.

Ron Delgado, the cast technician from Sutro State University Hospital, was supervising two young Salvadoran men. The Salvadoran cast techs were working on a tiny baby with a clubfoot deformity. One held the baby's foot while the other rolled cast padding. The mother, holding her baby's arms and torso, watched with eyes riveted on the hands of the cast techs. Delgado said nothing, just watched his pupils. This was the final examination after two weeks of training.

At last the cast was applied and the man doing the wrapping took the foot and gently molded the cast, rubbing and smoothing the wet plaster. Content, he took a single roll of green fiberglass and overwrapped the cast.

"Good job, Ron," said Stuart, giving the high five.

"They'll do well, Dr. Stuart," said Ron with a grin, "Just to make sure, though, can I come back next time to monitor their progress?"

"Yes, you can," said Stuart, "As long as you know that I know that you're more interested in monitoring your own progress with the girl who works in the clinical lab than observing how our techs do clubfoot casting."

"How did you know about that?" asked Ron.

"I'm something of an amateur detective."

Stuart left the clinic. He found the two Salvadoran orthopedic residents and congratulated them on being good learners. Then he went up to the operating room to find Kathleen.

She was still in scrubs, simultaneously supervising the packing of equipment and directing the operating rooms where surgeons were still working.

"Looks like you're still busy," said Stuart.

"The nurses' work is never done," she said, "I've got two of my San Francisco girls cleaning and packing up gear that needs to go back with us. Still have one room of plastic surgery going and Dr. Silverman is doing a carpal tunnel release. He has two more little cases after that. Then we can finish up here."

"Are your things packed?" Stuart asked.

"All my personal stuff is in my suitcase," she said, "I have street clothes in my locker here."

"The suitcases are all in the hotel lobby," he said, "Ours are set apart from the others since we're headed for the Arariel instead of the airport bus. I'm pretty much done."

"How about if I meet you in the hotel lobby?" she said, "Maybe three hours?"

"Okay," said Stuart, "I don't think that Wallace will sail without us."

Looking around to make sure that nobody was watching, she gave him a little kiss and he left the operating room.

On his way out of the hospital, Stuart ran into Margaret Goodman and Michael Pirelli.

"Hi, Dr. Stuart," said Mike, "We're pretty much done here. I want to thank you for a great two weeks. This was amazing. I learned so much and saw some cases that I'll never forget."

"I think I learned more in the last two weeks than any comparable time in medical school," Margaret chimed in, "What an eye opener. I have so much better appreciation for health care in developing countries."

"I'm glad you found this worthwhile," said Stuart, "And I definitely hope that you both will find time to devote to this sort of work during your careers. What are you two up to now?'

"We have a couple hours before the bus leaves for the airport," said Pirelli, "We thought we might just walk around the beach and the docks and take in some of the scenery."

"We'll be crammed into seats on the bus and on the plane for a long time," Margaret added, "I'd like to get a little exercise before we leave."

"Plus," Pirelli added, "there really hasn't been time to look around and see the sights of Acajutla."

"I doubt that we'll see the big tourist resorts, but we may catch a view of the beach," Margaret said.

"You're pretty far from the really nice beach," Stuart said, "But you may get a decent view of the harbor. Acajutla is a major port for El Salvador. You'll be impressed with how much shipping comes in and out of here."

"That sounds like it'll have to do," said Pirelli, "We'll enjoy what we can see and still be back to catch the bus."

"Be careful," said Stuart, "There are some sketchy parts of this town near the docks."

"He'll protect me," said Margaret, "He was an athlete in college."

Stuart knew that Pirelli had been a college baseball player. He was a pitcher who was known for his excellent fastball, but never could master a curve or a slider. The professional baseball scouts had no interest in a pitcher with just one pitch. Fortunately for Pirelli, he also had excellent grades. He choice of medical school and orthopedic residency would prove much better for him in the long run than a dream of a career in the major leagues.

19

Gabriella noticed that the guards were picking up their pace. Something was happening. The guards were hustling the captive girls through the showers. The girls were given shampoo and conditioner and ordered to make their hair look nice. Fresh, clean clothes were issued to each girl. The cage was swept and the portable toilet cleaned and disinfected.

"Something's going on," Gabriella said to nobody in particular.

"What do you mean?" one of them asked.

"Just look at those assholes," said Gabriella, "The men have their shirts tucked in. The girls have nice makeup and mascara. Two of them are cleaning their guns. They never clean their guns. And, look, the ugly one is actually sweeping the floor."

"Which ugly one?" someone asked, "They're all ugly."

"The one with the condor tattoo on his neck," said a girl.

They all had condor tattoos on their necks.

"Oh, that one," somebody quipped.

The girls locked in the cage shared an unexpected little giggle.

The gang member the others called Pablo, who seemed to be the leader of the guards, came over to the cage, put his hands on the bars, and spoke.

"Put on the fresh clothes," Pablo commanded, "Comb your hair. I want you to look nice today."

"Fuck you, Pablo," said the oldest girl.

"Do as he says," Gabriella cautioned, "Let's look pretty now."

Gabriella brushed her hair, pulled it back into a pony tail, and kept her eyes and ears on the guards. She found a pair of new sneakers that fit. She knelt next to the bars to put them on and tie them up. She could hear the guards better from there.

Most of the words were lost in the cacophony of voices inside and outside of the cage. She tried to concentrate on what they said. One word kept repeating in their chatter.

Jefe.

Jefe. The Boss.

The Boss was coming. That explained the showers, the clean clothes, the thugs cleaning their guns and sweeping the floor. If their leader was coming, it would disrupt the normal schedule. The guards would have their eyes on the Boss.

A visit of this importance might present Gabriella with an opportunity. She had no idea what might happen. She certainly didn't have a plan, but she would be vigilant. If a chance came, she would grab it.

Gabriella could tell by looking out the skylight of the warehouse that dusk was very close. Soon it would be dark. She startled at the sound of the overhead door to the warehouse beginning to move. The motor lifting the door was very loud. Opening this door was unusual.

The guards jumped into action with the first movement of the overhead door. Two of them with assault rifles positioned themselves on either side of the cage door. The rest, led by the one called Pablo, rushed to stand at attention.

Gabriella saw a large black Suburban parked outside the overhead door. Four armed gang members exited the vehicle. Two placed themselves outside the warehouse. Two more took up positions at the rear of the limousine. All four looked right and left, guns drawn. Satisfied, one of the thugs opened the back door of the limo.

El Jefe stepped out of the Suburban, looked around, took a deep breath of the sea air and strutted into the warehouse. Gabriella watched him closely. He was short and stocky, starting to go bald. He walked slowly, warily, looking left and right and straight ahead. Two of the men from the limo fell in behind him, putting their guns away as they came indoors. Pablo approached the Boss respectfully, gesturing as he welcomed the leader of *Los Cóndores*.

The Boss walked slowly toward the cage. The other gang members fell in behind Pablo. Gabriella noticed that only two from the limo remained outside. At least those were the only two she could see.

The Boss walked along the side to the cage, staring at the girls. Gabriella could see him well. He was a singularly ugly man, his face scarred from old acne and cuts from street fights. His eyes were black and cold. She watched, but never saw him blink.

Giancarlo Valdez studied the new shipment of girls. These were pretty ones, he thought. Some of them excited him. He felt himself getting aroused.

One of the young ones started to cry. Valdez was used to that. The little ones always cried. Most of the older ones looked down at the floor. That, too, was normal. Valdez made them afraid. He liked that. Giancarlo Valdez enjoyed making other people afraid. Fear was an aphrodisiac to him.

While most of the girls tried to move toward the far wall of the cage, one stood firm. She was the only one who kept her eyes fixed on his face. This one, Valdez thought, had spirit. He studied Gabriella carefully. She was certainly pretty. Nice flat belly, nice breasts. He watched her nostrils flare as she breathed. He could feel her hate. Oh, yes, this one was special. He had to see her closer, stare her down, watch her cry. He had to dominate this one.

"Not bad, Pablo," said Valdez as he walked along, studying the girls.

"Thank you, *Jefe*."

"Open the cage door," Valdez ordered.

One guard removed the padlock and another opened the cage. Most of the girls took a step or two backwards, trying to retreat to the other side of the cage. Gabriella didn't move, still staring at Valdez.

Valdez entered the cage, followed by Pablo and a handful of gang members. Valdez walked right up to Gabriella. He kept looking at her, unblinking. He knew the effect that his reptilian eyes had on other people. He savored the challenge of her stare, anticipating her tears.

Gabriella kept her eyes riveted on Valdez's. It was like having a staring contest with a snake. Inside, Gabriella was terrified. She thought her heart was going to jump out of her chest. With all her will power she held back her tears, maintaining control, eyes locked on his.

He could smell the musky odor of her body, the clean scent of her hair. This one was a prize indeed.

Valdez smiled. He took his eyes away from Gabriella, not even thinking that he had lost a staring contest. He wanted to congratulate Pablo on the acquisition of such an exquisite creature. Looking back at Gabriella, Valdez took his hand and gently stroked Gabriella's soft cheek.

Gabriella bit him. All the way down to the bone.

"Aah!" Valdez shrieked, "God damn it!"

He pulled his hand back quickly, blood spurting from his thumb. The surprise of the attack was more shocking than the pain.

Not understanding what had happened, the guards surrounding Valdez involuntarily took a step backwards. They couldn't see the wound on their leader's hand. His outcry made them recoil.

Gabriella was past them and out the door before the guards could react.

"Run!" yelled Gabriella as she sped past the thugs at the cage door, who were moving into the cage.

At first the other girls in the cage were as shocked as the guards. Nobody moved for a few seconds. Then one girl made a dash for the cage door. As soon as she sprinted past the shocked gang members, others followed. The girls collided with guards and each other, compounding the confusion.

Soon there were girls going in every direction, screaming in terror and desperation. The first instinct of the gang members was to aid Valdez, giving the girls precious seconds of freedom. Even the two men who had been standing guard outside the overhead garage door rushed inside to Valdez, leaving that large exit wide open.

Members of *Los Cóndores* were street thugs, not trained soldiers or police. They had no coordination, no teamwork, no discipline. Each guard went his own way, trying to help Valdez and catch the running girls. Most of them couldn't decide which task was more important. The hesitation allowed Gabriella and the other girls a few seconds head start.

Pablo was the first to gather his wits and take action. He saw the whole situation turning to disaster. His boss was not seriously hurt, but the prizes were escaping out the doors. He cursed the lack of discipline of the gang members. He needed to catch the girls quickly before they disappeared into the encroaching darkness. If he couldn't get them back in the cage, the whole operation could be lost.

Pablo stepped out of the cage, leaving Valdez cursing and holding his bleeding hand. Pablo began to issue orders, pointing to fleeing girls and shouting to specific gang members to catch them. He ordered the overhead garage door closed, trapping two or three girls still inside. Other guards rushed out into the dusk, following Pablo's orders, guns drawn

"Catch the girls!" Pablo shouted, "Stop them! Don't shoot them!"

Gabriella was out the overhead garage door and running full speed before one of the guards spotted her. She darted around barrels and containers and parked vehicles, never looking back. A momentary panic seized her when she heard footsteps behind her. She ran faster. Her heart raced. The pursuing guard shouted.

She recognized the voice of her pursuer. It was Esteban, the man she had slapped at the party she attended with Hector.

"Come back here!" he shouted, "Bitch!"

She feinted to her left, passing a public waste can. As she passed it on the right, she tipped it over. There was a crash and a clatter.

"God damn you!" Esteban yelled.

The maneuver gained her a few yards. She was ahead of him, but not out of his sight. She knew he had a gun. She remembered telling the other girls that the guards wouldn't kill them because they were only worth money when they were alive. She hoped she was right.

Esteban was a big man who drank a lot and smoked two packs of cigarettes each day. He knew he couldn't keep up with the teenage gazelle who was speeding away from him on the dock. He was already short of breath and the chase was just beginning.

Esteban was alone in his pursuit of Gabriella. He knew exactly which girl he was chasing. She was the sexy little bitch that Hector brought in. She had shamed him in front of his friends. He hated her and craved her at the same time.

He knew he would never catch her in a footrace. If she got away, he would have to face the wrath of Giancarlo Valdez.

The girl was faster than Esteban, but a bullet was faster than the girl. What if he just shot her? That would slow her down, to be certain. If he wounded her, he might catch her and take her back to the warehouse. She might be damaged, but still worth something on the market. If he could bring her to Valdez, the Boss could decide her fate. That would be an acceptable outcome. If he shot and killed her, he would be in trouble. He would have destroyed a valuable piece of property. He would be punished for that. What to do?

Esteban stopped, took aim, and fired at the fleeing Gabriella.

Gabriella startled at the sound of the gunshot. The bullet clanged off a shipping container sitting on the dock and ricocheted away. Momentarily off her stride, she quickly resumed her flight. Because Esteban stopped to shoot, she gained another couple of yards.

She never looked back and never stopped to look for a hiding place. She had no intention of stopping until Esteban was far behind her. She prayed for the darkness to become full. Then her chances of losing him improved. If he didn't shoot her.

Ahead she saw two people walking along the dock, a man and a woman. They didn't seem to have heard the gunshot. Gabriella altered course toward the couple, deliberately exposing her presence in the soft yellow glow of a streetlamp.

Margaret Goodman saw the running girl first. Margaret stopped and pointed.

"Look, Mike," she said, "That girl looks like she's running for her life."

Mike turned to watch. He saw the man chasing Gabriella a good forty yards behind, shouting and waving a pistol. The man stopped and took a shot. The girl kept running.

"That's exactly what she's doing," Mike said.

"We've got to help her," said Margaret. Waving her hands toward Gabriella she shouted "Hey, over here!"

Gabriella altered her course, still dodging around obstacles, but heading for Margaret and Mike. Esteban stopped, looked at Margaret and Mike, hesitated momentarily, and followed.

"Get away from her!" Esteban yelled, waving his pistol.

"Help me!" screamed Gabriella.

"Here!" shouted Margaret, "Mike, do something!"

Mike bent down and picked up a rock. As the thug with the gun came closer, the light from a dockside street light briefly illuminated him. He was about sixty feet away.

The perfect distance.

Mike Pirelli hit the gangster right in the forehead with an 87-mph fastball.

Margaret threw her arms around Gabriella protectively. Together they ran toward the hotel. Mike watched to make sure that the thug stayed down, then turned to join them.

When they had run six blocks or so, the three slowed to a walk. Looking behind them, they saw no sign of pursuit.

"What's your name?" Margaret asked in Spanish.

"Gabriella Cortez. They're going to kill me."

Margaret translated for Mike. In English she asked "What are we going to do with her?"

Mike hesitated a moment and replied.

"We'll take her to Dr. Stuart."

◆ ◆ ◆

"Detective Will Chen from Oakland PD on the phone for you, Duane," said the uniformed officer.

"Thanks," said Detective Duane Wilson as he picked up the phone on his desk, "Hi, Will. What's up?"

"We got some more information on *Los Cóndores*," said Will.

"You have my full attention." Duane sat straight up in his chair, grabbing a pen and pulling a pad of blank paper in front of him.

"We're pretty sure that we've located their headquarters," Will went on, "You know when I told you and your FBI buddy that *Los Cóndores* was getting into the retail cocaine market? They took over a few of the street corners vacated by the gang formerly known as the 8 Gangsta Blood. Not too many corners. *Los Cóndores* still doesn't seem to have that many members. But a few corners on a regular basis. They put their youngest members out on the street, like all the other gangs."

"Yes, I remember," said Duane, "Have you been able to follow these kids once they leave the street?"

"You got it," said Will, "Our folks in Narcotics have had their eyes on the corner salesmen. Once the kids have sold their shit and have their pockets full of money, they go to the headquarters to turn in the cash and get more product."

"Sounds good," said Duane, "Where are they?"

"Nice place, actually," said Will, "The corner dealers all go back to a pretty nice office in an industrial park not too far from the docks. We checked and it's rented to a company called LC Freight. They rent the warehouse adjacent to the office as well."

"LC. *Los Cóndores.*"

"Yeah," said Will, "Not terribly imaginative. Look, you're investigating a homicide, which is a bigger deal that our drug dealing. Do you want us to bust these assholes?"

"Oakland is your jurisdiction, Will," said Duane, "What do you think?"

"Honestly, I 'm not in a big hurry to get these guys off the street," said Will, "It's a game of whack-a-mole out there. If we sweep the *Los Cóndores* dealers off the street corners, some other gang will have their sales force on the same corners by the weekend. I'm more interested in *Los Cóndores* wholesale import business. If they're bringing in a lot of weight in product to sell to the Oakland gangs, we could make a bigger impact if we can intercept that. We know where they live. My inclination is to wait and watch."

"Actually, Will, I have a strong suspicion that these bastards aren't just bringing in cocaine," said Duane, "I think they may be bringing in people."

"You think your dead girl came in to Oakland with a load of cocaine?"

"I think that's a good possibility," said Duane, "If we can watch *Los Cóndores* and intercept their next drug shipment, we may be able to bust the next human trafficking shipment as well."

"We'd have to put together some sort of joint bust with the FBI," said Will.

"Walter Reynolds is a friend," said Duane, "I think he'll be a team player and not screw everything up like the Feds tend to do."

"Okay, Duane, we'll keep an eye on *Los Cóndores*."

20

"God dammit, get me a bandage!" yelled Giancarlo Valdez, clutching his hand, "This fucking thing is bleeding! That little bitch!"

Somebody found a roll of gauze and wrapped it around Giancarlo's hand. He looked at the fat bandage and wiggled his fingers. It hurt, but he was pleased to see that the hand still moved. Blood was seeping through the bandage.

It took nearly an hour and a half for *Los Cóndores* to bring order to the warehouse. Seven girls were locked in the cage. The girl who had bitten Giancarlo was still missing. So was Esteban, one of the gang members.

"*Jefe*, we have all but one of the girls," said Pablo, "Esteban is also missing. Somebody saw him chasing that last girl."

"I want her back," said Giancarlo. He hadn't decided what he was going to do with the girl when he caught her. He wanted to slit her little throat. Maybe rape her first. But she was worth a lot of money alive and he had promised her to the Client. Besides, the future the Client planned for her might actually be punishment enough for what the little bitch did to him.

"We'll get her, *Jefe*," Pablo reassured him.

"Will you?" hissed Giancarlo.

"Yes, *Jefe*," said Pablo.

"Which little bitch bit me?" asked Giancarlo, "And who brought her in here?"

"Her name was Gabriella Cortez," said Pablo, "And Hector Velasquez brought her in."

"Hector," murmured Giancarlo. That arrogant little shit. "Have Hector in my office first thing tomorrow."

"Yes, *Jefe*."

⚬ ⚬ ⚬

Stuart waited patiently in the hotel lobby. He was really looking forward to the trip home on the yacht. The cruise should last about five days. The Arariel could make much better time than a commercial freighter, which would take a week or more to reach San Francisco Bay. Five days with Kathleen should give them plenty of uninterrupted time together, time to maybe figure out where their relationship was headed.

"Hey, mister!" Kathleen interrupted his reverie, "Let's get out of this joint and take a vacation."

"I'm ready," Stuart said. "Took you a while."

"Yeah," she replied, "Our friend Dr. Silverman made a whole career out of three dinky hand cases. You can always count on surgeons to screw up your plans and complicate your life."

"Tell me about it on the cruise," said Stuart, "Let's go."

Just then Margaret Goodman and Mike Pirelli burst into the lobby, dragging a teenage girl. They went straight to Stuart and Kathleen.

"Dr. Stuart, you gotta help us," said Margaret.

"This kid's in trouble," said Mike, "We rescued her from an attacker. She says somebody is trying to kill her. We don't know what to do."

"Whoa," said Stuart, "Slow down. Mike, what are you talking about?"

"We were just taking a walk along the waterfront, enjoying the scenery," Pirelli said, "Margaret saw this girl running toward us along the dock, yelling. She was dodging around boxes and containers and stuff. When I looked, there was this man chasing her. He was yelling in Spanish, too. He was also waving a pistol around. He tried to shoot the girl."

"The girl was crying to us for help," said Margaret, "We just had to do something."

"And you obviously did," said Kathleen.

"Well, yeah, we did, I guess" said Mike "We got her and brought her here. It was the only thing we could think of."

"How did you get her away from an armed man?" asked Stuart.

"Well, I was a pitcher in college," Mike said, "I had a pretty good fastball and good command. I found a rock and, well, when the man got about sixty feet away, I let him have it."

Stuart couldn't suppress a smile. "You threw a strike?"

"More of a beanball," said Mike.

Stuart turned his attention to Gabriella. He smiled and addressed her in Spanish.

"I'm Dr. Stuart. This is Ms. Atwood. What's your name?" he asked.

"Gabriella Cortez."

"How old are you?"

"Almost fifteen."

"Where is your home?"

"A village called Cedros, in the foothills."

"Do you believe you're in danger?" Stuart asked.

"I know I'm in danger," Gabriella asserted.

"Can we take her to the police?" Margaret interrupted.

Gabriella scoffed.

"Not in El Salvador," said Stuart, "I don't know who this girl is afraid of, but you can't trust the police."

"I was kidnapped by *Los Cóndores*," Gabriella said, "They bribe the police."

"Ray, what are we going to do?" asked Kathleen.

Stuart thought for a few minutes.

"Mike and Margaret, go catch the bus," he said, "Kathleen and I will figure this out."

Mike and Margaret were eager to divest themselves of the problem. Relieved, they took off.

"See you back in San Francisco, Dr. Stuart," said Mike as they turned to go.

Gabriella jumped when she heard the words "San Francisco." She almost started to run again.

"What's wrong, Gabriella?" Kathleen asked.

"They, *Los Cóndores*, were going to send me to San Francisco," Gabriella stammered.

"We're not going to hurt you," Stuart assured her, "We'll try to get you back to your family in Cedros."

"I may not have a family," Gabriella said, her eyes downcast.

"Where are your parents?" Kathleen asked.

"My father ran away years ago," Gabriella said, "And Hector said my mother was dead."

"Who's Hector?" Stuart asked.

"He's, no, he used to be my boyfriend," Gabriella said, "He's the one who kidnapped me."

"And Hector told you that your mother was dead," said Stuart, "Do you believe that?"

"I don't know," said Gabriella, "Hector told me a lot of lies. I hate him. And I don't trust him."

"Do you want to go back to Cedros?" Kathleen asked.

"No," said Gabriella, "Cedros isn't safe. *Los Cóndores* will find me there. Hector is *Los Cóndores*. I, well, I hurt one of their leaders. I can't go back to Cedros. Not for a while anyway."

"Again, Ray, what are we going to do?" asked Kathleen.

"Well, we only have two options," said Stuart, "Either we leave her here or we take her with us."

Stuart looked at Gabriella.

"You have a choice," said Stuart, "Ms. Atwood and I are about to board a yacht that will eventually take us to San Francisco in the United States. That's where we live. You can come with us if you choose. Otherwise, we can leave you here, either at this hotel or with the police."

Gabriella looked back and forth from Kathleen to Stuart. He imagined the conflict as she made up her mind.

"I'm going with you," Gabriella said.

"Do you speak English?" Kathleen whispered to Gabriella.

"No."

"Come on," said Stuart, "The hotel manager said that he would drive us to the yacht in the hotel van."

"How are we going to tell Dr. Godfrey?" Kathleen asked, "Are we going to sneak Gabriella onto the ship?"

"No," explained Stuart, "We're just going to march up the gangway with Gabriella as if Wallace had invited her as a guest."

"That could be embarrassing," she said.

"Embarrassing to who?" Stuart replied, "He can't just turn her away. That would be inhospitable."

"Suppose we get her into San Francisco Bay," asked Kathleen, "What then? She has no papers. And she's a minor. How will we explain this?"

"Exactly as you say," says Stuart, "She is an unaccompanied minor requesting asylum. We can work with that. At least it'll buy us some time. Look at it this way. Let's get her on the yacht. We'll have five days at sea to make a plan."

On arrival at the dock, they were met by a member of the Arariel's crew. He had a clipboard which he checked. Of course, he didn't find Gabriella's name on it. Stuart explained that Gabriella

Cortez was a last-minute addition, but she would be joining the voyage as a guest.

"I'm sorry, Dr. Stuart, I wasn't informed," said the crewman, "I'm afraid we haven't a stateroom prepared for Ms. Cortez. If you give us a little time, we can make one up. Please be patient while we make accommodations."

"That won't be necessary," said Kathleen, "Ms. Cortez will be sharing my stateroom."

"As you wish, Ma'am," said the man.

"Just follow me, Gabriella," Kathleen whispered, "Do what I do. Don't worry about the language. I'll translate when we have time."

Stuart's cabin was luxurious and spacious. It had a queen-size bed, a desk, and a bathroom. There was a porthole window. Kathleen and Gabriella had a mirror-image room across the hall. The crewmember brought the suitcases.

"Dinner will be served in the dining room at seven," said the crewman, "We'll set a place for Ms. Cortez at your table. Now that you're aboard, we'll cast off in about twenty minutes. Dr. Godfrey will see you in the dining room."

"Thank you," said Stuart, "We'll get unpacked and freshen up."

When the man left, Stuart turned to Kathleen.

"Get comfortable and meet me in my cabin," he said.

When they were back together in Stuart's cabin, they all spoke Spanish. Stuart sat at the desk while Kathleen and Gabriella reclined on the bed.

"Gabriella, we're going to have to explain why you're here," Stuart said, "We work at the Project Raphael hospital here in Acajutla. I'm one of the doctors there. We'll say that you came to the clinic in desperation. We'll explain that you were being chased by a violent Salvadoran gang and you feared for your life. We'll tell everyone that we're taking you to San Francisco where we'll turn you over to the authorities and help you get asylum in the United States. If you don't want to stay in the United States, our government will send you back to El Salvador. Everyone on this ship will be speaking English, so we'll help you with translations. Generally, I don't want you to talk much. Just answer questions that Kathleen and I translate for you."

"What's Project Raphael?" Gabriella asked, "I never heard of it."

"Project Raphael is a medical mission for poor people in El Salvador," Kathleen explained, "North American doctors and nurses come there to see patients and do surgery. We're part of the group. If anybody asks, just pretend that you heard about the hospital and clinic in your village."

"Gabriella, do you know why *Los Cóndores* was going to take you to San Francisco?" Stuart asked.

"There were eight girls, including me, being held in a warehouse in a cage," Gabriella said, "The guards talked a lot. I tried to listen to what the guards said. I think they were going to sell us for slaves."

"And how did you think they were going to transport you?" asked Kathleen.

"I don't know," Gabriella answered.

"I think maybe she's right," said Stuart, "I think there's a human trafficking organization bringing girls into San Francisco. Gabriella may have been one of the victims."

"Dr. Stuart and Ms. Atwood," Gabriella said, "Do I have to go to San Francisco?"

"Yes, for now," Stuart replied, "We live in San Francisco and that's where this yacht is headed."

"What if I don't like it there? Will you make me a slave?"

"Kathleen and I will never make you a slave. I promise. Neither will anyone else on this ship. You don't have to stay in San Francisco if you don't want to," said Stuart, "You came to us rather suddenly. We didn't have a plan for you. Since this ship was sailing, we only could offer to take you with us. You agreed to that."

"I did," Gabriella said, "You two seem like kind people. I didn't see that I had much choice. If I stayed, *Los Cóndores* would surely catch me. If they didn't kill me, they'd put me back in the cage. I had to trust somebody."

"Please don't call me Ms. Atwood. I'm Kathleen. You and I are going to be roommates for the voyage," said Kathleen, "You can trust us. I admit that we don't quite know what to do with you right now. We'll have to make our plan on the way. It takes five or six days to get to San Francisco from Acajutla. We'll do what's best for you. You'll be part of the decision, every step of the way."

The crew of the Arariel set two tables in the salon. Dr. Godfrey shared his table with his wife and Bill Conklin. Stuart, Kathleen, and Gabriella sat at the other.

"Sorry about the extra passenger," Stuart said, "Gabriella was a kind of emergency addition. She came running up to the clinic just as Kathleen and I were leaving, pursued by a young man with obviously bad intent. It turns out that her whole family was killed by one of the Salvadoran gangs. The young man was about to add Gabriella to the dead when she found us."

"Wow!" said Godfrey, "What did you do about the guy who was chasing her?"

"He ran off when he saw us," Stuart lied, "I guess he didn't want to get involved with Americans. It's one thing to terrorize Salvadorans. Assaulting US citizens is a whole different matter."

"Couldn't you turn her over to the police?" asked Conklin.

"Bill," said Godfrey, "You should know better than any of us how corrupt the police are in El Salvador."

"Exactly," said Stuart, "Wallace, I knew you wouldn't mind if we brought her along. She won't be a bother, I'm sure. She'll share the stateroom with Kathleen. It's the right thing to do. I'm sure you would have done the same thing if you were in our position."

"I'm certain that he would," asserted Lois, casting an admiring glance at her husband. "Gabriella, you're welcome here."

"She doesn't speak English," said Kathleen.

"I see," said Godfrey, "My Spanish isn't very good."

"That's okay," Kathleen, "I'll do the translating."

"What are you going to do with her when we get to San Francisco?" Lois asked.

"We don't exactly have a plan," explained Stuart, "For now, I think we'll turn her over to the federal authorities. I would guess that she'll be classified as an unaccompanied minor seeking asylum. We do, however, have five or six days to come up with a better plan."

"Gabriella isn't the only minor on this voyage," said Godfrey, "We've got a little boy named Manuel Cuellar in the medical stateroom. He has A.L.L., acute lymphoblastic leukemia. I've arranged for him to be treated at the University of Minnesota. Modern medical science has come so far in the treatment of that form of childhood leukemia that we have better than eighty percent chance of a complete cure."

"Where is he?" Kathleen asked.

"He'll stay in the medical stateroom for most of the voyage," said Godfrey, "Daniella Santiago, our registered nurse, will be with him. You may see him running around the ship from time to time. One can't keep a rambunctious child confined, no matter how sick he is. He'll be out for exercise. But he and Daniella will take their meals in the medical stateroom. With his leukemia, he's susceptible to infection, so I think it's prudent to limit his contact with others."

"That's so kind of you, Dr. Godfrey," said Kathleen, "To bring these kids to the US for treatment."

"Thank you," said Godfrey, "With young Gabriella here, it seems that in your own way you're doing the same thing."

During the meal, Stuart noticed that Gabriella couldn't keep her eyes off Lois Godfrey.

21

HECTOR VELASQUEZ WAS scared. He knew that Gabriella had escaped from the warehouse. He also knew that she bit Giancarlo Valdez. Now he found himself summoned to Valdez's office. This could not be good.

Hector was admitted to the inner office. Valdez sat behind his desk, his right hand expertly bandaged. Pablo Ortega, the *Los Cóndores* captain in charge of the shipment of girls, stood out of the way in the corner of the office, his face grim.

Hector faced Valdez. There was a chair in front of the desk. Hector glanced at it.

"Don't sit down," said Giancarlo, "You're here to listen, not talk. You won't be here long enough to get comfortable."

Hector gulped, trying to swallow the lump in his throat.

"You failed me, Hector," Giancarlo said, "You brought me a vicious bitch. She bit me. The fucking bitch bit me."

Valdez held up his bandaged hand.

"Then the bitch escaped," he continued, "She ran to the Americans who were working at the clinic. And they kept her. They took the bitch on a yacht that sailed last evening. So, your vicious little bitch is gone."

"I'm sorry, *Jefe*." Hector stammered, "I had no idea. She was just a stupid village girl."

"Shut up," said Giancarlo, "It's your job to know what sort of goods you are delivering. This is the second time you've brought me defective girls, Hector. I haven't forgotten the sick one you brought me who died before she even arrived in Oakland."

"*Jefe*."

"I said shut up," said Giancarlo, "Not only did you bring me this violent bitch, but you cost me money, Hector. Do you have any idea how much we've been paid to deliver these girls? Do you? And do you know what we make when they die or run away? Nothing."

Hector looked down at the floor. He felt his knees starting to shake. He wondered if there was anything he could say. In his mind, he knew he should be silent. He had been a member of *Los Cóndores* long enough to realize what was happening. He understood. In his heart, though, he couldn't accept the situation as hopeless. He hoped for mercy, even though he knew that Giancarlo never showed mercy.

"You're worthless, Hector," Giancarlo went on, "Fucking worthless. You bring me damaged girls. You cost me money. You have no loyalty to me. You jeopardize our whole operation. What do you think I should do with you?"

"Please, *Jefe*," Hector pleaded.

"I'll tell you what I will do with you," said Giancarlo, "I'll use you to teach others. Pablo, take care of this worthless piece of shit.

Make sure that his body is prominently displayed so that everyone can see what happens to people who fail me."

◆ ◆ ◆

The Arariel's diesels caused a vibration that permeated the whole yacht. Gabriella found it soothing, like the purring of a contented cat.

The stateroom was like a dream. She sprawled out on the bed and inhaled the fragrance of the fresh sheets. In all her life, she had never experienced anything like this.

She was confused. One minute she was in the car with Hector, blindly in love. She was looking at luxury resorts and fantasizing about having her first sex on a big, wonderful bed. In an instant her whole life turned upside down and she was a caged animal, bound for a life of slavery. The love of her life turned into the devil incarnate.

Now she was on a fancy yacht, totally dependent on the kindness of strangers. Kathleen and Dr. Stuart seemed like good people, but then so did Hector at first. Things were changing so radically and so rapidly. She feared that she would lose her mind.

Could she trust these North Americans?

She looked at Kathleen, who was sitting in the stateroom chair and smiling kindly at her. Kathleen was a beautiful woman with long, wavy brown hair and soft brown eyes.

"Who are you, Kathleen?" asked Gabriella.

"I'm a nurse with Project Raphael. I live in San Francisco. I work in surgery. I come to Acajutla about five times a year. We perform operations on Salvadoran people who can't afford to go to hospitals. I'm not married and I don't have kids. I'm Catholic. I like to swim and exercise. What else would you like to know?"

"Why are you helping me?" Gabriella asked. She liked Kathleen's answers. The woman seemed honest and was clearly trying to put her at ease.

"I guess it seems like the right thing to do," Kathleen replied.

"Are you in love with Dr. Stuart?"

Kathleen blushed.

"We work together," Kathleen hedged.

"That's not what I asked."

"Well, yes, I suppose I am," Kathleen admitted, "But don't you dare tell him or anyone else."

"I won't tell," Gabriella promised, "It'll be our secret. What happened to Dr. Stuart's eye?"

"You ask a lot of questions."

"I'm on a strange boat with a bunch of strange people, most of whom don't speak a language I can understand. I'm on a trip to a place I don't want to go," Gabriella said, "I'm entitled to answers to a lot of questions."

"Yes, I suppose you are," Kathleen said, "Dr. Stuart was in a very bad automobile accident about four years ago. He lost his eye in the accident."

"What kind of doctor is he?"

"Well, he's a very good one," Kathleen said, "He's very smart. And he's a surgeon. He takes care of children and babies who have something wrong with their bones and joints."

"Like when a kid breaks an arm?"

"Yes, and more complicated problems than that," Kathleen said.

"Was he doing surgery on Salvadoran kids?" Gabriella asked, "Is that why he was in Acajutla?"

"Yes," Kathleen answered, "and he was teaching some young Salvadoran doctors as well."

"He seems like a kind man."

"He is, Gabriella."

For a few minutes they sat in silence, looking at each other. Gabriella felt safe with this woman. But she had felt safe with Hector, too. She would have to remain on her guard.

"Now, can I ask you a few questions?" Kathleen said.

"Yes, that's fair," said Gabriella.

"I know that you are fourteen and that you live in a place called Cedros," Kathleen said, "Tell me about your parents. And, do you have any brothers or sisters?"

"Cedros is a small village in the foothills to the east," Gabriella said, "Most of the people are farmers. It's dirty and small. There's not much to do. Most of the kids grow up to be just like their parents, farmers who work in the dirt until they die. My father wanted something better than Cedros. He left quite a few years ago, when I was little. I think he went to San Salvador to find a better life. I used to think that he would come back and take me and my mother to the city, but we never heard from him. Now that I'm older, I'm pretty sure he never planned to come back. That happens to some families, you know."

"Unfortunately, yes, that does happen to some families," said Kathleen.

"My mother was left to take care of me," Gabriella continued, "She took in people's laundry and cleaned their houses to make money. She made a lot of sacrifices to take care of me. I love my mother very much. She didn't understand that I wanted a more exciting life. We argued a lot, mostly about Hector. Now I know she was right."

"That happens when girls become teenagers," Kathleen reassured her, "In all families. Mothers and teenage daughters fight. That's part of growing up."

"I said some terrible things to my mother," Gabriella confessed.

"And every girl does the same," Kathleen said, "I said some horrible things to my mother when I was fourteen."

Gabriella started to cry.

"Hector said that my mother was dead," she sobbed, "I'll never be able to tell her I'm sorry. She was right about Hector. He's a gangster and a thug. I want to go back to my mother. I want to apologize and hug her and tell her I love her."

"You said that Hector was a liar," Kathleen tried to reassure the girl, "For all you know, Hector was lying about your mother. She may be alive and very worried about you."

"Do you think so? How will we find out?"

"I think it's possible," Kathleen said, "When we get to San Francisco, we'll see if the United States government, or maybe some friends we have through Project Raphael, can locate her."

"You would do that?"

"Of course," Kathleen said, "You said that you don't want to go to San Francisco. When we get into port, we'll see if we can get you home. Do you have other family?"

"No brothers or sisters," Gabriella said, "I have two aunts and an uncle. And my grandmother."

"Good," said Kathleen, "We'll see if we can work with that. Now, tell me how Hector kidnapped you."

"He came into Cedros with his friends," Gabriella said, "They're all members of *Los Cóndores*. You can tell because they all have a tattoo on their necks of a flying condor. They're a gang. They have nice cars and nice clothes. They have money to spend. And they have guns. People are afraid of them, so they get a lot of respect. Hector found me when I was walking home from school. He told me that I was beautiful."

"You are very beautiful," Kathleen said.

Gabriella ignored the compliment.

"Hector told me that he was in love with me," Gabriella went on, "He took me to restaurants and we ate real nice food, like we had on this ship tonight. He bought me some nice clothes. He took me to a fancy party where there was music and dancing and lots of interesting, sophisticated people. He let me smoke a cigarette once. I didn't like it. That made him laugh."

"And did you love him?" Kathleen asked.

"I thought so," Gabriella said, "I never was in love with anyone before. He kissed me and that felt really good. I let him run his hands over my breasts. That gave me a nice, tingly feeling. It was exciting."

"Did you have sex with Hector?" Kathleen asked.

"No," Gabriella said, "He said he was going to take me on a trip to San Salvador. I thought that we would probably have sex there. We were going to stay in a luxury hotel. But instead of San Salvador, he took me to Acajutla. He said that we were going to stay there one night in a resort, then go to San Salvador."

"But instead he took you somewhere else, didn't he?"

"Yes, he took me to this place on the waterfront," Gabriella said, "It was like a big warehouse. He opened the door and pushed me inside. There were some girls inside a big cage. Lots of *Los Cóndores* were there. They had guns, too. They pushed me into the cage with the other girls. And they laughed at me. All of them. Hector laughed at me, too. He called me a stupid girl."

"Who were the other girls?" Kathleen asked.

"Some were just like me, village girls who were betrayed by men they thought were boyfriends. The youngest were just eleven and twelve. They were just snatched off the street. So was the oldest girl, who was nineteen. They took her when she got off work."

"What did you do?"

"At first I just cried," said Gabriella, "Then I got mad. And I started to try to find a way out of there. Most of the other girls were afraid to try and escape. I forced myself to watch everything and to listen to what the guards were saying. One day, the one they call

El Jefe came to see us. I think he was there to inspect us. We felt like pieces of meat at the market. All the guards were on their best behavior. The guards were watching *El Jefe* more than they were watching us."

"Who is *El Jefe*?" Kathleen asked.

"I don't know," Gabriella said, "I'd never seen him before. He was a short, heavy man. One of the ugliest men I had ever seen. His face was all scarred up, with pits in it. And his eyes looked like a snake."

"Did you get a good look at him?"

"He came into the cage and stared at me. His face was only a few inches from mine," Gabriella said, "I'll never forget his face for the rest of my life. And his eyes were so cold, so cruel. I was so scared that I almost peed myself."

"But you didn't."

"No," Gabriella said, "I kept telling myself to keep calm, not to lose control. The pig got real close, then he reached up and petted my cheek. It was awful. And I bit the son of a bitch. Hard. I tried to bite his thumb off. It made him bleed. He yelled and backed away from me. The guards panicked. I had a chance and I ran away."

"Did any of the other girls get away?" Kathleen asked.

"I don't know," Gabriella said, "I just kept running. One of the guards chased me. I didn't look back. I saw your friends on the waterfront and ran to them. You know the rest."

22

STUART TOOK A stroll around the deck after breakfast in the salon. Both Kathleen and Gabriella looked better, rested after a good sleep. They planned to go below to their stateroom. Standing on the step, he saw Gabriella stop, freeze for a moment, and stare. Then she ran below.

Stuart heard the squeals of a child and watched a little boy run across the deck, pursued by the nurse. The little boy ran right to Stuart and began to jabber. He had a little toy stuffed parrot that he was determined to show Stuart.

"Pardon the child, doctor," the nurse said, trying to corral the little guy, "He just starts running whenever I let him out of the stateroom."

"That's alright," Stuart said, stooping to inspect the little toy, "I like kids. He sure has a lot of energy. Don't you, buddy? What's your name?"

"Manuel."

"Manuel, that's a good name," said Stuart, "I used to know a boy named Manuel. But he was little. And you're very big."

"Yes, I'm big," beamed Manuel.

"Come on, big boy," said the nurse, "Leave the good doctor alone."

Stuart lingered on deck for a quite few minutes, looking at the ocean and thinking. His mind was whirling with bits of data that hadn't yet consolidated into understanding. When he went inside, he knocked on the door of Kathleen's stateroom.

She let him in. Kathleen and Gabriella sat on the bed, leaving the chair for Stuart. Kathleen filled him in about the story Gabriella had told her the night before.

"Gabriella, Kathleen and I are going to talk in English for a few minutes. Is that okay with you?"

"Sure."

"I saw the little boy that Godfrey told us about at dinner, the one who he said had leukemia and was headed for Minnesota," Stuart said.

"Yes. I remember. Where did you see the boy?"

"Out on the deck," Stuart said. He paused. "Kathleen, I know this kid."

"What? How?"

"I saw him in the clinic on the last mission," Stuart said, "His mother brought him in for being pigeon-toed."

"Really?" she asked.

"I remember it well," Stuart said, "His name is Manuel. He was incredibly well behaved and happy. I had the medical student, Dennis Nichols, with me. The little kid was so good that I took the time to show Nichols the proper way to examine a child. The whole thing. Not just the bones and joints, but the heart, lungs, abdomen, eyes, ears, nose, throat, neurological. The little kid and I hit it off, just naturally. He was the last patient of the mission. I gave him the stuffed parrot that I used to distract the little ones. Today on the deck, it was the same. He saw me and came running to me, like we were old buddies. He still has the parrot."

"That's remarkable," Kathleen said.

"One of the things I always teach residents and students about pediatrics is that you start your examination from the doorway to the exam room," Stuart went on, "You just stand there and watch the kid. From the doorway you can tell if a kid is healthy or sick. That helps you a lot before you start talking to the parents or examining the kid."

"I've seen you do that in the clinics before," said Kathleen.

"Well, I just saw little Manuel running all over the deck of this yacht," said Stuart, "I can promise you that this kid is not sick. Combine that with the fact that I personally gave him a complete physical just a couple months ago. There's no way in the world that this kid has leukemia."

"What are you saying, Ray?" Kathleen asked.

"Right now, I'm just saying that there's something not right about the people on this yacht," said Stuart, "Don't say anything about this to Gabriella. And let's be very careful about what we say to anyone on this ship."

Stuart switched to Spanish and looked at Gabriella.

"You recognized the little boy on the deck," he said, "How do you know him?"

"He was in the warehouse where they kept us in the cage," she said, "He wasn't in the cage; they kept him in a separate room. I only saw him once or twice, and only for a second each time. But I recognize his voice. I'm sure he's the little boy from the warehouse."

⁂

Felipe Peña always looked forward to visits from the leaders in El Salvador. Felipe was very proud of how the *Los Cóndores* enterprise was thriving in Oakland. The wholesale cocaine business was well established. The gang was also now entrenched on a small territory of the town near the docks selling cocaine directly to customers. When Pablo and another man arrived in his office, Felipe was eager to see them.

"Welcome to Oakland," beamed Felipe.

"Greetings from El Salvador," said Pablo, who ranked higher than the other man. "*El Jefe* sends you his regards and his congratulations on the fine work you're doing here. The SS Hermione sailed from Acajutla yesterday."

"So, we should expect her in eight or ten days," Felipe said.

"Right," said Pablo, "Are you ready?"

"All is prepared," replied Felipe, "She can unload at the usual dock. There will be no interference from the authorities. The longshoremen will cooperate. We'll have the trucks ready to unload the containers."

"This shipment includes fifty kilos of product," said Pablo.

"We already have buyers for that," said Felipe, "Now that we're selling retail on the streets, we could handle twice that amount."

"Twice?" asked Pablo, "That's a lot of powder."

"Believe me," said Felipe, "We can handle it. We're only limited by the number of members of *Los Cóndores* here in Oakland."

"There are also seven girls on the Hermione," said Pablo, "Do you have destinations for them already?"

"Yes," said Felipe, "But we were expecting eight girls. I have orders for eight."

"There was a slight complication," said Pablo, "The one called Gabriella Cortez, a fourteen year-old, will not be included in the shipment."

Felipe examined some papers on his desk.

"A gentleman in Detroit will be disappointed," said Felipe, "But the gentleman will wait until the next shipment. Or make other arrangements. It's a problem for the Client."

"The money from the drug sales?" asked Pablo.

"Has been transferred to the bank in San Salvador," Felipe replied.

"Very good," said Pablo.

"There is one thing I would like you to discuss with *El Jefe*," said Felipe, "We could use more manpower. Can you send us some more men?"

"From El Salvador?"

"Yes."

"Perhaps," said Pablo, "There may be some young men who would like to move to the United States. You should know that *El Jefe* is very cautious about who he sends far away from his own supervision. These will have to be men that he trusts. Right now, generally, men that *El Jefe* trusts are doing very well in El Salvador."

"Do you think that *El Jefe* would allow us to recruit members locally?" Felipe asked.

"Here in Oakland? Salvadoran men?"

"Yes, there are quite a few young Salvadoran men here in Oakland or other East Bay towns," said Felipe, "The jobs that are available to them pay poorly. They're not respected in the North American society if they have poor jobs. The North Americans are very racially biased. I think that some of the immigrant men might jump at the chance to join us."

"I'll discuss this with *El Jefe*," said Pablo, "But you know how cautious he is."

"I also know how much he likes money," said Felipe, "I can assure you that we can employ many more men here. With a larger work force, we can expand our territory. The expansion will increase the money we return to *Los Cóndores*. "

"We'll discuss this with *El Jefe* when we return to El Salvador," Pablo repeated, "You're doing good work here, Felipe. Don't get overly ambitious."

23

ON THE THIRD day of the voyage, the crew re-arranged the salon to make one table for six. Godfrey and all of his guests could now dine together. Stuart thought that Gabriella was behaving herself well. She always sat next to Kathleen, who whispered running translations to her. Gabriella said nothing, but listened intently. Stuart was deeply troubled by the little boy's presence on the yacht. His suspicions were consolidating, but he didn't have a plan of action yet. It was essential that he maintain a façade of normalcy.

"Have you two figured out what you're going to do with Gabriella when you get to San Francisco?" Lois Godfrey asked.

"Well, we think so," said Stuart, "Now that we've had a little time to think and talk."

"In safety," Kathleen added, "Thanks to you, Dr. Godfrey."

"Please call me Wallace, or Wally," smiled Godfrey, "We're just friends here, Kathleen. We're not in the operating room."

"Thank you, Wallace," Kathleen replied.

"What is your plan?" Lois asked.

"Well, it turns out that young Gabriella here has family in El Salvador and she misses them," Stuart said, "For some reason, sight unseen, she's decided that she doesn't want to stay in San Francisco."

"The uninformed certainty of teenage girls everywhere," added Kathleen, "Now that she feels safe, she wants to go back to her family and friends."

"What about the people she says are trying to kill her?" Lois asked.

"Well," says Stuart, "With a little time and distance between them, Gabriella now seems to think that maybe she can avoid them if she gets back home."

"I hope so," said Lois.

"Now that we've talked, our plan is to contact Customs and Immigration when we land," said Stuart, "They may take her into custody or, hopefully, they may let her stay with Kathleen until things are worked out. We'll see if the federal authorities can make contact with her family in El Salvador. Then we plan to send her home."

"If you need help, Project Raphael has extensive contacts in El Salvador," Dr. Godfrey said, "We know people all over the country. Our network of health professionals is our source of referrals to the clinic. I'm sure that we could use that network to contact her family. Isn't that possible, Bill?"

"Er, yes," said Bill Conklin, "What's her last name again? And where is she from?"

"Her last name is Cortez and she's from a little village called Cedros in the foothills," said Kathleen.

"I'm afraid I never heard of Cedros," said Conklin.

"We can find it," Godfrey said with confidence.

"But there's no reason to worry about that now," said Stuart, "Wait until we get home. I'll let you know if we need your help."

"Okay," said Conklin, "Thanks."

After dinner, Lois Godfrey and Conklin retired to their respective staterooms. Kathleen took Gabriella to the bar area, where a large screen TV was located. They were scanning various video offerings. Gabriella was wide-eyed at the miraculous technology she was seeing for the first time.

Stuart and Godfrey went out on deck for a stroll. Godfrey lit a cigar and sipped on a cognac.

"This is a marvelous way to travel, Wallace," said Stuart, "So peaceful. Nothing really to do."

"I love it, Ray," replied Godfrey, "I know it's an indulgence, but when I get back to San Francisco, there's nothing but nonstop work. I have my practice, which is super busy. The rich clientele I cater to is also very demanding. People think that plastic surgeons work banker's hours. They have no idea. My patients think nothing about calling me in the middle of the night because they think that their chin is sagging or that their breast implants have shifted. Sometimes I think that, if I was really honest with myself, I would admit that I go on Project Raphael missions just to get away from them. Even in Acajutla, business meetings can be stressful, too. Not in the same way as stress in surgery, but stressful nonetheless. I can always count on the voyage to and from Acajutla, though. Being out here on the ocean is healing, rejuvenating for me. There are days when I wish the voyage would never end. No destination, just sail forever on calm seas."

"The seas are calm indeed," said Stuart, "I would have thought we'd have had some big waves, some storm."

"Oh, they happen, Ray, they happen," said Godfrey, "We stay fairly close to the shore, never really go out into the deep stuff. We're rarely farther than ten miles away from the land. Most nights you can see the lights on the buildings on the shore from the deck of the Arariel."

"And where are we now?"

"Off the Baja peninsula," Godfrey replied, "Tomorrow we'll put in for provisions and fuel."

"Do you tie up at a pier or use the dinghy?" Stuart asked.

"We've got to tie up to refuel," Godfrey laughed, "The crew will walk into town and buy provisions."

"I noticed a dinghy and a Zodiac on the second deck." said Stuart, "What do you use them for?"

"When we're at anchor in a harbor, we use the dinghy to run in to the shore," Godfrey explained, "It's our primary lifeboat, should we need it. The Zodiac is mostly a toy. I use it from time to time if I'm going to scuba dive on coral reefs. It's got a dinky little gasoline engine and a gas can like the one people keep in their garage for the lawnmower. It'll only go about twenty miles before it runs out of gas. But it's fun. We don't want the Arariel close to coral reefs."

"Do you dive often?" Stuart asked.

"Never on a Project Raphael mission," Godfrey answered, "Sometimes when I take the Arariel on vacation. Ray, let me change the subject. Are you enjoying the cruise? That teenager complicated your plans, I imagine."

"Yeah," said Stuart, "I have to admit that I didn't plan on a terrified girl throwing herself on my mercy just before the ship left the dock."

"What's going on between you and Kathleen?" Godfrey asked, "I thought for a while that this little voyage might be a romantic one for you two."

"It might have been, Wallace," Stuart said, "I was hoping that we could spend some quiet time together, talk, maybe figure out if there's a future for us."

"Are you in love with her?"

"Maybe," said Stuart, "I've known Kathleen for years. We worked side by side in the operating room in San Francisco. We tease the hell out of each other, exchanging insults and making fun of one another. She's the best damn OR nurse I've ever known. We have this chemistry together in the operating room."

"Does the chemistry extend beyond the operating room?"

"I think it might," said Stuart, "You know we hadn't even spoken to each other since my car wreck. Not until you signed me up for the last mission. Now we're dating. Other than the cases I did at Project Raphael, we haven't worked together in the OR. Instead, I'm seeing her outside of surgery. I like it."

24

"I'M REALLY GETTING scared," Gabriella said.

The statement came out unprovoked and uninvited. Stuart knew that teenagers sometimes blurted things out for no apparent reason, but it always surprised him when it happened.

It was the afternoon of the fourth day at sea. The Arariel had been fueled and provisioned in the morning and they were once again heading north. There was a mild squall and a little chop on the ocean. Nobody wanted to be on deck. Godfrey, Lois, and Conklin were drinking at the bar and chatting in the salon.

Stuart, Kathleen, and Gabriella were gathered in Stuart's cabin. He thought this might be a good opportunity for them to make a few additional plans.

"Why are you scared?" Kathleen asked.

"Why is that little boy on this boat?" Gabriella asked, "Why was he in the warehouse with us girls? Was *Los Cóndores* going to sell him as a slave?"

Stuart was struggling with questions about the little boy himself.

"Gabriella, I need you to think back to when you were in the cage in the warehouse," Stuart said, "This is very important. How do you think *Los Cóndores* planned to transport you girls to San Francisco? You said maybe on a ship."

"Let me think," Gabriella said, "I thought that I told you everything that I can remember that was important."

"How about things that you didn't think were important?" Stuart asked, "Did they ever talk about trucks? Or airplanes? Or the names of ships?"

"I don't remember them talking about those things," Gabriella said, "One of them might have said something about a box."

"Did they use the word 'box'?" Stuart asked, "Might they have meant 'container'? Did they say *contenador* or *caja*?"

"You're right, Dr. Stuart," Gabriella said, "They said *contenador*. I remember now thinking that was weird. I guess I forgot."

"If they were going to send you girls to San Francisco, they would have to make sure you had food," Stuart said, "Did you see any stores of food or water in the warehouse? How did they feed you girls when you were in the cage?"

"There were lots of bottles of water," Gabriella said, "Lots and lots. They gave us little bags of food."

"Did the bags of food come out of boxes labeled 'M.R.E.'?"

"Yes," said Gabriella, "How did you know that?"

"I think that I know how they planned to send you girls to San Francisco," said Stuart, "M.R.E. stands for Meals Ready to Eat in English."

"I guess that makes sense," said Gabriella, "We just opened the box and everything was ready to eat."

"They were developed for soldiers who needed to have food on the battlefield," Stuart explained, "Now you can buy them easily. People use them on vacations and when they're camping. Very convenient. Not great taste, but convenient."

"The boxes of food weren't as good as my mother's cooking," Gabriella said, "But they tasted all right."

"I think that *Los Cóndores* planned to put you girls into a shipping container and load you onto a freighter," Stuart said.

"What's a shipping container?"

"It's a very large metal box that companies use to ship products around the world," said Stuart, "They are stacked inside freighter ships. That's what the big cranes in the harbor are for, to move the containers from the docks to the ships and back."

"What about the little boy?" Gabriella asked, "He's not in a container. He's on this boat with us."

"Manuel was already on this yacht when you escaped from the warehouse. I think that the plan was always for him to go to North America on this boat."

"Why?" asked Kathleen.

"I don't want to talk about what I'm thinking," said Stuart.

Nobody said a word for a few minutes. Then Stuart rose and walked toward the door.

"I need to go on deck for a few minutes," he said.

"It's raining, Ray," said Kathleen.

"I know," he replied, "It'll just be a few minutes."

Outside on the deck, there was a light breeze and a mist of water that hovered between rain and fog. Stuart looked to the west and saw what he thought was sunshine and maybe lighter sky. He made his way up to the bridge of the yacht where the ship's captain was at the helm.

"Hello," Stuart greeted the captain.

"Hello," said the captain, "Dr. Stuart, right? Want to take the wheel for a while?"

"No, thank you," said Stuart, "Just came to enjoy the view."

"Not much to see right now," said the captain.

"The waves are smaller than I expected," said Stuart.

"It's not really a storm," the captain explained, "No big front moving in. Just a little sprinkle. I can't even call it a squall."

"Do you expect that the sky will clear?"

"Oh, yes," said the captain, "The rain will stop around sunset. Then we'll have calm seas and clear sky. The stars should be spectacular tonight. No moon and very little ground light."

"I would have thought that there would be lots of light from the shore," said Stuart, "Aren't we just west of Los Angeles?"

"We passed L.A. two hours ago," said the captain, "You can't see anything of the shore right now because of the overcast. Besides, once we get north of Santa Barbara, it gets pretty dark along the coast."

"Well, if the sky is going to be clear and dark and it's not raining, maybe I'll bring Miss Atwood on deck tonight for a little star gazing," Stuart said, "Thank you, captain."

Stuart lingered on the deck, ignoring the mist. Facts, suppositions, theories, and suspicions swirled in his head.

When Stuart returned to his stateroom, Kathleen was alone.

"Where's Gabriella?" Stuart asked.

"She and I discovered last night that this yacht has a large library of movies that you can watch on the big TV in the salon. Some of the movies are in Spanish," Kathleen said, "This morning, Gabriella and I were playing with the TV in our stateroom and figured out that you can also play the movies in the stateroom. So, she went to our cabin. She's sprawled out on the bed, watching some teenage romance movie. Just like an American teenager. To be honest, I think she wants a distraction to keep her mind off what's really going on here."

"I'm glad she's found a distraction. You and I need to talk and I'd prefer that she not hear what we have to say."

"What's going on?" Kathleen asked.

"I'm afraid that a lot of inconsistencies are resolving and the conclusion is very, very disturbing," Stuart began, "Let me walk you through my observations."

"Go on."

"Let me start with things that I saw on our previous mission that struck me as weird that have nagged at my mind," Stuart said, "When I first came to Project Raphael, Wallace gave me a grand tour of the facility. The tour included the clinical laboratory, which is state-of-the-art and truly remarkable for El Salvador. There is a machine in the laboratory called a Maxwell FSC."

"Never heard of it."

"It's pretty sophisticated for the kinds of patients we see at Project Raphael. It does tissue typing, the kind of stuff they need for transplant surgery."

"Transplant surgery?" said Kathleen, "We don't do that."

"I know," said Stuart, "The Maxwell FSC can do other things, but it's a more powerful machine than we need at Project Raphael. Now, bear with me. Do you remember on the last mission there was a little kid, four or five years old, that Wallace had on the yacht? The kid supposedly had a brain tumor. Wallace was bringing him back to the States and had arranged for surgery in New York."

"Sure, I ran into the little guy when I went to the bathroom the night we had dinner on the Arariel," Kathleen said, "Cute little scamp."

"Okay," said Stuart, "Wallace told me that the boy had a meningioma. That's a benign brain tumor. Depending on where it is in the brain, it can be removed and the patient is cured. I remember questioning the diagnosis, but Wallace said they had sent the kid to San Salvador and had an MRI confirming that it was a meningioma."

"I remember that."

"Meningiomas are tumors of adults," Stuart said, "Mostly older people. To see one in a four or five year-old with no obvious symptoms, well, the correct term is 'unbelievable.' Now we've got a little boy on board this yacht that I personally examined a few months ago. Wallace says he's got leukemia. That, too, is unbelievable."

"What are you saying?" Kathleen asked.

"I'm saying that we've seen two healthy little kids on this yacht," Stuart said, "Neither one of them could possibly have had the diseases that Wallace claimed they had. And I'm saying that Project Raphael has a fancy piece of laboratory equipment that is used for tissue typing, a kind of test that we don't need for plastic surgery or orthopedic cases. We both know that thousands of people die all over the world each year while on waiting lists for organ transplants. There are far more people who need transplanted kidneys and livers and hearts and lungs and whatever than there are organs available. Worldwide, it's well-known that some rich people can buy an organ on a kind of medical black market. People crushed by poverty will happily sell a kidney for cash to feed the family. All over the developing world, there are rumors among the poor that rich people might steal their babies for use as organ donors. Now, I've never seen any proof about stolen babies, but, if people will sell their kidneys, is it possible that they may also sell their children?"

"Are you saying that little Manuel is about to become an involuntary organ donor?" Kathleen asked.

"I hate to say it, but, yes," Stuart replied, "I don't think that little Manuel is going to Minnesota for treatment of leukemia."

"Oh my God," said Kathleen, "Are you sure?"

"I'm pretty sure," said Stuart.

"Does Dr. Godfrey know about this? Is he part of it?"

"I've been trying to think of any scenario that plays out with Wallace as an innocent nonparticipant," said Stuart, "And it's tearing me up inside. But Wallace is the one who told me about the kids' diagnosis and where in the US they were going for treatment.

He told the lies. There's no way that Wallace doesn't know what's going on."

"Oh my God," Kathleen repeated, "What are we going to do?"

"I'm afraid that it's even worse," Stuart said.

"How could it possibly be worse?" she asked.

"There was something else I noticed on our last mission," Stuart said, "You know how we ship equipment and supplies for the missions in containers? One of the containers is twenty feet long and the other forty feet long. Well, I saw the containers when they were being unloaded at Project Raphael. The forty-footer seemed too short inside. I didn't think anything of it at the time."

"But now you think that *Los Cóndores* was using our containers to smuggle girls into San Francisco," Kathleen said.

"That theory also fits the facts," said Stuart, "Back at home, I was consulted by the San Francisco Police Department about a body they fished out of the bay. It was a teenage girl. She probably died from tuberculosis. She was Salvadoran. I think she was a victim of human trafficking. What if she was in one of the containers? The gang that kidnapped Gabriella is called *Los Cóndores*. Gabriella said the gang members have a tattoo of a condor on their necks. Well, the men who unpack our containers at Project Raphael all have tattoos of condors on their necks. And most of them seem to be packing pistols. The company that they work for is LC Freight."

"LC" said Kathleen, "*Los Cóndores*. My God. Do you think Dr. Godfrey is involved with human trafficking as well? I can't believe it."

"I don't want to believe it," Stuart said, "Maybe he doesn't know about the trafficking. God, I hope he doesn't know. I've known Wallace Godfrey for twenty years."

"As have I," Kathleen said, "He's one of the kindest, most dedicated doctors I've ever known. He's vain and egotistical, but I can't believe he'd be involved with something so, so evil."

"I hope it's not true, Kathleen," said Stuart, "I hope there's a better explanation."

"What are we going to do, Ray?" Kathleen asked, "Are we safe on this yacht?"

"I think that you and I are safe," Stuart said, "Nobody knows that we suspect anything. But I'm worried about Gabriella. They may not want her telling stories. What worries me even more is little Manuel. We need to get to the authorities before Manuel arrives in San Francisco. The only thing we can do is get Gabriella and ourselves off this yacht."

"How? When?"

"Tonight," said Stuart, "And I have a plan. There are some risks, but I think it'll work."

25

SUPPER ON THE yacht that evening was important for many reasons. The food was exceptional. The chef prepared steak *au pouvre*, using some exquisite filet mignon he found when he went ashore for provisions. He paired it with a fine French Bordeaux, which everyone except Stuart and Gabriella enjoyed. Stuart found the conversation to be subdued. That was a relief.

"Will we make it to San Francisco tomorrow?" Kathleen asked.

"I believe so," said Godfrey, "I spoke with the captain. He expects clear skies and calm seas all night tonight and tomorrow. If we maintain our current speed, we should be at the dock by suppertime."

"Where do you berth this yacht, Wallace?" Stuart asked, "She seems rather large for most of the marinas I know. Do you tie her up in Sausalito?"

"Actually, I have a berth at Oyster Point," said Godfrey, "You're right, the Arariel is too big for the main marina. There's another marina farther south from the one you know. Not too many people even know it's there. Only a few berths, but all of them accommodate larger yachts."

"It's actually very convenient," Conklin added, "Easy freeway access. A quick trip into downtown or to the airport."

After an elegant dessert of German chocolate cake, Stuart, Kathleen, and Gabriella excused themselves and retired to their staterooms. Stuart followed the girls into their cabin.

"Get some sleep," Stuart said, "Meet me in my stateroom at 2 A.M. Don't knock, just come in. Wear the warmest clothes you've got. Make layers."

"Why?" asked Gabriella.

"Can you swim?" Stuart asked her.

Gabriella looked frightened.

"No."

"You'll be alright," Stuart assured her, "Kathleen and I will take care of you. But we can't stay on the Arariel any more."

"We're afraid that you may be in danger," Kathleen said, "You know about the girls in the cage and you know that the little boy was in the warehouse. There is something bad going on here. We don't want you to be on the yacht when it lands in San Francisco."

"So, we're getting off tonight," Stuart said, "All three of us."

"Getting off?" Gabriella asked.

"Yes," Stuart said, "We're going ashore a little early."

"Do we have to swim?" Gabriella was on the verge of panic.

"No, no, we won't be swimming," Stuart assured her, "We're going to take one of the small boats on the upper deck."

"The lifeboat?" Gabriella asked.

"No, the smaller rubber boat," said Stuart, "They call it a Zodiac. We'll take it into shore. You'll be safe once we're on land. Don't worry. Kathleen and I will make sure you're safe on the water. You'll have a life jacket and you won't have to swim. Both of us are good swimmers. Now, try to get some sleep."

"What about the little boy?" Gabriella asked.

"We'll be ashore before this yacht arrives at the dock," Stuart explained, "We'll notify the police and they'll be there to help the boy. American police aren't like the police in El Salvador. Besides, I have a good friend with the police who I trust. He'll make sure that Manuel is protected."

None of them could sleep. Stuart knew that they wouldn't. Things kept running over and over in his head. No matter how hard he tried, he couldn't escape the conclusion that innocent children were being transported out of El Salvador, probably to be used as involuntary organ donors.

There were alternative explanations for the trafficking of the girls that did not include Project Raphael, but none that so well fit the facts. He hoped that he was completely wrong.

There was little that Stuart could not leave behind in his stateroom. He needed his passport, his wallet, and the Swiss Army knife that he always carried. The rest was superfluous. He almost left behind the prosthetic eye. It would be a nuisance on the escape trip, but it would be expensive to replace. The glass eye went into a pocket with a zipper. He wore his eyepatch.

Promptly at two, the door to the stateroom opened. Kathleen and a trembling Gabriella entered silently. Stuart put his finger to his lip to remind them to keep silent, then motioned for the girls to follow him into the corridor.

The Arariel was asleep. The only sound was the rhythmic purr of the engines.

Stuart heard snoring as they passed Conklin's stateroom on their way aft. There were no voices, no footsteps save their own.

Stuart slipped out onto the deck. The sky was clear and there were billions of stars. The night was moonless and the ocean was opaque. He found a box containing life jackets. Quietly, he removed three. Passing two to Kathleen and Gabriella, he motioned for them to remain hidden. Soundlessly, Stuart crept forward. Looking up near the bow of the yacht, he could see a single crewman on the bridge, hand on the wheel. The man looked bored, glancing occasionally at the navigational instruments but mostly gazing out on the black sea.

Stuart moved silently aft, mounted a ladder leading to the upper deck. Crouching low, he made his way to the Zodiac. He easily untied the little craft, which had a small outboard engine and a tank of gasoline. He detached the engine and the tank, then tested the weight of the empty Zodiac. To his relief, it was not at all heavy. Stuart slid it over the edge of the upper deck and it came to a soft landing on the main deck. He was happy to see a shadowy Kathleen emerge and place a restraining hand on the little rubber boat. Grabbing the outboard and the gas tank, Stuart descended the after stairs onto the main deck.

In another box on the deck, Stuart found a stout rope. One end was fixed in a knot. This he secured to a cleat on the starboard side.

He put the outboard and the gas tank in the Zodiac, then quietly pushed the craft over the side. The yacht was making good headway and there was a strong pull on the rope when the Zodiac contacted the water. Stuart quickly threw a couple of loops around another cleat. The Zodiac, thus lashed, remained firmly alongside.

Stuart motioned to Kathleen and Gabriella. He spoke in Spanish and in a whisper.

"Kathleen, lower yourself into the Zodiac," Stuart said, "Be ready to help Gabriella."

Kathleen nodded wordlessly and seized the rope. Stuart supported the rope on the back of the yacht, although the cleat held the rope fast. Kathleen gave a thumbs up when she was inside the Zodiac.

"Now you," Stuart whispered to Gabriella.

Her eyes conveyed pure terror. Stuart tightened her life vest in a gesture that was more reassuring than mechanically necessary. He looked into her eyes, then gave her a gentle hug. The hug got firmer as Stuart lifted her off her feet. Gabriella gasped.

"Come on," he whispered, "Kathleen will help you into the boat. Grab onto the rope."

Trembling, Gabriella seized the rope. Stuart lifted her legs over the rail.

"I've got you," Stuart whispered, "Let your foot slide down until you get to the Zodiac. Kathleen will take you then."

Stuart saw her lips part in what might become either a word or a scream.

"Don't talk," Stuart said firmly, "I'm right here and Kathleen is right there. Now, let go of my neck with your other hand and use it to hold the rope."

Tremulously, Gabriella complied. She now had both legs and both hands off Stuart. She wrapped both legs around the rope and grasped it with both hands. She held on like her life depended on it. She didn't move at all. Kathleen reached up and grabbed a leg, gently pulling Gabriella. Slowly, Gabriella relaxed and began to move toward the water. Sliding into Kathleen's arms, Gabriella arrived in the Zodiac.

Stuart released a sigh of relief, then hoisted himself over the rail, sliding down into the little rubber boat. He took out his Swiss Army knife and cut the rope.

The Zodiac drifted free as the Arariel cruised unknowingly to the north. Little sparkles in the water marked the yacht's wake. Stuart was a little surprised at how quickly the Arariel distanced itself from them.

Even a calm sea is not entirely flat. Gentle swells raised and lowered the Zodiac. The sea was black and merged imperceptibly with the sky. Glorious stars glowed and twinkled, but provided no useful illumination. On the surface the only light was from the gradually vanishing Arariel.

They sat in silence watching the yacht disappear. Stuart looked at the stars, trying to remember something of the astronomy section of the physics class he took as an undergraduate. Somewhere up there was the North Star. He would need to find it if they were going to get ashore. There was something about following the line of the cup of the Big Dipper.

There were two small paddles in the Zodiac, but they just drifted while Stuart tried to figure out a course. There were no visible lights from the land. Everything was black ocean and black sky. For now, it didn't seem to matter in which direction they drifted.

Stuart knew that the Arariel was on a heading due north. That helped him to find the North Star. Once the yacht's lights were gone, the star would be their only guide to navigation. Without it, he knew they would wander aimlessly. When he was sure that the Arariel was long gone, he attached the little outboard, pulled the cord, and was thrilled when the motor started up.

"We can talk now," Stuart said.

"It's beautiful," said Gabriella. She lay flat on her back, her eyes fixed on the heavens. Her fears were temporarily replaced by wonder.

"Which way do we go?" asked Kathleen, ever practical, "Everything looks the same. Which way did the Arariel go?"

"We're going east," said Stuart, pointing over the bow of the Zodiac, "As lovely as the stars are tonight, I won't be happy until we beach this thing in good old California."

"How do you know we're headed in the right direction?" Kathleen asked, "Do you have a compass?"

"Well, I don't exactly have a compass," said Stuart, pointing to the sky, "I'm pretty sure that really bright star is the North Star. I'm taking a bearing from it. Just like the ancient sailors did. I know which way is north, and I go ninety degrees clockwise. All I have to do is keep the North Star to our left. Then we'll be going east. And east will be California. It's important that we stay on course. We don't have a whole lot of gas for the motor."

"I hope you know what you're doing," Kathleen replied, "You look like a pirate with your eye patch."

"Aargh!" he said.

"Where's your sword, Captain Kidd?"

"Not a sword, Lassie, it's me cutlass," he retorted, "I left it with me brace of pistols on the Arariel."

"And the compass."

"But I've still got me dagger."

"Your Swiss Army knife?"

"Aye, Lassie."

"Dear God, I'm stuck with a one-eyed pirate and no compass," Kathleen teased, "Pray tell me, good captain, where in California do you think will we land?"

"Well, we passed Los Angeles and we haven't gotten to San Francisco yet, so we're somewhere between L.A. and San Francisco," Stuart said," I really can't be more accurate than that. The ancient mariners had no way to establish latitude, and neither do I."

Gabriella was puzzled listening to the conversation.

"Are we lost?" she asked, "Lost at sea?"

"No," Stuart replied, "We're not lost. We know what we need to know. Just relax and enjoy the trip."

They puttered along silently in the Zodiac for perhaps an hour. Stuart emptied the gas can into the little outboard. Gabriella pointed ahead and to the left.

"What's that?" she asked, "I see a light. It twinkles, but not like the stars."

Stuart and Kathleen strained to follow Gabriella's pointing finger.

"It's a lighthouse," said Kathleen, "Pretty far in the distance, but I think that's the light of a lighthouse."

"Yes, you're right," Stuart agreed, "And I think I know which one. That's Pigeon Point, in Pescadero. We want to stay south of that."

"Why?" asked Kathleen.

"The beaches there and to the north are mixed with lots of rocks," said Stuart, "And lots of mussels on the rocks. Mussel shells are sharp. They'll tear the fabric of this little Zodiac to shreds. Not to mention the soles of our feet. A little farther to the south there are some sandy beaches at the base of the cliffs. We'll want to beach the Zodiac on the sand, not the rocks."

"You said cliffs," said Kathleen, "I've driven along that part of the coast. It's a long way down to the water."

"I know," said Stuart, "There are some trails that people use to get down to the beach. We'll find a trail and hike up to Highway One."

"And then what?" Kathleen asked.

"We'll find someplace to make a few phone calls," said Stuart.

"It's pretty deserted down there," Kathleen said.

"There's a youth hostel at Pigeon Point," said Stuart, "Once we get up on the cliff, we can hike there, if we don't find something first."

The first tiny rays of sunrise poked over the coastal mountains as they approached the shoreline. They could faintly hear the sounds of the waves breaking on the shore. The ocean remained black and there were no lights on the land save for the lighthouse on the cliff.

All three of them had their eyes fixed straight over the bow of the Zodiac. Nobody could see much, but the anticipation demanded their full attention.

The little outboard motor coughed once and died.

"Shit," said Stuart.

"What did he say?" Gabriella asked, getting a little nervous.

"It's a thing that surgeons say," Kathleen explained, "There's no good Spanish translation. Just be quiet and let him work."

Stuart yanked the chord over and over. It was futile. The motor was out of gas.

"Kathleen, grab a paddle," Stuart said, "We're going to have to make our landing the old-fashioned way."

"Aye, aye, Captain Kidd," she teased, handing a paddle to Stuart.

"Aargh!" replied Stuart.

"Where's the treasure buried, Captain?" asked Kathleen, dipping her paddle deeply into the water.

"On the beach, me matey," Stuart said, "It's all on the beach."

"What's going on?" Gabriella asked.

"Captain Kidd just ran out of gas," Kathleen said, "We're close to the beach. We'll paddle the rest of the way in. Don't worry. We're almost there."

"Who's Captain Kidd?"

Stuart and Kathleen made slow progress, but it was progress. They could hear the sound of the breaking waves getting closer, even if they couldn't see much.

"Oh, shit!" yelled Stuart, "Kathleen, paddle backward!"

"Huh? Backward?"

In the trough of a wave, Stuart saw the rocks just ahead and to the left. He had only moments to try and turn the Zodiac to the right.

Not enough time.

A wave picked up the little boat and dropped the bow right onto the rocks. There was a hissing sound that could be heard above the waves as the air rushed out of the Zodiac. Razor sharp mussel shells sliced right through the inflatable hull.

"Kathleen, bail out to your right," Stuart commanded, "Gabriella, come to me."

Kathleen slipped over the side. Stuart watched her bob in the water, flick back her hair, and begin stroking for the beach. They had run aground on the last outcropping of rocks before the small sandy open beach to the right. Two or three yards more to the right and they would have been fine. In the dim light before dawn, Stuart couldn't guess the distance to the beach. He grabbed Gabriella by the life jacket and drew her close to him. She was shaking with fear.

"Gabriella, do you trust me?" Stuart asked, holding her face close to his.

Gabriella nodded.

"Grab onto of my life jacket and hold on tight," Stuart said, "You're going to ride while I swim. It's just a short way to the beach."

Gabriella grabbed the orange vest as tightly as she could. Stuart slid backward over the rapidly deflating Zodiac.

The water was icy cold. The sudden chill took Stuart's breath away. He knew that nobody voluntarily swam in the Pacific Ocean off this part of the California coast without a wetsuit. He knew there was not much time before hypothermia would begin. It would start with an overpowering fatigue. He would be unconscious when his heart stopped. He sent off a quick, desperate prayer for strength and endurance.

The life vest kept Stuart's face out of the water most of the time. He got an occasional mouthful, but never stopped swimming. Gabriella clung to him, an expression of terror on her face. Stuart had no idea that his eyepatch had slipped down around his neck, putting Gabriella only inches from the empty eye socket.

Gabriella's teeth were chattering, as much from fear as from the cold water. Still, she maintained a desperate grip on Stuart's life jacket.

Stuart employed a backstroke. He stayed near the surface, letting each wave carry them closer to the shore. Occasionally, he would let one foot drop down, feeling for the bottom.

"Ray, Ray!" came Kathleen's voice ahead and to the right. "I'm right here, Ray! I'm on the beach! Swim to me!"

Stuart angled toward her voice. He lowered a foot and the strong undertow pulled him out toward the sea. Stuart let himself drift out a little, then flattened out on the surface and pulled hard on the backstroke.

At last he felt sand under his feet. Stuart dropped both feet into the sand and braced himself against the undertow. He put an arm around Gabriella. When the wave receded, he walked backward toward the beach, never turning his back to the ocean. When the water was shallow enough, he put his other arm under Gabriella's legs and carried her. She didn't relax her grip on the life jacket until he set her gently onto the sand.

"Oh, Ray!" said Kathleen when she ran up to him. She threw her arms around his neck and kissed him hard. Locked in each other's arms, they collapsed in the sand next to Gabriella.

All three of them sat in the sand, shivering in the cold, holding on to each other for both warmth and consolation. After nearly an hour, the light was sufficient for them to see that they were alone on a little beach perhaps thirty yards long and fifteen feet deep. The cliff looming above them was at least fifty feet high. There was no obvious path to the top.

"I don't see a path," said Kathleen.

Stuart realized that his eye patch was around his neck and pulled it back in place covering the empty socket. He stared at the rocks above them.

"There is no path," he said, "But there are lots of cracks and spaces between the rocks. Gabriella, look up there. Do you think you can climb up those rocks?"

"Yes, Dr. Stuart," she replied, "I can't swim, but I can climb. If you and Kathleen can do it, so can I."

Carefully and slowly, they ascended the cliff, which was nearly vertical. Stuart took the lead, testing each new rock as he climbed. Gabriella followed, making sure to use the same rocks on which Stuart had put his weight. None of them dared look down to the beach.

At last, Stuart felt some scraggly weeds in his hand as he reached the top. He pulled himself up and lay prone. He extended his hand. Gabriella seized it and he pulled her to the top. Kathleen followed, pulled the final yard by Stuart's strong arm.

The morning's light was brighter. The three of them stood up in the weeds and took in the spectacular view of the ocean. There was a fairly stiff breeze blowing up from the beach which chilled them, but they were at least beginning to dry out. Behind them was the empty winding asphalt of Highway One. Other than the lighthouse to the north, they saw no buildings.

"See, we made it," Stuart said, "No problems. Just like I planned it."

"Yeah, right," said Kathleen.

"What are you two saying?" Gabriella asked, "Speak Spanish!"

"You don't need to know everything," Kathleen replied, "There are some communications between doctors and nurses that must be confidential."

They trudged along the highway, headed toward the Pigeon Point Light Station. It sat on a small, sharp peninsula and stood majestically near the tip. The white tower stood as a guide and a beacon to ships and now served a similar function for the three hungry and thirsty hikers. A grey-black cupola topped the white concrete. They saw no people. When they came close, they found a dirt path bounded on the left with a short wooden fence, which ran along the cliff. To the right was a stout rope suspended between posts. There was a building to the left of the light tower and some smaller ones to the right.

As they approached the buildings, they saw occasional people darting in and out of the lower buildings. Still closer and they picked up the unmistakable smells of bacon and coffee. They picked up the pace and followed their noses to a building with a big open kitchen and a small group of college-age kids.

"Hi," greeted a pretty African-American girl, "Welcome. Want some coffee?"

"Hey, where'd you come from?" asked a young man with long hair in a pony tail, "No offense, but you look like you just washed ashore on the beach."

"Yes, yes, oh God yes," Kathleen accepted the girl's offer, "I really need some coffee."

Stuart addressed the young man.

"What I need first is a phone," he said, "Then maybe a bathroom."

26

"I'M QUITE CERTAIN they're not on board, sir," said the captain of the Arariel, "The Zodiac is gone."

"Damn," said Godfrey. This was a problem, "Any idea when they left?"

"Sometime after midnight, sir," said the captain, "I made my regular inspection of the ship at midnight. All was quiet and all our guests were in their staterooms. After midnight, I just had one crewmember on the bridge. He didn't see anything."

"And where were we at that time?" Godfrey asked.

"Midnight? Off the coast of Monterey. Shall I notify the Coast Guard, sir?"

"Thank you, captain, but I'll take care of that," said Godfrey. Notifying the Coast Guard was the absolute last thing he was going to do.

Deep in thought, Godfrey proceeded to the salon where he sat down with Conklin. Lois was sleeping in, giving the two men a chance to talk. A crewman served their breakfasts.

"It's true," said Godfrey, "All three of them left sometime after midnight last night. Stuart, Atwood, and the girl. They took the Zodiac."

"Do you think they made it to shore?" Conklin asked.

"We must assume that they did," said Godfrey, "We're not far off the coast. We were near Monterey at midnight. That's a good-sized city and the beaches are good. North of Monterey there are good beaches and scattered small towns. We don't know exactly when they jumped ship, but we must assume that they made it ashore."

"How much do they know?" asked Conklin.

"I have no idea," Godfrey admitted, "I didn't know that Stuart had any suspicions at all."

"They must know something or they wouldn't have fled in the middle of the night," said Conklin, "I bet that damn girl told them about the container. I knew she was trouble the minute she came aboard. Do they suspect that the little boy isn't what we told them?"

"Why would they?" asked Godfrey.

"He was in the warehouse with the girls," Conklin said, "Maybe the girl saw him."

"Christ, I don't know," said Godfrey, "These idiots we hired in El Salvador have made a colossal mess of the whole thing."

"What are we going to do?" asked Conklin.

Godfrey scratched his chin. He had been desperately thinking since he got the news that his guests had disappeared.

"We've got to get the little boy out of the United States as quickly as possible," he said, "We dock very close to the airport. I'll make a few phone calls. We'll have a limo at the dock when we arrive. We can whisk the boy and Ms. Santiago right off to the airport. We'll have the plane ready for takeoff. The plane usually refuels in Houston, I think. We need to get the hell out of US airspace as quickly as possible."

"I agree," said Conklin, "We can arrange for the plane to refuel in Monterrey, Mexico. We should be able to keep the aircraft away from the US authorities until it unloads in Saudi Arabia."

"What if we had the plane land in Cairo instead of Riyadh?" said Godfrey, "Ms. Santiago and the boy could travel to Saudi Arabia by boat or even overland from Cairo. That way the authorities should never learn about the hospital in Jazan. The boy and the nurse will simply disappear into the Cairo crowds. Yes, I think that will work."

"What about the container?" asked Conklin.

"That could be a much bigger problem," said Godfrey, "The Hermione is at least two days behind us. It's much more likely that the girl told Stuart and Ms. Atwood something to make them suspicious about the girls in the container. Unfortunately, they have plenty of time to work with the authorities to intercept that shipment. Kathleen knows the name of the ship we use. It won't take long to figure out the dock where it's supposed to land."

"We're fucked," said Conklin.

"Don't give up so fast, Bill," said Godfrey, "Do you know how to contact the leader of *Los Cóndores* in Oakland?"

"No," said Conklin, "Valdez is very secretive. He doesn't like me much. He prefers dealing with the person he knows only as the Client."

"It's better if Valdez doesn't know a lot of names," said Godfrey, "The man is scum, subhuman you might say. Do you know if the captain of the Hermione is part of our organization?"

"Yes, bought and paid for," replied Conklin, "He may not know all the details, but he knows that the contents of the containers are special. My guess is that he suspects the cocaine, but not the girls."

"Good," said Godfrey as the solution became clear to him, "Here's what we're going to do. Get word to the captain of the Hermione to expect guests when he's off the Farallon Islands. We'll take our cargo off the ship while it's still at sea. If the cops are waiting on the dock for the Hermione to land, they'll find an empty container."

"How are you going to arrange that?" asked Conklin.

"Leave that to me," said Godfrey, "Give me an hour, then I'll have the Client contact Valdez in El Salvador. He can coordinate with his people in Oakland. We still have a good chance to win this game."

Gabriella's nose was pressed against the back window of Stuart's Jeep. Though she was exhausted, her eyes were wide open.

"This is San Francisco?" Gabriella said.

"Part of it," said Kathleen, "We call it the Sunset District. This is the part of the city where I live. The street we're on is called Sunset Boulevard."

"The houses are so huge," Gabriella said, "Which one is yours?"

"You'll see soon," said Kathleen, "I don't think of my house as particularly huge."

"That depends on what you're comparing it to," said Stuart, "Gabriella, we need to take you for a drive around San Francisco."

"You mean there's more?" Gabriella asked.

"Much more," said Kathleen, "Are you hungry?"

"Oh, yes," Gabriella said, "The bacon at the place by the lighthouse was good, but I could definitely eat more."

"There's not much food at my house," Kathleen said, "But we'll get some. More than food, I need some sleep and a hot shower. Ray, just drop us off in front of my house and you go back to your place and take a shower. I'll call you when we're ready. I need to get Gabriella some clothes and I need to stock the kitchen. All that comes after the shower and the nap."

"Fair enough," said Stuart, "You know, the Arariel is scheduled to dock in just a couple of hours."

"Try to forget about it," said Kathleen, "It's out of our hands. Let's just hope your friend in the SFPD gets there in time."

Gabriella felt safe for now. She was eager to see the house where Kathleen lived. The time for scary thoughts and worrying could wait.

◆ ◆ ◆

Bill Conklin couldn't believe how well things were going. He kept looking from side to side and behind him, fearing some catastrophe was about to occur. But here he was, at the general aviation terminal at San Francisco International Airport.

Everything had gone perfectly. A limo was waiting for them at Oyster Point. He, Nurse Daniella Santiago, and little Manuel Cuellar were inside the limo and driving away before the Arariel was fully tied up. The ride to SFO was smooth and swift, unusual given the normal San Francisco traffic. Daniella Santiago had little Manuel well sedated and curled comfortably in a stroller. The American authorities accepted Manuel's forged papers without even a hint of suspicion. Of course. When one was dealing with precious commodities on the international market, one could afford the best forgers.

Cleared to go, Conklin and Nurse Santiago, who was pushing the stroller, arrived at the departure gate. Conklin would not be making the trip. He handed Santiago papers with detailed instructions about who would meet the plane in Cairo and who the contacts would be between Cairo and the hospital in Saudi Arabia. Daniella Santiago was quite experienced in the transportation of patients and donors to the hospital. She had escorted people from literally all over the world. Conklin smiled at the Gulfstream G550 private jet standing ready on the tarmac, the stairs lowered. A uniformed blonde-haired woman approached.

"Mr. Conklin?" the woman asked politely, "I'm Gloria Savage. I'll be your flight attendant today. Ms. Santiago, I presume. And who is our sleepy little traveler today?"

"I'm not going on the flight," Conklin told her, "but we've got a few changes in the route. May I come aboard and pass the new itinerary to the pilot?"

"Of course," replied Ms. Savage, stepping aside to allow Conklin to ascend the stairs.

Daniella Santiago lifted the sleeping little boy out of the stroller and followed Conklin up the gangway. Ms. Savage brought up the rear, carrying the stroller.

Conklin turned into the cockpit. The two pilots were pointing to the cockpit instruments and talking to one another. The pilot in the left seat was unfamiliar.

"Excuse me, Captain," Conklin said, reaching into his pocket for an envelope of flight instructions.

The pilot rose from his seat. He was tall and thin and very black.

"Mr. Conklin, I'm Special Agent Walter Reynolds, FBI," said the pilot, "You are under arrest for human trafficking."

Conklin shot a look at the still open door to his left, the gangway still leading to the ground. Ms. Savage had left the stroller blocking the door.

Reynolds displayed a Glock 9mm semi-automatic and pointed it right at Conklin.

"Just give me a reason, you bastard," Reynolds said.

The tone of Reynolds' voice told Conklin that the FBI man was serious.

Pistols appeared in the hands of Ms. Savage and the co-pilot. Uniformed police officers appeared at the foot of the gangway.

Unaware that his life had been saved, little Miguel Cuellar slept through the whole thing.

♦ ♦ ♦

Stuart's phone calls to SFPD and the FBI set the authorities in rapid motion. Duane Wilson and Walter Reynolds asked Stuart if he and Kathleen could hang on to Gabriella for a few days. Once the authorities dealt with the traffickers, there would be plenty of time to sort out Gabriella's immigration status.

That arrangement was more than acceptable to Stuart and Kathleen.

Stuart found Kathleen and Gabriella jabbering happily in the kitchen. Gabriella wore a colorful rib knit tie dye dress. It was a virtual kaleidoscope of purple and blue and green in fabric. Gabriella was grinning from ear to ear.

"We just had time for a little trip to the store," said Kathleen, "I bought Gabriella that dress and a pair of sandals. We just got enough food for tonight's supper. Tomorrow we'll shop in earnest."

Stuart couldn't suppress his grin.

"You two look a thousand percent better than when I dropped you off," he said, "If I wasn't an eye witness, I'd never believe what you've been through. What's for supper?"

"We're making shrimp scampi," beamed Gabriella, "Kathleen is teaching me."

"Have you ever had shrimp scampi before?" Stuart asked.

"No, but it smells wonderful and sounds delicious," Gabriella replied, "And we're going to have some fresh asparagus to go with it."

Kathleen owned a duplex house in the outer Sunset district. It had a nice dining area with a table for four. The conversation was light during supper, with Kathleen telling funny stories to Gabriella about the adventures she and Stuart had in surgery, both in San Francisco and on medical missions. Gabriella almost danced rather than walked as she cleared the supper dishes from the table.

At nine o'clock Kathleen could restrain herself no longer.

"Did they catch them?" she whispered in English.

"Yes," Stuart replied, "I heard from Detective Wilson that the FBI stopped the plane before it could take off. Conklin and the nurse are under arrest and little Manuel is safe. I'll be meeting with Duane Wilson tomorrow morning."

Kathleen made the sign of the cross.

"Thank you, Lord."

Gabriella re-appeared in the dining room.

"Are you praying?" Gabriella asked.

"Yes," Kathleen said, switching to Spanish, "Dr. Stuart just told me that the North American federal police just arrested Mr. Conklin and the nurse. They saved the life of the little boy who was on the yacht with us."

"I'm glad," Gabriella said, sighing with relief, "I was really worried about the little boy."

"Now I think I'll be able to sleep tonight, knowing that Manuel is safe," Kathleen said.

"Maybe we all will," Gabriella said.

Stuart rose from the table, ready to leave.

"You two are shopping in the morning," he said, "And I have a meeting with Duane. How about tomorrow afternoon for a tour of the city with Gabriella? Maybe supper in Sausalito to cap off the day?"

"We're going to need more than just the morning for shopping. In the first place, I plan to sleep late. Let's postpone the city tour. We'll meet you for supper," said Kathleen, "By the way, I'm impressed that Gabriella gets the first-class treatment. You never take me to Sausalito."

"You're invited tomorrow. Quit your complaining."

27

Dr. Yousef Al-Saffar saw the concern on the face of his friend and colleague, Ali Darwish. Something was very wrong.

"Why the grim look, Ali?" the doctor asked.

"The American FBI seized Nurse Santiago and the donor that she was bringing from El Salvador," said Ali, "They got William Conklin, too."

"Who's William Conklin?" asked Al-Saffar.

"He's a financial guy who helps facilitate transportation for donors from El Salvador," Ali responded.

"How much does he know?"

"Very little," said Ali, "He knows where our hospital is located and some of the payment channels, but not much more. Nurse Santiago has far more knowledge."

"I know Ms. Santiago," Al-Saffar replied, "She's totally committed to the mission we have here. She'll never betray us."

"What about the loss of the donor?"

"Well, now that's a medical issue," said Al-Saffar.

The doctor walked to his desk and turned on his computer.

"Give me a moment, Ali, to look at the database," Al-Saffar said.

"What will you tell the patient who is waiting for the heart transplant?" Ali asked.

"Nothing," replied Al-Saffar, "The patient doesn't know that we have a donor. This is a heart transplant, remember? Normally, the recipient of a heart transplant is on call with a bag packed. We only notify our heart patients a few hours before we expect them to report here. That's one of the reasons why we do such extensive medical work-ups on our patients before we look for a donor. Most of our patients have access to private aircraft. This particular recipient is in Vienna."

"How difficult will it be to find another donor?" asked Ali.

"Not difficult at all, my friend," smiled the doctor, "I've got one already. And not too far away. There is a perfectly compatible donor in Lagos. We can have her here in a few days."

"Are you worried about the American FBI?" asked Ali.

"Only a little," said Al-Saffar, "The Americans will only have a few pieces of the puzzle. The FBI has no jurisdiction in Saudi Arabia. Even if they think they have evidence to pursue us, they'll need to work through Interpol or some such agency. We have enough contacts and influence here in Saudi Arabia that we'll have ample warning of any police inquiry. Frankly, I think this will just be a minor inconvenience."

♦ ♦ ♦

"Understood, *Jefe*," said Felipe Peña, "When the police come to meet the SS Hermione at the dock, they'll be lonely and disappointed. We can do this, *Jefe*. You can count on me."

Felipe broke the phone connection. He was seated in his office in Oakland. He had little time and much to do. Giancarlo Valdez had called with an emergency change of plans. The operation was blown by some teenage girl who escaped from the warehouse in Acajutla. For a minute, Felipe wondered which of Giancarlo's boys had brought that girl in for shipment. He knew that it didn't matter. *El Jefe* had, no doubt, disposed of that fellow by now.

He had the names of two men with boats at the Oyster Point marina in San Francisco. Each had a forty-foot motor yacht suitable for ocean sailing. Felipe decided to take both of them. He would need three of his men in each yacht. They would divide the girls between the yachts. He alone would guard the cocaine.

Felipe had little time to waste. The rendezvous was tomorrow night. He decided which of his men would come on this mission. He had to choose which weapons they would need. This was an impromptu undertaking. There was no time to plan for unforeseen contingencies. Better, he thought, to have extra firepower. It would be at night, so they would need the handheld radios they used at the San Francisco warehouse attack.

Felipe called the men with the yachts. He explained the plan and they agreed to a price. The men with the yachts asked very few questions. They were both expecting the phone calls. They were acquaintances of Dr. Godfrey. He had contacted them from the Arariel.

♦ ♦ ♦

Duane Wilson reserved a small conference room at police headquarters for this meeting. Stuart was the last to arrive.

Three people were already seated at the table. Special Agent Walter Reynolds, a female Coast Guard Lieutenant Commander and Detective Will Chen.

"Dr. Raymond Stuart," Duane said, "Let me introduce Lt. Commander Noreen LeBlanc from the Alameda Base and Detective Will Chen of the Oakland Police Department. You already know FBI Special Agent Walter Reynolds."

Hands were shaken all around. Before Duane could start the meeting, Reynolds spoke.

"Dr. Stuart," Reynolds began, "I want to personally thank you for the information you gave to help us take down that bastard Conklin. You saved the little boy's life."

"I'm glad I could help," said Stuart, "But, to be honest, I need to give credit to a fourteen year-old girl named Gabriella Cortez from El Salvador, who escaped from the warehouse where the victims were being held. She recognized Manuel from the warehouse. Without her help I would have never quite gotten my mental arms around the magnitude of the evil that Conklin was involved with. It's beyond my imagination."

"Believe me, I understand," said Reynolds, "When I came face to face with that bastard and saw that innocent little kid, well, it took every shred of my self-control to just arrest him and not put a bullet right between his eyes."

"Where is Manuel Cuellar now? The little boy," Stuart asked.

"We have him in protective custody," said Reynolds, "He's safe. He's so young that he has very little to tell us. The State Department is contacting his family in El Salvador. We'll get him home as quickly as possible."

"I met his mother in the clinic in Acajutla," Stuart said, "She's a nice woman, loves her son. She'll be worried sick."

"Excuse me," Will Chen interrupted, "How do you happen to know this kid?"

"His mother brought him to the Project Raphael clinic because he's pigeon-toed," Stuart said, "That was several months ago. Manuel was particularly friendly and cooperative. And perfectly normal. So, when I ran into him on the yacht Arariel and they told me he had leukemia, I knew it was a lie."

"You figured out that Ms. Santiago was taking the kid out of the country to be an organ donor?" asked Lt. Cdr. LeBlanc.

"Not just from his being pigeon-toed," Stuart chuckled, "I had more data than that. Sometime I'll explain."

"Okay," said Duane, "What we need to deal with is the fact that there's a ship coming into the bay in the next day or so and it is carrying a container full of young girls who are about to be sold as slaves."

"Which ship are we talking about? Do we know?" asked LeBlanc.

"Yes," said Stuart, "They're on the SS Hermione."

"How do you know that?" she asked.

"Ms. Kathleen Atwood is in charge of loading all the medical and surgical supplies when Project Raphael does a mission to El Salvador. She told me that Project Raphael always ships their two containers back and forth from Acajutla and Oakland on the same ship, the SS Hermione."

LeBlanc tapped a few keys and looked at the notebook computer in front of her.

"Salvadoran register, medium sized coastal freighter, due to dock in Oakland day after tomorrow," she read from the files.

"We can be ready for them when they tie up," Chen said, "I can have a full SWAT team right there on the docks. We can take the freighter, the girls, and the whole *Los Cóndores* gang."

"Human trafficking is a federal crime," said Reynolds, "The FBI should take the lead on this."

Duane did not want the meeting to get into a jurisdictional dispute. He knew that the Coast Guard had jurisdiction on the water, that the FBI was primarily responsible for policing human trafficking, and that *Los Cóndores* was an Oakland gang.

"SFPD is conducting a murder investigation," said Duane, "We can't get into some sort of bullshit turf battle here. There are bad guys and crimes enough for all of us. We need to work together. That's the whole reason I called this meeting."

All nodded in agreement.

"And we're forgetting something really important," said Duane, "The people on the yacht know that Dr. Stuart and his friends jumped ship. They have to assume that he has alerted us to what's going on. Most likely they know that we've caught Conklin and Santiago."

"They may not know," said Reynolds, "We rounded up the pilot, the copilot, the flight attendant, everyone on the plane. We're holding them all incommunicado until this whole thing is finished."

"That's wishful thinking, Walter," said Duane, "Conklin wasn't supposed to make the flight. He'll be missed. Most likely, they have somebody who was expecting to meet the plane. We need to assume they know that we've got Conklin and Santiago. I don't want to blow this because we were naïve."

"There may be seven girls locked in a container on that ship," said Stuart, "Their lives are at stake."

"How do you know these things?" Chen asked.

"Gabriella told me that there were seven other girls. The others ran when Gabriella got out. She doesn't know if any other girls made it."

"I suggest we assume that no other girls got out," said Duane.

"Still, they'll know that their plan is compromised," said LeBlanc.

"Exactly," said Duane, "So the bad guys will have to make a Plan B. And that's another reason why we're here. We don't have much time. We need to figure out what their options are and prepare to counter them. We're going to need the cooperation of all of our agencies."

"The obvious move, if they think we're on to them, is to dock the Hermione somewhere else," said Chen, "Maybe San Francisco, or maybe sail right across the bay, up the delta, and tie it up in West Sacramento."

"The Coast Guard can have eyes on the Hermione right now," said Lt. Cdr. LeBlanc, "That's easy. Our aircraft can follow the ship wherever she goes and we can position our ships anywhere to shadow or intercept her."

"The FBI can certainly have a welcoming party for them once we figure out where they plan to land," said Special Agent Reynolds, "Assisted by the local law enforcement, wherever they decide to dock."

"Let me play out a different scenario," said Duane, "I haven't been able to sleep or think about anything besides this case since Dr. Stuart called me. Let's look at what we know. Somebody is using a medical charity to smuggle people out of El Salvador to become involuntary organ donors, while young girls are brought into Oakland and sold off as sex slaves. A gang that calls itself *Los Cóndores*, based in El Salvador, but with a branch in Oakland, is involved, but maybe just as hired muscle. *Los Cóndores* is also in the cocaine business and probably responsible for a mass murder in San Francisco. I can't believe that these street thugs are smart enough to run a human trafficking organization. There's somebody higher up making the plans. Now, if I was the criminal mastermind running this organization and I thought that the cops would be waiting for me at the docks, I wouldn't try to bring the girls ashore in the shipping container at all."

"How would you do it, if you were a criminal mastermind?" Chen asked.

"I'd try to get the girls off the ship before it made port," said Duane.

"How the hell would you do that?" Chen asked.

"I'd take them off while the Hermione is still at sea," said Duane.

"Do you have any idea how difficult that would be?" asked LeBlanc, "It's not easy to get into a shipping container in the hold of a freighter that's at sea."

"That's one reason why you're here. Is it possible?" Duane asked.

"Whew," said LeBlanc, thinking, "That depends on a lot of things. Is the crew of the Hermione part of the criminal organization?"

"Dr. Stuart, do you know?" asked Duane.

"I don't know," Stuart said, "Project Raphael uses the same freighter for each mission, so my guess would be that at least the captain knows that some smuggling is going on."

"Let's assume that the crew is in on the scheme," said Duane, "If some or all of the crew will help, can they get the girls out of the container?"

"Yes, it's possible," said LeBlanc, "One way or another, they'll need some experienced sailors to do it."

"What about taking the whole container off the Hermione while it's at sea?" Chen asked.

"Highly unlikely," said LeBlanc with a smile, "The idea of arranging to transfer a shipping container from one ship to another in the middle of the Pacific on short notice is, to say the least, improbable. I don't think we need to make plans to thwart that."

"But they could get the girls out of the container while it's still in the hold of the Hermione," Duane said.

"It would be difficult, but probably possible," said the Coast Guard officer, "Don't forget that, if they can get the girls out of the container, they have to transfer them to another vessel in order to get them ashore."

"If you were the traffickers, Commander, how would you do this?" Duane asked, "We're cops. We don't even know what questions to ask."

"If I wanted to get a bunch of teenage girls out of a container and safely ashore, I'd use the lifeboat on the Hermione," she said without hesitation, "Then I'd transfer the girls to other craft, probably split them up, and return the lifeboat to the Hermione. Most merchant crews are very good at lifeboat drills. They know how to get the lifeboat back aboard as well. They've done it many times."

Duane was pretty impressed with the Coast Guard officer. She sure seemed to know her stuff.

"What if Duane's wrong?" Reynolds asked, "What if they're still planning to bring the ship into some port or another?"

"If they're also shipping cocaine, they may need to dock the ship," Chen added.

"I think we can accommodate both possibilities," said Lt. Cdr. LeBlanc, "We'll keep an eye on the Hermione. If she stops offshore, we'll know. If she puts into port, we'll know that, too. We'll be able to give you enough time to meet the Hermione if she ties up somewhere. And we can get our ships out the Golden Gate faster than you think."

"Can you keep an aircraft over the Hermione continuously without raising suspicion?" Duane asked.

"No," said LeBlanc, "We don't need aircraft."

"Are you saying that you have satellite coverage?" Reynolds asked.

"I didn't say that," said LeBlanc with a grin.

"You must have a satellite," said Reynolds, "How else can you watch the Hermione?"

"That's classified," LeBlanc replied, "Trust me, Agent Reynolds, we can take care of this."

"Do we have enough evidence to get a warrant?" Will Chen asked, "What I have on *Los Cóndores* could get me a warrant for their Oakland headquarters, but a warrant to search a ship at sea? No chance. Walter, can you get a federal warrant?"

"Our evidence is pretty thin," said Reynolds, "I'm not sure I can get a federal judge to give me a warrant based on the words of a runaway teenager and an orthopedic surgeon with only one eye."

"Don't worry, boys, we're the Coast Guard," said Lt. Cdr. LeBlanc, "We don't need a warrant."

Now Duane really liked Lt. Cdr. LeBlanc.

28

AFTER SPENDING HIS day with law enforcement, Stuart arrived at Kathleen's house at six. Supper reservations were at seven, so they had plenty of time to get across the Golden Gate Bridge to Sausalito.

There was nothing more that he could do about the girls in the shipping container or Wallace Godfrey today. Stuart resolved to keep his mind on Kathleen and Gabriella. They all needed a happy, relaxing evening.

Kathleen and Gabriella were resplendent in new dresses. Shopping boxes were stacked in the corner of Kathleen's living room, straggling bits of tissue paper protruding from the sides.

"Wow," said Stuart, "You two look great. A successful day at the stores, I guess."

"Oh, Dr. Stuart," bubbled Gabriella, "Today has been incredible. I couldn't have dreamed this. You can only dream about the things you can imagine. I could never have imagined this. Is everyone in the United States rich? San Francisco is nothing like what I thought. We spent all day in stores. Kathleen bought me so many new clothes. I've never seen anything like these, never. We ate lunch in China town. Wonderful, amazing food. You just sit there and they bring food to your table. If it looks good, you just point to it and they give it to you. You don't even have to talk in Chinese or English or anything. Just point!"

"Dim sum," said Kathleen. Stuart nodded.

"Are you still full of dim sum or do you want some supper?" Stuart asked.

"Oh, we burned off the dim sum and we're both famished," Kathleen said, "Let's go."

Gabriella giggled and sighed and oohed and aahed as they drove across the Golden Gate bridge. The sun was going down over the Pacific. Sailboats glided into the bay under the bridge as people returned home after a glorious day on the water. A few huge container ships headed into and out of the port.

They ate at a restaurant which stood on a pier right on the water. The rays of the setting sun caused the waves to sparkle. Gulls and cormorants flew and landed on docks and the masts of berthed boats. Sea lions poked their heads up above the water and dove down again in search of food. Gabriella couldn't get over the playful creatures.

Stuart thought that Gabriella was just a little kid watching the birds and the sea lions. Watching her now, it was hard to imagine that she could also be a very brave and feisty young woman. She ate her supper with relish, savoring fabulous seafood dishes that she never heard of before.

Darkness had fallen when they left the restaurant. They took a few minutes to stroll along the water, watching the lights of the city of San Francisco come on and sparkle. Stuart could see the sparkles reflect and amplify in Gabriella's eyes.

Stuart looked at Kathleen. She wasn't looking at the city or Gabriella. She was looking at him.

Stuart was genuinely happy. There was a sense of deep, rich serenity in his heart.

◆ ◆ ◆

Felipe Peña watched his men load weapons onto the two motor yachts. The owners were white men he didn't know and therefore distrusted. The one who owned the boat Felipe would ride on was called Jack and the other was Phil. Felipe wondered for a moment why rich white men would get involved in activities like the one planned for tonight. Perhaps such willingness to get involved was how they got to be rich.

Felipe was impressed with the elegance of Jack's boat. Big, comfortable seats, fancy wood paneling, a well-stocked bar. Not bad, not bad at all. Felipe decided that he needed one of these. He wondered how much it cost. Perhaps he could buy one with his share of the profits from the cocaine and the girls who waited outside the Golden Gate.

It was dark. They used minimal light on the yachts. Those few lights gave dim illumination in the marina, but no other boats were moving. The only signs of life came from the muffled conversations of people in the marina who lived on their boats.

Jack gave Felipe a quick orientation. Jack would handle the boat, but Felipe and his men might have to pitch in with ropes and fenders when they left the dock and when they rendezvoused with the Hermione. Felipe's men were young and strong and fearless. He was certain they could do what was required.

Jack showed Felipe the controls and instruments on the bridge. The radar screen was most important. It would show the locations of the other boats and ships. It would also lead them to the Hermione once they were out in the ocean. Jack gave Felipe a pair of binoculars which he hung around his neck. Felipe would serve as the lookout once they got close. Felipe also had a bright flashlight. He knew the signals to exchange with the freighter.

The engines of the two motor yachts gurgled to life. All interior lights were extinguished. Only the running lights revealed that the boats were moving. They slowly trolled out of the marina and into the bay.

There was a slight breeze and, as usual, the bay air was cold. Felipe noticed with relief that there was no fog on the bay. At least not yet.

⬥ ⬥ ⬥

Duane Wilson and Walter Reynolds waited in Duane's office, staring at the telephone. They both jumped when it rang. Duane was faster.

"Yes," Duane said.

"The Hermione is stopped five miles west of the Farallon Islands," said Lt. Cdr. Le Blanc, "Meet Lt. Jacobs on the USCGC *Tern* at the dock near the Golden Gate Bridge Welcome Center."

"Thank you," said Duane.

"Good hunting," said LeBlanc, "Get those girls, Duane."

"Aye-aye, Commander."

Duane and Walter dashed out of the office. They found a pair of uniformed officers just getting into their patrol car.

"Officers, this is an emergency," said Duane, "Take us to the pier near the Golden Gate Bridge Welcome Center. Lights and sirens. Let's move it."

Slicing through the city traffic, Duane and Walter arrived at the pier before the 87-foot coastal patrol boat belonging to the Coast Guard got there. They watched the boat come in, noting the 50-caliber machine gun mounted on the foredeck. The crew brought the boat alongside smartly.

Duane and Walter jumped aboard. A young African-American woman wearing khakis, a baseball cap, and a flak vest greeted them. Duane noticed the pair of silver bars on her collar.

"Lieutenant Susan Jacobs," she said, offering her hand.

"Detective Duane Wilson, San Francisco Police. FBI Special Agent Walter Reynolds."

"Find a seat and hold on tight," Lt. Jacobs said, "We've no time to waste. Petty Officer, cast off!"

The patrol boat roared away from the dock. Despite the light chop in the waves, they quickly achieved a speed of twenty-five knots. A petty officer second class wearing a helmet and flak jacket approached.

The petty officer handed Duane and Walter flak jackets.

"You might need these," the petty officer said, "Helmets are below deck, if you want them."

"Thanks," said Duane, "We'll wait on the helmets."

"You armed?" the petty officer asked.

Duane and Walter showed their semi-automatics.

"Want something bigger?" asked the petty officer, indicating the M4 carbine slung over his shoulder.

"No," said Duane, "We're fine with what we've got. You folks with the fifty caliber and the M4s should give us all the firepower we'll need."

"Oh, we're not all of it," said the petty officer with a grin. Then he turned away to his other duties.

"Lieutenant, I've got two vessels just ahead of us, bearing three-five-zero, speed thirty knots," said the Chief Petty Officer looking at the instruments.

"Those would probably be the bad guys. Most of the recreational vessels have gone in by now. I don't know of any commercial vessels that are supposed to be here. How long before they reach the Hermione?" asked Lt. Jacobs.

"Forty minutes, Lieutenant."

"I want maximum speed," said Lt. Jacobs, "We can't catch them, but we'll get there before they can do much damage."

♦ ♦ ♦

Felipe was cold. He couldn't see anything in the dark. He was ready for this mission to be over.

"I've got the Hermione on radar," said Jack, "She's three miles away, straight ahead and dead in the water. Looks like they're waiting for you."

Jack pointed to a white blob on the radar screen.

"See, that's the Hermione," Jack said, "And that's Phil's boat over to our right."

Felipe looked to his right and was reassured that the other yacht was on station. He pointed to another white spot on the screen.

"What's that?" Felipe asked.

"Oh, some other boat," said Jack, "Bigger than mine, but not like a freighter. You see these things on radar all the time. It's the Golden Gate, you know. There's a fair amount of traffic all the time."

"How about that one?" Felipe pointed to another unidentified blob of light.

"Probably a small freighter," said Jack, "These things are out here. There's nothing to worry about."

"I'll take your word for it," said Felipe, "Listen, when you get to the Hermione, I want you to pull right alongside."

"You going aboard?" asked Jack.

"Yes," said Felipe, "They'll drop a rope ladder and we'll go aboard. You stay here until we return."

"You're paying the bill, so whatever you say."

Felipe looked uneasily at the waves as the yacht raced along. The idea of climbing a rope ladder onto a freighter in the middle of the ocean didn't appeal to him one bit. But those were his orders. And he knew from experience in *Los Cóndores* that the consequences of disobedience were far worse than falling off a ladder into the cold water.

Felipe had his men check their weapons. He planned to leave one man on board the yacht while he and the other boarded the freighter. Likewise, two of the *Los Cóndores* gang on the other motor yacht would board and one stay behind. According to the message from *El Jefe* in El Salvador, the captain of the Hermione and most of his crew were friends. The sailors would take him and his men to get the girls and the drugs. Felipe would decide how to get the girls to the motor yachts. If it looked safe, they'd use the rope ladders. The girls were too valuable to drop in the ocean. They might have to lower the girls down on ropes, securely tied up. If all that looked impractical, they would use the Hermione's lifeboat.

Felipe saw a shadow of even greater darkness ahead. The night was dark, but this was a huge shape of greater blackness on a background of black.

He used his flashlight to blink a signal. Watching the big black shadow, he was relieved to see a light on the deck returning the signal. Just as planned.

The yacht slowed, turned, and snuggled alongside the hulking metal mass of the freighter. A rope ladder tumbled off the deck and splashed into the water. Jack nudged the motor yacht closer. At Jack's direction, the *Los Cóndores* men deployed plastic fenders over the port side of the yacht to prevent the smaller vessel from damage when it bumped into the freighter.

Waves made the yacht move up and down. So did the Hermione. Felipe watched uneasily as the two vessels bobbed in the water. Felipe couldn't swim. He wore a life jacket, but it seemed to afford flimsy protection against the prospect of being crushed between the motor yacht and the freighter or freezing in the cold ocean.

His man caught the ladder and hauled it onto the bow of the yacht. The man with the ladder would be the one to stay on the yacht, holding the ladder while Felipe and his other comrade ascended.

Glancing behind him, Felipe saw the second yacht hovering behind Jack's, fenders deployed. When Felipe and his man were up on the deck of the freighter, the second yacht would take their place.

29

On the USCGC *Tern*, Duane was standing right next to Lt. Jacobs. Using the radar, the Coast Guard patrol boat crept within a hundred yards of the freighter. Duane had a pair of binoculars. He could see the little running lights on the motor yachts and the big black wall of the immobile freighter. The Coast Guard boat sailed without running lights. Still, he wondered that they hadn't been spotted.

"Why don't they see us?" Duane asked, "How are they letting us get this close?"

"Nobody on the yachts is looking at the radar," Lt. Jacobs explained, "Pulling alongside the freighter in the dark with moderate seas is tricky."

The crew of the USCGC *Tern* was at battle stations. One man was on the foredeck manning the fifty-caliber machine gun. The others not involved with operating the boat held M4 carbines. Duane and Walter drew their pistols. Walter had gone below and found helmets for both of them.

Straining at the binoculars, Duane couldn't see any of the people on the motor yachts or on the freighter. That all changed when the *Tern's* searchlight came on, casting blinding light on the scene before him.

"United States Coast Guard," said Lt. Jacobs with impressive authority. Her voice was amplified by a tinny speaker, "You on the motor yachts, move away from the freighter. Stand by to be boarded."

In the bright light, Duane could see the men on the lead yacht freeze momentarily. In seconds, they sprang into action. One man was on the bow, working with a rope that hung down from the freighter. He dropped the rope and scrambled back into the yacht. Another grabbed a rifle. A third disappeared belowdecks. One remained at the steering station.

Duane saw the unmistakable flashes of gunfire from the lead yacht. There were quick flashes from an automatic weapon and one large flash. At a distance of eighty yards, the sounds were distinct but slightly muted.

Duane and Walter ducked instinctively behind the pilot house. In a second, Duane remembered that the men shooting at them were street thugs from Oakland, not US Marines. Most of these morons weren't very good marksmen even on the land. Firing from a bobbing boat on the ocean wouldn't improve their skills. It was unlikely that they could hit anything on the patrol boat. Duane stood up and stepped out on deck.

"What are you doing?" asked Walter, "Get back here, fool."

Something splashed into the water and exploded. It was a rocket propelled grenade. It wasn't even close to the *Tern*.

"I don't think these assholes can hit anything out here on the water," Duane said.

Just then a spray of bullets ricocheted off the pilot house. The searchlight exploded. Everything became pitch dark. Duane sprawled on the deck next to Walter.

"You hear what I'm saying?" Walter said, "I don't care who's doing the shooting. When there are bullets in the air, get your black ass down."

"Return fire on the lead yacht," ordered Lt. Jacobs calmly.

The Coast Guardsman on the .50 caliber opened fire, aiming between the running lights of the yacht. At the same time, a few other crewmen opened up with M4 carbines.

Crouching next to Walter, Duane felt outgunned.

"When I joined the SFPD, I never expected to get into a damned naval battle," Duane said.

"My Mama didn't raise me to be no Horatio Hornblower, either, Brother," Walter replied.

All hell cut loose with racket. Both sides were firing in the dark, aiming between the running lights of the yacht and in the direction of the flashes from the small arms.

Duane looked up and saw the lights of the second yacht moving away from the freighter. Muzzle flashes appeared from this vessel as well.

Duane and Walter, crouching, made their way out of the pilot house and onto the deck. There was only the open deck, surrounded by a rope barrier that would provide no protection at all against incoming fire. Duane was fighting mad. He fired his pistol, knowing that at this range he was unlikely to be effective. Still, it felt good to vent his anger at these men who were trying to kill him. He wished he had taken the petty officer up on the offer of the M4.

Another large flash from the yacht alongside the freighter signaled that another rocket propelled grenade was on its way. Launched by an untrained street gangster from a yacht bobbing on the waves at a target in the dark, the chances of hitting anything were minimal.

Minimal chances are not zero chances. The rocket exploded against the lightly armored hull of the patrol boat.

The Coast Guardsman manning the fifty-caliber was knocked off his feet with the impact of the rocket. Another man, dropping his M4 into the ocean, reeled away from the side and fell into Duane's arms. The man was bleeding profusely from his thigh. Duane knelt beside him, applying pressure to the gushing wound. Immediately, another Coast Guardsman appeared.

"I'll take this," said the Coast Guardsman, "Help me get him below."

They dragged the wounded man behind the pilot house and below deck. The Coast Guardsman, who was the boat's medic, quickly cut away the wounded man's pants and expertly applied a tourniquet. The bleeding slowed. The medic applied a thick gauze dressing.

"Keep pressure on this," the medic ordered Duane.

While Duane pushed on the pressure dressing, the medic produced a needle, some tubing and a plastic bag of IV fluid. Swiftly starting the IV infusion and taping the needle in place, he took a blood pressure and pulse.

"He'll be OK," the medic told Duane, applying a pressure dressing to the wound, "You can stop pressing now."

With the impact of the RPG round, the crewman at the helm veered to the right and the patrol boat spun away, losing speed.

"Damage report," demanded Lt. Jacobs.

"Hull is breached, Lieutenant," said the Chief Petty Officer, "Above the water line. As long as we keep our speed down, we'll be OK."

Drenched in blood, Duane crawled back onto the deck. This time he picked up an M4 carbine. Walter was prone on the deck, shooting his pistol at motor yachts he couldn't really see.

"You okay?" Walter asked.

"Yeah," said Duane, "Son of a bitch."

"That guy gonna be okay?" Walter asked.

"Yeah, the medic says he'll make it," Duane replied.

Lt. Jacobs remained calm and in command. Duane watched her receive reports from her crew. She assured Duane and Walter the patrol boat had been damaged but was in no danger of sinking. Speed was going to be compromised, though.

"Keep up the fire on both yachts," she commanded, "Raise the *Bertholf* and tell them we're damaged."

The crewman was back behind the fifty-caliber. Tracer bullets from the machine gun tracked a path toward the motor yacht.

Suddenly there was an explosion as the diesel tanks and engine of the lead yacht, the one on which Felipe was riding, ignited. For a few moments the whole scene was brightly illuminated. Duane saw debris and bodies launched into the air in the blast. Then the light turned dull orange as flames consumed the rest of the sinking hulk.

Duane continued to pump bullets in the direction of the other yacht, which was fleeing toward the Golden Gate.

"Lieutenant, the freighter is underway!" shouted a crewman.

Lt. Jacobs grabbed the microphone.

"To the SS Hermione, this the United States Coast Guard," she said, "Heave to and stand by to be boarded."

The freighter continued to slowly increase speed.

Duane was afraid that they'd blown the mission. Sure, they disposed of a yacht full of gangsters, but the other yacht was getting away and, most importantly, the freighter with the girls in the container was also escaping.

"Shit," was all he could say.

The sky lit up as a red star shell flare illuminated the scene.

"Where the hell did that come from?" asked Walter.

"Holy shit," said Duane, "Look over there!"

Duane pointed off to the right. In the eerie light of the star shell, a large warship was visible, painted white with red stripes.

"That's USCGC *Bertholf*, out of Alameda," said Lt. Jacobs, "Cops aren't the only ones who bring along backup."

A male voice boomed from the 418 ft. cutter.

"SS Hermione, heave to and stand by to be boarded."

Duane thought momentarily that it sounded like the voice of God. But the freighter kept on going.

"Motor yacht heading into the San Francisco bay, heave to!" boomed the voice from the big cutter, "Halt right now or you will be fired upon!"

Duane looked left at the fleeing motor yacht, straight ahead at the freighter, and to his right at the big Coast Guard cutter. It was a maritime game of chicken. None of the vessels was slowing or altering course.

"Boom!"

Duane saw a flash from the deck of the *Bertholf* as the fifty-seven-millimeter gun put a round across the bow of the Hermione.

Almost simultaneously, a racket of noise and flashes erupted from the side of the cutter. Twenty-millimeter rounds flew out of the Phalanx weapon system, a high-tech Gatling gun, at 3,000 rounds per minute. The second yacht seemed to vaporize in a hail of bullets, fragments of boat, bodies, and flames.

"What the hell was that?" asked Walter, staring at the demolition of the motor yacht.

"That was the wrath of God," said Duane, "I guess that's what you get for fucking with the United States Coast Guard."

The SS Hermione stopped its engines and slowed its progress.

Duane watched with satisfaction as an inflatable boat full of armed coast guardsmen launched from the stern of the *Bertholf* and made its way to the freighter. He knew that he was watching a boarding party and that they would take over the SS Hermione.

Duane Wilson's first naval battle was over.

♦ ♦ ♦

Gabriella fell asleep on the short drive between Sausalito and Kathleen's house in the outer Sunset.

Stuart saw her head leaning on the window in the back seat of the Jeep, eyes closed, an innocent smile on her face, breathing regularly.

He carried the sleeping teenager into Kathleen's house, depositing her gently onto the bed in the guest bedroom. Kathleen remained with the girl to tuck her in while Stuart found a comfortable seat on the sofa in the living room.

"Do you want anything?" asked Kathleen, slipping quietly into the living room.

"No, I'm fine," said Stuart, "Your company and some private conversation in English would be welcome, though."

Kathleen sat down beside him and snuggled up close.

"I've become quite attached to her, you know," said Kathleen, "What are we going to do about her?"

"Duane Wilson said that we'll have to report her to Immigration," said Stuart, "I have no idea how to do that. I thought that in a day or two I'd ask Walter Reynolds how to do it. He said the FBI would help once the smoke clears on the apprehension of the traffickers."

"Is that finally over?" she asked.

"Maybe," he replied, "The Hermione was supposed to enter the Golden Gate tonight. Duane will probably tell me. Then I'll give it a day or so and call Walter."

"And that will be the end of it? The criminal stuff? The horrors and nightmares?"

"Not quite," said Stuart, "But close. What would you like to do about Gabriella?"

"You're going to think I'm crazy," she said.

"I already know you're crazy," he interjected.

"I want to keep her," said Kathleen, "I want to have her live here. I never use that bedroom. I keep it for guests, but I never have any guests. I want to have her as the daughter I never had. I want to send her to school. I want to dress her for her prom, watch her graduate."

"Have you talked to Gabriella about this?"

"No."

"She said she didn't want to be in San Francisco," said Stuart, "She wanted to go home to El Salvador. To be with her family."

"Now that she's seen something of San Francisco, she may have changed her mind."

"What about her mother? She must be worried sick about Gabriella," he said, "We have to be fair to that poor woman."

"I know," sighed Kathleen, "But it breaks my heart. Maybe we could bring her mother here, too."

"If that didn't work, we could visit Gabriella when we go back to El Salvador on missions," Stuart suggested.

"What makes you think there will be any more missions?" she asked, "If Project Raphael is involved in human trafficking, there's no way that it won't be shut down."

"Wallace told me that there is a board of trustees," Stuart said, "He said that he established it so the program could continue after he's no longer involved."

"It seems a pretty safe bet that Dr. Godfrey will no longer be involved," Kathleen said.

"Yeah, I know," said Stuart, "Conklin is going to be history, too. But maybe the board of trustees can figure out some way for the work of Project Raphael to go on. The hospital and clinic really are doing a lot of good."

"It'll take a lot of work and more than a little luck," she said.

"Let's enjoy the time we have with Gabriella," Stuart said, "Maybe the authorities will let her stay with you while they look for her mother in El Salvador. The federal government works very slowly in these things, I should think. And Gabriella deserves special leniency considering how she came into this country and how her cooperation led to the breakup of a particularly evil trafficking ring."

"You're right," said Kathleen, "We'll take it one day at a time. I'm gonna enjoy every minute I get as a foster mother."

"Most people wouldn't want anything to do with a fourteen-year-old girl," Stuart commented, "She was really sweet tonight, but Gabriella has shown that there is a bit of the hellcat in her. We need to be careful that we stay on her good side."

"Ray," Kathleen changed the subject, "What about us?"

Stuart knew exactly what she meant, but didn't know how to respond, so he asked.

"What do you mean, about us?"

"Well, after what's happened, I don't think we can rely on Project Raphael missions. What are you and I going to do? Will I still be seeing you? Is tonight about the beginning or the end?" she asked.

"I hope it's a beginning."

"Ray, I've got to ask," Kathleen said, "Why didn't you ever call me after the car accident. I called you so many times. I even wrote letters. Why didn't you respond?"

Stuart pulled back a little, so he could look directly at her.

"There is something you don't know, Kathleen, something nobody knows," Stuart said, "Something that makes me ashamed and guilty. I haven't been able to share it with anyone except my priest. He says that I am forgiven, but God help me, I don't feel forgiven."

"What is it, Ray?"

"The car wreck wasn't an accident," he said, "It was a suicide attempt. I ran the car into that tree on purpose."

Kathleen gasped.

"Why?"

"I've battled depression on and off since I was Gabriella's age. It's a reaction that I get often when I think I've been hurt. It's a form of selfishness. I see that now. In this case, I thought I was in love with a woman. She didn't love me. She was happily married to another man. There was no chance that we would be together. And I felt sorry for myself. I didn't want to live without her. I couldn't see how many wonderful blessings I had. I could only think about the thing I wanted and couldn't have. It was selfish. And I'm very ashamed."

"You never knew that I loved you, did you?" she asked. "I still love you, Ray. I'm glad you survived the crash."

"I'm very grateful right now that I survived. I've never been this happy," he said.

"I'm gonna do everything I can to make sure that you never get depressed again," she promised.

30

THE SAN FRANCISCO office of the FBI is on the thirteenth floor. Stuart was not a superstitious man, but he wondered if there was some significance to that. He smiled to himself and thought that the rent might be cheaper. Good for the taxpayers.

Duane Wilson was already waiting in Walter Reynolds' office. Stuart greeted both men and hands were shaken.

"We got the girls," Walter said, "I knew you'd want to know. There were seven of them, just like you said. They're all alive. Physically, all of them will be okay. I doubt that any of them will ever get over the emotional damage."

"We owe you and Ms. Atwood and especially the Salvadoran girl our gratitude," said Duane, "Not only did you save the lives of seven innocent girls, but you helped us to break up an extensive human trafficking ring."

"We also seized fifty kilograms of cocaine from the container that held the girls," said Walter, "A kind of bonus for us and the Coast Guard."

"We had a small naval engagement just outside the Gate. The Battle of the Farallon Islands," Duane said, "Two Coast Guard cutters against two motor yachts full of *Los Cóndores* gangsters and a rogue freighter. We had one man wounded. They lost about eight bad guys. That's only a guess, since the Coast Guard blew their boats to smithereens and we'll never know how many of the bastards were on board."

"The seizure of the cocaine gave the Oakland police all they needed to shut down *Los Cóndores* in the east bay permanently," Walter continued, "When Will Chen and his unit raided the Oakland headquarters of *Los Cóndores*, they found elaborate records of the human trafficking operation, including the names and addresses where the gang shipped the girls. These books will help us enormously nationwide. These bastards will get caught and get punished. And, with a little luck, we may be able to rescue some of the other girls that they brought into the US in previous shipments."

"The girl whose body we found in the Bay was in their books as well," said Duane, "Now she has a name. She was Carla Torres. She died in the container on the way to Oakland. We don't know where she came from, but we can work with the authorities in El Salvador to contact her family."

"Now the mystery of the girl in the Bay is solved," said Stuart.

Duane nodded in agreement.

"*Los Cóndores* kept detailed records of all their activity in the Bay area. It was amazing. We found out that they owned the warehouse where the 8 Gangsta Blood were massacred. They had it as a backup in case Oakland PD busted their headquarters on that side of the bay. The details of the ambush of 8 Gangsta Blood were all recorded. That case is also now solved."

"I guess it all ties together, doesn't it?"

"It seems that way," said Walter.

"Project Raphael is right in the center of the whole, horrible mess," said Stuart.

"There are a few details we don't understand yet," said Duane, "But Project Raphael is the common denominator. William Conklin, the business manager of Project Raphael, seems to be a link between *Los Cóndores* and Project Raphael. He made sure that the right officials were bribed and the containers were delivered and modified to accommodate the girls and drugs. The containers went south with medical equipment and supplies and came north with girls and cocaine. There is no evidence, though, that *Los Cóndores* paid Conklin. In fact, it looks like the other way around."

"What do you mean?" asked Stuart.

"It seems like Project Raphael was shuttling money to *Los Cóndores*," Duane said.

"That doesn't make sense," said Stuart.

"I think that we still don't have all the data, here," said Reynolds, "There is another player mentioned in the *Los Cóndores* books. This person is referred to only as the Client, never named."

"Are they talking about Conklin?" Stuart asked.

"We're fairly certain that Conklin is not the Client," Duane said, "The Client may be farther up the organizational chart than Conklin. It may be that *Los Cóndores* itself is just hired muscle. That might explain why Project Raphael is paying them."

"Where's Conklin now?" Stuart asked.

"We're holding him in solitary in the county jail," Duane said, "It looks like most of the charges against him will be federal, but I'm pretty sure that I can get the district attorney to file against him for first-degree murder in the case of the girl we found in the bay."

"And the nurse?" asked Stuart.

"In federal custody," said Reynolds.

"Are either of them talking?" Stuart asked.

"They each say only one word," said Duane, "Lawyer."

"Shit."

"What about Dr. Godfrey?" Stuart asked, "Wallace Godfrey is the founder of Project Raphael. What's his role in all of this?"

"The FBI, with the help of SFPD, is investigating Dr. Godfrey," said Duane, "He's mixed up in it for sure."

"At this point, we don't think we have enough hard evidence to get a federal indictment of Godfrey," said Walter, "As long as Conklin and the nurse won't talk, we're going to have trouble nailing Godfrey."

"Maybe I can help," Stuart offered, "Each time a patient, adult or child, comes to Project Raphael, or each baby that's born there, there are lab tests. Blood work and urinalysis. The lab in El Salvador includes a machine that does tissue typing. My guess is that each patient is tissue typed and their data entered into the computer. They have a bank of potential donor data right at the hospital. If they have a potential recipient, all that's needed is to run it through the computer and see if they have a match."

"Are you sure of that?" Walter asked.

"Quite," said Stuart, "I saw the machine myself. There's no real medical reason to have that machine in the lab at Acajutla. We don't need tissue typing for any of the clinical work that's actually done there. With what we know now about Project Raphael's criminal activity, it's the only explanation that fits the facts."

"Have you personally seen anyone at Project Raphael do the things you describe? Have you seen anyone looking up tissue typing data for a potential transplant? Do you have some documentation, perhaps computer records?"

"Of course not," Stuart said.

"Then I'm afraid that even a poor defense lawyer will completely discredit your testimony in court," said Walter, "And Dr. Godfrey can afford a very good lawyer."

"Godfrey also lied about the children he smuggled on his boat," Stuart protested, "He made up false diagnoses and claimed that he had arranged for treatment for them in the US. These are all lies."

"Do you have some written document recording these diagnoses and treatment arrangements? Can you prove that these children were going to be transplant donors?"

"No."

"Perhaps you're beginning to see, Dr. Stuart, "said Walter, "what we're up against. Right now, we can prove that Dr. Godfrey had the boy Manuel on his yacht. Perhaps without the permission of the boy's parents. We might make a case for kidnapping, but that would be a Salvadoran charge. Maybe we could get him on unlawful transporting a minor. Assuming that you're right, we can convict

Dr. Godfrey of making the wrong diagnosis. That's incompetent, but not criminal. The US Attorney, if she takes this to court, wants a conviction. With what we have now, I don't think I have enough to go to the US Attorney and ask for an indictment."

"For the love of God, man, what will you do?" Stuart asked.

"Our best hope is that we can cut a deal with Conklin or Ms. Santiago, get them to testify against Godfrey," Walter said.

"If they won't testify, Godfrey will walk," Stuart said, "Is that possible?"

"Sorry, Dr. Stuart," said Duane, "But it's very possible."

Gabriella was going to take her grand tour of San Francisco. Dr. Stuart was coming to Kathleen's house, but they weren't going to drive around in his Jeep. Kathleen told her they were going to ride on the bus, maybe a streetcar, and, if she was lucky, maybe something else.

Gabriella was thrilled. Everything she had seen so far about San Francisco seemed dazzling. On the other hand, Gabriella couldn't really allow people to know how different, how unsophisticated she really was. She needed to at least look like she fit in. She was a poor girl from Cedros accompanied by two older North Americans. Her plan was to make it look like she, the very mature teenage girl, was leading the tour for her visiting aunt and uncle.

Carefully planning her outfit, she dressed in tight jeans, new Nike sneakers, and a light blue short-sleeved top that said "Pink."

She had seen North American teens on the street when she and Kathleen went out, so she brought along a black Adidas hoodie. It was nice and warm out and she didn't know why she should have the hoodie, but the US kids did it and so would she. She tied the sleeves together around her waist. When she looked in the mirror, she thought she looked very American.

Dr. Stuart parked his Jeep on the street in front of Kathleen's house. The three of them made the short walk to the bus stop, where they boarded a colorful orange and yellow bus that said "Muni."

The bus took them to a street called Irving. It reminded Gabriella of the China town where Kathleen took her for lunch when she first got to San Francisco. There were lots of Asian people, markets with dead animals hanging in the windows. In that regard, she was familiar with those markets. They had them in El Salvador, too.

The most interesting things on Irving Street were the people. The people came in all sizes and colors. There were black people, Asian people, white people, and people who looked like Salvadorans. All sorts of languages were spoken. She recognized lots of Spanish. Most of the people spoke English. She knew what that sounded like, but couldn't understand the words. There were lots of other languages that she couldn't understand at all.

Another thing struck Gabriella as very unusual. A lot of the people were very fat. Before she got to the United States, she had only ever seen three or four fat people. Now there were fat people everywhere. She wondered if the North Americans thought fat people were beautiful.

On Irving Street, they boarded a kind of train that Kathleen called a streetcar. It ran on tracks embedded into the concrete street itself and some sort of wires strung up above the street. The streetcar took them past a bewildering collection of buildings and neighborhoods. All of the houses were immense. Not one had a thatched or corrugated metal roof. Surely, she thought, everyone in San Francisco was rich.

The streetcar rumbled into a very dark tunnel and she had no idea where they were. Eventually, the car stopped at a brightly lit underground station. Kathleen motioned for her to get off. Gabriella followed Kathleen and Dr. Stuart.

Dr. Stuart put a little card into a machine. There was a gate that opened and she walked through when Dr. Stuart told her to. Then they walked over to what looked like a staircase, but the steps were moving.

"What's that?" Gabriella asked.

"We call it an escalator," Kathleen smiled, "Just pick a step and hop on. Watch me."

Kathleen stepped calmly onto one of the moving stairs. Gabriella watched her ascend.

"Come on," Dr. Stuart said, "Your turn."

Gabriella hopped onto a moving stair with both feet. She grabbed onto the rail, which she discovered was also moving. At the top of the moving staircase, she jumped off, joining Kathleen on a beautiful brick patio surrounded by hundreds of people.

"Where are we?" Gabriella asked.

"They call this the Embarcadero," Kathleen answered.

"Embarcadero, that's Spanish."

"Lots of things in San Francisco are Spanish," Kathleen pointed out, "The name San Francisco itself is Spanish."

They walked through the streets. Gabriella was afraid her head might fall off from turning so much from side to side. All pretense of being the sophisticated San Francisco teen giving a tour to her rural aunt and uncle were lost. Gabriella was spellbound and the whole world could see it.

Soon they came to a place where brightly colored boats were moored.

"Are you up to a little ride around San Francisco bay?" Dr. Stuart asked, "On one of these cruise boats?".

"It's a really good way to see San Francisco," Kathleen reassured her.

With that promise, Gabriella agreed.

The cruise around the bay showed Gabriella the vastness of the bay area. Kathleen explained about the Pacific Ocean to the west, the entrance to the bay, which she called the Golden Gate. Gabriella loved sailing under the Golden Gate bridge.

"Hey, that's where we went to dinner," Gabriella exclaimed, pointing to Sausalito on the north end of the bridge.

Perhaps the best part of her day was being with Kathleen and Dr. Stuart. By now she was certain that Dr. Stuart and Kathleen were in love.

Her thoughts came back to her mother. There were so many things she wanted to say, so many hugs she wanted to give, so much forgiveness she needed to seek.

Eventually, they came back to Kathleen's house. Dr. Stuart got back in his Jeep and said that he had an errand to run.

31

Lois Godfrey answered the door when Stuart rang the bell. She was heavily made up and dressed as though she was ready to go out.

"Hello, Lois," he said, "Is Wallace at home?"

Lois looked at him with a vacuous expression.

"Yes, he is," she said, "Wally is taking me on a long cruise on the Arariel."

"Well, that sounds like fun," Stuart commented, "Where are you going?"

"I don't know," she replied, "Someplace warm with beaches and palm trees and five-star hotels."

"When do you leave?"

"Very soon," she said.

"Can I talk with Wallace?" Stuart asked.

"He's in the library."

"Thank you. I know where it is," he said.

Stuart opened the door and let himself in. There were two large briefcases on the desk. Godfrey was slipping a laptop computer into one of them.

"Hello, Wallace," Stuart said.

Godfrey looked up, surprised. Stuart saw the color drain from his face. He looked trapped.

"Ray," he said.

"Why?" Stuart asked.

"How much do you know?" Godfrey replied.

"I think I know it all," said Stuart, "The girls, the transplant donors. I just want to know why."

"You should understand. You're a doctor," Godfrey said, "We start in medical school with fantasies about serving our fellow men and women. The only reward we expect is the gratitude of those we've healed. Sometime during our residency, we realize that not all of our patients are grateful."

"So what?"

"Some of the patients don't follow sound medical advice," Godfrey went on, "They don't take the medicines we prescribe; they don't take care of their incisions. They don't keep follow-up appointments."

"We all learn that, Wallace," said Stuart, "We learn to compensate for human nature, to anticipate the consequences of patient noncompliance."

"If we're observant," said Godfrey, "we see that there are different kinds of patients. The chronically noncompliant, the ungrateful ones are all in a single class. They're stupid, poorly educated, unmotivated. They make no real contribution to society."

"That's not for us to judge."

"Oh, but it is," said Godfrey, "When we're in practice for a while, we may be blessed to see a different class of patient. These people are highly intelligent, motivated, creative individuals. They get it. They are excellent patients because they are excellent people. Once I got into private practice, I began to see such people, to get to know them. I've treated major movie stars, titans of industry, artists and musicians whose names are known all over the world."

"Congratulations," said Stuart, "What does that have to do with human trafficking?"

"I'm getting there, Ray," said Godfrey, "When a famous person needs medical care, how do they select a doctor? I'll tell you. They go to the doctor who has successfully treated other famous and talented people. You can find the names of those doctors in the newspapers, magazines, on TV."

"The famous people, and some that are not so famous, are a better class of people," said Godfrey, "And they seek you out because you're a better class of doctor. There are excellent people in this world, Ray, and the doctors who care for them are excellent as well."

"Of course, the doctors become richer as well."

"It's not just about money," said Godfrey, "although money is the way that we often measure our success. It's really about talent, intellect, creativity, the things that elevate humanity. These are the people who make a difference, the ones who advance society."

"You're a plastic surgeon, for God's sake," Stuart replied, "You do face lifts and breast augmentations."

"I'm not alone, Ray," Godfrey said, "Think about it. Every specialty has doctors who are sought after by the superior people in the world. These are the doctors who make sure that the very best people are the ones who procreate and thrive."

"You speak like there is some kind of organization of the famous doctors who treat the famous patients," Stuart said.

"Oh, but there is," said Godfrey, "There is. Every specialty is represented. Doctors from every country and continent. We form a network. We communicate. We collaborate. We're dedicated to promoting the very best in the human race."

"So, you take innocent children and use them as organ donors?"

"You know how the organ transplant game is played, Ray," said Godfrey, "The bleeding hearts and the so-called ethicists insist on all these rules and all these lists. Do you really have any idea how hard it is to get on a transplant list? You have to practically be a saint. Any little shortcoming, any little bad habit, and your disqualified. Even if a person is flawless, he or she winds up with a long wait. There's no guarantee that someone on the list will even get an organ before they die from their disease. The time on a transplant list is an ordeal. It's impossible to be productive while waiting on a list like that. During the whole time, the world is deprived of the benefits of these superb individuals."

"Your solution is black-market organ transplant," said Stuart.

"Black market is a judgmental term."

"Using innocent children as donors is judgmental."

"Realistically, donating an organ is the only productive thing that some of these people will ever do. It's an opportunity for an otherwise worthless person to make a contribution to human progress."

"What about the trafficking of girls for sex slavery?"

"Providing good health care to superior people costs money, Ray," said Godfrey, "As I pointed out, not all excellent people are rich people. We need a revenue stream to maintain our health care organization and our transplant program."

"The girls that you kidnap and sell for sex slaves, I suppose that you consider them to be disposable people, too," said Stuart.

"They'll be forgotten," said Godfrey, "The money we get for them supports a noble cause."

"If you're so proud of what you're doing, why hide it from the public?"

"The public is too stupid to understand what a great thing we're doing. The public, and the laws are unenlightened."

"Now that your enterprise has been exposed, you're running away," Stuart said, "It doesn't sound like you're so proud of what you've done."

"Not running away, Ray, relocating," said Godfrey.

Stuart had heard as much as he could stand.

Stuart hit Godfrey so hard that Stuart's feet left the ground in the follow-through. Godfrey went down like a bowling pin, hitting his head on the bookcase behind him as he fell.

"Pretty good punch, Dr. Stuart. Was that what you call a left hook or a cross?"

Stuart turned to see Lois Godfrey standing in the doorway of the library. She held a pearl-handled pistol in her right hand, pointed right at him.

"Surprised?" she asked.

Stuart was speechless.

"Did you think that Wally was capable of running an organization like this all by himself?" Lois asked, "Or perhaps the pathetic William Conklin? Wally's a good doctor as you can tell by looking at me. But it takes a good businesswoman to really make an enterprise as complex as ours work."

"Are you behind all of this," Stuart stammered, "The whole human trafficking, the organ donors?"

"Oh, heavens no, I couldn't do it all alone," Lois answered, "Wally has the medical mind. He's the one who communicates with all the best doctors in the world. Wally's the one with the ideals. He's the one who wants to preserve the race of super people. No, Dr. Stuart, I'm just a person who likes to live well. I'm good at details. I'm the one who works with the Salvadoran gangs. *Los Cóndores* is a convenient business partner. They have contacts throughout Central America and are very efficient at obtaining the people that we need. They find people who won't be missed or in places where the local authorities will be unable or unwilling to investigate disappearances. They are ruthless, violent, and will do anything for money. Their drug dealing provides us with a distribution network. They lack the intelligence to understand the real business. They don't ask a lot of questions. In fact, they don't even know my name. They just call me the Client. It's an arrangement that's been working successfully for years now. You might consider me the CEO of this business, but I rely on others to make this work."

"Do you agree with Wallace," Stuart asked, "I mean, about the superior people and the idea of using poor people for spare parts?"

"I have no such ideals," Lois answered, "The business that we run providing girls to customers makes us enough profit to cover the expenses of the organ transplants. Plus, we get a little cut of the cocaine money for providing secure transportation. We've been doing very well financially. It's just business, Dr. Stuart."

Stuart observed that the pistol she held was a 25-caliber automatic. It was a pretty little thing, the sort of weapon a woman of style might carry in her purse. However, it was not the sort of pistol that would kill anyone, unless the shooter got lucky and hit a vital organ. Stuart decided to mess up her aim.

Stuart rushed at Lois and she fired quickly. He felt a burning in his abdomen, but kept moving, knocking Lois down. The pistol slipped from her hand.

"Don't move," Duane Wilson charged into the library, his 9mm automatic drawn.

"Jesus Christ, what took you so long?" asked Stuart, "She shot me."

♦ ♦ ♦

Kathleen was there when Stuart woke up from the anesthetic.

"Hey, Doctor," she smiled, "You've just gotta play the hero, don't you?"

Stuart groaned.

"Ray, you're in the hospital at Sutro State," she said, "Lois Godfrey shot you. You've had surgery. You're going to be fine. You lost a few loops of bowel, but you won't miss them."

"Godfrey," was all that Stuart could say.

"They're both in jail, Dr. Stuart," said Duane Wilson, who appeared to Stuart out of the fog.

"We got them, Dr. Stuart," Walter Reynolds chimed in.

"By the way, Ray," said Kathleen, "You broke Wallace's damn jaw. And Ray, there's someone else here to see you."

Out of the mist, Stuart saw Gabriella's face. She had been crying.

Impulsively, Gabriella leaned on the hospital bed, sprawled right on top of his incision, and hugged Stuart as hard as she could.

The pain was excruciating, but Stuart held her tightly.

32

Stuart took in a deep breath of cool ocean air. The morning fog was still thick and it was cold on the beach below his home. He felt remarkably good, considering that it had only been two weeks since Lois Godfrey shot him.

Kathleen and Gabriella were wonderful nurses, helping him to recover after surgery. Stuart was grateful for their help, but was not comfortable with fawning attention. After a few days at Kathleen's house, he was happy to get home to his own place by the ocean.

Tentatively, at first, he tried jogging in the sand. There was no pain, so he increased the pace. He was thrilled that he could run.

After his run, Stuart climbed the steps that led up the cliff to his home. He was surprised to see a car parked in front of his house, but quickly recognized the government-issued sedan that Walter Reynolds of the FBI drove.

"Hey, Doc," Reynolds greeted Stuart, standing at the top of the stairs, "A little chilly for a walk on the beach, don't you think?"

"Just the way I like it, Walter," Stuart replied, "Bracing air. Clears the lungs and the mind. What are you doing here?"

"May I come in?" Reynolds asked.

"Sure," said Stuart, "I'll brew us some coffee."

"Thanks."

"What's up?"

"You've done a lot to help us with this whole human trafficking case. You deserve to be kept informed. Let me begin with an update," Reynolds said, finding a chair at the table, "The nurse, Ms. Santiago lawyered up and won't say a thing. William Conklin, it turns out, doesn't know that much about the organization or the extent of the network. He's cooperative, but not useful. Your friend Godfrey is full of this 'excellent people' bullshit."

Stuart smiled.

"Lois Godfrey is a different story," said Reynolds.

"You can say that again," Stuart said, "I didn't think that she had any brain at all inside that pretty head of hers. She turned out to be nasty."

"Not just nasty, but very, very smart," said Reynolds, "She has no principles at all. She'll even sell out her husband. She's willing to share everything that she knows in exchange for reduced charges and lenient sentencing."

"She's up to her brow lift in human trafficking," Stuart said, "She's involved in the death of the girl they found in the bay."

"She's got some leverage and she's using it," said Reynolds.

"Nuts," said Stuart, "I was hoping she'd go away for the rest of her life."

"The real reason I wanted to talk to you is what our FBI guys found on the computer you took from Dr. Godfrey," said Reynolds.

Stuart poured the coffee.

"Go on."

"Project Raphael and the El Salvador trafficking are just a small part of a larger operation," Reynolds said.

"What?"

"There are files on the computer that suggest that a worldwide network of doctors, hospitals, and clinics are connected," said Reynolds, "They're all dedicated to this notion of superior humans, who must be protected, healed, and allowed to procreate and dominate for mankind to make progress. There appear to be thirty or forty doctors, representing almost every continent on earth."

"Some of the things Wallace Godfrey said suggested as much," Stuart recalled, "It sounds like they've got a kind of eugenics society of doctors."

"The worst part of the network is the trafficking in black market organs," said Reynolds, "It seems that the black market is blacker than anyone thought. These people don't just buy kidneys from poor people, they also kidnap live subjects, harvest the organs, and dispose of the bodies of the donors."

"It's monstrous."

"The hospital where the organ transplants are done is a private facility in Saudi Arabia," Reynolds continued, "It was the destination for the Salvadoran victims mentioned on Godfrey's computer. We know that the donors are sent there and never come back. Unfortunately, that's about all we know."

"What do you mean?"

"Dr. Godfrey's computer doesn't contain all the data," said Reynolds, "It looks like he doesn't have clearance to see all of it. We know some of the names of the doctors in the eugenics society, but not all. We know about the registry of DNA for the Salvadorans who were patients at the Project Raphael clinic. We have details on the Salvadorans who were sent to Saudi Arabia as donors. We don't have the names of any of the organ recipients or the sources of transplant donors outside El Salvador. We suspect that El Salvador is only one of many places where these doctors get victims to use as donors."

"Was any of this on the radar of law enforcement before?" Stuart asked, "There's a lot of international cooperation when it comes to human trafficking, I understand."

"We have a lot of cooperation," said Reynolds, "There were hints and rumors, but this organization is well hidden from law enforcement. Nobody knows much about it."

"These bastards must be stopped," Stuart said.

"It looks to our FBI computer geeks like the headquarters, or at least the worldwide computer servers, come out of this hospital in Saudi Arabia," Reynolds said.

"Can you get the Saudi government to shut them down?"

"That's a little tricky, Doc," Reynolds replied, "The Saudis have their own ways of dealing with things. It's hard to tell sometimes who has influence in their society."

"I get it," said Stuart, "Then you have to get somebody inside that hospital, get access to the computer data, and shut these assholes down. You need to do it fast, if they're still killing people for donors."

"It takes a long time for us to infiltrate an undercover agent into an organization," Reynolds explained, "Especially if we're not going to involve the local government and law enforcement."

"I could get in," said Stuart.

"You mean you could join the eugenics medical society?"

"Hell, no. Nobody would believe it. Besides, just being one of the eugenics doctors wouldn't be a reason for me to visit this hospital in Saudi Arabia. I would need a different reason."

"You want to join the hospital staff over there?"

Stuart laughed.

"I doubt that they're looking to start a pediatric orthopedic program, Walter," he said, "I wouldn't go there as a doctor, although my medical training might very well be valuable once I got inside."

"I'm not sure I like this," said Reynolds, "You're not a trained law enforcement agent. This could be damn dangerous. You're a civilian. Besides, you're still recovering from getting shot."

"I've recovered just fine from the wound," Stuart argued, "I'm a trained physician and I know my way around hospitals. I'll sign a waiver for the FBI. I think I should go in as a patient, not a doctor."

"A patient?"

"Sure. Wallace Godfrey was always bragging about how rich and famous patients referred each other to their own doctors. I'll pose as a wealthy patient who's in need of a transplant. I'll get an appointment and travel there for a medical evaluation. Once inside, I'll see how much information I can bring out."

"It sounds risky and complicated," Reynolds said, "What sort of patient would you be?"

"I'll pose as a musician," said Stuart, "Somebody who plays guitar professionally and maybe also sings. Many of the songwriters and studio artists are famous and valuable, but don't have faces that everybody recognizes. The eugenicists might still consider them to be 'excellent' people because of their artistic contributions. I think that a cover like that could get me in the door. That's all I need."

"Can you pretend to be a musician?"

"Wait until you hear me play the guitar."

Kathleen found the people at the Immigration and Customs Enforcement to be very friendly and helpful. Maybe it was because of the recommendations from the FBI and the US Attorney, but everybody was eager to help Gabriella. The girl was a hero, no doubt, and the country owed her a debt of gratitude.

Gabriella stayed in Kathleen's home. More than two months had passed, which was fine with Kathleen. The slow grinding of the bureaucratic wheels was welcome. When Kathleen went to work, she dropped Gabriella off with a social worker who was employed by the immigration agency. The social worker set up a kind of school for Gabriella, including teaching her English. Kathleen picked Gabriella up after work.

"Good afternoon," Kathleen said in English when Gabriella got in the car.

"Good afternoon, Miss Atwood," grinned Gabriella proudly, "How are you?"

"I'm fine. I had a good day at work," Kathleen said, "What was the best thing you learned in your private school today?"

Gabriella looked puzzled. Kathleen had exceeded her English comprehension. The girl switched to rapid-fire Spanish and giggled.

"The police here are so much nicer than the Salvadoran police," Gabriella gushed, "I can't believe that your police provide a tutor and feed me lunch."

"You're a hero, don't forget," Kathleen responded, "You helped put the bad people in prison and you saved the lives of seven girls and a little boy. You deserve a little reward."

Gabriella sat quietly for a few minutes, looking out the window of the car.

"Have the police found my mother yet?"

"I'm afraid not," Kathleen replied, "Some American agents and the Salvadoran police went to your house in Cedros, but no one was there."

Gabriella shivered.

"Is my mother dead?"

"We don't know that, Gabriella. We mustn't give up hope."

Tears streamed their way from Gabriella's eyes down her cheek. Kathleen pulled the car to the curb, leaned over and hugged the sobbing girl.

Stuart was no stranger to the FBI office in San Francisco. He knew his way to the conference room. On arrival, he saw Reynolds with a tall, grey-haired, distinguished man.

"You're looking rather, well, casual," said Reynolds, pointing to Stuart's stubble of beard.

"Just preparing myself for you to accept my offer," grinned Stuart, "Haven't had a haircut since I came back from El Salvador."

"Dr. Stuart, meet Agent Dieter Irresburger, from Interpol," said Reynolds, "Herr Irresburger, this is Dr. Raymond Stuart, the man I've been telling you about."

Hands were shaken and the men were seated.

"The jurisdiction of the FBI is limited to the boundaries of the United States," said Reynolds, "A human trafficking ring based outside the United States should be pursued by international law enforcement. I've shared the information that we learned from the Project Raphael investigation with *Herr* Irresburger. He knows everything that we do about the organization and the hospital in Saudi Arabia."

"I also understand Agent Reynolds' concern about sending a civilian undercover in this situation," said Irresburger, "You realize, Doctor, that Interpol has very little information about this trafficking ring."

"All the more reason why you should allow me to go into the hospital," said Stuart, "This is a reprehensible international crime.

It should be stopped as quickly as possible. You need data and I believe that I can get it for you."

"That's precisely what Agent Reynolds said that you would argue," said the Interpol agent, "To a great extent, you are correct, Doctor. If you could get inside the hospital and gain access to the computer system, it is possible that we could shut this organization down. It would be dangerous, though."

"I'll take the risk," said Stuart, "Lois Godfrey told me that this operation has been going on for years. Why do you know so little about it?"

"Probably because nobody would ever suspect a bunch of doctors of doing something so barbarous," Reynolds said, "Doctors are supposed to be the good guys."

"Even good guys can get seduced by bad ideas," Stuart said, "I think that Godfrey got swept away with a little fame, a little flattery, and a lot of money. Next thing he knew, he was believing in some class of superior people, and he was one of them. In the end he was nothing better than a modern-day Nazi, dedicated to his own sort of master race. For the sake of all that is holy, all that I hold dear about my profession, I've got to stop this."

"Agent Reynolds says that you suggest that you pose as a musician and songwriter with kidney disease," said Irresburger.

"Right," said Stuart, "I can get complete medical records from the hospital where I work, all authentic, even though they would be fictitious. I found out where the hospital is in Saudi Arabia. A surgeon friend of mine found the name of the head of the transplant program. Another doctor did a little research and figured out how to make a patient referral. I'll go to the hospital as a prospective patient for a medical evaluation. Once inside, I'll get as much information as I can."

"If you can get inside," said Irresburger, "and gain access to the computer system, you might be able to insert a bug for us. The bug would open a channel through the hospital's cyber security and allow Interpol access to the entire computer system."

"Can you get me to Saudi Arabia?" Stuart asked, "I can get the appointment, but can you provide transportation?"

"The hospital is in Jazan," said Irresburger, "It's on the Red Sea, just north of the border with Yemen. There's a regional airport. It's also a port city. We can get you flown in on a private jet."

"Passport?"

"Easily provided," said Reynolds, "Courtesy of the FBI. You'll be travelling as a US citizen. You won't need forgeries. Your papers will be genuine. We'll create a whole history for you on the internet in case the good doctor in Jazan wants to listen to some of your favorite songs."

"I'll be in Jazan as well," said Irresburger, "I'll be your contact on the ground, if something goes wrong. And I'll arrange for your escape after you plant the bug."

"How?"

"Leave that to me," said Irresburger, "Will you need anything else?"

"Just one thing," said Stuart, "I'll need a new guitar. I'll want something to play in my hospital room. That should convince the staff that my identity as a musician is real. I suspect that, once I've planted this bug, I may have to scoot out of there and the guitar may get left behind. I'd prefer not to lose my own guitar, since I'm so fond of it."

"I'm sure that the Bureau can afford to spring for a damn guitar," said Reynolds.

"Don't be too sure, Walter," said Stuart with a smile, "It's got to be believable for a professional. I've always wanted a Taylor acoustic-electric. That may set the Bureau back a couple of grand."

33

"Dr. Stuart, are you growing a beard?" asked Gabriella.

"Maybe," Stuart replied, "Do you like it?"

Gabriella looked at him for a while, then tilted her head to get a slightly different angle and looked some more.

"Kinda," she said, "It makes you look more interesting."

Kathleen laughed.

"You mean he looks like a rock star instead of a professor of surgery," Kathleen said.

"I could have been a rock star," Stuart protested.

"I believe you could," said Kathleen, "I've heard you play, you know. I'm glad you chose to be a surgeon, though. It's a hell of a lot more stable. But, what's with the scruffy look? Are you going back to work looking like that?"

"I need to talk to both of you about that," Stuart said, "I'm going to go away for a few days. It could be a while before I get back to the hospital to work."

"Where are you going?" asked Gabriella, "You promised to take me to the zoo."

"We're going to the zoo tomorrow," Stuart assured the girl, "I can't tell you where I'm going or exactly when I'll leave or come back."

"Can you tell me?" asked Kathleen.

"No."

"Why?"

"I'm doing a little work for the government," said Stuart, "I'll tell you after it's over."

"Does this have something to do with *Los Cóndores* and the bad people who hurt the girls and the little kids?" Gabriella asked.

"Yes, it does," Stuart said.

"I thought that all those bad people were caught," said Gabriella.

"Not all of them," said Stuart.

"Are you going to El Salvador?" Gabriella asked, "Will you go to Cedros and look for my mother?"

"I'm not going to El Salvador," Stuart said as gently as he could, "I know that you're worried about your mother. We are, too. A lot of people are trying hard to find her."

"Are you up for a field trip?" Agent Walter Reynolds asked on the phone.

"Sure," replied Stuart, "Where are we going?"

"We gotta get you a new guitar," said Reynolds.

"It's approved, then," Stuart said.

"Yep, the whole thing," said Reynolds, "I suggest that we start with the guitar you want, then we'll take some photos for your documents. I have an identity for you, which we really should discuss. How about if I come pick you up and we'll go shopping."

"Better if I come to your office," said Stuart, "The music store I want is downtown."

Stuart selected a Taylor 714 with a sunburst finish. It came with a hard case. Stuart added a soft leather strap, a tuner that clipped on the headstock, a Shubb capo, and a handful of picks. The bill came to $3,700. Reynolds almost choked to death.

"You plan to leave this thing when your job is over?" Reynolds complained, "Jesus, Doc. You're spending the taxpayers' money here."

"Do you really want to start a conversation about how the government spends the taxpayers' money?" Stuart asked.

Stuart was grinning, caressing the new guitar when they left the music store and headed to the Federal building.

Reynolds closed and locked the door to his office. He pulled a chair over next to his own so that they could both see the computer screen on his desk.

"Your cover identity is that of Neil Wayman. He was one of the guitarists and songwriters for a band called The Lost Tribe back in the late eighties and early nineties."

"I remember them," said Stuart, "Good band."

"Jesus," Reynolds rolled his eyes. "You look a little like him. You two are about the same age. Our boys in the computer lab did some photo manipulation and we can make photos for album covers that put you in the picture where Wayman was. Not even an expert will detect the substitution."

"Neil Wayman is a real person," said Stuart, "who's very much alive."

"Mr. Wayman is also a patriot," said Reynolds, "who's more than happy to allow his name and photographs to be used for this operation. When we told him that we were working with Interpol to catch some human traffickers, he was delighted to cooperate."

"Good for him."

"Do you know any of the songs from The Lost Tribe?" asked Reynolds.

"One or two."

"Well stop and buy a couple CDs on your way home and start practicing with the fancy new guitar we just bought you," said Reynolds, "We want you to be proficient with their songs."

"I can do that."

"I like the scruffy beard," said Reynolds, "You'll look perfect for the passport photos we'll be taking today. The hair is an improvement. Not quite long enough for a rock star, but at least you don't look like a Marine anymore. Don't get it cut before the mission."

"Sir, yes, sir," Stuart mocked.

Reynolds shoved a stack of paper to Stuart.

"This is your homework," Reynolds said, "It's background on Neil Wayman and The Lost Tribe. Now, you said that you can get some medical records fabricated?"

"Not a problem," said Stuart.

"Get started," said Reynolds, "It's also time to refer yourself to the Al Saud Medical Center in Jazan, Saudi Arabia."

"I'll get on that right away," said Stuart.

"Let me know when they schedule your appointment," said Reynolds, "We need to let them set the date. I'll give your phony papers to Interpol. They'll take it from here."

"Shall I assume that you and the FBI are done with this?" Stuart asked.

"Remember, our jurisdiction is only in the United States," said Reynolds, "We've done what we can. Good luck, Doc. Let's catch these bastards."

"You got an appointment in Jazan in ten days," said Agent Irresburger, "I'm impressed."

"It was easy, actually," Stuart replied, "I just got on the phone, explained my situation to an intake nurse. She took down the data over the phone. Then I Faxed the medical records that I had fabricated at Sutro State. She called back the next day with the appointment. I made my calls to Jazan with the phone you provided through Agent Reynolds."

They were meeting in the parlor of a suite at the Hilton on Union Square. Stuart admired the spectacular view of the city. He smiled to himself, realizing that San Franciscans always judged a place at least in part by the view.

"What's impressive, *Herr* Irresburger, is this suite you have," Stuart said.

"International law enforcement does have its little perks," said Irresburger, "We can't meet at the FBI any more. Officially, the FBI is out of this operation."

Irresburger took a passport from a stack of papers. He opened it, looked at Stuart and back at the document.

"Excellent," Irresburger said, "The stubble of beard and the longer hair make you more credible."

"Thanks. You should see my new guitar. Now, that makes me credible."

Irresburger pointed at some other papers.

"This is how we'll transport you," he said, "You're going to fly Turkish Airlines from San Francisco to Istanbul. Then you'll fly from Istanbul to Riyadh, also on Turkish Airlines. We have you flying business class. It's twenty hours of flying and we want you rested when you arrive. You'll be met at the airport in Riyadh and flown by private jet to the regional airport in Jazan."

"Who will meet me?" Stuart asked.

"An Interpol agent," Irresburger said, "The agent will display a sign saying Wayman. Once you land in Jazan, a car will take you directly to the hospital. If you need a hotel in Jazan before your appointment, we'll take care of that."

"Will I have a contact in Jazan?"

"Yes," said Irresburger, "I'll be your contact in Jazan. You'll use the phone that we gave you to contact me. If you look at that phone under 'Contacts,' you'll see the name Jessica. That will be my cell phone."

"Where will you be?"

"I'll be registered in a nearby hotel," said Irresburger, "You don't need to know which one. If you need me, text or call."

"Sounds like cloak and dagger stuff," Stuart said, "Like out of a thriller movie."

"Doctor Stuart, this is no movie," Irresburger said, "We're dealing with international human traffickers. They've killed plenty of people. They won't hesitate to kill you. The steps we've taken are essential not just to the success of the mission but to your own safety."

"I understand."

"Once you get inside the hospital, you'll need to get access to the hospital computer system," Irresburger went on, "This is going to be difficult. We don't know exactly what sort of computer system they have. To get inside, you are going to need a login identity and a password. Unfortunately, we haven't yet been able to hack into the system and get one of those for you. I'm afraid you're on your own to get access."

"That may take some luck," said Stuart, "I won't have much time once I get inside. They have the fake medical records from Sutro State, but they'll be running their own tests to assess my condition and determine if I'm a candidate for a transplant. I can't imagine that it will take more than a day and a half before they know that I'm perfectly healthy."

"We understand," said Irresburger, "If you can't get to the computer system, bail out of there. If you can log in, I want you to insert a thumb drive into a USB port in the computer. You'll get a prompt asking if you want to install. Hit enter."

"What is it?"

"It's called a Trojan horse," said Irresburger, "It will create a hole in the cyber security system that will allow Interpol hackers full access to all their data. Once you've installed it, remove the thumb drive and get the hell out of there."

"Won't the hospital security find the thumb drive?" Stuart asked, "I'm guessing that they're going to search my belongings. Won't they be suspicious?"

Irresburger reached into a bag and retrieved a rectangular box. It had three buttons and a needle gauge.

"Do you know what this is?" Irresburger asked.

Stuart laughed.

"It's an old-fashioned guitar tuner," he said, "I haven't seen one of those for years."

"Like maybe in the '90s?" smiled Irresburger.

"Maybe."

"Well, consider it a throwback old favorite from the heyday of The Lost Tribe," said Irresburger, "Tell them you use it for sentimental reasons. The thumb drive will be inside the tuner box."

Stuart took the box and studied it.

"It actually does work, you know," said Irresburger, "You can tune your fancy new guitar with it. Go ahead and open it up."

Stuart snapped open the plastic box. Nestled in among the wires and the batteries was a small thumb drive.

"This is like some sort of James Bond movie," Stuart said, "How did you make this?"

"Don't ask."

"How do I get out of Jazan, assuming that I can actually install the Trojan horse?" Stuart asked.

"I'm working on that," said Irresburger.

The Al Saud Medical Center was a three-story structure adjacent to North Corniche Park with a beautiful view of the Red Sea. There was a central section of the building and two wings, one north and one south. The entire first floor was used for business offices, diagnostic services like imaging and laboratory, physical and occupational therapy, records, and information technology. The second floor of the central section housed the surgical suites, interventional radiology and cardiology, and, on the top floor, the board room and offices for the most important medical and administrative staff.

Inpatient units were on the second and third floors, north and south wings.

Dr. Yousef Al-Saffar watched as the caravan of vehicles arrived in front of the medical center. Today his special patient, Khalid Al-Quatani, was being admitted. The entire third floor of the south wing had been cleared and reserved for the terrorist and his entourage. Al-Saffar watched them set up a perimeter of armed guards and escort their leader inside the building.

Al-Quatani himself was ensconced in an oversize suite with a wonderful view. The normal hospital security staff was banned from the third floor of the south wing and greatly diminished on the second floor of that wing. Men with AK-47s guarded the elevators and stairways throughout the south wing, including the ground floor. The normal security guards were intimidated enough that they were happy to patrol other sectors of the medical complex.

For his part, Dr. Al-Saffar just wanted to get the transplant over with and Al-Quatani out of there. The doctor had no religion and could care less about the Islamic fundamentalism that the terrorist group Quabdat Allah espoused. The doctor also had no political point of view, really. He believed that there were superior people in the world and that his job was to save and preserve those individuals. Khalid Al-Quatani was not a superior person. Just a dangerous person.

He walked over to the south wing. After being searched and scanned by the terrorist bodyguards, he entered the room with his loathsome patient.

"How are you feeling?" Dr. Al-Saffar asked.

"Weary and sick," said the terrorist.

"Have you been taking your insulin as I prescribed?"

Al-Quatani just glared at him.

"When was your last dialysis?" the doctor asked.

"Two or three days ago, I think," Al-Quatani replied.

"Listen," said Al-Saffar, "we have a few days before the transplant is scheduled. I'm going to use that time to get you into as good a condition as I can. You'll get daily dialysis, proper control of your diabetes, and monitoring of a few of your lab tests. The donor arrives later today. We have a few tests to perform on the donor as well."

"Is all this necessary?" asked Al-Quatani.

"Given your circumstances, it's essential," said the doctor, "You and I both want to do this transplant once and only once. We both want this operation to succeed, so you can get on with your life and your mission and I can get on with mine."

"Very well," said Al-Quatani, "For the next few days, my life is in your hands."

◆ ◆ ◆

"Play me something on your new guitar," Kathleen asked.

The three of them sat on the deck of Stuart's house by the ocean. The sun was setting peacefully over the Pacific. The fog was still offshore and the whole scene was lovely.

"I've never heard you play, Dr. Stuart," said Gabriella.

Stuart went inside and emerged with his new Taylor guitar. After quickly checking the tuning, he began the instrumental introduction to a power ballad by The Lost Tribe. Then he began to sing and play the rhythm chords. Both Kathleen and Gabriella watched and listened intently.

"That was beautiful," said Gabriella, "You're good!"

There were tears in Kathleen's eyes.

"I didn't think I would ever hear you sing again," she whispered.

"What was the song, Dr. Stuart?" Gabriella asked.

"It's a song by a band called The Lost Tribe," said Stuart, "They were popular in the US about thirty years ago."

"I never heard of them," Gabriella said.

Stuart laughed.

"I'd be shocked if you had," he said.

"I never heard you play any of their songs before," said Kathleen, "I didn't think you were a fan of that sort of music."

"I didn't used to be," Stuart said, "I've been learning a lot of their songs lately. It's an acquired taste. The more I play them, the more I've come to appreciate them."

"Does this represent a new Ray Stuart?" Kathleen asked, "The beard, the longer hair, back to singing, and nineties rock?"

"Maybe. I'm getting used to not shaving and playing different songs."

"Does this have something to do with the secret trip you're planning?" Kathleen asked.

"Yes," he said.

"When do you have to go?" Gabriella asked.

"Tomorrow."

34

Agent Irresburger met Stuart outside the international terminal at San Francisco International Airport.

"You ready?" the Interpol agent asked.

"All packed and ready to go," said Stuart, "I memorized all the information you and Agent Reynolds gave me. I've got my medical information, cell phone, guitar and tuner, a couple of paperback books, and nothing else."

Irresburger slipped Stuart a piece of paper.

"Study this on the plane," said Irresburger, "These are your final instructions. When you have inserted the package into the computer, send a text to Jessica on the phone. Your message will be 'hugs and kisses.' The hospital is located just north of the Tourist Edge Marina. In slip number 39 you will find a thirty-two foot, green Sea Ray Sundancer. The name on it will be *Jessica's Dream*. The keys will be under the seat at the wheel. Take it out of the marina. Make a heading due west for ten miles. The boat will have charts, radar, GPS, and all the instruments you'll need. It's big enough to handle any weather you should encounter in the Red Sea, but small enough that you should be able to handle it yourself.

Your destination is Thoo Alraka Island. You'll be met there and extracted back to the US."

"Do you want me to leave as soon as the drive is in the computer?" Stuart asked.

"Yes, send the text and depart immediately."

"Will you meet me at the marina?"

"Possibly," said Irresburger, "I'll be nearby and will try to meet you at the boat. Just in case, you need to know how to get to the rendezvous in the boat, even without me."

"Okay," said Stuart, "I can do this."

"You have a long flight," said Irresburger, "Use the time to memorize the instructions on the paper. Then swallow the paper."

"Are you kidding?"

"Wash it down with a stiff drink." Irresburger said.

"I don't drink," said Stuart.

"Then wash it down with a carbonated cola," said Irresburger, "That's even better. Cola drinks will dissolve anything."

᛫ ᛫ ᛫

The Al Saud Medical Center sparkled in the afternoon sunlight. Stuart emerged from the car and the driver brought the suitcase and guitar case to the front of the modern medical facility.

Stuart studied the building. It had a cream-colored exterior featuring lots of windows of tinted glass. Everything was immaculately clean and neat. The medical center radiated a sense of excellence and optimism. Totally first class.

Three men approached from inside the building. All looked young, fit, and professional. One wore the uniform of a security officer. All smiled and appeared friendly.

"Mr. Wayman?" asked a man in a suit.

"Yes," Stuart replied.

"I'm Ahmad," the man replied, "Welcome to the Al Saud Medical Center. We've been expecting you. Mazin will take your belongings to your room."

A young man in a short-sleeved shirt and khakis picked up the suitcase and guitar and started inside.

"You understand that the safety and health of our patients are our primary concern," Ahmad continued as they began to walk to the front door, "Please allow Officer Rahal to escort you though our security entrance."

Stuart looked around. He could only see one or two uniformed security guards on the hospital grounds. They had radios, but did not seem to carry weapons. However, to his right were three men in baggy Middle Eastern garb, each with his face covered, carrying AK-47s and a bandolier of ammunition. These men paid no attention to Stuart, but seemed focused on guarding the entrance to the south wing of the building.

"Pardon the inconvenience, Mr. Wayman," said Officer Rahal, "But please empty your pockets into the dish. Do you have any metal inside of you?"

The officer pointed to scanner very similar to those used by the TSA in American airports.

"Yes," said Stuart, "There are steel rods in both of my legs. An auto accident four years ago."

The officer motioned Stuart into the scanner. Stuart placed his hands on his head and the scanner whirred and rotated.

"Please step outside, sir," the security man said, "I see that you also have an artificial eye."

"Yes," Stuart replied, "Also the accident."

Stuart was led to the second floor of the south wing. There was a bright, wide hallway, tastefully decorated with soothing artwork. Stuart guessed that the unit held about twenty rooms. There was a brightly lit, modern nursing station. Staff nurses with their heads covered in scarves prepared medications, spoke on phones, or worked at computer terminals.

Stuart was shown to a private room with a large hospital bed, a comfortable reclining chair, a small desk with its own chair, and a private bathroom with a shower. One of the nurses came in with him, took his vital signs, and showed him around. The man who had taken his guitar and suitcase arrived in a few minutes and delivered his belongings.

"Please make yourself comfortable, Mr. Wayman," said the nurse, "It's not necessary that you wear a patient gown at the Al Saud Medical Center. There are pajamas, a bathrobe, and slippers in the closet. We understand that many people aren't comfortable in the gowns that American hospitals require."

"Thank you," Stuart said. The Saudis got that one right.

"Mr. Darwish, our administrator, will be here to see you in about half an hour," the nurse said as she left the room.

Stuart unpacked his suitcase. While everything was neatly arranged, he knew that the bag had been searched. Likewise, he opened the guitar case. The guitar had survived the trip in perfect condition. Before leaving San Francisco, he had loosened the strings on the instrument. He sat on the bed, removed the tuner, and began the process of putting the guitar back in tune. This activity gave him a good opportunity to inspect the tuner. The thumb drive was right where it was supposed to be.

Stuart was still playing the guitar when a polite knock at the door announced the arrival of Ali Darwish. The financial expert took a seat in the desk chair.

"You play very well," Darwish said, "I couldn't help but admire your skill from the hallway."

"Thank you," Stuart replied, "Are you a fan of The Lost Tribe?"

"I'm afraid not," Darwish said, "My taste runs more to classical music. Are you comfortable here?"

"This place is very nice." Stuart said, "You're here to make sure that I can afford to be here, right?"

"Mr. Wayman," Darwish smiled, "we've already established that you can afford to be here. You have kindly paid your fee for this evaluation visit in advance. If it turns out that you do require a transplant, we'll talk about the costs. That decision, of course, is up to Dr. Al-Saffar."

"When do I see the doctor?" Stuart asked.

"Later this afternoon, I believe," said Darwish, "You understand that the Al Saud Medical Center and its doctors do not accept money from insurance companies."

"Yeah, I heard that," Stuart said, trying to stay in character, "Seems a shame that I've paid the premiums all these years and just when I need it, they can't help. Why don't you people at least take some of their money?"

"As soon as a health care facility accepts money from an insurance company," Darwish explained, "the facility also must accept the rules and regulations that the insurance company dictates. Insurance companies are only interested in their own profits. They impose rules which cut their own costs, often at the expense of good care for the patients. That's unacceptable to Dr. Al-Saffar and to the medical center as a whole. We insist that our patients receive only the highest quality care. We're very selective about which patients we treat. We like to think that we have the highest quality patients and they deserve the very best care."

"Thank you, Mr. Darwish," Stuart said, "I guess I'm lucky that you agreed to see me at all."

"Do you have any questions?" Darwish asked.

"Not really," said Stuart, "Do I have to wear pajamas all the time?"

"No," Darwish smiled, "Keep your identification band on while you are here. If you are scheduled for tests or to see the doctor, please wear the pajamas. Otherwise, you may dress as you like."

"Is it OK for me to walk around? This is a really beautiful place."

"You are free to go anywhere in the hospital or on the grounds," Darwish said, "except the third floor. The third floor is where the private offices are located. Right now we have some unique patients on the third floor, who must remain in isolation from the rest of the patient population. It's for their health and the health of others that we must keep them separate."

"Fine," said Stuart.

Darwish rose, handed Stuart a business card and prepared to depart.

"If there is anything I can do to make your stay more comfortable, please feel free to call me," Darwish said.

Stuart took the next hour to inspect the hospital. All of the rooms on the second-floor south wing looked similar to his own. One of the rooms was locked from the outside. Stuart made a mental note that it was Room 212. He wondered who might be inside. The central section of the building on the second floor was the surgical suite. It looked just like hospitals at home and, of course, barred curiosity seekers from admission.

Stuart was back in his room by four o'clock and dressed in pajamas when Dr. Al-Saffar arrived.

"Dr. Yousef Al-Saffar," the doctor smiled and extended his hand, "Mr. Wayman. My daughter is a fan of your music."

"That's nice to know," Stuart grinned.

Al-Saffar produced a CD and asked Stuart to sign it for his daughter.

"Perhaps before you have to return to the United States, I could bring her in and you could play a song for her," Al-Saffar suggested.

"I'd be delighted," Stuart said.

"She's seventeen and a fairly good musician herself," Al-Saffar said, "Things are changing rapidly for young women in Saudi Arabia. Many careers are becoming possible that used to be closed to women. She has these wild ideas about becoming a rock star."

"Doctor, lots of teenagers have those kinds of dreams," Stuart said, "If I may offer some advice, try to get her to follow in your footsteps and become a doctor. That's a safer path and she'll make a far greater contribution to humankind that way."

"Getting to the reason you're here," Al-Saffar said, "I read your medical records. The hospital in San Francisco was kind enough even to send some slides of your kidney biopsy. You have membranous glomerulonephritis."

"What's that?" Stuart asked.

"Nobody knows for certain," Al-Saffar smiled kindly, "Our best guess is that it is an auto-immune disease. It's a fairly common cause of renal failure."

"Did I get it from using too many drugs in my younger years?"

"No," said Al-Saffar, "Drug use may cause other health problems, but not membranous glomerulonephritis. In any event, the biopsy shows that your kidneys are almost completely destroyed. Right now, you probably think that you're fine, but very soon you'll need to go on dialysis. A person can get by with very little kidney functioning for a while, but eventually you'll cross a threshold and will need either dialysis or a transplant."

"That's what my doctor at home said," Stuart said, "I don't want to go on dialysis if it won't cure my disease. We're trying to get our band back together. I'm still touring and playing to decent audiences. I can't be tied to some damn machine. If I'm going to have to have a transplant anyway, why not get on with it?"

"Is that why you've come to Al Saud?"

"Partly," Stuart said, "The hospital at home said that I'd have to wait until I'm sicker to get a transplant. Even then, I'd have to go on a list and wait years, maybe, for a transplant. My doctor said that I might get care quicker here. He also said that you have a reputation of being probably the best transplant surgeon in the world with the highest success rate."

"Tell your doctor that I appreciate the flattering words," Al-Saffar said, "Now, if you would please remove your shirt, I'd like to examine you."

The physical examination was expert and thorough. Stuart could tell that Al-Saffar didn't miss a thing. When he was looking at Stuart's abdomen, he pointed at the recently healed scar.

"You've had surgery recently," Al-Saffar said.

"It's all in the records," Stuart lied, "I had a blockage as a result of the old injuries."

"A bowel obstruction?"

"Yeah, I guess. A blockage."

"When was that?"

"Three months ago. It's back to normal."

Al-Saffar grunted and finished the physical examination.

"You seem to be generally healthy and fit," Al-Saffar said, "That's good. We'll be doing some tests over the next two or three days. I'll come by every day and keep you informed. Any questions?"

"Not really," Stuart said, "Thank you, Doctor."

Stuart had little appetite for his dinner. He couldn't quite calm down. What was he thinking when he volunteered for this undercover mission? He was a surgeon, not a secret agent.

It took intense concentration to stay in character as a professional musician. He knew way too much about medicine and how hospitals worked. Sooner or later he would make a slip and expose himself as a fraud. All he wanted to do was plant the bug, get out of the hospital, and go home to Kathleen and Gabriella.

He couldn't stand to be alone in the room. He donned the bathrobe and set out for a stroll in the hall.

"Can I help you, Mr. Wayman?" asked a nurse he passed in the hall.

"Thank you, but I'm fine," he said, "Just getting my muscles stretched out with a little walking."

He walked slowly, stopping to look at the paintings on the wall, but checking everything on the nursing unit. He saw a nurse come out of the room with the locked door, carrying a used dinner tray. She set the tray down on a cart in the hall, then took a key and re-locked the door. Stuart noticed that there was a blue metal disc on the ring with the key. When the nurse disposed of the dinner cart, Stuart watched her hang the key with the blue disc on a hook behind the nursing desk.

When the dinner trays were cleared and the cart sent back, presumably to the kitchen for washing, the nurses scurried about, assembling and distributing medications. The nursing shift ended with most of the staff sitting in front of computers, finishing their daily documentation.

Stuart alternated watching boring movies on the TV in his room with little casual forays into the hallway. After sunset, there was very little activity. The number of nurses on the evening shift was much smaller than during the day. Stuart observed several times that there was no-one at all at the nursing station.

He had no hope of sleep. Morning would bring lab tests, probably an MRI of his abdomen and kidneys, possibly other tests. He had fake data of a kidney biopsy from Sutro State, complete with re-labeled microscopic slides of someone else's sick kidneys. Stuart had little time to accomplish his mission. It wouldn't take long for Dr. Al-Saffar and his staff to realize that Stuart's kidneys were perfectly normal and that he was a fake.

Stuart lay down in the bed and closed his eyes, trying to rest. He reminded himself of why he was there. He thought about the little children on Wallace Godfrey's yacht, stolen from their families, their healthy organs used for spare parts, and disposed of without a shred of remorse. He thought about the girls like Gabriella, tricked or kidnapped, sold into slavery to finance a monstrous international enterprise. These thoughts strengthened his resolve.

He hadn't expected the people at the Al Saud Medical Center to be so, well, normal. Mr. Darwish was pleasant and cordial and friendly. The nurses seemed to be competent and caring. Dr. Al-Saffar was obviously a highly skilled professional. Somehow, he had thought that we would be dealing with sinister, bitter, nasty villains like in the movies. These people seemed like dedicated health professionals.

These people were shockingly like himself.

But not like himself. Like Wallace Godfrey. Smart, talented professionals whose ethics and souls had been corrupted by a seductive ideology of eugenics.

This was the beautiful, shining face of evil.

35

STUART TOOK AN early morning shower and put on the pajamas and robe. A phlebotomist came before breakfast to draw his blood and the nurse brought a container for him to urinate in. After breakfast an orderly came with a gurney to take him to the MRI suite on the first floor.

Like everything at the Al Saud Medical Center, the imaging suite was bright, spotless, and totally modern. The orderly parked Stuart on his gurney in a holding area.

Right away Stuart noticed the dark-skinned teenager. The kid was parked next to him. Stuart thought he looked Indian.

Stuart gave the boy a little wave of greeting. The kid forced a wan smile and waved back without enthusiasm.

"Neil," Stuart said, pointing to himself.

"Manvik," the boy whispered, glancing at the orderly who sat lazily in a chair next to his gurney.

"America," Stuart said.

"Mumbai," replied Manvik.

"Speak English?"

"Little English," the boy replied.

"Why are you here?" Stuart asked.

Manvik covered his mouth and whispered.

"Kidnap."

The technologist called for Manvik and the orderly bestirred himself and pushed the gurney away.

Stuart felt like he had been punched in the gut. Mother of God, this kid was going to be an organ donor. Now he knew who was behind the locked door of Room 212.

The mission just got more complicated.

The afternoon brought a renal ultrasound exam and a lot more waiting. Some of the nurses asked for a sample of his music and Stuart obliged with an acoustic version of The Lost Tribe's greatest hits. The nurses applauded politely, but Stuart suspected that this was the first time they had ever heard American rock'n'roll.

All of the nurses on the unit wore white tunics, slacks, and headscarves. Some covered their faces, while others were content to keep only their hair concealed. At four o-clock a young nurse came to Stuart's room, where he was waiting dutifully in his hospital-issue pajamas.

"Mr. Wayman," she said, "I'm sorry to tell you that Dr. Al-Saffar has been delayed in surgery. He'll be making rounds late, probably after dinner."

"I understand," Stuart said, "Thank you for telling me."

He needed time to make his plan anyway. The test results would be known the next day, so he needed to make his move tonight. He figured that, if he watched the nursing station, an opportunity to insert the Trojan horse might present itself during the night shift.

He got out the guitar and the tuner. While he made a show of tuning the instrument, Stuart extracted the thumb drive from the tuner and slipped it into his pocket.

Dr. Al-Saffar arrived just as dinner was served.

"Hello, Doctor," Stuart said, pushing his dinner tray away, "The nurses tell me you had a long day in surgery. I hope everything went OK."

Al-Saffar sighed and took a chair. He had a binder in this hand with Neil Wayman's name on it.

"Everything is fine," said Al-Saffar, "We just needed a little more time. Thanks for asking. Now, Mr. Wayman, we have the results back from this morning's blood tests. They look absolutely normal. These are totally unlike the results you had in San Francisco."

Stuart looked at him, feigning surprise.

"Does that mean I'm cured?" Stuart asked with a big smile, "Can I go home?"

Al-Saffar scowled and snapped the chart closed.

"No," he said, "It means that there is probably a laboratory error. I'm sorry, but we'll need to repeat these blood tests first thing in the morning."

"I hope they show that the doctors back home were wrong," Stuart said, "No offense, Doctor Al-Saffar, everyone here has been great and this is a beautiful place, but I can't wait to get back to California."

Al-Saffar said nothing, just got up and left. Stuart could hear him speaking in a loud voice to the nurses in Arabic.

When the night shift of nurses came on, Stuart dressed in his street clothes, then put the bathrobe on overtop. He ventured into the hallway, aimlessly strolling, looking occasionally at a painting. There was only one nurse at the station. She was doing something with the computer. Stuart knew that meant that she was logged on. So much for needing a password.

The phone rang and the nurse answered. Then she got up and walked toward the end of the hall away from Stuart. He walked toward the nursing station, slowly as if bored. As the nurse got farther away, he picked up his pace.

Stuart slipped behind the desk and looked at the monitor screen. It was mostly in Arabic, with lots of numbers, but it was clearly on. He reached to the side of the computer and found a USB port. He inserted the thumb drive.

The computer whirred and the screen went blank. In seconds a prompt appeared in English.

"Install?"

Stuart hit the Enter key. Again, the screen went blank and the computer whirred.

He heard a door open down the hall. Leaving the nursing station, Stuart slipped back into the hallway. The nurse was approaching, but looking at a specimen bottle of urine she carried, not at him.

"Can I help you, Mr. Wayman?" she asked as she approached, noticing him standing by the desk.

"I don't want to bother anyone," he said, "But I would like some ice for the water in my room. If you tell me where it is, I'll be happy to get some."

"Nonsense," said the nurse, "I'll bring you some ice just as soon as I label this specimen and send it to the lab."

She disappeared into another room, carrying the urine. Stuart darted behind the desk and saw that the computer screen had returned to the Arabic letters and numbers. As far as he could tell, it looked the same as it did when the nurse left. Stuart slipped the thumb drive out and pocketed it.

He went back to his room, noticing that the nurse was back at the computer, tapping swiftly on the keys. He threw the ice from his bedside stand into the toilet, then lay down on the bed and turned on the TV.

The nurse was there in seconds with a decanter of fresh crushed ice.

"Here you go, Mr. Wayman," she said, "Having trouble sleeping?"

"I'm afraid that hospitals make me nervous," Stuart said. This hospital certainly made him very nervous indeed.

"I can call the doctor and get you something to help you sleep," she suggested.

"No, thanks, it's all right," he said, "This TV show is boring enough to put me under. I'll just sip some water and watch for a while."

Stuart waited half an hour. The hallway outside was silent. He got the cellphone and selected Jessica from the Contacts list. He texted "hugs and kisses" and sent the message. He sat on the bed, staring into the phone screen for perhaps three minutes, hoping for some sort of response. Nothing happened.

Stuart cracked open the door and looked toward the nursing station. It was deserted. Looking each way, he made his way to the station. He quickly snatched the key with the blue disc off the hook. Still seeing no-one, he moved to Room 212 and opened the door with the key.

The room was dark except for a dim light over the sink. The only occupant was asleep in the bed, blankets pulled up. Stuart recognized the teenage boy.

Stuart put on a light and touched the boy on the shoulder. The boy stirred and opened his eyes. Stuart put a finger to his lips.

"Sssshh," Stuart hissed, "Be quiet. I'm here to help you. Do you understand?"

The boy looked at Stuart, rubbed his eyes, and nodded in assent.

Stuart pointed to the kid, then back to himself, then to the door.

"Manvik. Neil. Out of here. Mumbai," Stuart hoped that the kid understood. It was pretty stupid communication.

Manvik rewarded Stuart with a big grin and a thumbs up sign.

Stuart motioned for Manvik to follow. The two crept toward the door. Stuart opened it a crack, then swiftly closed the door and turned the lock bolt.

There was a uniformed security guard at the nurses' desk, talking to the night nurse.

Stuart turned off the light, leaving only the one near the sink. Manvik stood right next to Stuart by the door. He could hear Manvik breathing rapidly.

Stuart put his finger to his lips and his ear against the door.

He could hear the guard and the nurse talking in Arabic. He could only try to imagine the conversation by the tone of the voices. It was impossible. Then he heard something that made him smile.

The nurse was giggling.

Stuart waited a few more minutes until the voices began to fade. Then he cracked the door and took a peek. The nurse and the guard were walking into a room, holding hands.

When they closed the door to the room, Stuart opened Manvik's door and motioned the teen into the hallway. Stuart locked the door of Room 212, put the key on the hook at the nurses' station, and motioned Manvik into this own room.

Manvik was dressed in hospital pajamas, so Stuart outfitted him in street clothes from his own wardrobe. Everything was baggy on the Indian kid, but Stuart did some creative tucking and belting. It wasn't great, but an improvement over the pajamas.

They turned off the light and closed the door to Stuart's room behind them and slipped down the corridor to the stairwell door. Quietly, they opened the door. A dim light illuminated the stairwell.

Stuart sensed that they were not alone. He glanced up and saw a man with an AK-47, his face hidden by a balaclava, standing in front of the door to the third floor. The man looked directly at Stuart.

Stuart motioned to Manvik and tried to look like he belonged in the stairwell. They headed down the stairs. The man with the rifle said nothing, just watched them go down. Nothing happened when they emerged on the first floor. No alarms. No shouting. No gunfire. Nothing. The man was not interested in people going down the stairs. He was there to prevent anyone from coming up.

The first floor was quiet. Stuart and Manvik made their way to the glass doors at the front of the building, just at the junction of the middle section and the south wing. Stuart saw uniformed, but unarmed hospital security guards walking a pattern in front of the center and north wings. Two men with AK-47s, ammunition bandoliers, and headscarves stood in front of the south wing.

Stuart didn't know who these armed sentinels were. It was apparent to him that they were more concerned, however, with keeping people out of the third floor, south wing. They didn't seem particularly interested in keeping people in the hospital.

Stuart and Manvik exited the hospital right in front of the armed guards.

"*Salaam Alaikum,*" said Stuart as he guided a trembling Manvik past the guards.

"*Wa-Alaikum Salaam,*" said the guard.

Stuart kept a firm grip on Manvik's arm and guided him across the street into the North Corniche Park. It was an open area with lots of palm trees and paths. As soon as they got out of sight of the hospital, they found a path and began to run to the south.

Soon they arrived at the Tourist Edge Marina. Stuart studied the numbers on the dock, looking for Slip 39.

Jessica's Dream was a beautiful boat. Stuart stepped off the deck onto the diving platform.

Manvik stood on the dock and looked at Stuart suspiciously.

"OK," said Stuart, motioning for the teen to come aboard, "OK."

"Mumbai?" asked Manvik.

Stuart understood. The kid thought they were going to sail all the way to India on this pleasure cruiser.

"Airport," said Stuart, motioning with his hand like a wave, "Airplane to Mumbai."

"Ah, airplane," smiled Manvik as he stepped onto the boat.

The keys to the boat were just where Irresburger said they would be, under the seat at the helm. There was, however, no sign of the Interpol agent.

Stuart checked the cellphone. There were no messages. He pressed the button to call "Jessica." No answer. No voicemail option.

They sat on the boat for an hour. Manvik explored the craft. He found some bottled water and some fruit in the refrigerator and helped himself. Stuart watched the kid lounging on the plush, comfortable benches and smiled.

The first rays of sunrise were peeking over the hills to the east. Stuart had waited as long as he could. He found the nautical charts, the GPS and radar. He found the life jackets and put one on himself and Manvik. The language barrier was way too great for him to explain what the jacket was for.

The engine rumbled to life in the most reassuring way. A quick check of the instruments found that the fuel tank was full and everything seemed to be in order. Stuart turned on the running lights. He went to the bow and pointed Manvik to the stern. When Stuart tossed off the bow line, Manvik did the same with the stern one.

Stuart pulled the boat out of the slip and out of the marina at a trolling speed. Once out in the open Red Sea, he sped up and set a course for Thoo Alraka Island, ten miles due west.

The Red Sea was calm. Other than *Jessica's Dream* there were no boats on the water nearby. Stuart enjoyed watching Manvik. The youth was fascinated with everything. While at the dock, he explored every inch of the sport cruiser, running his fingers over every object. Out on the water, he stood in the cockpit, his face to the wind, eyes wide open in wonder. Stuart wondered if the kid had any idea what was about to happen to him at the Al Saud Medical Center.

Morning light was improving with the rising sun at their back. Manvik startled when he saw the big black monster form first. Stuart saw him jump and followed Manvik's pointing finger out onto the water ahead of them.

A huge black shape was rising out of the water. At first Stuart thought it was a whale. He didn't even have time to think about whether or not there actually were whales in the Red Sea when the conning tower and antennae of a submarine broke the surface.

Soon the hull was above the water. Hatches opened and sailors rushed out.

Stuart turned *Jessica's Dream* to starboard and cut back the throttle. He and Manvik stared at the submarine in astonishment.

"Dr. Stuart," came a voice in accented English on a loudspeaker, "bring your craft alongside."

Who was speaking? How did they know his name?

Stuart kept *Jessica's Dream* idling at a distance.

"This is *Korvettenkapitän* Erich Holzer of the German Navy, commander of U-32," the voice said with authority, "Bring your craft alongside."

A German U-boat? If this was a trap or a deception, nobody would ever pretend to be a German U-boat. It had to be true. Stuart pushed the throttle forward and headed for the submarine.

Once aboard the U-32, Agent Irresburger came and shook Stuart's hand.

"Jesus, a German U-boat?" Stuart said, "Is this your idea?"

"Actually, I'm Austrian," said Irresburger with a smile, "When Interpol is in pursuit of human traffickers, everybody volunteers to help. The German Navy offered this vessel. It runs on hydrogen fuel cells and is essentially undetectable by normal anti-submarine technology. A perfect way to get in and out of the Red Sea."

"Nobody is going to believe this," said Stuart.

"Who is this?" Irresburger asked, gesturing to Manvik.

"His name is Manvik," Stuart said, "He's from Mumbai. I think he was about to become an involuntary organ donor."

36

"What do you mean, he's gone?" asked Dr. Al-Saffar, the color draining from his face.

The head of hospital security at the Al Saud Medical Center stood in the doctor's office, literally with his hat in his hand.

"The boy in Room 212 has disappeared in the night," said the security man, "The door was locked this morning, as normal. When the nurse went to deliver his breakfast, the room was empty."

"Where the hell did he go?" asked Al-Saffar.

"I don't know. The night shift of officers saw no-one leave the room or the hospital. We have searched the entire hospital and the grounds. The boy has vanished."

"People don't vanish," said Al-Saffar. As soon as he spoke the words, the irony hit him. This teenager had, to all appearances, vanished from the streets of Mumbai. Now he had disappeared from the hospital.

"The patient, Mr. Neil Wayman, the American, is also missing," the security man admitted.

Al-Saffar didn't care about Wayman. The man was just some overage rock musician. The boy from India was precious. Replacing him was going to be nearly impossible.

"Keep looking for them both," the doctor snapped, "Leave me. Don't come back until you've found them."

The security man departed in shame.

Without announcement, the men that Al-Saffar knew as Rashad and Jarra, aides to Khalid Al-Quatani, entered the office. They did not look happy.

Stuart pulled his Jeep to the curb outside Kathleen's house. Kathleen and Gabriella didn't wait for him to come inside. Rushing out the front door, they enveloped him with hugs right on the street.

"Where did you go, Dr. Stuart?" Gabriella asked, "Where's your new guitar? Tell us about your trip. Did you go to El Salvador? Did you find my mother?"

"Welcome back, Ray," Kathleen said softly, "Come on inside and have some tea."

Comfortably situated in Kathleen's living room with a cup of hot tea, Stuart gave his explanation. Agent Irresburger and Agent Reynolds had briefed him about what he was allowed to discuss.

"I wasn't in El Salvador, so I didn't have a chance to look for your mother," he began, "I was in the Middle East, helping our government to find more of the bad men who were kidnapping children and teenage girls. I made a new friend, a teenager from India. And I got to ride in a submarine."

"Did you stop the traffickers?" Kathleen asked.

"Oh, yeah."

"A submarine?"

"That's a very long story."

◆ ◆ ◆

Agent Reynolds' office on the thirteenth floor of the Federal Building was too familiar to Stuart. He was pleased to see Interpol Agent Irresburger.

"Did the Trojan horse work?" Stuart asked, "Was Interpol able to hack the computers?"

Irresburger grinned.

"It was a total success," the Interpol agent said, "Our computer hackers were able to download the records of the entire network. We know the names of all the doctors in all the countries who are part of the eugenics group. We have all their hospital and clinic information. We know which local criminal organizations they work with. We have names and locations of trafficked victims. We know who the patients are who have received transplants from trafficked donors."

"I'm curious," said Stuart, "Did the patients, the rich and famous people who received organs from involuntary donors, did they know where their new organs came from?"

"In some cases, we think they knew," Reynolds said, "The recipients aren't stupid people. They know that they were poor candidates for transplant and they know that their money bought them something they couldn't have gotten through normal channels. I don't know if they were aware that the donors were killed after the transplant surgery."

"My guess is that the recipients didn't ask a lot of questions about where their new organs came from," said Irresburger.

"Will the recipients be prosecuted?" Stuart asked.

"Probably not," said Irresburger.

"And the network?"

"Shut down," said Irresburger, "Your Dr. Al-Saffar was the head of the whole organization and personally ran the organ transplant black market. Ali Darwish, who you knew as the hospital administrator, was the overall boss of the human trafficking operation. Interpol is working with law enforcement in many countries to arrest people. Tracing and rescuing victims of trafficking will take months, perhaps a year. People will be punished. This network is out of business."

"It doesn't solve the world's problem of human trafficking," said Reynolds, "But we have stopped a particularly repulsive organization of modern-day eugenicists."

"It's the same in medicine," said Stuart, "None of us can eradicate all the ills in the world. We learn to be grateful if we can save or help the person that's in front of us."

"Speaking of saving," said Reynolds, "The teenager you saved in Saudi Arabia is back home in Mumbai with his family."

"Good," said Stuart, "I wonder if he really ever understood what they were going to do to him. I hope not."

"Dr. Stuart, do you remember when you were at the Al Saud Medical Center, that there were armed guards who were not part of hospital security?" Irresburger asked, "You mentioned them in your debriefing."

"Sure, I remember."

"Do you know who those guards were protecting?"

"I have no idea."

"It seems that while you were in the hospital, they had a very important patient there who had come for a kidney transplant," said Irresburger, unable to stop smiling, "The Indian boy who you rescued was supposed to be the donor."

"My God," said Stuart, "I was afraid of that."

"The recipient of the boy's kidney was supposed to be Khalid Al-Quatani."

Stuart was shocked.

"The terrorist?"

"Leader of Quabdat Allah, the Fist of God."

"Hasn't every country in the world been looking for that guy?"

"Yes, indeed," said Reynolds, "He was the most wanted man on the planet."

"Was?" asked Stuart.

"When you absconded with the kidney donor," Irresburger said, "Al-Quatani and his men took revenge on the transplant doctor. They beheaded him right in his office. They beheaded the administrator as well, just to emphasize their disappointment."

"Oh, my God," said Stuart.

"Without the doctor, Al-Quatani's health deteriorated," said Reynolds, "After they killed the doctor in Saudi Arabia, they went underground with their leader. We have it on excellent intelligence that Al-Quatani is dead."

"Quite a bonus, Dr. Stuart, don't you think?" Irresburger said.

"I probably shouldn't say this, but the world is better off without any of those three in it," said Stuart, "I couldn't be happier."

"There is also some bad news, unfortunately," Reynolds said, "US agents working in El Salvador found the remains of Gabriella Cortez's mother. She was buried just outside the village of Cedros. She was shot in the head."

"Oh, no," Stuart said, "Does Gabriella know?"

"No," said Reynolds, "We thought it might be better if you told her."

⁂

Stuart held Gabriella close to him while the girl sobbed. He knew that no words would help. All he could do was hold her. She had to cry this out. Kathleen stood by, just as helpless as he was.

Gabriella was fourteen and an orphan.

Gabriella clung to Stuart for a full fifteen minutes, then gently pushed away, drying her eyes on her sleeve. She sat down on a sofa and stared at the floor. Kathleen brought a box of tissues and a cold ginger ale and set them in front of her, but the girl seemed not to notice.

"What will happen to me?" Gabriella sobbed.

"We're here for you," Kathleen said.

"Will I be deported?" Gabriella asked, again wiping her face with her sleeve.

"You should be safe in El Salvador," Stuart said, "Dr. Godfrey and Mr. Conklin are in prison. *Los Cóndores* has been greatly weakened. The man who used to be *El Jefe* is dead, probably killed by one of his own gang members. *Los Cóndores* has problems of its own right now. You're past history to them. Our authorities think that the gang isn't a threat to you."

"Does that mean that they'll make me go back?" she asked.

"What do you want to happen?" Stuart asked.

Gabriella blew her nose, wiped her face, and took a sip of the ginger ale. After a pause, she regained some of her composure.

"I want my mother to be alive," she said, "I want to hug her and tell her that she was right. I want to tell her that I love her. I want to start over with my mother."

Stuart and Kathleen were silent. There was nothing to say.

"I knew this could happen," Gabriella went on, "I've thought about it over and over for the last months that I've been here with you. Still, when it all proves to be true, it's, well, it's hard."

"I know," said Kathleen, "There's no way to prepare for this, really. In your heart you hope that losing your mother will never happen."

Gabriella nodded and took another sip.

"I don't want to go back to El Salvador," she said, "There's nothing there for me. I have my grandmother, but she's old and hardly knows me. She lives in a different village. I wouldn't know anyone in her village. My friends are all in Cedros. They're all poor. I couldn't stay with them. I have no skills."

"You could go to school," said Kathleen, "We have friends in the Church. We might be able to arrange for you to go to a Catholic school."

Gabriella looked alternatingly at Kathleen and Stuart.

"Can I stay here with you?"

"In San Francisco?" Kathleen asked.

"Yes."

Kathleen and Stuart exchanged looks.

"Is that what you want, Gabriella?" he asked.

"Yes."

"Do you want to live in my house?" Kathleen asked.

"I would love that," Gabriella said, "I've come to love you."

"You'll have to go to school and you'll have to learn how to speak English."

"There's nothing I want more," Gabriella said, looking at Kathleen through eyes that were once again brimming with tears.

"I think it could be arranged, Gabriella," Stuart said, "I'm pretty sure that our government is so grateful for your help in catching those horrible human traffickers that they'll grant you asylum in the United States. Especially if you have an American family who is willing to take you in."

"Family?" Gabriella asked.

Stuart looked at Gabriella, then deep into Kathleen's eyes. "Yes, family," he said, "I like the sound of that."

ACKNOWLEDGEMENTS

Many, many thanks to my wife Marilyn for her editing and comments. Like most of our marriage, writing books has been a shared adventure. I couldn't do this without her help.

Thanks to Amy Glum, who read the story out loud with great theatrical voices. If readers have as much fun with this book as I did listening to her readings, it will all have been worthwhile.

Thanks to Mary Glum for her expertise in clinical laboratory science. Thanks to my son Rob for tips on sailing San Francisco Bay. Thanks to Bob Brach and Bill Meyn, my consultants in all things maritime and Coast Guard.